CANDLELIGHT REGENCY SPECIAL

Candlelight Regencies

MISS HUNGERFORD'S HANDSOME HERO

Noël Vreeland Carter

A CANDLELIGHT REGENCY SPECIAL

Published by
Dell Publishing Co., Inc.
1 Dag Hammarskjold Plaza
New York, New York 10017

Dell ® TM 681510, Dell Publishing.Co., Inc.

ISBN: 0–440–15312–3

Printed in the United States of America

First printing—May 1981

This book is for
Mary and Claydon Pattison
and for their nephew
Gene Schulman,
who is my handsome hero

MISS HUNGERFORD'S HANDSOME HERO

:: 1 ::

"Bucky, I vow I cannot bear it another minute. I am too vexed for words," cried Charlotte Hungerford with a great deal of agitation before she proceeded to belie her last statement by going on at length as to the cause of her utter vexation of mind.

"Where is she now?" young Lord Buckthorpe Vane asked mildly when he was finally able to insert a word of his own.

"Where do you think? Off to take the waters, of course," Miss Hungerford snapped peevishly and then, with a relenting shake of her pretty chestnut curls, begged her nephew's forgiveness. "Oh, Bucky, I am sorry! You've only just arrived, and here I am ranting, but really she is such a trial since father's death. I simply *will not* drink another glass of warm seawater because my stepmother has nothing better to do than imagine an apothecary's textbook of ills for us all." She tossed her head in a gesture of disgust, and Bucky noticed with some amusement how his aunt's firm jaw thrust itself forward with determination as her anger grew. He had seen the same family characteristic manifest itself in the face of his mother, Lady Helena Vane, who was Charlotte's sister.

"And Brighton, of all places!" she went on. "You know how I like peace and quiet. I *need* it, for heaven's sake. I swear I cannot write a line—

"Oh, do stop that vile habit of yours. It's filthy," Charlotte Hungerford interrupted herself to scold young Buckthorpe, who was inhaling a goodly pinch of snuff with much attendant scattering and sneezing. "You cannot even be neat about it; you get it all over yourself," she complained, twisting her pretty face into a moue of disgust.

The young man smiled tolerantly but made no answer. It was a raffish affectation of his to make a mess with his snuff, and he always secretly delighted in his aunt Charlotte's disapproval. Not that she complained very often. In fact, she was usually very indulgent, which was why he now weathered her impatience so well.

"I have got to start another novel," she was saying. "They've been clamouring for more ever since *The Madness of Maida* was published in the spring, but how can I begin when I have Fanny hovering about my shoulder like a breath of ill wind—"

"Has she got the wind, too?" Bucky interrupted serenely. *"That's* got to be from all the damned seawater."

"Bucky!"

"She wants a good purge and be done with it," he continued with seeming innocence.

"That is not what I meant, and well you know it, my lad. I never have any peace," Charlotte complained. "Either she hovers over me silently like a smothering hen on her chicks—following me from room to room even—or else she talks incessantly, describing her every ache and pain in the most minute detail—*and* the every ill of every chance acquaintance to boot. F'r instance, do you know that Lady Blanding's daughter-in-law's father has not passed water in three weeks due to the stone?"

"Naw! Really?"

"Really." She laughed in spite of herself at her nephew's pretense of hanging on her every word. "And the places that they've been lancing boils on old Mrs. Creevey are virtually unmentionable. Nevertheless, Fanny managed to mention every single one of them in the minutest detail over breakfast this morning whilst I struggled to down a plate of kidneys. Finally had to give up, too," she added with a face that mirrored lingering regret and perhaps hunger as well. "*I* totally lost my appetite, but not Fanny, mind. She had something from every dish on the board and then, somewhat miffed that I would not join her, trundled off to take those wretched waters at the spa."

"She's as healthy as a horse, though, isn't she?"

"Of course she is. You know it, and I know it, and so, deep down, does she, I'll warrant. But she has no occupation now your grandfather's died. Whilst she had him to dote on and fuss over, she was fine, and good company, too, in her sympathetic, not overly bright way, but now—" Charlotte Hungerford threw up her hands in despair.

"What you're sayin' then, Charlotte, is that she wants diversion."

"Exactly."

"So what d'you propose I do about it? Take her about on me nightly prowls?" Here Bucky Vane leered in anticipation of the debauches he planned for himself now he had arrived in Brighton.

"No, of course not, you little sot!" Charlotte laughed.

"I know," young Buckthorpe exclaimed brightly, one forefinger to his blond head in a dramatic indication of sudden thought, the humourous effect of which was unintentionally funnier for the fact of his exaggeratedly full lace cuff getting in his eye and causing it to water. "Ouch!" he winced.

"What? Are you going to put out an eye for me, so she shall have a new victim to nurse? How obliging of you, Bucky."

"Do shut up. Can't you see I'm in pain?" he retorted petulantly as he wiped his eye until it was bleary. "No," he said at last. "I was going to suggest gettin' her a job in a nice flash house."

"Bucky, if I cannot speak to you seriously, I shall send you packing right back to Wooton-Maggot," Charlotte threatened, knowing she had him well in hand with that threat.

"You wouldn't, Aunt Charlotte?" young Lord Buckthorpe Vane cried out in sudden alarm at the thought of being sent back to Buckthorpe Court, Wooton-Maggot, Wilts., to face the tedium of life with his elderly governor, the third Viscount Vane, his mother, Lady Helena, and a seemingly endless succession of younger brothers and sisters—known somewhat snickeringly as the "various Vanes" owing to the variety of their paternal ancestries. "For God's sake, anything but Wooton-Maggot," he pleaded earnestly.

"Then do behave," Charlotte commanded serenely "Actually, though, you're not far off the mark, my lad, when you mention flash houses," she mused.

"I'm not?" He gulped in surprise and dismay He hadn't meant to be taken seriously after all.

"Well, I do not recommend that she take on the whole of Brighton, mind you, but *one* man—one *husband* . . "

"Marry her off!"

"Can you think of a better solution?" she purred.

"No, you crafty little aunt o' mine. It's a damnably good idea," he agreed enthusiastically. "Only one trouble"—suddenly deflating—"who's going to do it? Marry her, I mean. She's nice enough, I suppose, but she's so *old*."

"Old! Why, she's not yet forty. She was far too young for my father, but then, with her penchant for fussing and mothering, I suppose a gouty elderly widower with one daughter already married and another yet to be raised must have been just her cup of tea."

"Not yet forty," young Buckthorpe repeated. "That sounds positively *ancient* to me."

"Yes-s-s, I suppose that it would to one who is not yet twenty," Charlotte mused, ruminating ruefully on the fact that she herself was closer now to thirty than she was to twenty. She glanced at her reflection in a mirror on the wall across the drawing room and looked away in haste. Thirty! Ugh! But never mind, she told herself. Fanny was the problem at hand.

"Nevertheless, dear boy, she needs a husband, and since I shall probably not get a word writ down whilst we're here in Brighton anyway, it seems to me that the summer season would not be entirely wasted if I could marry her off before she's turned me into a periwinkle with her blasted waters. To which end, I have sent for you, my pet. I don't go about much in Society, as you know, and when I do, it is always in Fanny's wake, so I am counting upon you to find some suitable man for her "

"And what, pray, constitutes a suitable man for Mrs. Fanny Hungerford, Wiltshire parson's widow?" Buckthorpe Vane drawled with deadened eyes. He saw his prospects for a carefree seaside summer fading amidst a pack of gouty elderly gentlemen suitors and titterings behind the fans of fat middle-aged ladies. Gad!

"Well, I have given that some thought already. Old—but not so old that he has no use for a buxom, active woman—"

A snicker from young Buckthorpe.

"And sick—but not so sick he's like to die on her."

"A slight case o' the pox," he suggested helpfully.

"I'll 'pox' you, me lad." Charlotte laughed and pelted him with the silken bolsters from beside her on the sofa. He caught one and sent it hurtling back across the room.

"Yoo-hoo," came a cheery cry from the central hall beyond the drawing room doors. It had the effect of stopping cold what had otherwise given promise of a damned good pillow fight of the sort in which aunt and nephew had often indulged in in bygone times and in which they still revelled occasionally, though one of them was nearing, and the other was well past, their respective majorities.

"Damn," Charlotte muttered, stuffing the cushions back into place.

Buckthorpe Vane tittered merrily. He loved his aunt's somewhat unladylike saltiness. She was a devilish good sport and far more indulgent than not, especially when he chose to exercise his share of the Hungerford family charm to get round her.

The drawing room doors opened just then, and Mrs. Fanny Hungerford, the subject of their interrupted discussion, made her bustling entrance upon the scene. She was a plump, youthful, round-faced woman in her late thirties, dressed in the simple but tasteful height of slightly provincial fashion. Her skin was creamy with high-coloured cheeks and eager eyes, like bright brown buttons. Her hair was jet black and as yet untouched with silver.

"Charlotte, you shall never guess who—" she burst out, breaking off immediately she saw young Buckthorpe Vane standing beside the mantel. "Bucky darling! So those are your boxes strewn about the hall! I should have known! Have you come to stay for long? But of course you have! Oh, what a charming surprise. Come, come, do give us a kiss," she insisted, extending her plump hands toward him and raising her lips in a pucker, eyes closed, head back. Dutifully the youth came forward and performed the ritual expected of him.

"Hullo, Stepgrandmama," he greeted her with a sly wink over his shoulder at Charlotte, who remained on the sofa, watching this scene with hooded eyes of a luxuriously honeyed shade of amber.

"Uh," cried Mrs. Hungerford with an exaggerated expression of pain and one fist striking her ample but modestly clothed bosom. "*Must* he call me that, Charlotte?" she appealed to her stepdaughter. "Surely I am too *young* to be a grandmother."

"At least he only calls you that in private, Fanny," she answered dryly. "*Me* he calls by my given name at home and insists on 'Auntie dear' in public. Which would you prefer?"

Young Buckthorpe snickered in delight, his mischievous blue eyes twinkling merrily.

"But he shan't anymore, shall he," his aunt continued pointedly, "or he shall 'Auntie dear' himself right back to Wooton-Maggot, shan't he?"

Buckthorpe winced.

The mention of his father's seat reminded Fanny of the further amenities expected of her. "How are your dear parents, Bucky?" she asked rather absently as she flounced herself down on a sofa across from Charlotte and settled in for a cozy gossip. She was delighted to have her young stepgrandson (that *is* what he was, and no denying it, she admitted ruefully—but only to herself!) amongst them. Charlotte tended to be so dry and was really no fun at all these days.

"Quite well, thank you." Bucky nodded.

"And all the various little Vanes?" This was a slip of the tongue, but it was virtually impossible not to mention the word "various" when speaking of Helena Vane's massive brood. Charlotte, with her superior vocabulary, thought of her nieces and nephews as the "variegated Vanes," which was a more precisely grammatical description. But then that was Charlotte Hungerford after all—always just a shade too precise and pedantic for everyone else's comfort, as she herself was well aware.

"Fine," Bucky was answering Fanny. "We've had a new one, don'cha know?" he drawled carelessly. " 'Nother gel."

"How nice," Mrs. Hungerford exclaimed doubtfully, but with a look of somewhat embarrassed interest. Really, she was thinking, poor Charles's eldest was too much! "Whom does this one take after?" she asked with some want of discretion under the circumstances. Which side of the family, would have been more politic phraseology.

"Lord Henley's groom, they say," Buckthorpe replied placidly, taking malicious pleasure in his stepgrandmother's startled discomfort.

Charlotte Hungerford listened to this exchange with ill-disguised amusement.

"Oh!" Fanny shrilled. "Oh, really." And then recovering with a devastatingly charming smile: "Still, it's a sight better than taking after Lord Henley himself, I daresay."

"Perhaps, but we've got ourselves one of those as well," he drawled.

"Oh, which?" she asked with what was now genuine interest.

"Three whelps back," came the even reply, which sent Charlotte's hand flying to stifle the whoop of laughter she felt coming.

"Ah, me." The elder lady sighed. "It's a wonder your father stands for it." As she shook her head, other portions of her ample person followed suit, jiggling gently and comfortably like a gelatin mold upon a plate.

"That's just the trouble. He *stands* for too much. He'd be all the better for lyin' down a bit more, I expect," young Lord Vane drawled earnestly.

Mrs. Hungerford clicked her tongue in disapproval. "I declare, Charlotte, this boy takes too much from your father's side of the family. His tongue is getting to be as sharp and as wicked as yours," she fretted.

"Blood will out," Miss Hungerford agreed with a pleased and tolerant smile, for this was an old, familiar complaint and had the ring of truth about it. She liked her eldest nephew very much

17

and saw a great deal of her late father Charles Hungerford's mischiefs, wit, and humour in Bucky, although physically he was nothing like his grandfather, being instead the spit and image of his own father, the senior Buckthorpe Vane, who was the third viscount and hence Charlotte's long-suffering, much-cuckolded brother-in-law.

Both father and son were tall and broad of build, with high colour, brilliant blue eyes, and thick blond hair, although the elder Vane still affected a powdered wig, which therefore hid that particular similarity in their makeup. Bucky wore his own hair closely cropped, owing to its embarrassing tendency to curl, and chose to dress like a somewhat dishevelled, rather foppish coachman, his thought being that the contrast of perfect tailoring, lots of lace at collar and cuff, all rumpled and coated with a liberal spattering of mud and the finest snuff gave him a sort of raffish, devil-may-care style in keeping with the bucks of his day and yet still with an individual air of his own. In the wilds of Wiltshire he was even considered something of a trend setter—"the Petronius of Wooton-Maggot," as Charlotte was wont to call him somewhat acidly, though he took it as a compliment.

His aunt saw all this with some affectionate amusement and tolerated his affectations, sensing that "this too would pass" and that one day he would take on, of his own accord, the more sober and sensible habiliment of a fashionable gentleman of mature tastes. Meanwhile, she reasoned amiably, let the pup have his day.

Young Vane winked just then, bringing his aunt out of her reverie, and, becoming suddenly, suspiciously contrite over his teasing of his stepgrandmother, crossed the room to sit beside Fanny Hungerford.

"Actually, Grandmama," he began confidentially as she groaned at the title, "actually the guv'nor's livid after this last brat. He's put his foot down flat and virtually put Mama in 'durance vile.' She's not to leave Buckthorpe Court for so much as an afternoon's ride without him accompanyin' her—and no guests at all! Says the next one's going to be his or it'll be nobody's."

18

"Well, it's about time. Helena's had her way far too long. This shall chasten her much, I'm sure," she clucked righteously.

"Oh, d'ya think so? I've put my money on Mother. Still, maybe you're right and the guv'nor shall have his way with her yet," young Vane drawled laconically.

"Well, after all, Bucky, he did once, you know," Charlotte reminded him comfortingly, for while his younger brothers and sisters might be an odd lot, Lord Buckthorpe himself was so obviously his father's son as to have earned the sobriquet "the Invariable Vane" from an otherwise cynical society.

"Yes, yes, that is true, Aunt Charlotte," he agreed somewhat philosophically. "They do say it's a wise child that knows his own father, which makes me, I suppose, the wisest child in my family."

"Actually you've got it turned round. ' 'Tis a wise father who knows his own child,' " Charlotte Hungerford corrected with a slight trace of the pedant in her nature.

"Haw"—Buckthorpe guffawed grimly—"nobody's ever accused the guv'nor of bein' a wise man."

"Poor Charles," Fanny Hungerford lamented suddenly and vociferously, drawing both aunt and nephew from their little colloquy, "how he should have suffered had he known of Helena's shocking indiscretions. Thank the Lord, he never knew," she moaned dramatically.

"Quite so," Charlotte muttered.

"Thank the Lord, indeed!" she went on, waxing even more fulsome on the subject. This, too, was a familiar lament. "Bad enough for any gentleman's daughter, one may say, but for a *parson's* daughter! It is really unthinkable!"

"Then pray do not think of it," Charlotte suggested rather acerbicly.

"Helena is such a disappointment. A clergyman's daughter and risen, by fortune, so far above her station as marriage to an honest viscount! But does she appreciate her happy lot? Not that hussey! Why, she behaves no better than a duchess! Oh, the shame of it! The disgrace!" Mrs. Hungerford lamented at length, a handkerchief pressed to the end of her red nose in dismay.

Charlotte had had quite enough of this display. "Tell Bucky about Mrs. Creevey's boils, Mother," she shouted across the room loudly enough to be heard over the elder woman's shrill laments. Buckthorpe Vane shot her a look of unmitigated horror.

"What? What?" Fanny Hungerford asked distractedly.

"Mrs. Creevey's boils, Mother," Charlotte repeated with precise enunciation as if her stepmother were slightly deaf. "Tell Bucky all about them whilst I give orders for tea." With that, Charlotte Hungerford escaped from the drawing room, leaving her nephew to his fate.

"Ah, she's gone," Fanny Hungerford whispered in relief immediately when the doors had closed on her stepdaughter's retreating form. "Really, Buckthorpe, dear boy, I am so glad you have come to stay with us. Charlotte has been impossible these past weeks."

"Oh?" young Buckthorpe prompted noncommittally. This was an interesting turn, he thought.

"She is no fit company at all, sour and grumpy and so mercilessly dry in her humour, always complaining that she wants peace and quiet. And she's forever scribbling away at that new novel of hers. There's simply no living with her, I tell you!" Mrs. Hungerford lamented.

"Maybe she does want peace, Grandmama—*Fanny,*" he amended hastily as he noticed the look she gave him.

"Peace! Fah! She'll have peace and quiet soon enough when she's dead and buried, and that's the truth. What she wants is a man, Bucky. A husband!"

Now this was a development indeed, young Buckthorpe Vane thought to himself, his eyes alight with the possibilities of mischief afoot. "A husband! Ah, I see. Now that's all very well, I'm sure, but for God's sake, Aunt Charlotte's never bothered much with men. Not that she couldn't, mind ya. She's pretty enough, the Lord knows, but she's got that devilish wicked tongue and—and—"

"And?" Fanny urged, wishing to get a man's point of view on

20

the girl, even if it was only Bucky's opinion. After all, it must count for something.

"She's too damned smart by half, Fanny," he finally blurted out in exasperation. "She makes a feller feel a fool. They *look* at her and fall head over heels. They *talk* with her, and it's like a cold bucket of ice water smack in the face." Young Lord Vane could envision countless admiring glances that he had seen directed toward his aunt in the years since he was old enough to notice such things, and no wonder! What with her elegantly coiffed chestnut curls, all gleaming red highlights in the sun; her slumbrous, honey-amber eyes, sensually hooded and surrounded by the longest, thickest lashes of any lady he had ever seen, Charlotte Hungerford was a real head turner.

She invited any gentleman with a connoisseur's eye and a libertine's heart to turn and look again as she passed by, haughty and serene in her bearing, high-bosomed and slim-waisted, long of neck, graceful of step; yet, whenever they spoke, she flattened their puffing male pride with a word and a glance, for her tongue could be very tart, and those hooded, inviting, honey-amber eyes could flash with anger, turning dark and menacing or cold and stiff with hauteur.

No, young Bucky thought with a shake of his head, there was no getting around his aunt's physical attractions, or her warmth and humour when she was disposed to be at her best, but never yet, to his knowledge, had any man seen her at her best, and now, at twenty-six, with a goodly quantity of successful novels to her credit, what man stood a chance? Now she was not only pretty, high-spirited, and haughty but independent financially as well. She had a name that was known in its own right and so needed no man's title to give her place.

He shook his head again. The more he thought about his aunt, the more he despaired. "Ice water smack in the face, that's what it is, Fanny, and it's terribly offputtin' ta a feller, ya know."

"I know," she agreed disconsolately, her curls shaking and the rest of her pleasantly ample person following suit.

"Aunt Charlotte's a born spinster, I'm afraid," he said. "A reg'lar Jane Austen, if ya ask me."

21

"Well, I am not asking you, Bucky. I am telling you," Mrs. Hungerford stated with renewed determination in her button-bright dark eyes. "I have managed to drag her down here to Brighton this summer for the express purpose of findin' her a husband."

"You have?" young Vane blurted out in surprise. It was an interesting trick—seeing both sides of a coin at once, so to speak.

"Certainly! You cannot imagine that I really *like* drinking warm seawater, can you? It is all for Charlotte's sake."

"But Charlotte don't like seawater either, so what's the point?"

"How dull you can be, boy." Fanny Hungerford clucked. "Lord Ned Darlington, of course."

"Ned Darlin'ton? What about him?"

"I declare, Bucky, that snuff has gone to your brains! Lord Ned Darlington," she repeated with more precise enunciation, "is the Duke of Axminster's eldest son."

"Yes, Fanny, I know who he is. What's he got to do with Aunt Charlotte?"

"He's mad for her."

"Is he?" This was the first Bucky had heard. Poor Darlin'ton, was his private comment.

"He is indeed," Fanny was answering smugly. "He's followed her around like a puppy all spring, and the more she pushes him away, the more he perseveres. He's lovesick, I tell you, *and* the heir to a dukedom."

"Fancy Aunt Charlotte a duchess," young Buckthorpe mused, trying to envision his spinster aunt in crimson and ermine.

"And why not?" Fanny Hungerford snapped indignantly. She had genuine affection for her stepdaughter and was mightily proud of the young woman's accomplishments. "If your mother could land a viscount, Charlotte ought to rate at *least* a duke, if not, in fact, a duke royal! Oh, not one of our dukes royal, of course," she amended. "One of those libertine vagabonds would never do for *our* Charlotte, but some nice Continental duke or prince—Protestant, naturally," she rambled on, losing her original point in her high hopes for the girl, which was natural after all, for she had raised her from the age of ten. Though she adored Charlotte, she tended to be rather in awe of the girl's prettiness, intelligence, and talent. Yet, like most ladies of her age, Fanny counted no young woman truly happy unless she was married—preferably with a title—and hence the origin of her despair over Charlotte Hungerford's impending spinsterhood.

"Ned Darlin'ton, you say?" Buckthorpe remarked thoughtfully.

"Yes. The moment I heard that he was going to be down here with the Duke of Cumberland and the regent's entourage, I knew what I must do."

"So you grabbed her by the forelock and dragged her kickin' and screamin' all the way from Wiltshire ta Brighton."

"Indeed," she agreed with a pleased pursing of her plump, ripe-lipped mouth, neglecting to add that she had fixed it with Neddy beforehand, the two of them being in cahoots like Romeo and Juliet's nurse—though, hopefully, with less dramatic results.

Bucky watched her thoughtfully for a moment. Yes, Charlotte was right about his stepgrannie. She was youngish yet, ripe and buxom enough to please some old duffer. It was a devilish interestin' situation, the young man observed to himself. Here he was being asked to play the maestro to two matchmaking enterprises at once. Could he pull it off? Get *two* ladies down the centre aisle and married off by the end of the summer? To tell the truth, Fanny didn't seem like much of a problem. All he needed was to find a suitable man, and he was sure Fanny herself could manage the rest.

But Charlotte Hungerford was another story entirely. There was, evidently, a suitable enough man in the picture already. But Bucky just happened to know that his aunt could not abide the sight of Ned Darlington. Seemingly impossible odds, them.

Still, that's what made a horse race, wasn't it?

When Charlotte Hungerford returned to the drawing room, her stepmother was indeed expounding on Mrs. Creevey's boils. No surprise there. What puzzled her was the faraway look of almost wicked amusement in the glittering blue eyes of young, handsome Lord Buckthorpe Vane. She was sharp enough to be suspicious.

"She's here." The young man sighed as he leaned his long, spare figure against the frame of the bow window in which he stood and stared diagonally across the street toward a particular door in the line of spanking new row houses, identical to the one from which he gazed and which housed for the summer himself and his two companions.

"Who's here?" came a rumbling, grumpy, curmudgeonly voice from behind a breakfast table set farther back in the room.

"His ladylove, naturally," answered another, deep, lighter baritone from the direction of the silver trays set out upon the sideboard. "Took a house across the street."

"First I've heard of it," came the rejoinder, slightly Germanic in accent and definitely testy in intonation. "What's the wench's name, Darlin'ton?" he called.

Another sigh came from the distracted young lord moping in the window. "Miss Charlotte Hungerford," he proclaimed as if the name should be etched in gold on the stained-glass windows of a shrine.

"D'ya know her, Cheng?" rumbled H.R.H. Ernest, Duke of Cumberland and Teviotdale, fifth son of mad King George III and his embarrassingly fruitful consort, Queen Charlotte of England, to the immaculate gentleman in black and buff who had taken a seat beside him and was proceeding to attack his breakfast with a will.

"Never laid eyes on her," came the reply, somewhat distorted, the words having to make their way through a barrier of bacon and egg.

"She pretty, Ned?" Duke Ernest called across the room to the young man in the window.

"Beautiful." He sighed.

"She anyone's daughter?" the duke persevered.

"Nobody's." Ned Darlington shrugged disinterestedly. "Just a country parson's gel. She's Bucky Vane's maternal aunt, though," he added helpfully.

"That whelp." The duke laughed, showing a fine, strong set of teeth and a goodly portion of scrambled egg as well. "One o' them 'variable Vanes,' eh?"

"He's the 'invariable' one o' the lot," Ned Darlington answered a trifle defensively, heartily wishing that he had said nothing at all.

"No matter," the duke mumbled into his tea. "The mother's a tart. What's the sister like?"

"She is a virtuous and proper lady." Darlington sniffed.

"Too virtuous and too proper, from what Ned tells me," said Sir Hannibal Cheng, Bart., leering over his teacup. "Ain't been in her bed yet, have ye, lad?" he taunted.

"Damn me, Cheng, shut up. She's the gel I'm going to marry," Ned Darlington snapped in exasperation. He had not meant to make such an admission, especially to these two cynical and worldly fellows, but he had allowed himself to be goaded.

"Marry!" both men shouted at once, spewing the table with incidental bits of breakfast in the process.

The duke wiped crumbs of egg from his luxuriant mustache and looked hard at Ned Darlington, with his one good eye starting from its socket like a well-coddled egg. "Why on earth d'ya have to marry her?"

"Because I love her, sir, and because I want her for my wife," Lord Darlington declared self-righteously and with an air of manly dignity somewhat weakened in its effect by a rather reedy tenor voice.

"Noble lad." Sir Hannibal Cheng applauded with mocking approval.

"I don't know why *you* mock me, Cheng, you of all people. You'd still be tucked up on your estate in Ireland if your wife hadn't died on you. You've known the joys of matrimony—and you've got an heir as well. If I don't produce a little Darlington, why, the dukedom will die with me," he raved emotionally, forgetting for the nonce that his father had already covered that contingency by siring several younger sons as assurance of the Axminster perpetuity.

As Ned Darlington spoke, a look of pain passed for an instant over the peculiar features of the first Baronet Cheng and then was lost. "There are pitfalls as well as pleasures in marriage, lad," was all he said in reply.

Duke Ernest saw the swiftly passing expression on his friend's face and cut in quickly. "Neddy lad, we've older, wiser heads than yours. We're only tryin' ta warn you."

"I don't need warning. I've got my heart set on Charlotte Hungerford, and that's that," Lord Darlington stated flatly, his arms folded across his narrow chest and his gray eyes fixed stubbornly on a certain house across the way.

"No sense sayin' any more," Hannibal Cheng said, throwing his napkin down beside his plate and rising for a second helping from the covered dishes on the sideboard. "He's as stubborn a buck as ever I've met, Ernest, and there's no helpin' it." He stood by the table and stared past his friend out into the sunlit road beyond. It was already a bustle of activity despite the early hour, carriages coming and going in a constant succession, and presented a not unpleasant sight to the eyes of the first Baronet Cheng.

The Duke of Cumberland regarded him thoughtfully. Sir Hannibal Cheng was a peculiar-looking chap indeed, as peculiar-looking in his way as Ernest Cumberland himself, what with his sabre-scarred face and one eye gone forever. Yes, he thought, but Cheng was more than that—a rara avis if ever there was one—being half Irish and half Chinese. If that wasn't peculiar, then the duke didn't know what was!

Cheng was a stocky, muscular man of middle height with broad shoulders, a wide, handsome, tawny face, fiercely blazing black eyes, and a lion's mane of thick black hair, which he wore unpowdered and chopped off at the top inch of his collar. He affected an immaculately tailored black and buff riding habit as his main and terribly rakish mode of dress, abjured jewellery and lace of any sort, rode a black horse, and had never been seen to enter a carriage on any occasion whatsoever, tolerantly deeming such conveyances necessary for women, children, and old men, but an abhorrence to anyone who called himself a *man*.

He had been to China and back seven times already in his

thirty-eight years, was said to be the richest gentleman in Ireland, and was now a widower with a small son called William—after the late King William III, whose grant of land on Bantry Bay had established Sir Hannibal's Chinese forebears on Occidental soil and begun their rise to fortune, if not fame. Cynics might hint that it was the legendary Cheng family fortune which endeared him to Cumberland's heart, for like all his brothers, the duke was ever in debt. But in truth, to imply such a thing was unfair to both men. Sir Hannibal Cheng was a man worthy of the friendship and trust of kings, and Duke Ernest of Cumberland, a man of good brain and no little integrity, was the most misunderstood and unjustly reviled of all poor old King George's sons.

In short, while Hannibal Cheng and Ernest Cumberland might be considered the unlikeliest of friends in the realm, yet true friends they were—both rather outcasts for their looks and diffident manners, both men of action with no tolerance for lies and indirection, and yet both men of the mind as well, with great intelligence but little purpose. They both, at this point in their lives, wanted occupation. At present none was in the offing.

In fact, Cheng's greatest moment so far in his life was well behind him, having occurred in 1796, when he and the men of his merchant ship *William and Mary* and the servants of his vast estate called Moondragon had fought off an invasion of Bantry Bay by a small fleet of French ships, which had tried to land a party of soldiers for the purpose of fomenting discontent amongst the Irish peasantry. This act of patriotism had brought him to the notice of the duke and had earned him his baronetcy from George III. Cumberland had much admired the fierce young Irishman *cum* Chinaman, and from thence their friendship had sprung.

Cheng came out of his reverie, tearing his vacant eyes away from the activities beyond the windowpane, and addressed the young man hopefully. "Does she have money at least, Neddy?" he asked. Perhaps this parson's daughter had some advantage yet.

"Not much from her father, I expect, but she writes."

27

"Writes?" Duke Ernest exclaimed. "What does she write? Letters? *All* women write letters. Damned perfumed things, and they always expect an answer, too, eh, eh? Ain't that so, Cheng?"

"They may expect what they wish. You'd never catch me writin' letters," he drawled easily. Cheng's accent was a law unto itself: well-spoken King's English laced heavily with Gaelic intonations and occasionally singsongy inflections which his friends owned must be the result of his proficiency in Chinese and Gaelic as well as the more acceptable Latin, Greek, and French which everyone was supposed to be able to muddle about in. He generally hid the fact that he was a genuine scholar, preferring to lay emphasis on his dashing and heroic image as a seafarer, adventurer in the China trade, and occasional warrior on behalf of his sovereign.

"She don't write letters, you blocks," Ned Darlington moaned in exasperation. "She writes novels."

"Novels!" the duke exclaimed. "You mean she's a scribbler? Like Jane Austen? Like that Mrs.—Mrs. What-d'-ya-call-her who wrote that *Otranto* thing? Oh, that *is* hard cheese, young feller. Them lady writers are all dried-up old spinster types. No," Duke Ernest said with great finality and a sudden slap of his napkin on his thigh for emphasis, "she's *not* the gel for you, my lad. You want a fine, buxom wench who's willin' and winsome. No scribblers for my Neddy boy."

With that, Ned Darlington turned heel and went flying from the breakfast room, a long drawn-out wail of exasperation sounding in his wake.

"Humph! What d'ye make o' that, Cheng?" Duke Ernest asked indignantly.

" 'Fraid there's no helpin' him. He's got it bad as it can be," Hannibal Cheng replied with a dismissing wave of his hand.

"Of course, we'll help him. We have to, damn it. He's our friend. We can't have him go runnin' off and committin' the foolish act o' matrimony on us, now can we, eh, eh?" The duke had a point there.

"No, I suppose not. But how?" Cheng asked with only the vaguest interest. After all, Neddy had money enough not to have to marry more, and if he liked the wench, what business was it of theirs?

"First thing, we've got ta get a look at this scribbler o' his. See for ourselves just how barmy-brained he is," Duke Ernest said firmly, with the air of a commander about to take the field. Hannibal Cheng nodded in reluctant agreement. There was nothing else to be done, it seemed.

Lord Ned Darlington flew from the house and his troublesome companions like a man possessed but almost immediately checked his hasty flight, for the brightness of the morning sunlight, the hustle and bustle of the postbreakfast carriages taking groups of fine ladies and gentlemen of Brighton down to the spa smote upon his consciousness like the sudden, unexpected appearance of a high wall before one's horse during a hunt; it does tend to bring one up short!

He had actually intended, with all the impulsiveness of his nature, to tear across the road to Number 10 Seaview Row, rap the polished brass knocker off the very door itself, push past the startled butler, find Charlotte Hungerford—charming, he imagined, in elegant and sensual dishabille and taking chocolate on a chaise in her boudoir—and throw himself prostrate at her feet, laying before her haughty and indifferent person his life, his fortune—or his father's, rather—and his eventual dukedom.

How could she resist? he asked himself quite seriously. Yet, of course, he reminded himself forlornly, he had several times already done just that—offered his all at the feet of his ladylove —and each time she had simply patted his head and said with infuriating calm, "Do get up, Neddy darling, and stop being so silly."

Silly! He was *dying* of love, and she called him silly!

If Ned Darlington had not been so silly, he would have seen that of all the fair ladies in the whole of England, Charlotte Hungerford was perhaps the very last to be swayed by a prostrate form and a servile manner.

In fact, Charlotte herself had said as much on page 83 of *The Romance of Rowena Renfrew.* To wit:

* * *

When a gentleman takes to his knees before a lady with his head bowed low in supplication, he runs the serious risk of displaying to her jaundiced glance whatever green stuff yet remains behind his ears from his salad days. The healthier the growth of lettuce she spies, the less likely the puppy to win his suit. And that is the way of a woman.

Now whether it was actually the way of Woman in general or not, it was most definitely the way of Miss Hungerford in particular!

Moreover, whether Lord Darlington would have heeded that advice is a moot question, for he had never so much as cracked the spine of one of Charlotte Hungerford's novels, and it had never once occurred to him that, finding her an inscrutable and mysterious goddess of haughty and enticing indifference as he did, the key to her mysteries might lie, like a treasure waiting for discovery, right within the pages of the books that she turned out with no great regularity but with ever-increasing success.

So now, on a bright early-summer morning, the young suitor found himself in a quandary as old as time itself. What to do? How to win her? How to gain the hand and heart of his ladylove?

At just that moment the door to Number 10 opened, and Mrs. Fanny Hungerford bustled out onto the step, stopping to pull on her gloves and survey the scene before her.

"Yoo-hoo," she called across the road in a shrill, flutey voice with an attendant upraising and waving of her plump little arms.

Lord Ned Darlington, at great risk to his booted toes from the hooves of a pair of chestnut geldings, hurtled himself across Seaview Row and greeted Mrs. Hungerford almost before the arm raised over her head had dropped once more to her side. As they rode off together in her carriage, hope burned with a renewed fire deep in the eager heart of the Duke of Axminster's eldest son. In Fanny Hungerford, he had himself a powerful ally, or so he thought.

::2::

Ernest, Duke of Cumberland, stalked the Esplanade with all the upright, soldierly bearing and swagger of the superior cavalry officer he was, his one good eye surveying the passing throng with much the same observant and slightly suspicious manner as he might inspect a company of German troops on manoevres in Hanover. That little kingdom he was destined one day to rule, owing to the fact that under Salic law, his niece, Princess Charlotte of England, heiress presumptive to the throne, was barred by her sex from inheriting that kingdom along with the others over which her male forebears held sway.

His was an unmistakable and striking figure in the summer sunshine, what with his deeply sunken, cloudy left eye, the sabre scars across his face, and the deep pit in his temple which was the result of a trephining operation but a few years earlier. His face, which some said mirrored his soul, caused many to avert their eyes as they passed, for his one good eye wore a perpetual squint against the brightness of the sun and his mouth a grim scowl that was only occasionally replaced by a leering show of square teeth beneath the full-flowing cavalryman's mustache. With his tall, solid, well-built person, Ernest was, of all his brothers, the finest of figure and most probably the best of brain and perspicacity. His tragedy was that his battle-scarred looks were against him and that his sharp tongue was quite as forbidding and unpopular as his scowl. Moreover, his politics and those of his elder brother, the prince regent, were quite at odds.

All this did not, however, prevent the ladies and gentlemen of fashion, riding and strolling along the Esplanade, from greeting him with some deference as they passed. He returned their attentions with polite, if somewhat distant, civility. But now, tired of such empty formalities, he turned his back and stood, arms akimbo, looking out toward the Channel; Sir Hannibal Cheng was beside him, leaning casually against the parapet with his back to that body of water and his elbows resting on either side, one booted foot crossed over the other at the ankle.

"Here comes Bucky Vane," Cheng informed his companion laconically as he spied a tall, robust young man in fine, if somewhat dishevelled, tailoring, strolling toward them in the middle distance.

"That whelp," Cumberland grumbled thoughtlessly, and then realized the implication. "Ah, the nephew, what?"

"So Ned says."

"See if you can collar him, Cheng. Don't mention nothin', though," he cautioned needlessly, since at this point Sir Hannibal Cheng was finding the whole matter rather a bore. He did not share his friend's Hanoverian love of intrigue, and whilst he enjoyed an occasional romantic lark of his own, he could hardly take Ned Darlington's plight seriously. No wench, he had come to believe in his thirty-eight years, was worth much serious effort on his part, and certainly not worth agonizing over! Of all the ladies he had ever known—including his own late little wife, who had been a cousin, part Chinese like himself, and a meek, yielding flower of a woman so frail as to have barely survived by a month the birth of their only child—not one had really been much different from another. Their company was needed primarily to satisfy the more earthy desires of his undoubtedly sensual nature or, in the case of his late cousin-wife, to perpetuate his line.

Thus far Sir Hannibal's greatest challenges in life had been taming the high seas to the prow of his ship and the winds to her sails. That a female might present, on dry land, a challenge of equal magnitude had never occurred to him at all, and perhaps never would have, had he not heeded Duke Ernest's request and hailed young Lord Buckthorpe Vane out of the throng moving along the Esplanade.

"Off to take the waters, Vane?" the duke asked with seeming casualness once greetings had been exchanged.

"Not likely," Bucky answered, making a face at the very thought. "Just off ta fetch me auntie, who's buyin' out Macready's in the town."

"Macready's?" Cumberland asked, his eye lighting up at the fortuitousness of it all.

"Bookseller's," Cheng informed him, although he refrained from adding that he himself was guilty of an occasional foray into that dusty and fascinating establishment.

"Ah, books! Yes, I see," the duke mumbled. "Scribbler o' some sort, ain't she, Vane?" he asked with studied nonchalance.

"Ladies' novels, Your Highness," Bucky explained, and, upon seeing the duke's dark scowl, made a mental note to drop the formality of his address in future. "You know the sort," he went on when he saw that more was expected of him. "Gothick stuff— dungeons, lost heirs, ghostly visitants, deflowered virgins—"

"Eh?" Cumberland leered with a sudden increase of interest.

"Nothing there, sir, I can assure you. All very sub rosa," Bucky added hastily, lest the duke think ill of his terribly proper aunt. Actually he was wrong on both counts: The duke would have admired her the more, and his aunt was really not as proper as Bucky liked to think.

The duke, his hopes of some spicy reading deflated, merely grunted a noncommittal "Oh."

There came then a slightly awkward silence as Cumberland's mind raced to find a new tack to try and as Bucky endeavoured to think of a way to escape the duke's less than easy company. Hannibal Cheng, seeing the discomfort of both men, and by reason of his inscrutably sardonic part-Oriental nature and his fey part-Irish sense of whimsey, refused aid or comfort to either of them. He simply stood Buddhalike and watched.

Finally, the duke, spying a rather pretty and lively young woman amongst the crowd, spoke up, "Now there's a fine-lookin' gel, lads, in't she?" He bowed and leered in the young lady's direction, at which action the female in question blushed crimson and tittered behind her hand to a less pretty, less well-endowed companion, who had until then escaped all notice.

"Buxom little wench, eh, Bucky?" he asked companionably. "Your auntie ain't half so handsome as that, I'll wager, eh? Eh?" He leered with a devilish wink of his good right eye and a sharp nudge in Bucky's ribs.

Hannibal Cheng winced at this tactless "subtlety," but he had no need to worry, for young Vane was not that subtle himself and therefore answered the question in all seriousness.

"On the contrary, sir," he said with solemn pride, "my aunt Charlotte is a damned sight more handsome and would not, I like to think, be caught dead either blushin' or titterin' behind her mitt. In fact, I'm afraid she'd be more than likely ta stare back in such a way as to make *you* blush."

"Humph," the duke grunted in displeasure. What kind of behaviour might that be? he was thinking testily.

"Sounds a Tartar to me," Cheng interjected dryly.

" 'Fraid so," Bucky agreed mournfully.

"Don't sound ta me the kind o' wench as would have a suitor," the duke put in ingratiatingly as he put his arm firmly about Bucky Vane's shoulders and steered him slowly along the Esplanade in the direction of the town. Buckthorpe, somewhat dismayed, had nought to do but be steered. After all, one does not lightly balk at the attentions of a royal duke.

Sir Hannibal, divining his friend's intent, bestirred himself grudgingly from his stance against the parapet and strolled along just behind them, his hands clasped at his back, his dark eyes wandering idly over the oncoming crowd.

"Oh, she has a suitor, all right," Bucky was saying, but Cheng heard no more, for he let his mind wander as freely as his eye. They had not gone far when his gaze was arrested by the fetching sight of a young woman dressed in the prettiest shade of light blue silk, trimmed with honey-coloured satin and ecru lace, tripping jauntily along the high street leading down to the Esplanade with a small parcel tucked in the crook of her arm.

She was slim and shapely with a full bosom and light, graceful carriage, her head high and regal. From under her very simple, very fashionable bonnet peeked a goodly number of thick chestnut curls. But it was her expression that really held Sir Hannibal's notice once her general appearance had attracted it, for a delightful smile played upon her lips, and as she came closer, he saw that same smile lit up her large, bright eyes as well. Most remarkably, that charming smile, rather than being directed toward some lucky companion or even the pleasant, bustling Brighton scene in general, was instead turned totally inward. She looked so delightful in her expression because of some thoughts within her own pretty head or some scene being enacted before her own mind's eye.

How unusual, Sir Hannibal Cheng thought to himself. A pretty woman who actually *thinks* as well!

Even more of a miracle, this interesting creature did not turn off in some distant direction, but rather stepped onto the Esplanade directly into his path and that of his companions, who were still strolling just ahead of him. Perhaps he would do her the honour of a greeting as she passed, he thought.

"So there you are," the young woman in blue called lightly and with a merry twinkle in her eye. "I expected you a good quarter of an hour ago. It is well that I did not buy out the shop, as you said I would, or I should never have managed." Without any further ceremony, she thrust her small parcel into Bucky Vane's hands and laughed wickedly. There was just a hint of the scold in her voice and a hint of the parent as well, which Sir Hannibal instantly ascribed to their rightful causes. This was Bucky Vane's aunt! This was the scribbler! This was the woman Ned Darlington wanted to marry!

To say that Sir Hannibal Cheng went dizzy would be no exaggeration. He stood behind his two companions—in fact, had almost banged right into them when they stopped to speak with the lady in question—and literally swayed on the heels of his high-topped, gleaming black boots.

Those bright eyes of hers, now he saw them closer, were a peculiar shade of amber that reminded him of a particular variety of Oriental jade. They were thickly lashed, large, and very expressive. Her voice was firm and very pleasant, her whole manner completely self-assured, or so it seemed to him at the time. In short, she was really a rather remarkable example of her sex, he decided. He was certainly right in that, for any woman who had the power to make Sir Hannibal Cheng's head swim as it was swimming at that moment must be a remarkable example of her kind indeed!

He could not quite hear what the three of them were saying, owing to the slight buzzing in his ears that attended upon his swimming head, but suddenly he felt those great amber eyes turned full upon him, and he had to come, perforce, to his senses. She was staring up at him quite frankly between the shoulders of his two companions, just as Bucky Vane had said she was likely to do, and he, Sir Hannibal Cheng, first Baronet Cheng of Moondragon, found that he was indeed colouring, for he could feel the heat rise in his wide tawny cheeks. Seeing the slightly quizzical bemusement in her expression, he chose to interpret it in accordance with his present embarrassment.

Who the devil is this half-witted, funny-looking Chinee feller? he supposed she must be asking herself. Why does he look so dull and stammer so?

Suddenly the impact of who she was struck him all over again. This was Darlington's wench. Gad, poor Neddy! No wonder he'd gone barmy. No wonder he'd lost his head, poor devil. And then, with a groan of dismay, the first Baronet Cheng realized that Lord Ned Darlington was not the only poor devil in Brighton who'd lost his head to Charlotte Hungerford!

Now, truth to tell, poor Sir Hannibal cannot really be blamed, but he might have saved himself a great deal of subsequent bother had he not so drastically misread the undeniably bemused expression on Miss Hungerford's pretty face.

She had come down the high street from Macready's with her thoughts intent upon an exchange of witticisms between her latest heroine, Lady Viola de Villiers and her slightly wicked hero, Renaldo, Duke of Dalmatia (all of Charlotte Hungerford's heroes were slightly wicked), when she saw her nephew making his way up the Esplanade toward her, intent on the conversation of a tall man of soldierly bearing whose scarred face and bristling mustache indicated that he could be none other than the unsavoury Duke of Cumberland.

It was then that she noticed, between the shoulders of the two taller men, another face, and at that moment all thought of the wicked Duke of Dalmatia fled from her inventive mind. Gone, too, was the heretofore utter perfection of Sir Berry de Groat's wavy black hair; the enticing devilment in the dark eyes of Maida's lowborn lover, Ravenstock, and even the firm, square jaw of Laird Angus MacPherson, Lord o' the Isles, were as nothing before the impact of the face that hovered, disembodied, behind the left shoulder of her nephew.

Now there was a face to conjure with! she thought. There was the face of a hero! Handsome yet imperfect; powerful, strange, and far from the common lot of faces. Neither Maida nor Lady Viola nor even Rowena Renfrew herself had ever had such a hero with which to dally. In fact, no face out of Charlotte's wildest fancies, or depicted in her most passionate novels, could match that wonderful face.

The hair was black, straight, and thick; the eyes were wide and very dark brown, alert and sharp, with a real mind behind them. The mouth—oh, the mouth! So wide and firm, strong and romantically grim; the lips straight and not overly full, but quite full enough to bruise when they kissed an eager mouth. Gad, Lady Viola would die for the kisses of such a mouth!

The face was broad, the nose good, high-bridged and not too small, the cheekbones high and wide, the skin tawny, almost like a lion's, with a cast to it that suggested the exotic and romantic. This was no callow, pastey-faced English puppy with ruddy cheeks and thin blood. This was a man!

She did not quite remember later on just what it was she had said to her nephew as she approached. She had been quick enough, however, to thrust her little parcel of books into Bucky's hands at once, lest by holding it, she betray the fact that she had begun to tremble quite violently.

God alone knew what it was she had said to the Duke of

37

Cumberland upon their introduction; she had hardly taken any notice of him at all, which was in itself a tribute to the charms of Hannibal Cheng, for Charlotte Hungerford had always harboured a secret longing to meet the celebrated and notorious one-eyed duke. His reputation for outspokenness as well as utterly depraved and wicked deeds insured that he must be, in theory, if not in actual fact, a man after Charlotte's own heart. His reputed bravery in battle, his hideous scars and dramatic appearance ranked him high in her esteem as a hero of exceptional proportions. However, all of this was as nothing in the light of the exotic being who stood behind the once-fascinating royal duke.

At last, throwing all discretion to the winds, she had dared stare up directly and expectantly into the utterly magnificent and virtually godlike countenance which loomed up before her.

Who are you? she asked herself as she gazed into the stranger's sombre face, so stiff, regal, and disinterested—the exotic face of some prince of Araby perhaps, or even—

Who are you? she wondered as she looked deep into his wide, melting Oriental eyes—some Persian adventurer perhaps, or a maharajah sailed westward from the emerald shores of Serendip?

Now, had she dared to pose those extravagant questions aloud to Sir Hannibal Cheng, and had he, in his somewhat shaken condition, had the presence of mind to answer articulately, he might, in all truth, have replied: "No, Miss Hungerford, I am no prince of Araby, nor even a maharajah from the Isle of Serendip, but I am a true descendant, may it please you, of the last emperor of the Ming Dynasty of Imperial China."

Had he answered thus, Miss Hungerford would have fainted dead away!

Charlotte Hungerford had spent some hours now in a state of agitation that was at once wonderful and bewildering, joyful and frightening, for poor Charlotte had done at last exactly what Maida and Rowena Renfrew and so many other of her heroines had done before her. She had fallen in love. And like most of those other rather impetuous ladies of her mind's devising, it had been at first sight, total, complete, and every bit as startling and agonizing as missing one's step and falling full tilt down a steep flight of stairs.

Perhaps it even served her right! After all, look what she had put poor Maida through before the revelation of Ravenstock's true birthright proved him to be a worthy match for her. And think of the agonies suffered by Lady Isobelle Stuart before she was finally carried off to a life of bliss as the wife of Angus MacPherson, Lord o' the Isles, in the last chapter of *Isobelle of the Isles.*

Charlotte shuddered as she bethought herself guiltily of poor Lady Viola de Villiers and what tortures of love and despair she had so recently and calculatingly been planning for that noble, long-to-suffer young woman before her ultimate triumph in Society as the rightful Duchess of Dalmatia. If this was what it was really like to fall in love—and though Charlotte had been smitten often enough, she had never really been *in love* in her life—then she was not only a lady novelist, but a lady torturer as well, to have ever put so much as one of her beloved heroines into such a painful position as this!

Just as she was coming to grips with the agony of this new revelation and wondering at its ultimate outcome, young Buckthorpe made his appearance on the scene, entering the parlour, tout sheet in hand, and intent upon the latest entries for Newmarket.

After the most perfunctory exchange between them, he threw himself upon a settee and buried his nose in his paper.

"Bucky darling, you do have the oddest friends," Charlotte Hungerford remarked at length, keeping her eyes on her needlework lest they betray the concern behind her seemingly casual statement.

"How so, Auntie?" Buckthorpe asked with no great interest, his own eyes continuing to scan an appraisal of a certain dark horse entry. He hoped that politely discouraged, she would kindly shut up.

"Well, that fellow Cheng, for instance," she proffered tentatively and with a slight inner trembling.

"I hardly know the chap," Bucky mumbled.

Damn him, he was no help at all, Charlotte thought. "You must know something of him, I should think," she persisted a trifle tartly.

"He's half a Chinee, I think. Comes from Ireland. Mother was a Wallace. An aloof sort o' fellow. I don't much like him." Really! How could a fellow handicap a race under these conditions? Bucky fretted to himself.

"A gambler, I suppose, and a libertine," Charlotte suggested, half in hope and half in fear. He must, after all, have some wicked vice or flaw—but not *too* wicked, of course.

"No, not really," Bucky contradicted. "Likes his wenchin' I expect, as which of us don't? But he's a sailor o' sorts—China trade. Captains his own merchantman, I understand."

"Does he? How odd," Charlotte remarked thoughtfully, a faraway gleam in her eye. How *romantic,* is what she was actually thinking.

"Hasn't been about much until recently. Very thick with Cumberland, though. Has a small son, I think," young Buckthorpe drawled, dredging up the few morsels of gossip he had heard of the peculiar Chinee baronet since his arrival in Brighton.

"He's *married?*" Charlotte shrilled with far more alarm than was wise to display. She felt her heart drop like a lead weight within her heaving breast.

"Widower. Young son," was all the reply her nephew felt moved to muster, for his thoughts were intent upon the racing form. With the sound of hooves on grass-green turf occupying the ear of his imagination, he did not hear Charlotte's quite audible sigh of relief at his welcome intelligence.

A widower, she thought. Thank God! Suddenly her mind was off and spinning just as it did when a novel was abrewing. She imagined the stalwart, bereft young baronet, grieving like a medieval knight beside the tomb of his lost bride—his heart empty and aching, his fevered brow in need of the cool, soothing hand of consolation and the tender caresses of a new love—a love such as Charlotte Hungerford's, for instance!

"Ouch," she cried as, in her vexation, she stabbed herself smartly with her needle.

"What *has* got into you this afternoon, Charlotte?" Bucky asked impatiently, putting down his paper and really looking at her for the first time since he had entered the room. "You've been as nervy as a cat all day. Is it that time o' the month, eh?"

"I *have* not, and it *is* not, you little beast," she snapped. "Moreover, if you ever make such a vulgar remark again, it's back to Wooton-Maggot for you, me bucko!" Which threat served to shut Buckthorpe Vane tighter than a North Sea clam!

Oh, but she wanted him! She wanted Sir Hannibal Cheng, Bart., with her whole being; he was the most gorgeous, romantic, striking man that she had ever seen in her life! He made every hero out of every book she had ever read—including her own— look pale in comparison.

"I shall do it, Bucky. Yes, I shall indeed! See if I won't!" Charlotte Hungerford exclaimed aloud, the conviction of her words somewhat abated by their rather indistinct utterance, which was owing to the fact that her pricked finger was still stuck, unnoticed, in her mouth, where she had lodged it to stop the pain and stem the flow of blood.

"What shall you do, my dear?" her nephew asked tolerantly, finding his aunt, when in such a distracted and vehement state, to be rather fetching in her way.

"Marry him!" she blurted out unthinkingly and with instant regret.

"Marry who?" he asked in bewilderment.

"Whom!" Charlotte corrected.

"Whom, then," Bucky conceded and then added hopefully, "Ned Darlington?"

"What? What?" She looked across at him in a glassy-eyed daze and then said, "Oh, no, not that fatuous dolt," with a dismissing wave of her hand. "No—I shall marry *him*—to—to *Fanny,*" she added brightly, the germ of a splendid and terribly devious idea coming to full form.

"Ned Darlington?" Bucky repeated, completely at a loss.

"Young Ned Darlington and *old* Fanny Hungerford?" Had Aunt Charlotte taken leave of her senses?

"Stop talking of Neddy Darlington, you simpleton! No, Sir Hannibal Cheng."

"Hannibal Cheng marry Fanny? *Our* Fanny?"

"Of course. Do you not see that it is perfect? He is old— probably about her age, in fact—yet not too old—"

"But he ain't sick, so far as I know," young Vane broke in protestingly. "Though if he *is* sick, I'll wager it's the pox," he added with a devilish twinkle in his blue eyes. Charlotte shot him her Wooton-Maggot look, and the light fled his eye like the guttering of a candle flame.

"No, he is not sick, I grant you. He looks the perfect picture of health, in fact, but he is a widower with a child to raise, which is even better. Fanny is marvellous with children. Why, she practically raised me and see how well I've turned out," she answered with total unselfconsciousness. "She's just the thing he needs."

Young Buckthorpe looked askance at his aunt. "What makes you think Cheng will agree to all this? He seems a happy enough fellow to me just as he is." What man in his right mind marries if he don't have to anyway? Bucky wondered.

"Ah, but is he? Perhaps his reserve hides an aching, lonely heart!"

"Oh, bosh! Now you sound just like some silly gel out o' one o' them novels you write. Besides, even if his heart were lonely and aching, why Fanny and not some licentious, mad young thing like Lady Caroline Lamb or an agreeable strumpet like them Wilson gels are said to be?" he asked merrily before burying his nose where he felt it really belonged—in the latest racing news.

Somewhat chastened by that not unjustified rebuff, and shaken to her very core by a reminder of the quality and variety of the competition against which she must scheme, Charlotte returned without a word to her needlework. But whilst her hands flicked across the canvas, she was spinning spiderlike a new plot for a

42

new adventure for a new heroine. This time the heroine was Charlotte Hungerford herself.

That same afternoon found Sir Hannibal Cheng, the unwitting object of so much secret desire, skulking about in the dim, dusty interior of Macready's Bookseller's establishment like an embarrassed bull in the proverbial china shop. Having refused all offers of assistance with a wave and a growl, he hemmed, hawed, and browsed til his hands were grimy and his nostrils itched with the accumulated dust of ages.

But, damn it, try as he would, he could not find whatever obscure shelf or stall he supposed must be given over to ladies' novels, though in his search he had found innumerable copies of *The Compleat Angler,* Pepys, and endless Boswells, the memoirs of a score of doddering generals, and God alone knew how many histories of Rome, Greece, and other older, longer-dead civilizations. He even came across a copy of *The Military History of the Ming Dynasty* by his own late father, William Ch'engkung Cheng, and a few odd volumes by his maternal grandfather, the Irish military historian Valerian Wallace, the contents of whose personal library Sir Hannibal had inherited with much pleasure some years earlier.

Now all this was very gratifying in its way, but where the devil did they hide the ladies' novels? At last, grimy and testy with frustration, he was forced to mumble a sotto voce question in the general direction of the clerk.

"I beg your pardon, Sir Hannibal, but I could not hear you," the young, rather supercilious clerk remarked loudly enough for all to hear. "Will you please speak up?"

Resisting a strong urge to kill, Cheng enunciated with a menacing distinctness that frightened the young man just a trifle, "Ladies' novels! Where are the ladies' novels kept, you ass?" There was that in his eye and aspect which made the clerk quake and make no protest to the objectionable animal with which he had just been compared. Instead, he merely pointed in the direction of the large left-hand bow window of the shop and stammered something about novels of Romance and the Gothick.

"Sick aunt," Cheng muttered as he stalked toward the long row of stalls filled to overflowing by a plethora of books of a romantic nature. He hugged a copy of one of Grandpapa Wallace's books of famous battles as proof of his personal reading habits, slowed his step appreciably, and edged himself between the low stalls in the window like a crab scuttling sidewise up to something that looks both dead and edible, but that may prove to be, upon closer inspection, both alive and predatory.

He had just put his trembling, anxious fingers to the spine of a copy of *The Madness of Maida*, his heart quickening alarmingly at the very sight of the name Charlotte Hungerford in gilt letters below the title, when suddenly there came a sharp, insistent rapping on the glass panes of the bow window just at his back.

Sir Hannibal Cheng started as if he had been shot and, dropping his books, he turned, white-faced and horrified, toward the sound. He had not felt such a shock since that time, long ago, when he was fifteen and his father had caught him with his hand up the parlour maid's skirts.

There, on the other side of the shopwindow, his already grotesque face pressed even more grotesquely against a dusty pane, was the leering countenance of H.R.H. Ernest, Duke of Cumberland. Gesticulating wildly, he motioned Hannibal Cheng to come out at once. When he saw his usually phlegmatic friend behaving in such an erratic manner, there seemed nought else to do but obey his summons, and so, with many an inward oath, Sir Hannibal turned heel and fled Macready's with all the haste of a man obeying a royal command, which in a sense it was after all. Miss Hungerford's books would have to wait.

"Gad, Cumberland," he called as he came out onto the pavement, "what's got into you? You'd think you'd seen a ghost."

"No such luck, Cheng! No such damnable luck," he shouted over his shoulder as he strode down the street, dodging passersby with somewhat more agility than grace. Cheng stretched his legs to their fullest extent, trying to catch up with his taller companion as the duke turned an agitated, blood-drained, angry face back toward him and growled by way of explanation, "I've just seen *Garth!*"

"*Garth!*" Sir Hannibal Cheng repeated, stopping dead in his tracks.

"And that damnable whelp," the duke snarled, adding a string of oaths more suited to some low gambling hell than the fashionable streets of Brighton.

Garth! Cheng thought to himself. And after all these years. Now this *was* a pretty pass!

::3::

By the time Sir Hannibal caught up to the duke, they had gal-
loped the length of the Esplanade in record time and were already rounding the last turn into Seaview Row like the two best
bets at a racing meet. Sir Hannibal could see that the huge bulk
of Cumberland's closed travelling coach was stopped before the
door of their digs at Number 17, the horses freshly harnessed and
champing at their bits, the driver already in the box and only
awaiting the word to set off. The household servants were strap-
ping the last of several travelling boxes into place in the boot.

"You are—ah, *we're*—going on a journey?" Sir Hannibal
asked casually, amending the pronoun pointedly as he recognized some of his own impedimenta being loaded into place.

"Damned right, we are," the duke rumbled under his slightly
puffing breath.

"May I ask where?" Cheng pursued mildly. He was neither
surprised nor annoyed, being used, after all these years, to his
friend's unthinking high-handedness and mindful, too, of the
trust that such behaviour implied in a man such as Ernest Cumberland.

"Yes, ya may ask where, if you're that slow, man! Weymouth,
naturally—or Melcombe Regis, to be specific. Where in blazes
d'ya think I'd be settin' off for after telling ya I'd just seen *Garth*
and that damned young whelp, Thomas? I'd supposed they must
be in London—or better yet, China—but they ain't, damn them"
Here the duke let fly with another colourful and linguistically

46

eclectic string of obscenities of the sort for which he was justly infamous.

"And so you are going to run off and tell Princess Sophia."

"I'll do more than tell her, Cheng. I've got to head her off. She's comin' here in the next day or two. The regent's invited her ta the pavillion, but she's taking a house near Hove for the season. Says the activity in Brighton would be too much, but that she can visit from Hove if she improves. It's all nonsense if you ask me! I thought she was better off where she was—the sea air's just as good to breathe in Weymouth as here—but she would have it so. But *now,* if that whelp is goin' ta be skulkin' about, why then, I want her safe in Weymouth, where she belongs, damn it." The duke, ever the martinet, tended to protect his younger sister, the princess Sophia, with a fierceness borne of a deep, if rather wrongheaded, affection. In fact, on more than one occasion the demonstration of that overzealous and overprotective love he had for his semi-invalided sister had got them both into considerable trouble. Now, Sir Hannibal Cheng, out of his own feeling for both of these infuriating royals, decided hastily that he had indeed best go along on the duke's impetuous mission.

"Well, Cumberland, I suppose I shall join you after all. Nothin' like a hot, dusty bounce in a closed coach in high summer ta make anything else in life seem like beer and skittles," Cheng drawled nonchalantly, with a dry look askance of his companion just to let him know that Cheng considered himself to have had an option in the matter.

The duke, to his credit, got the point at once and harumphed politely, "Ah, yes. Well! Thanks, old fella. I'd appreciate the company, don'cha know. Damned glad ta have you along."

They had slowed somewhat in the stretch, as it were, but now the two friends put on a sudden, final burst of speed and hurtled themselves across the row and through the open front door of Number 17, each bent on the completion of a final ablution or two before their leave-taking.

Cheng scowled at his image in the mirror of his shaving stand. Yes, with Garth back in the picture, Ernest was certainly going to need a keeper. There was nothing more easily calculated to make the Duke of Cumberland see red in his one good eye than General Garth and the boy Thomas—nothing, that is, save the politics of his eldest brother, the prince regent! But that was neither here nor there; Cheng *never* meddled in his friend's politics. His friend's family concerns, however, were another matter entire. There he felt free to be of whatever service he could.

It was quite late in the evening when the princess, who had been reading a novel in the drawing room of Gloucester House, Melcombe Regis, was informed of her brother Cumberland's unexpected arrival. She greeted this intelligence with mingled delight and alarm, both feelings tinged with a touch of an even deeper and more subtle apprehension. For many years now, Cumberland, of all her brothers, had been the forbidden fruit. The old fear still held tight.

Minutes later the duke himself appeared in the doorway, his un-English-looking cavalryman's mustache abristle like the upraised hackles on a dog and his good eye squinting furiously in agitation. He looked so fierce! Until he saw his sister, that is, at which instant his fury abated and he melted.

"Sophy," he murmured affectedly. He had not seen her since their brother George had become regent, and that was a year or more already.

"Ernest, dearest, dearest brother," Princess Sophia whispered as they met in the centre of the room and embraced, kissing with all the warmth of their volatile Hanoverian natures. At last she pulled away, holding herself at arm's length from him, looking into his battle-scarred face with her prominent blue eyes darkening in urgency and concern. "But why have you come? I shall be in Hove but two days hence—and for the whole summer. Something has happened." She clutched her chest, having a tendency to cramps and coughing fits, and wondered if the news she was about to hear warranted another attack so soon after the one that had aided her escape from her mother at Windsor. "Is it Father?" she asked.

"No, no," the duke replied with a wave of his large hand. "He is as ever. Nothing is amiss with the family. . . ."

"Then why—" she began, her hand loosening its grip on the fabric of her gown.

"We have come to urge you not to come to Brighton, dearest Sophy."

"We?" she interrupted again.

"Cheng is with me," he said, and that intelligence brought a momentary smile of delight to the princess Sophia's face. She liked Sir Hannibal very much.

Not to be diverted, the duke went on with his mission, muttering like a tame bear, trying to be gentle and tactful despite his large size and blunt nature. "That whelp is there—" he blurted with total want of discretion.

"Whelp? Whelp? What whel—" Here, light dawning, Sophia trailed off, her face twisted into a painful grimace. "Oh, Ernest, you poor, dear fool," she said at last and with great kindness.

"The king's Garth is with him," Cumberland growled, looking away as, to his own surprise, he heard himself using the family's old and affectionate nickname for General Thomas Garth, King George's former and favourite equerry. "You are not to see him, Sophy, or the boy," the duke mumbled sombrely, gripping her hand in his, though he could not look her in the face as he said it.

"I am what, Ernest? I am not to what?" Princess Sophia asked mildly and yet with implied intensity.

"You *ought not* to see him," her brother corrected himself in a whisper, his face still turned from hers so that the deep scar on his temple was wholly visible to her.

"Ernest, you are my dear brother, as loving and loyal to me as any brother might be, but I am a woman now and will have my way at last." She spoke gently but with great conviction. "I know already that they are arrived in Brighton, and I have chosen to summer by the seaside at Hove for the very purpose of seeing him if I chose—and the whelp," she added with a painful smile. "This is the very first summer of my life that I am free, dearest Ernest, and with an income of my very own, thanks

49

to the regent getting through Parliament a bill allowing us girls our own money to spend as we please! Imagine! We poor wretched sisters of yours have never dressed ourselves but in the clothes our mother has chosen, or eaten but what she has ordered to be served us, or slept—save once or twice perhaps"—she smiled sardonically at that remark—"but where she would have us sleep. We have gone through hell these few months past in declaring our so much belated independence from the queen, and *now,* this summer—this summer of my thirty-fifth year—I am going to live as *I* wish to live—alone by the seaside, discreetly, but near enough to Brighton that I may see the prince, my brother, and you, and to see the king's Garth. The king's Garth and . . . *that whelp!*"

The Duke of Cumberland groaned.

"I *will* see him, Ernest. I will see that whelp, as you call him. After all, for good or ill, he is *my* whelp, *my* son, Ernest, and saving my dear good brothers and sisters, a blind, mad old father, and a tyrant of a mother, he is all that I have in this whole wretched world. The only thing that is mine—or that could have been mine," she amended with a wry, ironic smile, "had I not been born—what I was born."

"Oh, Sophy, my poor lovely little Sophy." The duke sobbed brokenly and suddenly. He who had raced posthaste across the dusty highroads of the south coast all day and evening to protect his invalid sister from the evils of this world found himself locked, for his own aid and comfort, in her gentle and affectionate embrace.

They clung like that for minutes, and Sir Hannibal Cheng, inadvertently glimpsing their intimacy through the partly opened drawing room doors, turned discreetly away and followed his boxes up the stairs to the bedrooms above. He would see the princess Sophia in the morning.

Cumberland, he knew, would retire for the night without calling upon him again. He would certainly wish to be left to his own devices after leaving his sister, for no man—least of all the Duke of Cumberland and Teviotdale—wishes to face another

50

while red-eyed from weeping. As far as the duke would ever know, Cheng never saw him shed a tear.

"You sent for me, Your Highness?" Sir Hannibal Cheng asked with a tentative smile as he entered a sunny, cheerful morning room, tucked like a pleasant surprise into a spare corner of the otherwise stuffy and old-fashioned Gloucester House by-the-sea.

"Indeed I did, Sir Hannibal," the princess Sophia exclaimed, raising her hand for him to kiss. She lay back upon a comfortable chaise dressed in a too-girlish white Indian muslin gown, surrounded by newspapers, novels, and several as yet unopened letters that had arrived by messenger just that morning. The various paraphernalia of letter writing—quills, inkpot, sand caster, wax, paper and the like—were set out on a small portable writing desk near to her hand. "Here," she ordered cheerfully, "make room in all this clutter and sit by me. I want to have a look at you in the light." With nervous fluttering, she moved her slippered feet and a few papers to make a place upon the end of the chaise for her guest.

"How long has it been?" she asked at last with amiable heartiness and a deep sigh, promptly answering her own question, "Too long, I expect. And you have a son! William, isn't it? Pray, how old is he now? Is he quick? Handsome as your own wickedly handsome self?" she asked, holding his hand with a sort of desperate affection. Cheng, not a little embarrassed, answered her amiable questions as best he could.

"William is nearly four now, and yes, he is very quick. Speaks both English and Chinese quite well. The Gaelic will come later, I expect. As to handsome, I think not very."

"You must *dote* on him," the princess cried effusively, lost for the moment in her deep-felt attachment for her own son, that secret son called Thomas, whose parentage was a scandal, whose existence was an embarrassment, that son whom she was forbidden to see—and yet whom she saw.

"I am afraid, Sophia, I find it hard to dote upon him. Children ain't my strong suit, if the truth were known," Sir Hannibal

51

contradicted her honestly but without much thought for her own sensitivity in that area.

He rose from his place on the end of the chaise to cross the room and scan the lawn for a sight of the duke. He was growing impatient now of their tedious chatter; he really had nothing more to say to this woman, though he liked her well enough and felt terribly sorry for her empty life. Still, what could he do?

"Ernest is out riding, I think," Sophia remarked as if divining the question in Sir Hannibal's mind. She sensed his restlessness, yet she could not bear to dismiss him just then. Instead, she watched him stealthily for a moment, and then, taking up a novel, she began to read.

Sir Hannibal looked up at length, realizing that he had gone into a brown study and left his companion to her own devices for an unconscionably long time. One was supposed to amuse the royals of one's acquaintance after all, certainly not ignore them. "What are you reading, Your Highness?" he asked to be social.

"A novel." The princess laughed in an overanimated attempt to hide her sorrowing mood from him. "A *ladies'* novel, of just the sort that you big brave soldiers and sea captains eschew with a passion."

"Oh? What's it called?" he asked with seemingly idle curiosity.

"*The Madness of Maida.* It's all the rage now, I understand. Lady Harcourt's daughter recommended it, and I am enjoying it no end. I used to be forbid the reading of such stuff, but since I have been set free—don't you know?—I have become quite the free spirit." She flashed him a mischievous smile that was like the ghost of her old, girlish self.

Cheng smiled at her warmly. She had beauty yet, poor soul. She could still be charming. "I am happy you are freer in your life now, Your Highness," he said gently, "but your brother *is* worried."

"He has no need. I know quite well what I am about." She paused. "This book is really terribly good, you know," she added firmly, to change the subject.

"Who's it by?" he asked, taking her hint.

"A Miss Charlotte Hungerford," she said, glancing at the spine.

Cheng's heart skipped a beat. "Really! Miss Hungerford," he remarked with a great show of merely casual interest. "Fancy, I just met that lady yesterday at Brighton," he said and strode across the room to look over Sophia's shoulder at the page of printed words, as if by some magic they might conjure up the author herself. He had dreamt of her that morning in his last doze and had cursed Ernest Cumberland roundly as he shaved. This jaunt to Weymouth was, after all, keeping him from any chance of glimpsing his fair secret fascination on the streets of Brighton.

"Did you indeed?" Sophia asked with interest. "Pray what is she like? She cannot be old, I think, for her books are quite passionate and impetuous," she went on.

"Are they?" Cheng mused. Indeed! How very promising. "No," he replied, "she is quite young, in fact, and exceptionally handsome; very proper. A parson's daughter, so I'm told."

"Is she in Brighton?"

"For the summer, they say, in company with her nephew, the younger Lord Vane, and her widowed stepmother."

"Sounds very proper. Fit company, you think? Socially, that is?" Sophia pursued.

Cheng shrugged. "Ned Darlin'ton's in love with her. What higher recommendation?" he asked with a twisted smile, neglecting to add who else loved the lady in question.

"When is Neddy not in love, I wonder?" Sophia smiled and added, "But really, Sir Hannibal, you know I think I should quite like to meet this lady. For tea one afternoon, if possible. Do you think you could arrange it?"

Sir Hannibal's heart fluttered in his chest. Arrange it! Why, I'd sail to the edge of the world to arrange it, he cried out to himself, although his actual reply to the princess was something more studied: "I see no bar, Your Highness, to making such an arrangement. I shall call upon Miss Hungerford immediately upon my return to Brighton and see what can be done." He bowed formally with the mocking deference of a courtier and made Sophia laugh in delight.

"D'ye have any odd books of hers lyin' about?" he asked casually, his eyes wandering to the bookcases that lined the room.

"Why, yes! Two or three in the shelves to your right," she replied in mild surprise at his interest.

He found them readily. "Mind if I borrow 'em for the day? If I'm goin' on a royal mission to capture the person of a real, living lady author, I'd best be supplied with forehand knowledge, don'cha think? I might have to pass a quiz, what?" Here he leered with an appropriate air of conspiracy, took up three of Charlotte Hungerford's earlier books, and tucked them under his arm. "But I'm tiring you," he said with a sudden and solicitous show of concern for his invalid companion. "I had better take my leave before I do you harm.

"By the way," Cheng called sotto voce from the doorway, which he had leapt to with unseemly haste, "if you want to get Ernest onto another hobbyhorse than yours, talk to him about savin' Ned from committin' matrimony with 'that scribbler,' as he calls Miss Hungerford."

"Thanks for the tip. I shall," the princess whispered conspiratorily and waved him good-bye, knowing how he must wish to be away.

Cheng smiled one last time and was off in haste.

Night had fallen, and all of Gloucester House was dark and still. Everything was in readiness for the next day's removal from Weymouth. When viewed from the highroad and parkland, the house seemed to sleep soundly, and all its inmates, even down to the huge mastiffs in the yard—the keeper's night dogs—slept the sleep of the just. But had one chanced to be sailing by moonlight in Weymouth Bay, one would have spied a lone light shining from beyond the panes of one single upper window, glimmering faintly like some furtive signal to a lover lost at sea.

And had one actually been able to peer within that square of glass, one would have seen a huddled figure, handsome, muscular, and naked save for the counterpane that covered his lower torso and drawn-up knees, bent over the last pages of a novel—a *ladies'* novel, no less—whilst the candles in the stick beside his bed burnt, unnoticed, down to the very last half inch of their lengths.

Their long nightmare was over at last. Free to be once more the man he could be, Sir Berry de Groat took Rowena in his strong, muscular arms without hesitation, bruising her willing mouth til it bled, and the warm, salty taste of her tears and her blood mingled on Rowena's lips with the passionate taste of his own hungry kisses. He seized her against his heart and held her yielding, supple form close to the pulsing, savagely throbbing bulk of his strong, warm body. Rowena thought surely that he would pull her into him and lock her—Love's slave, Love's prisoner—deep within the very heart and soul of him, just by dint of the sheer power and animal fervour of his ferocious desires.

Instead, he raised her up, sweeping her tiny slippered feet off the rich pile of the luxurious carpet, and carried her in his powerful arms into the chamber beyond. There, upon the couch that once had been her bed of pain and helpless torment, Rowena yielded herself to that passion that had so long lay buried like a treasure within the depths of her hungry, longing soul.

From that moment on and for all time, Rowena and Sir Berry de Groat were one.

Finis.

By damn, that little wench is somethin'. Cheng smiled to himself, his eyes blazing as he closed the book with a decisive snap and dwelt on the images that those last paragraphs had suggested to him.

"No wonder she don't care a fig for Neddy Darlin'ton," he exclaimed with the air of an alchemist discovering at what phase of the moon to boil the newts' tongues for greatest effect. "That puppy don't have enough blood in his veins ta turn somersaults, let alone tame a hell-fired female the likes of the wench who turns these things out." It's true the prose was a trifle florid, and there were a wee bit many adjectives. She wanted the depth of a Dante or an Aeschylus perhaps, but what the hell, she *was*, after all, only a *woman!* What could one expect? Moreover, she was writing for women—silly, flibberty things who think only about gowns and jewels, children and gossip. No, on the whole he thought that Miss Hungerford acquitted herself quite well as a writer; not so much for the writing, mind, which was overblown, but for the ideas she got across! And if she is, he leered to himself, as passionate as the heroines that she writes about . . . If she's anything like this Rowena Renfrew, why then, she's my kind o' woman, he thought smugly, with the kind of secret joy in his heart that a man feels when he spots what he knows for a certainty will be the winning horse in the Derby stakes.

"Yes," he mumbled sleepily as he slid down under the covers, "Charlotte Hungerford." And "Charlotte Hungerford," he repeated like a litany til he slept—and even after he slept—as he dreamt . . .

::4::

Charlotte Hungerford sat at her desk in the little study at the back of Number 10. The window on her right-hand side over-looked a long, narrow garden that separated the house from the mews beyond. To either side were vine-clad brick walls, and over them were glimpses of the greenery of neighbouring gardens: a very pleasant vista to look out upon whilst pondering the turn of a phrase or the fate of a heroine, both of which problems were simultaneously occupying her at that particular moment.

A rap at the door interrupted her train of thought, and as she called upon the intruder to enter, she hoped that it was not Fanny. They had had words at breakfast over Fanny's *eternal* wheedling and cajoling to get the girl out and into Society, whatever *that* beast might be! Charlotte was still smarting from it and wanted neither more of the same nor a maudlin scene of contrition and "making up" which would end in Fanny red-nosed and tearful and Charlotte saying sincerely things that she really didn't feel at all.

But it was not Fanny Hungerford as luck would have it.

"Mornin', Auntie dear," young Buckthorpe Vane greeted her with a toothy grin of good cheer. He had not been present at the breakfast contretemps, else he would have been more wary. His face, however, was such a relief after what she had expected that Charlotte greeted him almost exuberantly.

"Bucky darling, do come in," she cried. "Why, I'd have thought you were long up and well away from here by now, but by the look of you—" She broke off with a look of dismay and a wiping gesture across her mouth meant to convey that he should perform such an operation on his own visage. As Charlotte shook her head in a pleasantly exasperated expression of helplessness, Bucky took pains to wipe his breakfast egg off his face with one elegant lace cuff.

"Out late, lay abed, rose late. Just left the groanin' board this very minute as a matter o' fact."

"As I can tell. You have jam on your cheek as well," Charlotte remarked with a waggle of her forefinger in the general direction of his cheek as he crossed the room and bent toward her.

"Oh, yes." The offending jam was removed from Bucky's left cheek and deposited upon his right cuff in a flash of lace and a small cloud of snuff. He planted a dutiful toast-and-butter kiss upon his aunt, and, pulling back, stood before her desk and made a mock salute. "Honourable Lord Buckthorpe Vane wishin' to make a report, Captain, sir—*ma'am,*" he amended with great affectation of dismay at the "slip."

Charlotte went along with his little charade. "At ease, Lieutenant. Permission to speak," she said, at which command Bucky whipped out a soiled-looking, much-folded scrap of paper, scribbled all over with smudgy lead pencil jottings. Charlotte winced at the mere sight of it.

"A report on the eligible men of Brighton with an eye towards marryin' off one Mrs. Fanny Hungerford, widow." Young Vane grinned in delight at his own wittiness. "Requirements as stated in original orders: One, Must be old—but not too old. Two, Must be sick—but not too sick.

"Lord Vane wishes to report that havin' skulked about the spa and the baths these three days past, havin' loitered in the gamin' halls and dallied in the pits o' vice, all out o' the goodness of his kindly heart and in the very best interests of his dear stepgrannie, he has come up with the followin' list of fine and noble gentlemen as possible fish for Fanny's fat little hook." He grinned, and for an instant Charlotte saw her father's ghost cross his grandson's handsome face.

"First, a Mr. Hugo De'Ath, Esquire, of Wadebridge Abbey, Cornwall. Widower, late forties, small son named Ambrose. Of

French Huguenot background. In Brighton to take the waters for his tummy. Rumoured to have ten thousand a year."

Charlotte said nothing.

"Shall I go on, Auntie dear?"

"By all means, Nephoo." She nodded.

"Second on the list, Lord Wolverhampton, son of the Earl of Bletchley. Bachelor, of four and fifty summers. In Brighton—and here's the good part, Auntie love—in Brighton to find himself a *wife*. Plagued with gout and severe attacks of the *emeraudes.*" Bucky grinned with relish as Charlotte bridled somewhat. "Not much capital it seems til the old Bletch takes off, but what the hell, Fanny don't take much keepin', do she?" he asked happily, clearly taken with the idea of marryin' his grandmama off to the only son of a belted earl.

"Any more 'fish' on your list, Mr. Walton?" Charlotte asked.

"Just one. Sir John Pilkingtown—"

"Pilkingtown?"

"Yes, d'ya know him?"

"I do indeed. He was old when Moses parted the seas. I said *old* and *sick*, Bucky, not ancient and dying. He's not likely to live through the wooing, let alone the honeymoon."

"Well, well, as you say," Bucky conceded. "How about this De'Ath fellow? Haven't heard a bad word about him from anybody, and they do say he has ten thousand a year."

"Sounds very good on paper, Bucky, I agree, but I'm afraid you can forget the squire right off. Fanny, who has met him, it seems, says that he is completely taken up by a lady of questionable reputation," Charlotte stated with a prunelike pursing of her pretty lips.

"Oh? Who is that?" Bucky asked with the keen interest rich young men generally have in ladies of questionable repute and—hopefully—even more questionable virtue.

"I have no idea." Charlotte sniffed self-righteously. "I do not gossip."

"Well, hoity-toity, me dear Auntie, an' more's the pity," Bucky remarked with a flap of his wrist in disdain. Spying the dark look that she gave him just then, he changed tack. "Then what's wrong with old Wolfie? What possible objection can you have to him? He's fifty-four—certainly young enough—and ain't like to die o' gouty legs and a sore arse, is he? What better combination? And lookin' for a wife yet!"

"He is a bachelor," Charlotte remarked somewhat grimly.

"And what of that? Would you rather that he have six wives like Pilkingtown? In fact, he's had none and is in the market at last. Ain't that promisin'?"

"Oh, Buckthorpe Vane, you are a wonder! Of course, Lord Wolverhampton is in the market for a wife—a *rich* one. He has lost his mother's inheritance in gambling and—" She shut her mouth like a vise.

"And what, Charlotte?" Bucky prompted, sensing that there was something his aunt was not saying. Sometimes the things that she was inclined *not* to say were the very best things of all, bless her devious little heart.

"As I say, he is a bachelor," she remarked circumspectly.

"Well, what of that?" Bucky brayed in absolute frustration. "So, for the devil's sake, am I."

"That is not the same thing." She sniffed. "He is an *old* bachelor. He—he has lost his fortune by *virtue*—an ill choice o' words that—of his being a bachelor. His—his profligacy . . ." She trailed off with a shiver of disapproval. Would he not stop being so dense and read between the lines? Had she to spell it out?

"What?" Bucky laughed. "Was his flash house tab as high as all that?" Really, he had no idea his auntie could be such a prude.

"No, his . . ."

"His what, Aunt Charlotte? I say, this is not like you! You may be a parson's daughter, but you were never so priggish as all this. A bloody—"

"Bucky, watch your tongue!" shrieked Charlotte.

"—a bloody bluestocking maybe, but never really such a prig as all this," her nephew went on severely, in spite of her protest against his swearing. "Now do stop beating about in the hedgerow and be clear, for God's sake."

"His beautiful young men, as if you didn't know," she blurted out at last.

60

"Haw-haw! I didn't know. So that's it, is it? You *are* a little prig."

Charlotte glared at him darkly, her cheeks red with fury, as much for being laughed at by her nephew as for the information she had been forced to impart to him. "I do not like havin' to speak of such a thing to you. It is not proper. Moreover, I vow, I thought you knew about him all along and were just pulling my leg."

"Well, I didn't know, and I'm glad you spoke up. So that's why he pinched me arse t'other day as I was chattin' with him at the baths. I thought he was just bein' friendly—in an odd sort o' way, mind, but now . . ."

"You keep away from him," Charlotte cried out in alarm.

"Indeed, I will, Auntie dear. Have no fear o' that. I save me virtue for the whorehouses, where it belongs." He grinned. "By the by, that sort o' explains his *emeraudes,* don't it?" He flashed her a mischievous look of ineffable charm.

"Oh, you silly! That is absolutely disgusting." She laughed, throwing up her hands in a gesture of submission. "I give up on you." And she sat giggling til her sides ached.

"Well"—young Vane sighed at last when their mirth had subsided—"I suppose it's back to work for me. It ain't easy huntin' up likely prospects, ya know."

Charlotte looked at him shrewdly, playing with a curl over her temple. "Actually," she drawled, "you can stop hunting, dear boy." She tried to make her turnabout seem casual.

"Oh, why? Given up on your little scheme?" Bucky suggested hopefully.

"No, not likely. It's just that I've already found the right man. I partly mentioned it t'other day, I believe," Charlotte went on casually, her eyes straying to the garden beyond the window-panes, for she did not dare to meet her nephew's gaze directly.

"Oh, who the devil was it? I forget." Bucky was perched on the edge of her desk now and looking straight down at her. She felt terribly self-conscious.

"Oh, just that—that—*Irish* baronet fellow—you know—Sir

H-Hannibal Cheng," she mumbled, idly fingering her pen as she spoke.

"Cheng? Oh, God, yes, I remember now. Really, Charlotte, you can't be serious."

"And why not?" she asked indignantly.

"I—I can't say that I like it at all. I don't think it's a good idea," Bucky remarked doubtfully. There was a ring of concern in his voice.

"Go on," his aunt prompted warily.

"Well, I've met him once or twice now and he's rather *likeable*. I don't know him *well*, mind, but somehow I'd hate ta see him trapped into this little scheme o' yours. It don't seem fair."

"Why, pray?" Charlotte asked in annoyance. "Why do you think that way about him in particular, though you have not scrupled to mention these others—Squire De'Ath and Sir John Pilkingtown, for instance?"

"Because I know him partly," Bucky answered with a look of pain. "Because he's young yet, and happy and free. Lord, Charlotte, he was married once, and he's escaped— Leave him be, poor feller. These other chaps *are* old and *are* sick, and truth ta tell, a nice fat little woman like Fanny'd probably do 'em more good than harm. But poor Cheng! It'd be like puttin' the noose round his neck twice in a lifetime, so ta speak." An eloquent plea, that, Buckthorpe Vane thought with a certain amount of pride in his oratory. He hoped that when the time came and some wench and her ambitious mother were tryin' to hook him, some fine fellow like himself would say as much on his behalf.

"Noose!" Charlotte was exclaiming in fury. "Noose?" She was taking her nephew's remarks far more personally than she should have or than he had expected, for of course, he had no way of knowing that Charlotte's was the noose in question—not Fanny's at all!

"The noose o' matrimony, pet," Bucky explained blithely. "They hung him once, and it didn't take—leave him be."

Charlotte was furious now.

"I say, Bucky, you are a marvel. Where is your sense of loyalty? Here I am planning a happy marriage for the man—and with a fine, willing wife—and you talk as if it were a public execution. For goodness sake!"

"Where's me sense of loyalty?" Bucky cried, leaping up from his perch and crossing the room with his arms waving in exasperation. "Why, with me own sex, I suppose, now you mention it! Let him plan his own happy marriage if he's for it, but set Fanny's cap, if you must, for some old duffer who's too sick to run and too tired ta care, not a man with his whole life ahead of him." The truth was that Bucky felt a certain sympathy for Cheng; was he not himself likely to eventually be victim of such female scheming as this? Was he not himself rich, young, and eligible? Perish the thought!

"I think I have heard quite enough, Lord Vane," Charlotte snapped, piqued all the more because it was she who sought to trap the man that Bucky defended so vehemently. To understand her nephew's sympathy with Cheng's plight was at this time beyond her ken. "I shall consider your most eloquent plea for mercy at my leisure." As far as she was concerned, their interview was at an end.

"Besides," Bucky blurted out in one last desperate defense of a fellowman, "he's a Chinee, after all. Maybe Grandmama Fanny won't have a Chinee."

"Nonsense, dear boy," Charlotte chided with a patronizing sniff of disdain at the very idea. "He is as much Irish as the other, and we are really not, are we, so prejudiced as all that? Besides, it is not as if he were a Catholic, after all, is it?"

For that Bucky had no answer. He gave it up with a shrug and left to seek solace at the gaming tables. There was no helping it once Charlotte had got a flea in her ear like this. Poor Cheng would just have to make the best of it and fend for himself, he supposed.

After Buckthorpe Vane made his mournful exit, Charlotte Hungerford spent the next quarter of an hour in a brown study, her blank eyes fixed on the white marble wood nymph at the end of the garden. Bucky could be such a bother at times. Perhaps she should send him packing back to Wooton-Maggot and be done with it. But no, she decided at last, it was convenient having him here. He could still be useful in his way.

Her reverie was interrupted just then by another rapping at the study door. *This* will be Fanny, she thought in dismay, but again she was wrong. It was merely a maid who gave a perfunctory curtsey to her mistress and announced: "Sir 'annibal Cheng to see Miss 'ungerford."

Charlotte's mouth, as one may imagine, dropped open. It was too good to be true. "Sir Hannibal Cheng?" she exclaimed in shrill disbelief. "Here?"

"Not *'ere*, miss. In the drawing room," the maid replied calmly and with the simple logic of her kind. "And that's the name 'e give," the girl said flatly in something less than the best servantly tone.

Charlotte recovered herself with a frown. She must remember to sack this snip. "You may tell Sir Hannibal that I shall join him in a few minutes," she ordered in her most chilling and dignified tones.

The moment the door shut, Charlotte bolted from her seat at the desk, tore through another door in the room, raced up the backstairs like a dog on the scent, and dove into her bedroom at full tilt, thus frightening the life out of an upstairs maid, who very nearly became a downstairs maid by virtue of the fact that she was just then hanging out a window, intent on airing the bed linen and incidentally flirting with the butcher's boy in the kitchen garden below.

Charlotte took no notice of the unfortunate girl's momentary plight, however, for she merely stopped to wash her face in rose water, pat her already perfect curls into even greater perfection, and assure herself by a last look in the glass that her morning dress was fashionably tight in the bodice, sufficiently low in the bosom, and sheer enough in the sunlight to show a suggestion of delicately tapering limb. She pinched her cheeks to a becoming red, bit her lips for the same effect, and, after taking a deep breath, made a slow and stately descent of the front stairs and a graceful, elegant, and nonchalant entrance into the drawing room.

Sir Hannibal Cheng was standing in the bow window, looking out across the row toward Number 17. He was in *her* house now, nervous as a cat and not at all sure of what he was going to say to her. He was feeling more and more the fool with every passing minute, and so he stood there fighting a mounting urge to cut and run.

"Sir Hannibal! How charming."

Sir Hannibal turned and gaped at Charlotte Hungerford. She stood in the doorway of the drawing room looking like an angel, in a pink and white striped dress with little black satin ribbands —very tight under the bosom and very low above it—and really rather sheer all over, what with the early-afternoon sun filtering through the fanlight in the entrance hall behind her. She was ravishing—absolutely ravishing—and a whole host of decidedly unchaste thoughts crowded in upon Sir Hannibal as he gazed across the room at her, hardly daring to brave the frank look of those devilishly handsome amber eyes.

"Miss Hungerford," Sir Hannibal got out at last.

"Yes," Miss Hungerford agreed wittily.

"I—I have come on a mission—a—a mission of—" Here he dried up completely, his brain addled by her huge, melting amber eyes. By Jove, no gel should be allowed to look like that at a man.

"A mission, Sir Hannibal?" she asked with some slight regaining of her own composure. She was, after all, the huntress and must keep her wits about her if the prey chose to enter her drawing room.

"On—on behalf of—" he went on in a blank daze. Damn it, why could he not speak? he asked himself in quiet fury at his own wretched state.

"A mission—on behalf of?" Charlotte repeated with mounting suspicion and the beginnings of genuine anger as she leapt to a certain dismaying conclusion.

Sir Hannibal nodded mutely.

"You are not, sir, here on behalf of that ridiculous young puppy Lord Ned Darlington, are you? You cannot be! I will not have it!" Here Charlotte Hungerford waxed suddenly furious at the profound indignity of having the man she adored pressing the suit of another man!

"Oh, no, no, you mistake me, Miss Hungerford, you mistake me entire," Sir Hannibal hastened to assure her in some alarm. He found himself recovering his wits rather swiftly under the effect of her fury. By God, what a wench! She was magnificent, one minute as demure as a kitten, the next spittin' like a proper cat. He loved it! Gad, but she did set one up on one's toes.

"I am sent on a *royal* mission," he explained with an exquisitely engaging and absolutely dazzling show of his strong white teeth. Ah! good, he was thinkin' again—actually *thinkin'!* By usin' the old noodle, he'd answered one question for himself already: Charlotte Hungerford would marry Ned Darlington when the cat could lick its ear—which, as everyone knows, is never. Hah, one fly out o' the jam already. Now if he could just get his own hand in . . .

"A royal mission," Charlotte was prompting him, her curiosity piqued.

"Her Highness the princess Sophia is, it seems, quite a fan of your novels, and when I happened to mention that I knew you—" Sir Hannibal began. Encouraged by her lack of interest in Darlington, he had regained his waning composure and was becoming almost voluble. Charlotte, however, hardly noticed this, for at the mention of a possible royal patron she was unable to contain herself. She broke in at once.

"You mean—you actually mentioned to the princess that you know me?" she asked in dazzled amazement. He had really noticed her t'other day on the Esplanade, had spoken of her to someone—to a royal, in fact. How marvellous!

"Well, I—I—mentioned you in passin'—that we were acquainted, that is. She was reading some ladies' novel and merely wishin' to be polite, mind, I asked the title and the author. It was some thing or t'other of yours, and so I mentioned you, that's all," Sir Hannibal amended in embarrassment and for fear that she would think him impetuous, presumptuous, or—worse yet—smitten with her!

66

"How kind of you," Charlotte murmured in subdued delight, envisioning the dedication of her next book, *Lady Viola's Revenge:*

Dedicated, by gracious permission,
to
H.R.H. Princess Sophia

What a coup *that* would be! The Lord only knew how well regarded her books might become under the patronage of royalty. She looked at Sir Hannibal with shrewder eyes, suddenly seeing he might actually have a good brain behind those distractingly beautiful eyes.

"The princess Sophia, as you may know, has never been strong and is a semi-invalid at this moment. This season she has taken a house by the seaside at Hove, where she plans a quiet and restful time, leaving the madding crowds of Brighton for others of stronger constitution and more sociable disposition. She is, however, an avid reader, and when she mentioned your latest work—*Maida something-or-other?*—" he inquired blithely, not at all like a man who had nearly ruined his eyes in reading that very book in a bouncing coach careening over the roads between Melcombe Regis and Hove whilst Sophia gave him curious glances and the duke ragged him to a faretheewell about his choice of reading matter.

"The Madness of Maida," Charlotte was correcting him politely, trying not to be annoyed that he did not know the title of the current most popular book in all of England, there being some little vanity in her makeup, especially where her literary successes were concerned. Even her passion for Sir Hannibal could not change that.

"Ah, yes, that's it. *The Madness of Maida,* of course," he went on smoothly, for he had sensed her pique at his ignorance and was enjoying her reaction. "Good title that, what?"

"I rather thought so," she agreed, somewhat placated by his flattery.

"Well, the princess Sophia would be delighted if you could

come to tea one afternoon next week. Say Monday, perhaps?" he suggested, wondering how the devil he'd get from Wednesday to Monday next without seeing her again. "I should be happy to escort you to—"

"Why, Monday would be—" Charlotte exclaimed and then bit her tongue in vexation. She must not be too anxious. He would take it for ill breeding or some attraction to the idea of his company on the journey. That would never do! "I think, rather, that that afternoon would suit admirably and—" she corrected herself coolly, only to be interrupted in her remarks by a flutey voice from the hallway without.

"Yoo-hoo, Charlotte pet, wherever has Bucky got to?" came that shrill voice, followed almost immediately by the appearance of its owner in the person of a plump and bustling Fanny Hungerford, drawing off her gloves as she came rushing pell-mell and breathless into the room. "Oh, Oh! Pray forgive me. I did not dream that we had a visitor," she cried out and then clamped her mouth shut in fascination. Who on earth was this strange-looking person? Fanny, whose own taste in men was as prosaic as Charlotte's was exotic, rather ran to bulky, ruddy-faced, silvery-wigged English squire types. She was completely taken aback by her first sight of the bird of exotic plumage who sat upon the sofa beside her stepdaughter.

"Fanny darling," Charlotte greeted her with rather mixed emotions—part of her wanting to be alone awhile longer with Sir Hannibal and another part happy to be getting on with her plans in such an unexpectedly hasty manner. "Do come and meet Bucky's friend, Sir Hannibal Cheng, first Baronet Cheng of Moondragon in Ireland."

"Ohhh," Fanny cooed as she heard his pedigree recited—not nobility, of course, but at least he had a title. "How delighted I am, Sir Hannibal." Who *could* he be?—and *what?*—she pondered as she looked at his strange features and colouring.

"Sir Hannibal has taken a house across the row at Number Seventeen with the Duke of Cumberland and young Lord Darlington—for the season," Charlotte informed her, divining that Fanny could not place him and wishing to get that blank stare of vague curiosity off her stepmother's face as soon as possible, lest Sir Hannibal think that she was dull-witted.

"Oh, *has* he? How charmin'. We're quite the neighbours, then, I see," Fanny shrilled agreeably, nodding her head like a Dresden pagod, for she had just placed Charlotte's visitor in her mental catalogue of the Brighton social scene. This was the famous Chinee baronet.

"Indeed, we are quite the neighbours, Mrs. Hungerford," Sir Hannibal agreed with a tight smile that hid his great desire cheerfully to strangle this buxom and intrusive old cow. He wanted to be alone with Charlotte Hungerford, and here he was having to be polite to her stepmother. Still, there being really no help for it, he determined to make himself as agreeable as possible.

"I am so happy that you have come in at this time, Mother dear," Charlotte purred. "I had been hoping that you and Sir Hannibal might become acquainted. You two have so very much in common."

"We *have?*" both Sir Hannibal and Fanny blurted out together and with similar expressions of mingled wonderment and horror. Neither wanted to have anything in common with the other.

"I should say that you have." Charlotte smiled serenely. "You are both of an age—I shall not say what age, mind—" She smiled prettily, almost coyly, like a cat in the cream, as both her companions frowned darkly. Age was a sensitive subject after all. "Moreover," she went on smoothly, "you both share in a common experience of life—a blow from which few ever recover completely." Waxing somewhat dramatic, with a throaty quaver to her voice, she added, "Unless, of course, they are fortunate enough to find *another* to ease them in their abject sorrow—"

"Abject sorrow?" they both exclaimed, again as one, and for the same reason. So far they shared only their reaction to Charlotte's curious and utterly mystifying remarks. Certainly neither Fanny Hungerford nor Sir Hannibal Cheng had ever felt a moment of truly *abject* sorrow in the whole of their really rather comfortable and satisfactory lives.

"I am referring to *bereavement,*" Charlotte said emphatically and with a testy edge to her voice because they had yet, the blocks!, to take her meaning. How *could* they if they would go on interrupting her thought? she fretted to herself. "You are widow and widower respectively," she explained, "drowning, as it were, in the veritable *tidal wave* of your utter grief and loneliness. Such a commonality of suffering—and occurring in middle age"—here Fanny blanched, and Sir Hannibal sucked in his stomach "—is bound to draw you together, is it not?" she asked almost indignantly.

Fanny and Sir Hannibal gazed about in rolling-eyed wonder, finally electing to nod tentatively and mumble an "oh, yes, indeed" or two as they each tried to figure out whether they dared admit to such a callous breech of refined sensibility as a placid contentedness with their current spouseless lots in life.

Sir Hannibal for one had loved his little cousin-wife well enough, but never with anything akin to the sort of passion that a Charlotte Hungerford would find necessary to a marital attachment, and her death, while affording him much sadness and no little remorse, had been no bar to his continued satisfaction with his own existence. He had mourned the required while, taken a trip to China, and come back whole.

Fanny, on the other hand, had been genuinely attached to her rather elderly parson and did really miss him, though not for himself quite so much as for the simple fact that she had been deprived of someone to dote upon and fuss over. She was by nature an excellent nurse and a fond, effusive mother. Her husband gone, she had transferred the entire burden of her interest to her stepdaughter. At any rate, she was certainly *not* the abjectly grieving widow that Charlotte evidently expected her to be.

Really, what *had* got into Charlotte?

When young Lord Buckthorpe Vane returned to Number 10 Seaview Row and appeared upon the scene, he was amazed to find that rather odd feller Sir Hannibal Cheng sprawled at his ease in a giltwood fauteuil with one booted foot crossed over the other at the ankle and his third glass of sherry in hand. He wore a slightly silly grin upon his sardonic face, denoting some inwardly enjoyed jest of his own, or else the sherry had gone to his head.

Fanny was on her fourth sherry, and by the way her laughter shrilled and her overstuffed and rather fauteuillike person jiggled at every mild jest of the Chinee baronet, Bucky guessed that she'd soon be on her fifth.

His aunt Charlotte sat between these two rather inebriated souls like a cat with a mouse under its paw: contented, secure, not quite ready to strike. She had had two glasses perhaps, by the look of her eye and the tilt of her head, and remained silent, watching the amiable badinage between her companions in just the way that cat might relish the vain struggles of her captive mouse—or mice, in this case.

Bucky was damned if he could guess just how she'd managed it, but manage it she had, for now, a mere two or three days after she'd first mentioned trying to get Fanny and Sir Hannibal together, she had them not only together but as soused as a tripe into the bargain. He could only shake his head in admiration at her conniving and, after a deep breath, step forward and enter the lists himself.

"Oh, my Bucky darling," Fanny shrilled ecstatically as young Buckthorpe, wincing, submitted himself to his stepgrandmama's profusion of sticky sherry kisses and pillowy embraces. "Would you believe, Sir Hannibal, that this is my very own grandson, this big, wonderful boy right here?" she called across the room, all the while grasping Bucky to her like a slippery fish as he struggled to escape the stranglehold that she retained on his head.

"I would if you say so, ma'am," Sir Hannibal replied agreeably but with no diplomacy whatsoever.

"Well, he's *not!*" Fanny exclaimed in petulant fury as she thrust the offending, but entirely innocent, Bucky unceremoniously from her. "I'm far *too young* to be a grandmama," she stated flatly, indignant that Sir Hannibal had been so ungallant as to imply otherwise. She really did not like this fellow at all!

Bucky groped for safety on the sofa beside Charlotte and leant over to plant a buss on her cheek that gave him the opportunity to whisper in her ear, "By Jove, you are a fast worker, Auntie dear."

Charlotte gave her nephew a pointedly too sharp pinch on the cheek and said acidly, "Pour yourself a sherry, Bucky dear, and be a good boy." It was her Wooton-Maggot tone of voice, and so Bucky, thinking better of his next remark, said no more. Taking his cue from Sir Hannibal, he drank himself into oblivion.

At a considerably later hour of the day that companionable little party finally found sufficient use of its several pairs of legs for it to divide and its individual members to go their divers ways.

Bucky, somewhat the worse for his sherry (he had caught up nicely, thank you!), was nevertheless bent on giving Sir Hannibal the seven steps of decency and therefore accompanied the Chinese baronet to the front door.

"Your grandmama's quite the gel, Bucky," Sir Hannibal remarked cheerfully as they stood upon the steps before the house and breathed deeply of the cool evening air. (Not a good idea that, for they each reeled back under a sudden surge of horrible aching about the temples, and each resolved therefore to try not to breathe at all for a while if he could possible avoid doing so.) "Yes, quite the gel," he repeated when his eyes uncrossed and the throbbing subsided.

"Sir Hannibal, for God's sake, be careful. She's settin' you up, don'tcha know," Bucky whispered urgently, shutting the door behind them in haste and with such a bang as to set their fuddled brains to jiggling like a jelly. The die was cast. If Buckthorpe Vane had been torn between loyalty to his aunt and the duty that he owed to another poor fool of his own sex, this was it! His own sex won out, God bless 'em every one, man and boy, he thought sentimentally.

"Settin' me up, boy?" Sir Hannibal repeated blithely. "Who pray is settin' me up, and for what, pray?"

"Charlotte, Sir H., Charlotte," Bucky whispered, desperately afraid that he might be overheard through one of the windows in the front of the house. "Me aunt Charlotte. She's set on marryin' off Fanny this summer, and she's decided you're to be the Benedick."

"Oh, that." Sir Hannibal scoffed with a quiet, dignified belch. "Yes, I know."

"You know?" Bucky exclaimed, suddenly more sober than he had been in hours.

"Well, I may be a bit tight, old boy, but I'm not stupid. I could see the whole thing a mile away."

"And you don't mind?" Bucky asked in wonderment.

"Mind? No, why should I mind? It's really rather a good idea, in fact." With that, Sir Hannibal grinned enigmatically and set off across the row to Number 17, leaving Bucky alone on the steps of Number 10 to contemplate at his leisure the relative sanity of Chinee baronets.

::5::

"Ahh, Bucky darling, how my head does ache," Fanny Hungerford whispered as she arrived in the breakfast room early the very next morning.

"Ain't used ta tipplin' like that, are you, Grannie?" Bucky grinned.

"Ugggh," Fanny moaned dramatically.

"Head's really as bad as all that, eh?" young Vane asked with a trifle more sympathy. He had had too many bad mornings himself not to feel for a fellow sufferer.

"No, that was for the 'grannie,' dear boy. If you want to get on my good side again, though, just fetch me some tea and a bit of egg, there's a lamb. Some dry toast, too. And mind you don't—ooohhh"—Fanny winced as Bucky, in his enthusiasm to serve her, upset the silver covers on the sideboard with a great deal of resultant clangour—"mind you don't bang about too much. Every sound is a torment to your poor *step*grannie this morning."

"I think me poor Fanny don't know how to hold her liquor." Bucky grinned good-naturedly as he set a plate of eggs before her and poured the milk into her tea. "Enough?"

"Oh, yes, quite," Fanny replied. "I expect I held more sherry yesterday afternoon, my boy, than I have held all these twenty years past. I slept for hours last evening and had no proper supper at all—only some biscuits and milk in the mid of night. I feel utterly wretched. How can people drink so much as they do? It certainly cannot be for enjoyment."

"I think one has to work up to it actually. Develop a tolerance the way one does to pickled trotters and marriage vows and things of that nature. Actually the governor don't have no tolerance at all, though it don't stop him goin' through a bottle o' port before teatime and a bottle o' sack after dinner," Bucky observed. "No wonder he don't much appreciate the clatter o' little feet; must sound a bloody army to him, now I think on it."

"Well, I for one have no desire to build up a tolerance"— Fanny sniffed—"and I am heartily sorry that I ever started."

"Bravo, for a teetotaler, Fanny"—Bucky applauded her noble intent—"but why on earth did you do it, drink so much, I mean?"

"Well, Charlotte sent for the sherry. I only meant to be amiable, plus—"

"Plus?" Bucky prompted, all ears.

"Ah, I thought that if I cultivated this Cheng fellow, he being Ned Darlington's friend, I thought I might get us all together for a drive or a ramble on the beach or some such thing. In that way I can push Neddy on Charlotte whether she likes it or not. Perhaps then she shall see how that boy dotes on her and begin to take him seriously." Fanny was nothing, if not persistent. She would have Charlotte married to Lord Ned Darlington whether Charlotte liked it or not!

Now young Vane had his doubts as to the success of this venture, though he said nothing to discourage her. Why spoil her fun? "Oh, I see. Is that why you invited Cheng to call?"

"I, invite Sir Hannibal? I hardly even knew he existed save for an idle word from Ned or a scrap of gossip whilst taking the waters until I came in upon him—as large as life—settin' with Charlotte on the drawing room sofa."

"Oh?" Vane's ears pricked at that.

"My understanding of the matter is, Bucky dear, that Sir Hannibal came to call. Something about visiting someone in Hove on Monday next. Charlotte was really most annoyingly circumspect about it all," Fanny remarked with a look of vexation crossing her pale, plump face. Her bright eyes flashed indignation. "What right, I ask you, does she have keeping her own counsels like that? It is not proper for a young, unmarried woman to be so secretive."

"Yes-s-s, Charlotte can be like that at times. It is most arlnoyin'," her grandson agreed thoughtfully, chewing slowly on a rubbery bit of kidney the way a cow ruminates over its cud. He could not shake the feeling of something in the wind. He might just have to pry a bit.

"I need your dear help, Bucky my boy," Fanny was saying with an engaging look of helplessness.

"What? How?" He looked at her with sudden, suspicious alarm.

"Nothing deep, nothing hard," Fanny assured him hastily. "It's only that I have just sent round to Number Seventeen to ask Neddy Darlington if he will ride out with me this morning. I merely want you to come as well and get Charlotte to join us, that's all. There's a good boy," she coaxed with a cajoling purse of her lips, her plump cheeks dimpling prettily.

She did have a way about her, did Fanny, young Buckthorpe noted as he found himself acceding to her request. After what Cheng had said to him last evening, maybe Charlotte's scheme was not so farfetched after all. Perhaps Sir Hannibal did hanker after plump, fussy, doting little ladies like Fanny. Stranger things than that . . .

When Charlotte arrived at the breakfast table a few minutes later, she found herself beset with suggestions that she looked ever so pale, must be off her feed, and might benefit from taking the sea air.

"No, no, no, a thousand times *no,*" Charlotte insisted with upraised hands. "I have work to do. If I want air, I shall open a window—and I am not off my feed," she mumbled, stuffing her already full mouth with additional bacon to prove the point. "Really, you two would try the patience of Grisel."

"Griselda at least had a husband, which you do not." Fanny sniffed righteously.

"I shall let *that* lie, but I shall say this: Not only do I not want to ride out, but I certainly do not wish to do so in the company of that insipid and fatuous fool Lord Ned Darlington. Really, Fanny, I wonder at your taste in men," she snapped peevishly.

"He is a *charming* young man and fairly dotes on you, Charlotte," Fanny retorted, a trifle hurt. "How can you call him names when here you sit, six-and-twenty and still a spinster with no expectations? No, not a suitor to your name, saving young Darlington!

"People laugh at you," she went on. "Gentlemen call you a scribbler and a bluestocking, which you *are,* I suppose, if the truth be told," she conceded as she caught Charlotte grinning. "They liken you to Jane Austen—"

"That's damned good likening in my book, Mama." Charlotte smiled tolerantly.

"Jane Austen is an *old maid,*" Fanny burbled vehemently, wringing her napkin in her lap like an old facecloth, "and very like to die an old maid. I want more than that for you. I want you married and happy."

"I want me happy, too—and if marriage will help me to that happiness (about which possibility I have *many* reservations, mind you), then, by God, I will marry—"

"Oh," Fanny shrilled happily.

"—but not Lord Ned Darlington," Charlotte stated emphatically.

"Ohhh," Fanny moaned, "you wicked, wicked girl. Bucky, I vow, I cannot do a thing with her."

"No more can I," young Buckthorpe remarked with a shrug of seeming nonchalance as he ruminated quietly to himself on the fact that for the first time Charlotte Hungerford had admitted to the mere possibility of marrying. That in itself was a remarkable turnaround for his aunt, but the turnaround that was about to follow was so abrupt as nearly to set poor Bucky's head aspin. It happened thus:

The butler entered with a note for Fanny.

"Ah," she exclaimed, "Lord D. has sent over his reply." She tore the vellum and read aloud, and with some difficulty, owing to the gentleman's bad hand, the product of Neddy Darlington's childish scrawl and not much better literary effort:

77

* * *

Dear Mrs. H.,

Would adore to ride out if only for sun and your nice company (not to say that of my heart's desire which you know well). If we can drive toward Hove, all to the better since my friends, Duke Ernest and Sir H. Cheng, may be returning hence via that direction and we may meet them upon the road. Doing so, why not take tea at some little inn?

Shall be across in half an hour.

Yr. obed. servant,

Neddy D.

"There, Charlotte! Ain't that a nice note and a jolly suggestion? To ride out into the countryside and take refreshment at an inn along the way? And he calls you his heart's desire, imagine. D'you see now what a lark you shall be missing?"

Bucky, knowing just how much Charlotte hated such larks as that just suggested, awaited her frigid retort with secret glee. Instead:

"And who ever said that I shall be missing it?" Charlotte asked with a shrug as she rose from the table. "I shall just take my leave to change into something more suitable for a ride out in the country so as to be ready when the carriage comes round. Bucky, do close your mouth. You look like a fish—and *wipe* your mouth as well," she scolded as she crossed to the door. There she stopped briefly and, turning to her two flabbergasted companions, said, "By the way, Fanny, I was right about Lord Ned's being a fatuous fool. That is probably the most ill-composed note I have ever heard tell of. He must have had an idiot for a schoolmaster—or else his schoolmaster had a block for a pupil. I shudder to think of his Latin if that is an example of his English!"

The door shut then, leaving young Buckthorpe and his stepgrandmother to ponder on the bizarre and unexpected *volte-face* of Miss Charlotte Hungerford.

"What do you make of *that?*" Fanny exclaimed.

"I don't know," Bucky drawled thoughtfully. "Late pooberty, perhaps?" he suggested absently, forgetting himself for the moment.

"Bucky!"

"Oh, sorry, Fanny," he said, recovering himself hastily. "Early change o' life, d'ya think then?" he asked to make matters deliberately worse.

"BUCKY!"

He shrugged, too thoughtful even to enjoy his own mischief. "You figger it out then, Stepgrandmama," he said, helping himself to more kidneys and beginning to ponder the relative sanity of English lady novelists.

Actually, even Charlotte had to admit to herself that it was an agreeable little group that rolled away from Number 10 Seaview Row that morning and took the westward road along the coast toward the little seaside town of Hove, less fashionable than her famous sister town of Brighton.

Bucky, his tailoring as perfect as ever, his toilette as careless, and his whole aspect subtly redolent of this morning's breakfast, sat across from Charlotte with his back to the horses. Lord Darlington, undeniably handsome, though in a rather too ruddy and overly English way for Charlotte's exotic taste, was impeccably attired in dove gray, periwinkle blue, and white. He sat beside Vane and therefore across from Fanny, though his eyes tended to stray from her and rest upon the more agreeable face and form of his cool and distant ladylove.

Fanny, who burbled and simpered to her companions and nodded to every passing acquaintance, was in her glory, wearing dusty rose silk trimmed in white Belgian lace, a dusty rose bonnet accented with small white plumes upon her glossy black hair, and shading her pale complexion from the sun with a beautiful white lace and ivory parasol. She looked quite lovely and, knowing it, was as happy as a lady could be.

Charlotte wore a soft green muslin morning dress piped and embroidered in ivory silk and a bonnet to match, trimmed in ivory silk flowers and green ribbon rosettes. It was a very simple toilette and, as Darlington had been quick to remark, a very fetchin' one as well.

At this, she had merely smiled and gone back to her contemplation of the scenery.

They had been riding for some time and had got beyond the fringes of Brighton into the countryside when Fanny broke off her near-steady stream of idle chatter about this one and that and remarked to the company in general and to Charlotte in particular, "Oh, there they are. That is the Huguenot gentleman, Mr. De'Ath, I spoke of t'other day, and there the lady—if one may call her that—whom he has been awooing." She nodded with great want of subtlety toward a couple driving just ahead of them on the same road, alone in a spanking new phaeton.

"What a remarkable lady," Charlotte remarked when they had driven on out of hearing. She was in her early forties, lavish in her dress and utterly beautiful. Such women are books written about.

"Remarkable's hardly the proper word." Ned Darlington sniffed rather censuringly. "Notorious, you mean."

"Oh?"

"That 'remarkable lady,' as you term her, is none other than the celebrated Clotilde du Roc," he said with the sort of priggish disapproval that made Charlotte dislike him so.

"She was a courtesan in France before the Revolution. She lives by her wits and by her lover's fortunes," Darlington added. "She's a whiz at gamblin' and tarot readin' and Lord knows what other vices, and she's not a fit person to speak to. I pity that poor chap De'Ath, bein' trapped in her toils as he is."

"Really?" Bucky commented dryly. "I was rather envyin' him, meself, for a lucky devil, what?"

Ignoring Bucky's suggestive leer, Lord Ned went on with a supercilious air that Charlotte loathed. "You ladies should have cut her as we passed," he chided.

"Cut her?" Charlotte exclaimed indignantly. "On the contrary, I should like to have settled in for a good chat. By the look of her person, she was fascinating enough to warrant it, but by what you say of her life, it should be worth a whole book.

Moreover, Neddy, if you think about it, you are rather a hypo-crite, you know."

"I?"

"Charlotte!" Fanny squeaked.

"You would have me in company with your dear friend Cumberland, who, the rumourmongers would have it, is a villain and a pervert par excellence and the murderer of his valet, if I remember aright, these two years since. What kind of consistency is that, may I ask you?"

"Oh, really now," Ned Darlington retorted with as much spirit as Charlotte had ever seen him muster—which still wasn't very much—"That is not true at all. He did nothing of the sort. He is outspoken and has many enemies who malign him; his politics are at odds with the regent's, but he is a good man!"

"I agree with you, and I do not believe he killed the man. I merely wish to point out to you that by your own standards, his reputation is quite enough to warrant a lady's keeping her distance, eh, what?" Charlotte replied, ending with a mocking imitation of his manner of speech. "You see, Neddy, you really are a fool and a proper bore into the bargain."

"Charlotte, that is quite enough." Fanny squealed in alarm. "Really, Lord Darlington, I don't know what Charlotte is about this morning. Pay her no mind. She has been rude to us all by turns."

Bucky gave Charlotte a little kick on the foot, shaking his head with a slight grin as she glared at him. What a naughty girl, he seemed to be saying.

"Oh, it's quite all right, Mrs. Hungerford." Neddy sighed with the air of a martyr. "I am used to Miss Charlotte's way with me by now. She don't realize yet the abject desperation of my devotion to her," he said disconsolately and with a pathetic look in Charlotte's direction.

"Indeed I do, Ned Darlington, and I find it an utter bore. You evidently know absolutely nothing about me for if you did, you would know that I should find being loved in abject desperation an insupportable proposition. You are a spineless, proper prig, and I cannot bear it," she snapped at him with a petulant slap of her hand upon her knee and a moue of fury in his direction. Bucky almost expected her to stick out her tongue at the poor besotted swain before she was through.

"Hard cheese, old chap. I think she means it," Bucky remarked to his seatmate with a rather callous relish of the poor fellow's plight.

"Shut up, Vane," Neddy growled, thus putting an end to further conversation for a time.

On the outskirts of the town of Hove the carriage pulled into the courtyard of the Green Bull Inn, where Charlotte took delight in scrutinizing its curious inn sign portraying not a green bull, as one might assume, but rather, a hapless and headless Tudor-looking lady dressed all in green and carrying her head under her arm like a washerwoman's bundle.

"How delightful," Charlotte exclaimed with animation as Bucky helped her down from the carriage. "The Green Bull Inn or the Green Boleyn, if you read the rebus aright. I like this place already."

Set free from the carriage before the others, Charlotte left the rest of the party without a word, bent on exploring the lower rooms of the Green Bull Inn by herself. She exited the premises finally, through a door that led beneath a leafy bower and down onto a grassy terrace set about with little white iron chairs and tables.

Beyond that was the sea, banded by a broad swath of firm, dampish sands upon which groups of holidaymakers were walking in small troops.

Charlotte stopped on the top of the terrace steps that led to the beach and, taking a deep breath, surveyed the scene. What a glorious day, she thought to herself, suddenly glad that she had come along after all. It was even worth putting up with Lord D. and Fanny just to enjoy this wonderful vista of sea and sky and golden sands, the rocks, the sounds of waves, and the pleasant cries of the gray and white gulls wheeling in the air and swooping down to the surface of the water. There were also the shouts of children scampering along the edge of the surf ahead of their elders and the occasional creak and wheeze of a bathing machine being drawn into or out of the water on swollen, waterlogged wheels. Yes, it was a good day after all.

She stepped down onto the beach and started walking toward the water, deliberately taking a diagonal path that would make spotting her from the terrace a bit more difficult for her companions. She was enjoying this momentary solitude, feeling the shifting of the grains beneath her feet as she walked and the crackle, as well, of shells and the debris of the receding tides. Then, just ahead of her on the very edge of the littoral that marked the line of highest tide, she noticed a man and a boy standing, slightly stooped, with their heads close together as if they bent to examine some curiosity of the beach. They were intent upon their discovery, it seemed, and so Charlotte was able to observe them unnoticed until she was quite close.

"I say, have you come upon something interesting there?" she called out amiably once the distance between them had lessened to such an extent that not to speak would have been almost rude. Her simple question, however, brought about the most marked and amazing reaction, for the two of them, man and boy, started as if they had been shot, staring at her in mingled surprise and dismay as they immediately straightened up and drew slightly apart. They looked for all the world as if they had been caught at something.

The elder of the two recovered himself more quickly. "Why yes, miss, now you ask. I was just pointing out to my young master the anatomy of this crab that the tide has washed up onto the sands." He was a small, fine-boned, and fragile-looking man of thirty or so, dressed all in shabby brown wool with a yellowish white shirt and stock. He had about him the dejected air of a poor governor, and that, in fact, was just his lot in life. His face was swarthy and Italianate of feature, his eyes black, small, and piercing—and quite shifty, for they did not once, after the first startled gaze, settle themselves full on Charlotte.

Charlotte, who as a consequence of all this shifty-eyed awkwardness had taken an instant and perhaps not unjustified dislike of this man, turned her smile toward the boy.

He was a bird of a different feather altogether, being fair and blond with large, frank blue eyes and those charming bright pink cheeks and bee-stung lips that very fair and handsome English children tend to have in youth. He was perhaps twelve and not overly tall for his age, though sturdy enough in his figure to give promise of future height. By general appearance he seemed to be the sort of boy that any mother would be proud to claim as her own.

"See, miss, how the gulls have pecked away at its soft underbelly, leaving the shell picked clean and still intact?" the child remarked instructionally and with a strange, subtle air that Charlotte was at a loss to define. If he thought to turn her squeamish with his graphic description of the crab's demise, he had picked the wrong young woman, Charlotte thought to herself, suddenly thinking that he might wish to send her packing with his remark. Instead, she merely agreed and stood her ground, observing that he spoke very well with a poise and subtlety beyond his years, and a circumspection about him as well.

She looked down at the small dried and brittle crab corpse and agreed with him genially that its innards had indeed been picked clean. Still, she thought, there must have been a hundred such crab shells littering the beach; she had stepped on a dozen such just in the last few minutes of her walk, and this one was of no more odd or impressive description than any of the others scattered about, which left Charlotte with a strange suspicion that they had been, these two, intent upon something else beside the novelties of the seashore.

"It is a remarkable find, young man, most fascinating! You must be having a pleasant holiday, I imagine, studying nature's wonders by the sea?" she said, ending her remark with a question so as to lead the boy on to further converse.

"That I am, miss, and count myself fortunate to have such a companion as I have in Mr.—" Here he broke off with a foolish grin at the stern glance he received just then from his tutor.

Charlotte saw that he had evidently almost made a mistake in mentioning the older man's name. An odd thing, that, and one she was determined not to let pass so easily. Therefore, although until the boy had hesitated to name his companion Charlotte had not cared who he was, now she was determined to know.

"In Mr.?" She smiled, offering her hand to the man so swiftly as to catch him off his guard. Her beauty and charm worked, and he responded more as a man than as a conspirator.

"Sellis, miss," he smiled smarmily, taking her hand readily enough. He was very slender, Charlotte noticed, scrutinizing him with more penetration. Almost bony, with a sharp, rather hooked nose, and thick, curling black hair. Had he not been so shifty in his manner, he might almost have been handsome in an odd way, Charlotte decided. He evidently knew it, too, for something in the directness of his last look at her over the handshake made her warier still. He looked at her with a little too much relish of her person for his station in life.

"And this is young Master?" she said, ignoring his appraising look and turning her attention once more to the beautiful young boy.

"Thomas, miss. Master Thomas." He smiled winningly and then prompted, "Miss?," thus playing Charlotte at her own game.

"Miss Hungerford, Master Thomas, and most happy to make the acquaintance of such a *bright* little boy as you," she purred with a gleam in her eye. He was an observant, clever little fellow, was this Master Thomas, of just the sort that must have inspired Shakespeare's Richard III to make the comment "So wise, so young, they say, do never live long."

"Well, Master Tom, we must be off now, don't you think? Good day to you, miss." With a curt nod from Mr. Sellis and a wave from his charge, they started down the beach, first in the direction of Hove town itself and then sharply up the sands toward a cluster of trees where, Charlotte could see, a small pony trap waited in the shade by a road.

Interesting, Charlotte remarked to herself as she turned and started to wander back along the beach in the other direction. What a strange, subtle air of circumspection there was about those two. Yes, she agreed with herself, interesting . . .

* * *

"So there you are, Auntie! Hold up! Wait for me," Bucky Vane called out across the sands as he plodded his way toward Charlotte with evident distaste for the task. "This deuced sand is playin' havoc with me boots," he complained as he joined her, his boots being the one article of attire upon which no errant speck was allowed to stray, a man's boots being like his gun and his dog, holier than holy. "Look at 'em, all scratched and covered in grit!" he ordered, holding one foot as high as he could for her inspection. Had he fallen from that awkward position onto the beach itself, he would hardly have minded the sand in collar and cuff at all. Such was the madness of his youthful affectation.

Charlotte was not impressed. "Thank God for bootblacks" was all the sympathy he got from that quarter. No one, after all, had asked him to go chasing across the beach after her.

"Ordinarily Ned Darlin'ton'd have been racin' down here after you, and glad to do it, I'm sure, but after the way you've treated him this afternoon, he says he's goin' ta ignore you entirely."

"Oh, happy thought."

"He means it. He's cryin' on Fanny's shoulder right now."

"Good, let him. It's an ample enough shoulder, I'm sure. Have you come down here to scold me, by the bye?"

"No, not really," Bucky conceded. "I'm really not much more taken with Ned Darlington than you are—and you're right, of course. He is a prig and a bore! It's just that you shouldn't say so, at least not to his face."

"No, perhaps I should not, Bucky," Charlotte agreed regretfully. "It's just that I do not suffer fools gladly, as they say. I like the company—when I choose to have it—of a few clever, witty and intelligent companions—"

"Guess that lets me out." Bucky grinned.

"Oh, you are awfully amusing, dear boy. Jolly good company indeed, as well you know. And Fanny, God knows, is a good enough soul in her heart. She only, as I say, wants occupation. . . ."

86

"Well, Auntie dear, you needn't fear about that. I think you've got that leetle problem well in hand, me clever wench," Buckthorpe remarked with a conspiratorial smile and a wink.

"Oh, have I?" Charlotte rejoined in surprise. "How so?"

"Your little scheme to match her up with Sir Hannibal Cheng?"

"Yes?" she tendered cautiously with a slight sinking sensation in the pit of her stomach.

"Well, it's workin' to perfection," Bucky exclaimed with malicious gusto.

"It is?" she squeaked.

"It is indeed," he insisted. "He's up on the terrace right now, whisperin' sweet nothin's into the ear that Neddy ain't bedewin' with his tears."

"Sir Hannibal is here already?" Charlotte cried and whirled around on her heel, suddenly taking direct aim on the Green Bull Inn, which they had left far behind in their rambling. "Did he ask about me—where I was?" she asked in a breathless burst that even someone less knowing than our Bucky would not easily have missed.

"What? What? Ask? Why, no, now you mention it. He made a beeline for Fanny." This was not strictly so, for Sir Hannibal upon his arrival at the inn had been crestfallen at the assumption that Charlotte had not come at all. Only when he heard Neddy tell Cumberland of his row with the lady in question did Cheng relax and join Mrs. Hungerford, whom, he had decided, he must perforce engage to charm for the sake of being in proximity to her aloof and disinterested young stepdaughter. "I mentioned that you were lost—probably out upon the sands—and asked if I should come and fetch you," Bucky drawled affably, stopping before the revelation of Sir Hannibal's reply.

"Well?" she prompted when he fell silent and remained so.

"Well, what?" he asked with seeming absence of mind.

"You dolt, what did he say when you asked if you should fetch me?"

"Oh, that! He said no."

"No?" She was undone.

"Yes."

"Just that? A flat no?"

"Oh, he may have said not to bother you or something like that," Bucky amended casually. "He made some jest to Fanny about how authors—scribblers, as he put it—like their solitary walks, and to leave you be."

"Oh!" she answered, utterly crestfallen.

"No, it was the duke sent me to fetch you actually."

"The duke! Really, did he?" she asked with renewed interest.

"Aye. Said you might be a scribbler, but you were the prettiest one he'd seen yet, and he wanted your company. So here I am sent to haul you back and damn the boots—and here we are," he added, looking up just then and seeing that they were approaching the steps to the terrace, well within hailing distance. "Halloo there," he called to their little party seated on a tree-shaded part of the terrace lawn around a table with cold drinks and plates of biscuits, fruits, and little sandwiches set out upon it. "Here's our errant scribbler returned from her ramble. Ah, food! Good, I'm famished," and he busied himself with the dainties at hand, leaving Charlotte to her own devices.

"Come, sit by me," the Duke of Cumberland rumbled good-naturedly, patting the seat of the little iron lawn chair beside him. He smiled warmly at her as she approached, crinkling up his good eye in such a way as unintentionally to turn his face into that of a gargoyle.

"I've saved ye a chair by me, ma dear." He leered again, that good eye twinkling with the amiable charm of the rascally roué that he was at heart.

"How kind, Your Highness." Charlotte smiled wanly, devastated by the fact that her handsome, wonderful hero, Sir Hannibal Cheng, had merely nodded and waved, only half rising from his seat, so intent was he on his conversation with Fanny. Neddy, of course, had virtually ignored her, and Bucky elected to stuff his face with fruit tarts. With no aid from that quarter, and on the theory of any port in a storm, she concentrated all her attention upon the duke.

"Some refreshment perhaps? A lemonade?" the duke asked

when she had taken her seat When she nodded her assent, he snapped his fingers for a servant to pour

"What have ye been doin' to my poor friend here? Breakin his heart, I fear?" the duke growled at her in a low and confidential tone of gentle chiding. "He's lovesick, lass. Smitten! Daft! He says he's goin' ta *marry* you, girl. It's that serious!"

"It is not serious, sir," Charlotte said softly, somewhat mindful that she could not talk to a duke royal as one talks to a Ned Darlington.

"You think not? I've seen Neddy in love a hundred times, gel, but this is the first he's talked of marriage."

"And he shall be in love a hundred times more, I am sure, ere he finally does marry," Charlotte suggested with a smile. "You see, Your Highness, Neddy is not really in love with me. He is in love with the idea of loving me. If he really loved *me,* he would not be silly and foolish and go about things in all the wrong way, but rather would study me and know me and win me by loving me as I need to be loved. Did he do so. why then, I should study him as well—

"He aims to *marry* you, and soon, if he can,   the duke stated insistently, ignoring all of Charlotte's high-blown rhetoric. What, after all, did this green gel know of love? "Don't that please you, Miss H.? Now, most gels would be hot to marry such a feller as Neddy—and be a *duchess* in the course o' time, what, what?" He nodded with an encouraging leer, as if she should be charmed by the prospect. "Mother o' a line o' dukes, eh, eh?"

Now *that* was a dubious honour indeed, Charlotte thought, making a note that she had just come upon another reason for not marrying Ned Darlington—the production of his offspring.

"You are quite right, Your Highness." She smiled agreeably "Most girls *would* be hot to marry—even such a fellow as Ned Darlington—if it led to a dukedom in the course of time. But I have no more desire to be a duchess, or the mother of dukes, than I have to be Lord Ned Darlington's wife, and so, you see, I have no intention of being either."

"Oh? Oh!" the duke puffed. "Yes, . see. It's like that, is it?"

"It is, Your Highness."

"And there's no more ta be said about it?" he asked, detecting the iron in her backbone. His mother—another Charlotte—could be like that too, damn her.

"No, Your Highness, there is not."

"Females do change their silly little minds 'pon occasion, ya know," he offered tentatively, testing if the iron could be bent.

"*This* female does not, Your Highness," Charlotte said firmly, looking the Duke of Cumberland straight in his good eye until, at last, she had to smile.

He grinned back, his mustache bristling and his teeth bared in that good-natured, gargoyle leer of his which was rather growing on Charlotte. "Stubborn wench, eh?"

"I have been called so," she agreed seriously.

"I think," he said at last, "that Neddy's got very good taste in choosin' you, Miss Hungerford, but I think that it'd be a poor bargain on your part if you chose him. He's a good lad, mind. I'd be a liar to say otherwise. But he's not a fit match for the likes o' you. Stick to your guns, gel." He nodded solemnly, and then, breaking into a smile, he raised his glass aloft and tipped it toward her with all the charm of the true prince that he was.

Charlotte smiled back and, imitating the duke's gesture, joined him in the unspoken toast.

Hours later, back at Number 17 Seaview Row, over a last glass of port before retiring, Sir Hannibal Cheng, who had been decidedly troubled by the scene he had witnessed, asked his friend the duke about the meaning of that toast he had observed.

"What? What? Oh, that! Nothin', old chap. Nothin' at all," Cumberland said with an infuriating gesture of dismissal.

"It must have signified *something?*" Cheng persisted.

"Well, only that we don't have to worry about Neddy, that's all."

"How so?" cried Cheng in alarm. Had Charlotte Hungerford told the duke that she would marry Neddy after all?

"We don't have ta worry about savin' him from matrimony," the duke explained and then went on to add knowingly. "Probably not a man in Christendom perfect enough for a wench like

90

that. I know the type. She's a born spinster, if ever I saw one—
and I've got six in the family, mind."

Cheng, listening disconsolately, tried hard to reconcile the
Miss Hungerford of his dreams and reason with the Miss H. that
the duke presented with such knowing finality.

"Perhaps it's just as well, though," Cumberland added
thoughtfully. "Saves some poor bloke's hide for 'im."

"How so?" Cheng asked again.

"Reg'lar Tartar, that one. Pretty gel, I'll warrant. Pretty
enough to be sure, but a rough un. Yep, a reg'lar Tartar, and
there's an end to it." With that, the Duke of Cumberland yawned
and, taking up a candlestick, withdrew to his bed for the night,
convinced for the nonce that he had summed up Miss Hungerford aright.

Poor Sir Hannibal, blasted with love, horrible at playing
games, though he had tried his best that afternoon, and cut to
the quick by the duke's harsh summation of his ladylove, was left
to sit with the port decanter in one hand and a glass in the other,
pondering his fate.

::6::

Charlotte's journey to Hove for tea with the princess Sophia on the following Monday afternoon had turned out to be beastly. She was riding, it was true, in perfect luxury and comfort, seated in an elegant carriage, being propelled by matchless horses, escorted by a postillion, footman, and driver, all liveried to perfection in the colours of the royal house of England. The royal coat of arms was emblazoned everywhere—but she was *alone,* and so it was all beastly; utter vexation!

Sir Hannibal Cheng had gallantly offered to accompany her. It was all arranged, in fact, but then had come the princess's carriage—an hour early—and with it a note from the princess Sophia in her own hand, asking that Charlotte come at once and alone. There had barely been enough time to compose a brief note to Sir Hannibal, begging his leave and explaining her hasty departure without him. Indeed, not even daring to trust such a missive to some brainless servant, she had sent the message across via the convenient pocket of her nephew, Buckthorpe Vane. That done, she had completed her toilette and left for Hove immediately in a fine state of misery.

Yet if one thing could distract Charlotte from this blow that fate had dealt to her plans, it was an afternoon spent in a royal residence in the gracious company of a real princess, dressed incomparably in the height of court fashion and surrounded by a bevy of fashionable waiting ladies and dashing courtiers. The tea itself must be a virtual wallow in rich cakes and jellies served on golden plate accompanied by the rarest of spiced teas drunk from the finest of china services, all presented by an army of butlers in breeches and powdered wigs. Marvellous!

Moreover, Charlotte imagined, the Lord knew what powerful men of the arts and letters, what statesmen of renown would be gathered at this little salon of the princess Sophia. She had never heard much, she must admit, of that particular princess and knew nothing whatever of Sophia's tastes and fancies in the elegant world that must revolve around her at court—Charlotte, after all, gossiped little—but surely this would be an elegant and intellectually stimulating afternoon affair. Perhaps she would even be invited one evening to some distinguished soiree. There was no end to the possibilities.

But if only Sir Hannibal had been invited . . .

Still, perhaps the princess had been right after all. In such company as must be gathering this afternoon at Hove, Sir Hannibal, a bluff man of action like the Duke of Cumberland, might well be out of place. She began gradually to console herself with that notion and look forward to the glamourous royal adventure to come.

However, the house that Princess Sophia had taken in Hove turned out to be just that—a house! Pretty, to be sure, and of fine old Georgian brick, whitewashed once, though now faded to a pleasant salmon colour, set in a small park and garden with the sea and beach at its back. But still a house!

Charlotte could not help but be a trifle disappointed. What was more, there was no congestion of carriages without, betokening the brilliant company gathering for this literary tea. Perhaps she was sent for early in order to have a private audience with Her Highness beforehand. Very flattering thought, that. Or perhaps all the others had arrived and their equipages were either sent away again or dispatched to the princess's own stables for the afternoon. Well, she would soon know all.

They pulled up to the simple front door, the footman helped her to alight, and a dowdy middle-aged, rather tired-looking lady-in-waiting greeted her politely and escorted her from the entrance through the house to the back. By the slightly run-down look of everything in sight, the house must have been rented furnished, and rather indifferently so at that. It was, moreover, as silent as her father's little church in Wiltshire—and easily as depressing. Neither the pleasant murmur of witty literary lions nor the boisterous guffaws of amiable statesmen resounded from the rooms ahead. She must be sent for very early indeed.

The princess Sophia, when Charlotte was presented at last, sat, or rather reclined, upon a chaise in an airy, modestly appointed back drawing room overlooking the gardens, lawns, and the sea. She did not rise from her invalid's place upon the chaise but had the weary waiting lady draw up a chair for her guest.

"Pray forgive my not rising to greet you, Miss Hungerford, but as you can see, I am not strong today," the princess pleaded civilly as Charlotte, after completing an elegant and much-practised curtsey, took the chair across from her.

"Sir Hannibal Cheng," Charlotte replied, "told me you have not been well. I am sorry, Your Highness, to hear it and can only hope that your indisposition is temporary." In truth, she was dismayed to see so young a woman so weak and unwell.

"Ah, would that it might be so," Sophia answered rather patly and then changed the subject at once. "Sir Hannibal," she declared. "I daresay you should have found the ride less tedious had you had that gentleman's company as an escort. But alas, I am so easily fatigued, I felt it best we talk alone, and after all, what is the subject of Romantick Novels to a man of Sir Hannibal's literary tastes?"

Charlotte, who knew nothing whatever of Sir Hannibal's tastes, literary or otherwise, took the princess's earnest remark for irony and laughed lightly. Their laughter, however mistaken, served to melt the slight air of reserve between the two ladies, who then, more at their respective eases, began such an exchange of inconsequentials as permitted each of them the opportunity and the leisure to survey the other's appearance and general style.

Charlotte, whose last hopes of partaking in a lively literary tea had just died a quiet death, saw to her further disappointment not the vibrant, attractive, and finely dressed youngish woman she had expected a princess of England to be, but rather a pale middle-aged lady whose figure, while good, was just a bit too thin; whose complexion, while firm and clear, was just a shade too pale for health; and whose fair hair was not dressed half so fashionably as her own. Her white muslin dress was very fine of fabric but utterly insipid in style and not at all suitable to a woman of five-and-thirty, especially when she looked far more like four-and-forty. It was what came from having one's aged mother still choosing one's clothing, though Charlotte had no way of knowing that such was the case with the princess.

And yet it was not hard to imagine by her features that Sophia had been considered beautiful in her first flush of youth, although to believe that she had been both high-spirited and willful as well took a great deal of imagination. Yet it was said that of all of King George's pretty daughters, this princess had been the most spirited.

Princess Sophia, for her part, saw her visitor as a very beautiful young woman indeed—direct of eye, poised of manner, a trifle rigid and defiant, she suspected, and most fashionably attired in light blue trimmed in lemon yellow with touches of black ribbon. Everything about her, Sophia decided, given certain minor changes such as colour of hair or eye or height, might have been a characteristic of one of her own heroines. She had the same imperious stamp to her looks and manner that charmed the princess so in Charlotte's females and that which caused her to enjoy each novel as it was published in turn.

There was, moreover, a quite personal and particular reason that Sophia loved Charlotte Hungerford's novels and that would in no great time cause her to have similar warm feelings for the authoress herself: her heroines had about them the same high-spirited character that Sophia had once, briefly, exhibited before she erred so very far from decorum as to be from that time on hedged round with watchdogs and keepers. Maida, Isobelle, Rowena, and the others struck a chord in her nature and carried her outside of what she was—what she had *become*—to what she had been and what she wished with all her heart that she could have remained.

Their tea arrived at last, a very homey and rather unappetizing affair, consisting of bread and butter, digestive biscuits, and, happily, jelly tarts. The tea was common black and weak into the bargain, served in an ordinary china service that looked as if it must have come with the house. No luxury over the tea either, Charlotte noted with the last hope of some vestige of royal glamour fading from her eye. In fact, she had rather the impression that the jelly tarts, which really were good, were a concession to her presence. A mournful tea indeed. The lady-in-waiting arranged things near to her mistress's hand and retired discreetly, leaving Sophia and Charlotte alone at last.

"I like your novels terribly, you know," the princess ventured, pouring the tea and handing a cup to Charlotte.

"I am honoured, Your Highness."

"Yes." Sophia sighed resignedly. "I suppose you are, but really, I cannot think why. I am just as ordinary a reader as any other who enjoys your books—or at least that is so whilst I am lost in the reading of them—and therefore, it should be no more an honour to have me as a fan than any other lady that you might meet. But still, I expect I cannot escape it and must perforce accept your remark in the spirit you intended—as a compliment." She sipped her tea, and Charlotte could see at once it was not the steam rising from its surface that gave the moist look to her hostess's eyes.

Charlotte could not help but be taken aback somewhat. After all, it was certainly a most unexpectedly emotional response to a terribly simple and rather pat remark. Still, it did seem to invite some intimacy from Charlotte.

"I think," she ventured at last, "that you are rather tired of being a princess, are you not?"

Sophy looked up, her eyes wide with a kind of relief. "Oh, yes," she breathed softly. "Heartily tired of it. And I love your books because they help me to escape—to be—to be Maida or Rowena or—" She blushed crimson then, for she had been about to say, "Even myself as I was then." Instead, she bit her tongue and looked away, embarrassed by her own impulsiveness. "But I should not say such things—to anyone—let alone a—"

"A stranger," Charlotte put in with an ironic smile. She found of a sudden that for herself, she did not feel strange at all in the princess Sophia's company, but rather as if she were with a pleasant, rather sad acquaintance, cheering her up over the tea-cups with a homey little chat.

"I was going to say that, yes," Sophia admitted, "but oddly, I find you are no more a stranger than Maida or Isobelle would be if I were able to invite them to tea. I *liked* them so much. They have cheered me so much with their impulsive daring and their brave high spirits. They are friends. . . ."

"No author, Your Highness, could ask for a greater compliment on behalf of her heroines than that." Charlotte smiled kindly, feeling a great warmth and an almost protective affection for this lady. They looked up then, their eyes locking for a moment, and it was as if an understanding sprung up between them—a sensitivity to each other's feelings that was too much to acknowledge.

"No, I suppose not," Sophia answered, pulling her eyes away and changing her tone to one of enforced and musical good cheer. "And now I shall ask a silly question and one that I expect you must hear a thousand times over: Where do you get your ideas? How do you think of such adventures? Such romance? And you know, you do not write enough," she chided with a wag of her finger and the hint of a twinkle in her eye. "We want more books from you!"

Charlotte, both flattered by the compliment to her talents and charmed by the increasing animation of her hostess, laughed a light, ironic laugh. "I might perhaps write more if I were free and at peace, but I am surrounded by a numerous household—or so it seems at any rate—and have been since the winter when my father died. It precludes my having the kind of solitude I crave for my writing." Here, prompted by the princess, she launched into an outline of her recent life, from her increasing popularity as a novelist, her father's death, and the subsequent taking under her own wing of Fanny's considerable bulk, even Bucky's pleasant but dubious presence. She also mentioned her hope of marrying off her amiable stepmother, though she mentioned not a word of her own sudden and heartfelt attachment to Sir Hannibal Cheng and her plot to use Fanny as her stalking horse. That would not have done. It did not sound very nice after all, and for the first time Charlotte realized that her conscience on the score of Fanny did bother her a bit.

"Peace and quiet," the princess repeated thoughtfully when Charlotte had finished what had become a droll and humourously exaggerated recitation of her current woes. "How I have longed for such simple luxuries as that, away from the gossiping and dreariness of my mother's court at Windsor." She sighed and then smiled brightly. "And you see, here I am at last, in the peace and quiet of Hove with not a thing to trouble me. After *years*, mind you," she added with emphasis, breaking then into a delightful smile that lit her whole face quite unexpectedly. "This little house! You cannot imagine how happy I am to be in this *little* house with only an equerry, a lady-in-waiting, and my dressers and cook for household, a few local people to serve when needed, and a gardener, coachman, and so on lodged well away from my sight. No *troops* of hangers-on and courtiers to plague one's every step and spy one's every action." She spoke intensely now, and Charlotte sensed some deep hurt behind Sophy's words. "God, the peace all this is to me," she exclaimed, snatching up another tart for emphasis and chomping on it like a schoolgirl.

"You saw, did you not, how I dismissed my lady after you entered and our tea was brought in? In my mother's house I had no such freedom. She would have stayed and heard our every word and retailed it back to my mother or any other who would listen—and they all do, you know. Imagine! But *now* I am free. I dismiss them all, everyone, whenever it amuses me." She ended with a defiant popping of the last of her tart into her mouth.

Charlotte giggled conspiratorily at the princess's vehemence and took another tart herself.

"And I may have any company I choose—my brothers even— or any local child that interests me, old friends long forbidden my society—and especially new friends, if I am fortunate enough to make them," she went on, first defiantly and then with a more solemn tone to her voice. Sophia checked herself suddenly, as if to change her mood before she lost control. "You are not, are you, Miss Hun— Please, may I? Charlotte?"

"Oh, indeed, Your Highness," Charlotte hastened to assure her.

"You are not, Charlotte, going to marry Lord Darlington, are you?" Sophy asked quite abruptly and with much concern mirrored in her face. "My brother Ernest and Sir Hannibal seemed to think—"

"Well, they may think what they like!" Charlotte retorted with great pique. "Indeed, I am *not* going to marry Ned Darlington," she exclaimed vociferously. Really, she was thinking, this is too much! Does everyone in Christendom know of Neddy's puppy love? And is it even bruted about amongst the royal family? But still, she could not be rude. Obviously the princess Sophia was asking with solicitude. "Your brother the Duke of Cumberland has already taxed me on this matter. The truth is, I do not care a fig for Neddy Darlington, though he is, I am sure, a decent enough young man and fit for some young woman's matrimonial aspirations; he is simply not for *mine.*"

"Ah," the princess sighed. "I am relieved to hear it. I was afraid you might be browbeat into it by your stepmother, who, I understand, promotes the connection shamelessly, or perhaps even by some others I could name. There is much gossip abroad, you know, and Ernest has carried it all right here to Hove."

"I begin, Your Highness, to see the extent of the gossip," Charlotte remarked dryly, "but I hasten to assure you, I am not one to be browbeat into anything, let alone marriage—which is a consummation devoutly to be wished only if it is a matching of two like-minded and loving souls. Neddy might be loving enough, but as to whether he even *has* a soul . . ." At this mild jest, even Charlotte, who had taken this topic with great heat and seriousness, had to smile a bit.

Sophia returned her smile and reached across the table to pat her companion's hand. "I am happy to hear you say so. There are too many ladies in this world who will marry whatever the cat drags in, so long as he has a title and thirty thousand a year."

She forbore to mention that her sisters and perhaps even she would have *paid,* had they had it, thirty thousand a year just to be married ladies with courts of their own. So far only the princess royal had become a wife and now held sway as Princess of Württemberg. Her four living sisters still languished unmarried, if not unloved. "Not, mind, that there is anything really *wrong* with Neddy. But he is so young yet, and I could see in a trice that he is no match for the likes of you. You should be bored to tears in a day, I fear." She looked with great warmth at Charlotte. "I should not like to see you unhappy in your loving, my dear," she murmured, a look crossing her face that Charlotte read easily as a memory of her own unhappy loving.

"How kind you are," she answered simply, and, sensing that she must change the princess's wistful mood, went on with spirit, "No, you are right. Boredom is a prospect utterly unsupportable to me, Your Highness. Neddy, poor boy, simply pales beside my Ravenstock or the dashing Renaldo, Duke of Dalmatia, of whom you will be reading, I hope, in the next year to come." It worked. Sophy's eyes lit once more, and she asked to hear more of the intriguing Renaldo of Dalmatia. From thence Charlotte was able to distract her moody hostess with lively chatter about the books they both enjoyed, current fashions, and a myriad of light topics. They laughed easily and often over small witticisms exchanged or comical people that they had known until, at last, it was time for the carriage to be brought round. Princess Sophia, in spite of her oft-cited invalid's weakness, elected to accompany her guest to the door, a signal honour under the circumstances and one that Sophy's small household attributed rightly to the good effect of this guest upon their mistress.

The two women, separated more by the look of age rather than actual years, were standing together in the small front hall, saying a last and amiable farewell when Charlotte, in absently gazing past her hostess's head, happened to notice upon the wall a group of framed portrait miniatures, some dozen in all, of rather handsome children. Amongst them, unmistakable to Charlotte's eye, was the pretty, ruby-lipped, ruddy-cheeked boy whom she had encountered on the beach near the Green Bull Inn.

The princess, seeing Charlotte's attention so suddenly distracted, turned to follow her gaze. "Oh," she exclaimed delightedly, "my darlings. I take them with me wherever I go. It is the whole group of us when we were young and happy children. Were we not a pretty brood of chicks?"

"Beautiful," Charlotte agreed absently. "But that boy is not, I think, one of your brothers," she said as she approached and put her finger lightly on the likeness in question. The face was unmistakable: a boy of twelve or so and undoubtedly the image of Master Thomas. "It cannot be," she explained, "for I saw that same boy not a week ago on the beach some miles from here with his governor. He is far too handsome a lad for me to mistake."

She could not be sure, but Princess Sophia's expression seemed to tense ever so slightly and her brow knit before she answered. "Handsome! Why, he was the handsomest lad one could imagine, was Ernest."

"Ernest!"

"Why, yes, my dear. You are exclaiming over my brother the Duke of Cumberland. He was a beautiful boy and a handsome youth. It breaks my heart when I see him as he is now—so badly scarred, his eye gone."

Charlotte looked back from Sophia's face to the miniature portrait on the wall. That boy—so fair and pretty—now Ernest of Cumberland? No, it could not be. She had seen the child but a few days since. No twin could be more alike.

"But—but I saw the boy. I *spoke* to him. His name was Master Thomas, and he was as like this portrait as a face could be," she protested in bewilderment.

"You cannot be right, my dear," Sophia said evenly, her pale face tight. "For one thing, there is no family in the neighbourhood with the surname of Thomas, save the gardener's family, and they are too poor to have a governor for their son. Take, if you will, the frame from the wall and read the legend on the back." She nodded toward the picture to insist further, and Charlotte, far too sure of her ground and too mystified by this

101

strange turn to think of the impropriety involved in daring to doubt a royal princess, lifted the little oval gold frame from the wall without more hesitation and turned it over in her hand.

On the back, written on the vellum backing in leaded pencil that had blurred somewhat with the passage of years, were the words:

H.R.H. Prince Ernest Augustus
1783 aetat. 12 years.

Charlotte turned the portrait over again in her palm. There was no question that this child was the Duke of Cumberland as a boy. Yet that boy on the beach, twelve in this Year of Our Lord 1812, could well have been the sitter for this portrait done in 1783. Charlotte's mind began to revolve with dizzying speed. It suddenly occurred to her that the duke, with his reputation for wickedness, might have a bastard son whom he had nearby for the summer, in order to see the child upon occasion. For surely the boy on the beach, if not the boy in the portrait, must be son to that boy now grown a man. If that were so, why then, she must be causing her hostess great discomfort, for the child must be her nephew—and surely an embarrassment to them all. She replaced the portrait on the wall thoughtfully, and erasing the quizzical look upon her face and in her eyes as best she could, Charlotte turned once more to the princess.

"How very foolish I have been! And of course, you are right. That portrait is of a boy long grown." She smiled lamely and placed her hand, bent at the wrist, high in the air where the Duke of Cumberland's head would be. "And though the wee lad I saw was every bit as pretty as that, I vow, he was no bigger than this." She dropped her hand to her shoulder's level. "Moreover, I was totally forgetting that the child I saw had *brown* eyes—very dark and not at all English-looking."

At this outright lie she could see the princess Sophia's face relax visibly. Clearly the lady was immensely relieved. "Now there you have, Your Highness, a perfect example of the utter pigheadedness of my temperament. Do you see now why my stepmother throws up her hands and Lord Neddy is much the better off without me?"

"Pray, do not alarm yourself, my dear Charlotte. It was, after all, such a little mistake. Now you see you were in error, why, all is well," the princess added smoothly.

"You are most forbearing, Your Highness," Charlotte murmured with a curtsey to hide the enigmatic expression she felt crossing her face. "I was afraid you'd think me mad—or worse yet, terribly rude."

"Oh, no indeed. The matter is quite forgot," the princess hastened to assure her with a slight twinge of guilt at the abjectness of the younger woman's concern. "Say so with me, my dear."

"The matter is quite forgot," Charlotte parroted as they came away from the portraits and said a last farewell on the steps before she was handed into the carriage by the equerry.

"You must come again," Sophia said with more feeling in her plea than mere politeness would warrant. "You will, won't you, my dear?"

"Why, whenever you wish it, Your Highness," Charlotte replied. The carriage rolled away just then, and the two ladies waved another and truly fond adieu.

Now, when Charlotte went off on her journey to Hove to take tea with her sovereign George's youngest surviving daughter, she had unwittingly left behind her in Brighton a certain nearly related female party to welter in an anguish of high dudgeon and deep consternation, that near relation being one Fanny Hungerford.

And who, pray, can blame the poor lady? For having returned from taking those wretched waters—far more a social than medicinal necessity as it happened—she rounded the corner of Seaview Row just in time to see, parked right before her very own doors at Number 10, a magnificent carriage with bewigged and liveried driver, footman, and postillion. The coat of arms of the royal household of England was emblazoned upon every possible surface. Now she had seen often enough in the row

Cumberland's rather unattractive but serviceable travelling closed coach, and this was not his or any other she had seen about the town. Whose was it? Before she could even begin to think of an answer, out of Number 10 tripped her very own stepdaughter, Charlotte, and without so much as a by-your-leave or even the slightest blinking of her amber eyes over the incomparable appointments of the vehicle before her, she allowed herself to be handed up into the carriage by the footman. She smoothed her dress prettily, oblivious to the throng of neighbours gaping at her, and at the snap of the driver's whip, the carriage and she in it were off down the row and out of sight.

Charlotte had not even noticed Fanny, though she had yoohooed and trilled til she thought her breath would fail and her hand drop off at the wrist. She hastened up the front steps and into the house in breathless agitation, threw off her bonnet, mantle, and gloves, and flounced into the drawing room. Tea was in order, she decided, though it was early yet—and scones as well, all hot and buttery to soothe her jangled nerves. She yanked at the pull by the fireplace with angry vehemence and heard, seemingly in answer, such a rapping and banging as to make her think that in her fury she had done some injury to the very structure of the house itself.

As it turned out, the bellpull was still in order, and the noise was not of her own making at all, but rather that of some visitor attempting to beat his way through the front door panels by means of the brass knocker upon them.

"Sir Hannibal," Fanny exclaimed when the agitated guest had been shown into the drawing room.

"Where is she?" he cried with neither greeting nor ceremony. "We had an engagement! What's all this about a royal carriage and Charlotte in it?" The Chinese baronet's eyes were blazing hotly, and Fanny, unlike Charlotte, who would have relished such a sight, thought that she might actually faint, so much did she tremble at the heat of his agitation.

"Sir Hannibal, pray contain yourself. I cannot think but that you have taken leave of your senses to behave in such a manner, and before me of all people, who am as blameless a soul as—"

She could not finish but snuffled into her handkerchief instead—a most eloquent gesture and one that brought the recalcitrant Sir Hannibal to heel at once. Please God, he thought to himself, don't let her cry and get all red-eyed on me.

"Ah," he snapped abruptly, "do forgive me. You are quite right. I have forgot myself. Shameful of me, but I was in me rooms preparing to come over here in a matter of moments for the expressed purpose of escortin' your stepdaughter to Hove—"

"To Hove!"

"Yes, Hove. She is to take tea with Her Royal Highness the princess Sophia in Hove this afternoon. I was asked to arrange it, and I expected to escort—"

"Thank heavens." Fanny breathed a great sigh of relief. At least it was not an assignation with Cumberland. She slumped against the mantel, where she still stood with the bellpull yet in her grasp. At that very moment the maid came up from below-stairs in response to her original summons, and Fanny gave orders for the early tea that she had wished.

"You will stay for tea, Sir Hannibal?" she asked, more out of civility than from any hope of his continued company.

"That is most kind," he mumbled absently. "A—a cup, perhaps, to calm me." Fanny was dismayed; she could not wolf down a plate of buttered scones and jam quite so heartily with Sir Hannibal looking on and probably gauging upon what portion of her already ample anatomy each scone would apply itself. Well, there was no help for it. She must be kind.

"As I say, I had intended to accompany her, was readying myself for that task in fact, when Neddy came to my rooms to say that Char—Miss Hungerford, that is—had just gone off in Sophia's carriage. I naturally came at once—"

"Naturally," Fanny agreed dryly. "And banged the very doors down, terrifying the life out of me in the process." She placed one hand over her heart, for she felt flustered and terribly overpowered by Sir Hannibal. He might be nice enough in his way, but Fanny did not like to feel flustered by any man. It was too unsettling. A little self-assurance in the male sex went a long way with Fanny. Give her a nice easy fellow who didn't quite know his own mind—a fellow like Neddy Darlington, for instance. He was such a manageable young man that she couldn't understand Charlotte's lack of interest for the life|of her.

"Tea, you say?" Fanny prompted as Sir Hannibal paced the room in a catlike and agitated silence.

"Eh? What? Yes, a cup," he snapped distractedly. Gad, why had she gone off without him? Was she snubbing him?

"No, Sir Hannibal, you mistake me. I mean, Charlotte. She is taking tea, you say, and in Hove?"

"Yes, Mrs. H. The princess Sophia is summering there. She has read Charlotte—that is, Miss Hungerford's novels and wished to meet her. I arranged the date and had volunteered to escort your stepdaughter. Of course, that was days ago. I—I expect she must have forgot," he added, somewhat crestfallen at the thought. How he had been looking forward to this afternoon, to an uninterupted ride in her utterly fetchin' company with no Neddy, no Ernest or Buckthorpe Vane, and especially no fat, simperin' Fanny Hungerford. He had been so sure, given an hour's span alone with her, that she'd begin ta notice him. Why, if she did, she'd see he was just the sort o' fellow she wrote about: dashin' and adventurous. Why, as a man, he had that Ravenstock feller beat. And as for Sir Berry de Groat! He could howl in the wilderness before he could hold a candle to Sir Hannibal Cheng. Yes, he was sure of it! What Charlotte Hungerford needed was a chap like himself, with all the earmarks of a hero—and a baronetcy to prove it. She might dream o' men like him and write about them, but he was real and in the flesh. Once she saw that, why, damn it, he'd win her for sure. But when? Blood and destruction, when?

"Yes," Fanny agreed, "she must have forgot. Oh, yes, Charlotte can be like that," she said, not knowing that Charlotte's note of explanation still resided in Bucky's coat pocket amidst all the lint, snuff, lost buttons, and old fantan counters it usually held.

The tea things arrived, and Sir Hannibal, still as jumpy as the proverbial cat, managed just barely to sit upon the edge of a settee and drink a cup without either spilling the tea or breaking the china. His eyes wore an expression of deep concentration so fearful to behold that Fanny said not a word, merely staring in silent wonder at this very peculiar fellow.

At just that time young Buckthorpe Vane, emerging from his room, where he had lolled long and slept deep in preparation for the coming evening's debauches, tiptoed down the hall stairs, bent on making his escape from the house before his stepgrannie could collar him to keep her company for the afternoon. He glanced into the drawing room, and what he saw surprised him so much as to make him—even at the risk of detection—stop in his tracks and watch.

Sir Hannibal Cheng *again* in Fanny's company—and the two of them staring at each other in a deep and mutual silence that, to Bucky's somewhat callow experience, seemed to betoken the throes of love. He was amazed and not a little troubled at the sight, for he had come by now to realize his aunt Charlotte was more attached to the rather dubious charms of the Chinee baronet than she would ever dream of admitting. He knew that she had only intended Fanny to be her stalking-horse, but from the way things looked in that drawing room, perhaps the horse was going to win the hunt instead of the crafty Diana who hid behind her.

Clearly, this was no time to deliver that note Charlotte had given him. Best leave well enough alone. He slunk past the doorway, thinking of his poor aunt. She wouldn't take the losing of her chance very well, but still, if she did lose, it would surely have been her own fault for having been so indirect and scheming.

For Fanny, Monday afternoon grew more unsettling with the passing of each tedious moment. Sir Hannibal was lost in thought, his eyes blazing, his tea cooling in the cup on his knee, leaving Fanny to wallow in a sick-at-the-tummy sort of yearning for another plate of scones.

But he took his leave at last, almost as abruptly as he had arrived, stopping only to kiss her hand and thank her fervently for her patience in putting up with his moods (as if she had had any choice, since he *would* stay!). He called her an admirable lady; he, in fact, behaved with all the abstracted and near to idiotic madness generally attributed to a man in love. Now that thought utterly devastated Fanny, for she knew that he was a widower with a small child. Had not Charlotte made their ages and situations in life quite clear, after all, to their mutual embarrassment? It was true the man must be lonely and in need of female companionship—a wife, in fact, she assumed, being as sentimental about matrimony as any other female of her age and situation. But, oh, dear, not Fanny! The Lord knew he did seem attentive enough, being so often in her company these two weeks past as to be a positive vexation to her. Charlotte, moreover, seemed to push it upon them both.

"Ah, woe is me." She sighed aloud over another cup of tea and the last of her scones, liberally smeared with jam and butter, as an added solace to her lamenting mood. "I could not bear it if he proposed, the poor man. How could I say him nay and break his heart? And yet, how could I say yes and break my own? Whatever shall I do?" she moaned, and answered her question by doing the only thing that occurred to her—she ordered more scones.

::7::

John Darlington, His Grace the seventh Duke of Axminster, was
by nature a placid man, much given to snoozing by the fireside
of an evening in a disordered but comfortable baronial hall littered with dogs and children and the sort of clutter and noise
generally associated with those two not terribly dissimilar species of animal. Yes, John Darlington thought to himself, he was
really a placid sort o' man and patient to a fault—but *this* was
too much! Neddy had gone too far this time and he, the seventh
duke, was having none of it!

No son of his—no *eldest* son at any rate—was going to play
fast and loose with the family fortunes like this: marry some
penniless bluestockinged scribbler with a sister known by all of
Society to be as free with her favours as any actress on the
boards. Who the devil did Neddy think he was? One of Farmer
George's dissolute brood? Another Cumberland, perhaps? He
grumped to himself angrily, thinking of that unfortunate friendship his son had developed with Ernest Augustus. Still, even that
was probably a passing thing—and certainly not a marriage!
Well, if Neddy thought he could live that sort o' life, pick any
wife he chose—the scalawag—then his father, John Darlington,
was just going to have to apprise him of a few salient facts, such
as from what purse the boy's rather liberal allowance poured
forth—and with what iron fist that same purse could be snapped
shut!

Gaming he didn't mind, or cockfighting, or bearbaiting. They
were a gentleman's prerogatives after all. And wenching was

fine—good for the skin and bracing for the wind. Riding to hounds or shooting birds was splendid; made a man of a lad, improved his eye. Fine! But marrying? No.

At least not at barely six-and-twenty—and not to anything less than an heiress! Money and a title—in that order. There were a damned sight too many little Darlingtons to provide for already without adding some penniless daughter-in-law to the brew. And no scribblers with dangerous modern ideas, given to using their brains for ought but pleasing men and doing needle-work; no parson's daughters with priggish notions of right and wrong, always hemming a man in and doing good works amongst the peasants, raising expectations and giving notions to rabble such as ought not to think at all! And no sisters of such a tart as that Lady Helena Vane, the toast of every loose-living gentleman and gentleman's gentleman in Wiltshire. That was that!

Upon his arrival from Axminster Hall, that illustrious, if rather damp and somewhat mossy, seat of the ancient Axminster duchy, the seventh duke had gone straight to Number 17 Sea-view Row, missing Sir Hannibal by scant minutes. Once there, he had invaded the premises in a fury not unlike that of the Chinee baronet's at Number 10. In fact, after a similar assault upon the door itself, he stormed in, and finding his son in the back drawing room, he laid down all the aforementioned law to a stricken and shattered Neddy with more passion than his son had ever seen him display—and certainly with more heat than was wise for a man of his years and health to muster.

Needless to say, Neddy had been floored—appalled, in fact. He had been thinking all along that his father was safely tucked up at Axminster Hall, from which place he rarely ventured anyway, and now here he was, appearing as suddenly as a genie from some Arabian bottle and with all the frenzied energy of a dervish, laying down the law about things that Neddy never even dreamt his father knew! Gad, what a shock!

Moreover, his father had always been such a placid man—well nigh comatose as a rule. It was shattering for poor Neddy to see such a change rendered in his father, and especially by any act of his, for he had always been able to get away with almost anything with the guv'nor.

He had never pestered Neddy about his little Latin and even less Greek. He'd been an absolute peach over his dearth of talent in mathematics and history—after all, he had said, how many times does a duke have to name a date or square a root? Let others be clever if they had to be; all that Life and Honour demanded of a man of Neddy's station was the squaring of one's debts, and the guv'nor had always squared 'em, too. Gambling debts, tailors' bills, flash house peccadilloes—why, his pater had been a bloody living saint!

And now this! He'd fallen in love at last and wanted to marry —settle down. No more flash houses or gamblin' hells. He wanted to be a good husband and a dotin' father. What nobler aims? Yet here was his pater in a veritable rage about it all. Why, he'd be happier to see him with a good case o' the pox than with Charlotte Hungerford for his wife.

In fact, that is precisely what the duke had said—"better the pox than a parson's daughter"—thus displaying a laudable talent for impromptu alliteration that even Charlotte might have admired. Poor Neddy had said nothing to any of this; he had listened for as long as he could and had then taken to his heels, running pell-mell from the room and right out the doors of Number 17. He had to think—he had to reason out what was to be done. That resolve boding hard work ahead, he stalked down to the Esplanade and brooded upon the sea.

The duke, on the other hand, was nearly done with his day's work. He had given the law—Hammurabi-like—unto his eldest son, and now he had only one more stop to make, one more set of laws to give, before he could find some rooms and lay down his weary, overagitated head. In the morning, if he outlived the apoplectic attack that he feared was on its way, he'd see the sights of Brighton, take the waters, and tend to his always questionable digestion.

* * *

Fanny had just done justice to the last of her second plate of scones and seen to the clearing of the tea things when there came another bombardment of the panels of the front door.

"Oh, now really, this is just too much! That man must simply learn to bridle his temper," she fretted indignantly. Lovesickness was one thing, but insanity was quite another!

"The Duke of Axminster, ma'am, to see Miss 'ungerford," the maid announced tartly.

Well, at least it was not that tiresome Baronet Cheng. Still, Fanny was in no mood to be sociable. "Did you not tell His Grace that Miss Hungerford is away from home?" she asked petulantly.

"I did, ma'am, but 'e's no' 'avin' it."

"Not having it?" Fanny repeated, mouthing the maid's slang expression with a sniff of disdain.

" 'E says 'e'll—" Here the girl's aitchless harangue was interrupted by the seventh duke himself, who intruded his corpulent person into the doorway with no ceremony whatsoever.

"I said, madam, that I would see any breathing body in the house if I could not see Miss Hungerford herself."

Fanny Hungerford rose in very righteous indignation, indeed, at this unmannerly intrusion of the duke. "Sir, you forget yourself," she squeaked.

"And if I do, madam, it is upon much provocation—much provocation indeed," he shouted, waving both jowls and one chubby forefinger for emphasis.

Provocation? Humph! Fanny's curiosity was piqued by now, and its being Neddy's father, whom she had never met, she decided to put up with this corpulent and not entirely uninteresting gentleman's boorish behavior for a while. "You may go, girl," she ordered with an abrupt shooing gesture at the maid.

"Now, Your Grace, we are alone. Pray be seated and make known to me the reason for this ill-mannered intrusion upon my household."

"Forgive me, madam. I am too agitated to sit, but I will

explain meself, by your leave. I am here concernin' my son, young Lord Ned Darlin'ton—"

"An admirable boy. He does you proud, sir," Fanny remarked stiffly and with a condescending nod of her head.

"He has done, madam, until just recently," the duke agreed solemnly. "However, I am here concerning my son and a lady o' this house, one Charlotte Hungerford, spinster—"

Fanny winced at that word "spinster." It was no favourite of hers. "Indeed, sir! You refer to my stepdaughter Charlotte, who does *me* proud," she put in with great dignity.

"Well, she may do for ought I know, ma'am, but that's neither fish nor fowl to me. I'll not have her for me daughter-in-law. She's no match for my Neddy," he blurted, a statement with which Charlotte herself could have found no fault.

Fanny, having little wit and less subtlety, took his remark at its face value and answered in all seriousness, "Is that not for Neddy to decide, and for Charlotte?"

"It is *not!*" the duke roared, banging his fat fist on the mantel to the accompanying jangle of crystal drops on the candlesticks.

"Sir, if you cannot restrain yourself, I shall be forced to have you evicted from this house," Fanny warned him evenly.

"What? Eh? Oh, sorry about that. Forgot meself again, what?" Here John Darlington looked at her with all the shame-faced guilt of a little boy.

Now Fanny, with her sentimental soul and motherly heart, saw the boy beneath the man at once, with the flickering of that expression across the Duke of Axminster's rotund and jowly face. What a precious child he must have been, she thought, and suddenly she was looking at John Darlington not through the eyes of a stern and protective stepmother to a grown and rather willful stepdaughter, but rather through the glazed eyes of a very female widow woman.

He was of the old-fashioned school of man, well fed, to put it nicely, and solid of build. He was not overly tall, but what he lacked in height he made up for in girth. He had the ruddy face of a country squire and the powdered wig worn by the men of Fanny's youth. Fanny had always been weak-kneed at the sight of a rotund and dignified man in powdered periwig, and she had lamented much the passing of that fashion.

If his jowls shook a bit when he spoke and his stays creaked when he moved, if his wind was short and wheezy and his gray eyes were a trifle bloodshot, these things escaped Fanny's notice in her general approval of his solid, earthy build and forthright, boyish manner. His booted feet and buckskinned legs were quite stout and well turned—no hint of gout—though other less than subtle indications pointed to there being some little trouble with his digestion. His hands looked strong, and his back quite straight. His colour, as she had noted earlier, was excellent—ruddy and attractive to her eye. In short, John Darlington at approximately five-and-fifty was a very desirable man to the likes of Fanny Hungerford.

"You obviously have much upon your mind, Your Grace, and I can see it would do you good to relieve yourself."

"Relieve meself, madam?" the duke cried, looking up in alarm. Had he committed some gross bodily indiscretion, that she should make such a suggestion? True, his digestion was not what it should be, but surely . . .

"Unburden yourself," Fanny amended discreetly, "of the troubles on your mind. Over a glass of sherry perhaps?" she suggested winningly.

The duke's eyes lit slightly. She was a deuced pleasant little woman, this stepmother. "Uh, ah, blackberry brandy, rather?" he asked a bit sheepishly.

Ah, Fanny thought to herself, she was right. Digestion! Poor man probably got whatever his cook would dish out, now his wife was gone. She'd have to see he took the waters and ate a decent meal while he was in Brighton. "Blackberry brandy it is, Your Grace. An admirable potation and one I often enjoy myself of an evening." Yanking on the pull again, she summoned the maid and gave order for the brandy and some digestive biscuits as well.

"And now," she said decisively as she stood up and extended her plump and not unshapely arms toward the duke, "forgive me, Your Grace, but will you have the goodness to remove your coat for the nonce?"

The duke was, needless to say, quite shocked—nonplussed, in fact. What had this lady in mind? he wondered, his thoughts revolving upon the ardent reputation of Lady Helena Vane. "Remove me coat, madam? Did you say, remove me coat?" He pulled further away, as if to flee for his honour if he had to. " 'Pon mine honour, madam, wherefore should I remove me coat?"

Fanny smiled a smile of ineffable charm, gentling this skittish duke as if he were a puppy in a thunderstorm, and purred, "Why, so that I may repair the button, sir, that you are about to lose. Unless I do mistake me, it is a very good gold one and of your old regiment—the Seventeenth, I believe?"

"Aye, ma'am, the Seventeenth Lancers," he answered proudly, his corpulent person swelling alarmingly at the mention of his sacred regiment.

"Yes, Neddy mentioned that, but even had he not, I should have taken you for a lancer by your fine, straight figga and soldierly bearing," Fanny cooed. "I daresay you sit a horse like a god," she went on, gesturing with a tiny and charming moue of impatience for him to get on with the doffing of his coat.

"You see how loose it is," she said, nodding toward the button in question, which really did hang by the barest thread from the blue fabric of his coat. "I imagine that you would be terribly sorry to lose it."

"What? Oh, oh, yes indeed, madam, ah, Mrs. Hungerford, ma'am," he stammered as he strove to regain his composure, which had been lost in the contemplation of Fanny's bright eyes. "It is indeed a button of me old regiment. Many thanks, dear lady." Then, utterly charmed by this sensible and superior female who knew a regimental button when she saw it, not to mention a well-seated lancer when she met met him, he doffed his coat with alacrity and placed it like a newborn babe across her extended arms. "You are *sure* it ain't any trouble, ma'am?" he added with sudden solicitousness.

"I can assure you, dear sir, it would trouble me more to watch a button coming loose and be forbidden to set things to rights." She smiled, taking some stout blue cotton from a sewing table near the sofa and placing it, with needle, thimble, and scissors, in her ample lap.

When the girl returned with the brandy, Fanny, whose practised eye had gone over the duke's coat like a miser in a counting-house, gave orders for some Dover chalk and a brush to be sent up from belowstairs.

"Pray do be father, Your Grace, and serve our brandy, if you will. I always think it is a man's prerogative to handle the spiritous beverages in the house, don't you agree?" Fanny purred as she slid the thread along her little pointed tongue and from thence into the eye of her needle.

"Oh, ah, yes indeed, ma'am, I do agree," though of course, he had never given the subject a thought from one year to the next. "I should be happy to do so," the duke exclaimed heartily, and leaping gallantly to the table where the girl had left the tray, he performed his part with ease, handling the decanter and glasses with such aplomb as nearly to make Fanny's head spin with the accomplishment of it all. He handed her a glass and, taking his own, resumed his seat across from her as if he belonged in just that spot, which was, after all, exactly what Fanny had intended.

She raised her glass toward his, sipped daintily, and, putting it down beside her, resumed her task, setting every button on the Duke of Axminster's coat to rights in such a manner as to leave no doubt the buttons would outlast the very seams themselves. She worked in silence, merely humming a pretty and romantic old air under her breath in a high, sweet tone that roused the most sentimental feelings of the duke and calmed his agitated nerves to such an extent that he quite forgot his reason for invading Number 10 Seaview Row in the first place.

He watched Fanny Hungerford at her work with a feeling of contentment and comfort as he had not had in years, not, in fact, since that day when his duchess, after seeing a pink and squalling eighth Darlington into this world, had let out a long-drawn sigh of relief and left for that other and presumably better world beyond our own. The duke had always rather resented Elizabeth

116

for this act of unwifely disloyalty, considering it damned selfish of her to run off that way, leaving him behind to cope alone.

Looking at Fanny, he asked himself just what more a man could want than his brandy and a good woman to sew his buttons on his coat. Some good lady, he ruminated, to shut up the eight or ten—he was never quite sure of the number—squalling brats that his wife had left in his reluctant care. Ah, Elizabeth, he sighed. No wonder she'd given up the ghost! Probably had some intimation that they didn't allow children into heaven and made straight for it. Thinking on the pack he'd left behind at Axminster Hall as he did, who could blame her?

The Dover chalk arrived just then, and Fanny set about, with a studied air of domesticity, to remove several aged spots of gravy and other prandial debris from front and cuffs, before returning the coat to the duke's hands in infinitely better condition than it had left them.

"You are a marvel, ma'am," the duke boomed in admiration as he surveyed himself in the glass over the mantel.

"La, it is nothing, sir, I can assure you," she answered with a dismissing wave of her hand, followed by a deep and thoughtful sigh. "I often think that it was Providence that my poor Charles should have been called before my humble self. I should have worried so who would look after him when I passed on. Oh, do not mistake me, Your Grace. My stepdaughter Charlotte was a wonderful daughter to him, and dutiful beyond expectation, but still, it is a man's *wife* who loves and serves him best, is it not?" Fanny asked, looking up with great, serious brown eyes into his face.

"It is indeed, ma'am," he agreed wistfully. "I have daughters, you know, but they are young and skitter-headed, and they giggle overmuch. The boys, of course, are worse," he confided more tolerantly. "Ruffians, the whole lot o' them." A noticeable glint of manly pride came to his eye. No nancy boys in his brood, thank God. Now if only his daughter had more sense . . . "Ah," he sighed as he went on, "the house is slack, the place a dustbin. It takes a woman's hand, I tell you, ta set things right."

"Oh, I do agree. Why, I was but a *girl,* of course, when I

117

married Charles, but I learnt ever so quickly. I had to, with him being a *widower,* poor man, and with a gel still at home—that was little Charlotte, you know. Of the other, I say not a word," Fanny remarked, holding a finger to her prettily pursed lips in a gesture of silence and closing her eyes for further emphasis.

What a fine, discreet little woman, the duke was thinking, and pretty into the bargain. Still on the sunny side o' forty as well.

"That'd be Lady Helena Vane, I believe," he put in.

"Ah, woe is me." Fanny shook her head. "I shudder when I think of that woman's reputation. It is the greatest consolation to me that poor Charles never had an inkling of how far his eldest had fallen from the roots of that uncorrupted tree whence she springs. I have always suspected," she added confidentially, "that it was something on the *mother's* side. I never knew the lady, mind, but still, one hears things, you know. Fortunately Charlotte was yet young when I married her father, and I took her for my very own. I have raised her to be a decorous and proper young woman of unquestionable virtue and superior accomplishments. She has, moreover, her father's wit and scholarship to her credit. As I have said, sir, she does me proud."

A dark look crossed the seventh duke's ruddy features at that, and his jowls shook somewhat. "Well, well, be that as it may, I—I—" By the gods, what could he say to this charming lady? How tell her that they could not marry? And then he hit upon it!

"The truth is, ma'am, Neddy's too *young* ta marry. I won't have 'im marrying yet, no matter how admirable the wench. I—I mean to say I am aware of the virtues and talents of your stepdaughter . . ."

"My stepdaughter?" Fanny broke in a pretended display of surprise. "Is *that* what this state of agitation has been all about, Your Grace? Is that why you have been so upset?" she asked in apparent wonder.

"It is, ma'am," the duke replied gravely. "The lad's too young."

"Well, well, be that as it may, you are his father, and that is your decision after all. Of *that,* I have nothing to say, but as to

118

my stepdaughter, sir," she said, administering the coup de grâce with a perfect nicety of timing, "I can assure you right now that she will not have him."

The duke was dumbfounded. "She won't have him? Why, Neddy's sworn to me that they'll be married before the season's ended."

"As you say, Your Grace, the boy is green," Fanny answered blithely as she sipped at her blackberry brandy. It was remarkable how she could forget—or choose to forget, rather—how she had, all the spring and summer, schemed with and encouraged that same green boy in pursuit of Charlotte. She went on smoothly, telling the duke such things as could only relieve his mind, and happy she was to do so, now she saw what a fine, stout man he was. "Neddy is as impetuous as my stepdaughter is discreet. She has told me many times—and told dear Neddy as well—that she will not have him. So let me assure you, dear Duke, that your concerns are for nought, and now, there's an end to it." She smiled winningly.

"Madam, you relieve my mind, and I thank you for it," the duke wheezed, slumping into his chair. And then, thinking again, he added, "She won't have him, eh? Why not? What's wrong with the lad, pray?"

"Your Grace," Fanny purred, "let me be frank in my speech. They are both of an age and therefore do not suit. Charlotte is wise enough to see that. She had, after all, the example of her own dear father, who took to wife a young woman much his junior in years. I refer, of course, to my humble self," she said, simpering slightly. "She sees, as clearly as do I myself, that it is no proper match if a man is not father as well as husband—and, dare I say it? *lover*—to his wife. There must be a goodly span of years betwixt husband and wife in order to insure true marital felicity, do you not agree?"

"Eh? What, oh, yes, ma'am. I should say so," concurred the seventh Duke of Axminster, fixing the "goodly span" betwixt himself and the plump little woman across from him at something over twenty years and wondering whether that would suit her ideas of true marital felicity as well as it did his own.

"You have no children of your own?" he asked rather unexpectedly, and Fanny, leaping on his expressed displeasure with his own numerous brood, was happy with the suitability of her reply.

"Alas, no, Your Grace. I have not been so blessed, although little ones seem to dote on me and *behave* surpassing well under my *firm* direction."

The duke listened and sighed in even deeper admiration of the widow Hungerford—in fact, kept on sighing long after he had taken his leave of her and gone off to find himself some rooms in the town. The more he thought on her, the more her amiable virtues, her discretion, and her domestic charms began to appeal. Moreover, she was a buxom little lady with a well-turned ankle, good teeth, bright eyes, and fine, sleek dark hair. She dressed well and still looked ready—what? Looked ready and was barren into the bargain.

The duke leered at that happy thought especially, for he was, despite his bulk, of a rather sanguine disposition when it came to females and the only barrier to domestic bliss that he had ever encountered was his late wife's embarrassing fecundity. For a wife to be both ready and barren, the duke surmised, would be true bliss. Absolute bliss!

"Sophy, my dear, why, what is this? I expected, from what the household says, to find you in fine spirits. Your lady—what's her name?—Mary told me that you had Miss Hungerford for a visitor and that you were very thick, the two of you. Now I find you weeping. Did that gel upset you after all?" The Duke of Cumberland, very concerned, crossed the small drawing room to his sister, comforting her with a great, gentle paw laid softly against her shoulder. Sophy, sitting red-eyed in a chair by the window, a crumpled handkerchief in one hand and a small gold locket in the other, made no reply.

She turned her face away, looking through the glass onto the lawn. In her mind's eye, she saw a small blond boy flitting in and out behind the trees, and she clutched the locket even more convulsively in her thin hand, the knuckles of which turned white with the effort. The boy was not really there, but he had been, and she ached still with the unfulfilled desire to hold him close to her. It had not been possible then, was less possible now.

"It was not the girl," she said at last, in what was only half the truth, for Charlotte Hungerford's remark about the painted miniature in the hall had upset her very much. Still, there was far more to her mood than simply that. "It was the king's Garth. He came this evening for an hour and—"

"He brought the boy," Cumberland rumbled angrily. God, how he hated that man. He had been the nemesis of their lives for a dozen years now.

"He brought the boy," Sophy acknowledged with a stiff nod. "He left him in the park with his governor. I did not meet the man, of course. I—I see the boy so rarely, even here, and it—it hurts sometimes. That is all."

"And Garth?" the duke growled. It was not the boy that troubled him. It was the power that Garth might have over them should he choose to wield it.

"He is a good man. As good a man as ever he was, though he has grown—so old. He is as loyal as ever—to the family—and to me."

At this, Ernest left her side and paced the room, growling helplessly under his breath like a caged and restless tiger. Sophy felt suddenly cold across her shoulder where her brother's hand had been so abruptly withdrawn. "Truly he is, Ernest," she insisted. "He would not harm us. God knows, twelve years ago he could have ruined us—ruined *me*—but he did not. He has taken the boy and done well by him."

"What else could he do?"

"He could have ruined us, as well you know. Instead, he has behaved with nobility, been as loyal and good as any of us could have wished. Whatever my sins, I—I brought no shame to this family by my choice of *him*, Ernest. Only *I* brought the shame. Only I myself was to blame, being so headstrong and willful— but if my act was wrong, as indeed it was, then at least in Garth I did not compound the sin. It was all me, all your poor, high-spirited, wrongheaded little Sophy."

121

"Dearest girl, no more," Cumberland pleaded brokenly. Why must she forever castigate herself with the past? Could it not be buried?

"Garth deserves only praise—and especially so from me."

"Praise," the duke snarled with bitterness. "I'd like to praise him, all right. Praise him into his grave."

"Do not talk thus, Ernest. I will not have it," she said firmly, a grip now on her wavering emotions. Her brother's bitterness toward General Garth, whom she once had loved, whom she once so briefly had cherished above all other men, was serving to focus her mind and stifle her own feelings of self-pity and sorrow. "Miss Hungerford is a very pretty young woman," she stated with a forced smile as she strove for a swift change of subject. "It is no wonder that Neddy is so taken with her. She will not have him, though, which I think is wise of her."

The room was growing dark, the candles had yet to be lit, but she could see the white of Ernest Cumberland's teeth as he leered his agreement with her remarks. "Aye, she is that—both pretty and wise. She is too much for Darlington. Way above his head. That kind o' gel must have a challenge." He added this last with an idea of himself in mind. He would keep his distance, of course, but damn him if he wasn't tempted.

"She is intelligent as well. I greatly enjoyed our afternoon. I shall invite her again very soon. She cheers me."

"You do not look cheered ta me," her brother rejoined sourly.

"She said one thing that troubled me, that is all," Sophy remarked, almost biting her tongue for speaking out. Still, the cat was out, and she supposed, in the long of it, it must come out. It was better that way.

"Go on."

Sophy drew in her breath and straightened herself in the chair. She felt tired now and longed to be resting on the chaise, but she did not want to move and upset the quiet of the room or by her stirring set Ernest to lighting the candles. She wanted it dark and quiet yet awhile. "She saw your portrait on the wall, the one of you at twelve . . ."

"Hah." The Duke laughed shortly. "The little innocent. The

boy before he grew a man and learnt what life was all about—"
At that he winced, feeling a pain deep within him that caused
his good eye to well with tears. He was glad this household of
Sophy's was so slack, that the candles were yet to be lit. The
gloaming hid his face from her—and his feelings as well.

"Yes." She smiled sadly to herself, sensing those feelings he
thought hidden from her even in the darkness. "The innocent."

"Well, what about it?" he asked, recovering his usual gruffness
of tone.

"She mistook the portrait for another boy, another innocent,
one she met on the beach at Hove in company with his governor.
. . ." She paused significantly.

"Oh," was all the reply that Cumberland could muster.

"Yes, just that. Oh. Miss Hungerford said he called himself
Master Thomas, but she must have mistaken his Christian name
for the surname, of course. She could not at first believe the
portrait was not of the same boy she had seen—so strong, she
said, was the likeness."

"Surely you insisted?"

"I did, naturally, since it was of no child but you. I did not
have to lie in that. But she lied then."

"*She* lied. I should not have thought her capable of a lie,"
Cumberland exclaimed thoughtfully. Something did not fit. He
was very concerned by now and feared for Sophy. No wonder
she was so upset.

"It was a white lie. She saw my concern. She is observant, and
I think she must have seen how anxious her remarks had made
me. She lied to spare my feelings, saying then that upon closer
examination it could not have been the same child after all. She
said the boy she saw had *brown* eyes, but the eyes of both of
you—the boy you *were* and the boy he *is*—are unmistakable and
too like not to notice. I knew that she was lying then and that
it was done for my sake. I was grateful to her, but nonetheless,
it has left me troubled," she said in a flat and toneless voice.

"This is his likeness, here, painted when he was eight," Sophy
remarked, clutching the locket in her hand and going on in that
same empty voice. "Ah, how foolish of me! You cannot see it,

of course. It is too dark. I sent them away when they came to light the candles, but never mind. The face even then, at eight, was very like yours. Now that he is twelve, he is so like you as you were as a youth. It—it cannot be hid. Not any longer, Ernest."

"It *can* be hid, Sophy. You shall have to have Garth send him away." Cumberland's words were like a blow against her heart, but it was, in truth, no more than she had expected.

"He brought him here to be near me—at *my* request and as a favour to me," she protested halfheartedly.

"And he was a fool to do it. You were a fool to ask it. It was no favour at all."

"Can I not have *any* life of my own, Ernest? Can I have nothing?" she pleaded, expecting no answer, for there was none really.

"Yes, Sophy, you can have a life," he whispered softly, "but—you cannot have the boy."

"Cannot have the boy," the princess repeated tonelessly.

"It is too dangerous," the duke warned her with a shake of his head that she could not see. It was totally dark in the room now. He could just barely make out her silhouette against the window-pane—rigid, the head held high, the long, fine nose at a haughty angle, the lips working slightly in emotion.

"One more week, Ernest. One more week, and I shall have him sent away, I promise." Her voice floated out into the room like the voice of a ghost. She still had enough of the old spirit in her to want her own way, only now it was tempered by a decade or more of knowing that she would not get it. Her only course lay in compromise.

The duke was filled with deep sadness for her; he did not reply for a long time, and it was actually only after a bat brushed against the window, startling them both with the thump of its body against the glass, that their silence was broken at last.

"A week then, little Sophy," he whispered against his better judgement. Leaving her where she sat, he went off to see about the lighting of the candles. It was a cowardly act perhaps, but he did not want to have to look into her eyes once they were lit.

124

* * *

Fanny Hungerford had a problem.

Fanny Hungerford was in love—in love with John Darlington, Duke of Axminster—and now, instead of pushing a future dukedom on her pretty and deserving stepdaughter, she found herself daring to aim so high as an immediate one for herself. It was unthinkable—Fanny Hungerford a duchess! Fanny, Duchess of Axminster, had rather a nice ring to it, but oh, dear, could it be possible? A squire's daughter, a parson's widow raised so high as a duchess? Never! Only in novels!

Yet . . . to be fair, it was not ambition that had made her fall, like a schoolgirl, head over heels in one brief afternoon. No, indeed, for truly Fanny was not an ambitious woman, and certainly not at all for herself, despite the elegant and appealing ring of Fanny, Duchess of . . .

No, it was the sight of that dear, wonderful, ruddy-faced, bewigged, and soldierly man, so stout of limb and straight of back, with his buttons hanging off his coat like a vagabond, spots on his cuffs, and plagued with the wind for want of someone to look after his diet, the poor dear man, left alone to look after eight or ten orphans ranging in age from six to six-and-twenty without the loving ministrations of a doting wife to look after him and see to his needs. It was enough to rouse every instinct of woman, mother, nurse, and wife in the ample and generous bosom of Fanny Hungerford—and rouse those instincts it did, the sight of John Darlington, seventh Duke of Axminster, leaving her red-eyed and full of trepidations.

"Fanny, you are ill!" Charlotte exclaimed as she put down her fork with a clatter on the dinner plate before her. "Bucky, look at her. She has not touched a bite." Bucky, who could not be accused of a similar lapse of appetite, stuck his own overladen fork hastily into an already full mouth and glanced from his tout sheet to his stepgrandmama. It was enough to make him stop in mid-chew and open his eyes wide in surprise.

"I say, you're right, Auntie," he mumbled through his fish. "Grannie, what's come over you?" he asked, waving his fork at her untouched plate.

"Oh, ohhhh," Fanny wailed, coming out of her til now silent reverie and blubbering into her napkin in abject misery.

"Oh, poor Fanny," Charlotte sympathized. "Do tell us what's wrong. It can't be as bad as all that, can it?"

"Mmmmmmmm, oh, I—I," Fanny whimpered.

"Go on, dear," her two companions urged, each patting her plump shoulders from opposite sides of the table.

She took a deep breath and plunged. "I—I have fallen in love—quite, quite dreadfully in love and—and suppose he will not have me?"

"Why, that is wonderful," Charlotte cried, greatly relieved that it was only love bothering Fanny and not something fatal. "That is nothing to cry over," she added with hearty fatuousness, forgetting for the moment her own pangs over a certain Chinee baronet.

"And what d'you mean, 'suppose he will not have' you?" Bucky added fiercely. "Of course he'll have you. Why, any gent'd be honoured to win a good little woman like my grannie, ain't that right, Auntie dear?"

"Indeed," Charlotte agreed loyally.

"But—but suppose I am not good enough? He—he is a *titled* gentleman, and I—I am only a—a p-p-parson's widow—" With that poor Fanny dissolved into tears and fled from the table with all the dramatic passion of one of John Darlington's several giddy daughters, leaving Bucky and Charlotte sitting utterly speechless.

Charlotte, having no knowledge of her stepmother's visit from the Duke of Axminster, had gone pale as the napery, jumping to the instant and understandable conclusion that the titled gentleman in question must be Sir Hannibal Cheng, Bart.

"It looks like she don't have a worry, Aunt Charlotte," Bucky assured her.

"No worry? Whatever do you mean?" she asked in alarm.

"It must be Cheng she means, of course—"

"Of course," Charlotte agreed with a tightness in the chest that actually hurt.

"He was here this afternoon, havin' tea with her—and I swear,

126

I've never seen a more dumbstruck, agitated chap in all me days," Bucky stated earnestly. "He's really for it. He's in love for sure, by the way he seemed today."

"H-how f-fortunate f-f-for F-F-Fanny," Charlotte stammered into her napkin.

Bucky looked across at his aunt's reddened, sobbing face. Women! "Well, ain't that what you wanted? Ta marry Fanny off ta some poor bloke and get her out o' your hair?" he cried in exasperation.

"Oh, y-yes," Charlotte wailed, "that was just what I wanted—to get Fanny m-m-married, but n-not to Sir Hannibal Cheng of all men."

"Well, that's what you told me," Bucky retorted with a curious mixture of sympathy and devilment in his tone. It was a rare thing to see Charlotte Hungerford hoisted on her own petard.

"Well, I didn't *mean* it. I only thought—"

"You only thought that if you used poor plain Fanny as your goat, you'd lure the wolf close enough to shut him up in your own paddock without running the risk o' chasin' him yourself and bein' rejected," Bucky interrupted succinctly. He had suspected as much for days now.

"Mmmmmm," Charlotte mumbled contritely. "Well, yes-s-s-s, something like that," she conceded at last.

"Hah, I knew it! Damn me, if it wasn't jolly rotten of you, you know," Bucky chided triumphantly, "and it serves you right to sit here like this, all in tears. You don't deserve any better, you nasty girl," he concluded with a softening of his tone. He really did feel sorry for her after all.

Charlotte jumped up just then and, throwing her knotted-up napkin at him, ran wailing from the table, her action accompanied by the guffawing laughter of young Lord Buckthorpe Vane.

"Women," he exclaimed, laughing til the tears rolled. "Oh, the silly dears! Women!"

::8::

It was ten o'clock the following morning, and the house, quite uncharacteristically, sounded with nothing more lively than the laconic footsteps of the housemaids. Bucky lay abed and wondered idly whether his aunt and grannie had taken poison in the night as being the only resolution of what he considered to be their rather silly and overheated female passions.

But no! A faint rapping by some hapless menial upon the door of his aunt's room across the hall from his own elicited just then a muffled "go away," followed by the sound of some solid object —a hairbrush, perhaps—rebounding off the inner panels. Good! Aunt Charlotte was alive and most definitely kicking. Best keep out of her way yet awhile, however.

What of Fanny?

Young Buckthorpe dressed with rather more haste than he was wont to take with his snuff-dusted finery and, on his way to the breakfast room, knocked upon his stepgrandmother's doors, which were just down the hall from his own small hole.

"Fanny, I say, Fanny. You in there? Still amongst the living, eh?" he called gently.

"Bucky dear?"

"The very same one and only darlin' lad o' that name, Fanny," he replied cheerily, relieved to hear her voice, however trembly and weak its tones. "May I come in?"

"I look a fright!" came the tentative reply.

"An' who don't at this ungodly hour?" he called back expan-

128

sively, as if it were six in the morning instead of a quarter to eleven.

"All right then, but don't dare look at me," she warned coyly.

Bucky opened the door and found himself squinting in agony against the unwelcome glare of a brilliant summer morning as it streamed through Fanny's open windows onto a breakfast table gleaming with sunstruck silverplate. "Ahhhh," he squealed, throwing his hands up before his eyes in a gesture of high drama. "I shall go blind. One don't want ta see the sun before one's had one's breaker, f'God's sake. Close the curtains."

"Nonsense, dear boy. Fresh air, sunlight. All very good; all very healthy," Fanny chirruped brightly as she motioned him to the table and poured a cup of tea for him.

He sat himself down across from her so as to keep his back to the morning sun, peering at her warily as he adjusted his eyes to the light. "Why, you don't look a fright at all!" he exclaimed indignantly. "You look positively blooming, fresh as a green cheese," he added graphically as Fanny winced.

"That is *not* the best of analogies, Bucky dear," she remarked with a grimace of pain, patting her freshly coiffed black curls and adjusting the neckline of her dressing gown with charming self-consciousness. She did indeed look splendid.

"Well, you know what I mean," he went on. "I saw you last blubberin' into the table linen with red eyes and screwed-up face, and I knocked just now hopin' ya hadn't taken poison in the night—"

"Taken poison! Whatever for?"

"You were in a bad way last night, remember?" Bucky chided.

"Oh, that! Just a fit o' the vapours, dear boy," she said airily, dismissing her tantrum of the previous evening with a wave of her hand. "Actually I feel quite wonderful! Better than I've felt in years!"

"You do look an awful wonder, now I notice, Grannie," Buckthorpe conceded through his toast.

"It's love, dear boy. I confess it! I am utterly, utterly smitten. La, what a tonic," she chirped. "Just wait til you meet him. I daresay you shall see just what I mean." She smiled dreamily, never thinking how hard it would be for a youth of twenty like Bucky to see the charms of a creaking elder of five-and-fifty such as the seventh Duke of Axminster.

"I have met him, of course, and he seems a very good chap if you like the type," young Vane remarked, an image of Sir Hannibal Cheng crossing his mind. What *was* it about the man, by the bye? Why should two fairly sensible women, one an old widow and the other a cool young spinster, both go so barmy over the fellow? He knew both the ladies well enough to be sure it was not the Chinee baronet's wealth; neither Fanny nor Charlotte was in the least venal. There was not a fortune huntress's bone in either of their bodies. What, pray, made that man catnip to 'em? Whatever the trait, he'd like to know what it was, for then he'd either bottle it for sale or cultivate it himself, whichever he deemed the more profitable course of action.

"You have met? I had no idea?" Fanny asked in surprise, knowing that the duke had just arrived in Brighton the day before.

"Fanny darling, your mind must be going," Bucky enunciated precisely. "We all took refreshments together only t'other day at the Green Bull Inn. Of course, I know Sir Hannibal."

"Sir Hannibal? Sir Hannibal Cheng? Why, whatever has he got to do with all this?" Fanny asked with a blank stare that left Bucky astonished.

"Well, ain't it Cheng you've gone barmy over? Ain't he the titled gent—"

"Oh, good heavens, of course not! I have no regard for that peculiar man. I only cultivated him at all to help bring Charlotte and Neddy together, since he is such a friend of Neddy's. Actually I think Sir Hannibal is a dreadfully odd and tiresome person. He has the strangest temperament," she remarked with a shake of her head, thinking back to his startling behaviour of the previous afternoon. "Really, I cannot think what was in Charlotte's mind when she introduced us. She has pushed us unconscionably upon each other, to what end I cannot tell."

"Indeed?" Bucky remarked noncommittally. "Yet it seemed

to me—I mean, I could have sworn that the two of you were a pair of lovesick dafts yesterday afternoon at tea," he added dryly.

"*He* may be in love! I daresay he is, in fact, and I do feel dreadfully guilty about it quite naturally, but what am I to do?" she asked with a philosophical shrug. "I am, after all, a lady of some sensibility, and I am, therefore, just heartsick at having to turn him away, of course—"

"Of course," Bucky agreed solemnly.

"—but there is no help for it. I cannot marry a man I do not love simply because he is foolish enough to attach himself to me unbidden and without provocation." She shook her head indignantly, sounding very much like Charlotte.

"Ohh, ah, has he mentioned marriage then?" Buckthorpe probed.

"Well, well, no, as a matter of fact, but the way he behaved yesterday—so distracted, so *heated*—I expect it shall be only a matter of time, don't you know? And I cannot accept, of course!"

"Indeed you cannot," Bucky agreed solemnly, entranced by the self-possession of this morning's Fanny. "But tell me, pray, if it is not Sir Hannibal—poor fellow, due for a letdown, what?—" he interjected with tongue firmly in cheek, "then just who is the chap you've fallen so hard for?" He sipped his tea and waited for her reply.

"Darlington." Fanny beamed.

"Neddy?" young Vane squeaked, upsetting his cup into its saucer and dribbling tea down his chin.

"No, you dullard, not *Neddy!*" she scoffed. "*John* Darlington, seventh Duke of Axminster." Here Fanny sighed, giving to those plain Anglo-Saxon syllables a degree of musicality hitherto undiscovered by other, less romantically inclined speakers of that good, plain English name. "He came by yesterday afternoon— soon after Sir Hannibal left, as a matter of fact—fierce as a lion, proud as an eagle, in order to tell me he would *not* have Charlotte for a daughter-in-law."

"Well, I can't say I like that," Bucky broke in rather hotly. "What's the matter with me auntie? Ain't she good enough for his fatheaded son?"

131

"Oh, never mind such concerns as that. After all, we know that she won't have *him*, so what's the odds? And, oh, Bucky, thank heaven she won't have him! You know how I've wished it—how I've pushed the dear boy on her. It's a blessing she's had so much sense as to refuse him, else I should be in a terrible pickle, shouldn't I?"

"I daresay you should, under the circumstances," Bucky agreed mildly. Gad, what a fascinatin' mornin'—and so enlightenin' about the addlepation o' the female brain, if brain it was they had up there, rattlin' about in their pretty little noddles, the dears.

"As it was," Fanny explained complacently, "all I had to do was inform Lord D. that Charlotte had no intention of marrying his son—which rather got his nose out o' joint, I could see—and that rather pleased me, you may imagine, for my Charlotte is good enough for a queen, let alone a mere dukedom. Anyway, no matter, for once I pacified him on the subject of his son and my stepdaughter, why, the rest was all cream." She giggled happily.

"I *may* well imagine," Bucky marvelled.

"Oh, Bucky, Bucky, the duke is wonderful—a trifle ill in the digestion, of course," she conceded, "and he needs a wife—there's no doubt of that, but . . ." Here she trailed off, lost in a reverie.

"The trick's goin' ta be how ta catch him, I suppose," Buckthorpe put in cautiously as he foresaw a new round of plotting and man catching. Really, it was going against his grain by now—all this female entrapment of his own poor sex. Would there never be an end to it?

"What? Catch him? Oh, no, dear boy. I shan't need any help with *that*, if that's what troubles you. I can do quite nicely on my own, thank you!" She finished her remark with a pretty little moue.

"Oh, you can, can you?" Bucky laughed tartly, feeling both amused and relieved by Fanny's simple confidence in her charms and powers.

"Indeed I can! We have already engaged to take the waters

together this afternoon and hear a concert at the spa ballroom after. Later we shall dine in some elegant supper rooms I have heard of that are noted for the digestibility of their bill o' fare. Moreover, the duke has promised to bring all the portrait lockets of his children for me to see, and we shall get on very well, I am sure," she added pertly, sipping her tea with the air of a very complacent lady.

"You are a worker, Fanny. You are a worker," her stepgrandson exclaimed in admiration.

"Oh, I've been known to wind a man upon my finger, Bucky, in me day," she remarked archly. "It is a joy to find that I can still do so. However . . ."

"However?" Bucky repeated with instinctive wariness.

"Charlotte!"

"Charlotte?"

"Bucky, for all her clever ways, that gel can't seem to wind *anything* about her finger—least of all a man or a wedding band. What am I to do? If she's still a spinster now, with me here to scheme her into marriage, what will happen when I have removed to Ax—to wherever I may live if I marry again," she amended discreetly.

"Ah." Bucky raised his eyebrows knowingly. By Jove, Gran was serious about all this.

"She shall be a spinster for sure; do nothing but write books and dry up like an old toad. Neddy's out o' the picture, of course, so I have *got to find a likely man.* . . ." Fanny fretted aloud, though more to herself than to Bucky, who listened to her intently nevertheless. "I really haven't all that much time, now me own cap is set—"

Young Lord Buckthorpe Vane, a faraway look in his eye, sucked his teeth and pried at bits of bacon with the point of his tongue until suddenly that faraway glaze of near imbecility was replaced by an intelligent gleam of inspiration. He thought his idea through once or twice just to test it. It passed with flags flying! It was an idea so ingenious as to make him wish he had gone up to Cambridge to read law as his father had wanted.

Perhaps he was wastin' a wickedly good brain in entertainin' idleness and the joyful vices of his youth.

"Fanny," he drawled nonchalantly, "why not Sir Hannibal Cheng?"

"The Chinee baronet? That peculiar fellow who bangs down doors and bellows at the top of his lungs? Why, he is as imperious as—as—well, I cannot think what. And when he is not bellowing, he paces about with blazing eyes and great red spots of anger on his cheeks. I really do not know what to make of him at all."

"Sounds rather a male version of our temperamental little Charlotte, don't he? Ya know, Grannie dear, the more you talk, and the more I think, the more it seems perfect. He's smitten, so you say, with your charming but reluctant little self, right? Therefore, it behooves you ta discourage his suit, ta put him off easy, so ta speak. Well, why not explain all this to Charlotte— throw yourself on her mercy, as they say—and ask her ta distract the good man for you while he forgets the heartache o' losing you?" How Bucky kept a straight face through all of this, he wondered to himself long after.

"Meanwhile, and here's the beauty part, mind, he's smart as brass buttons—even reads books, so they say, which ought ta gladden Charlotte's bookish little heart, bless her—and he's a widower. She might even find she likes him, though familiarity often breeds you know what! And the Lord knows, he ought to find *her* pretty enough. Everyone else does. Why, suppose they actually make a pair o' it? I think I can fancy Aunt Charlotte a baronet's lady, with estates in Ireland—plenty o' quiet in *that* backwater, I expect—and you know how she claims ta crave quiet. It'll work, I tell you. It's quite perfect."

"Yes, Bucky, it is—it may be perfect, I think," Fanny offered tentatively, as she thought the matter through. "But she might see through the ruse and realize I was matchmaking again. You know how she has abused me for my efforts on poor Neddy's behalf. She'd have fits if she suspected what I am about this time." Fanny sat tracing little cupid's hearts and arrows in the tablecloth with her fork. "Oh, Bucky, everything's a muddle."

"Nonsense, Fanny! You stick to your dukey, and *I'll* handle

Charlotte. You don't even have to say a word. You know how easily I can get round me favourite auntie dear. She won't suspect a thing."

"I believe she's your only 'auntie dear' as well," Fanny commented dryly. She looked at him askance.

"Well, be that as it may," he conceded airily, "had I ten thousand aunties, she should still be me favourite. Shall I arrange it all, Grannie?" he pressed eagerly, for he was finding the whole situation a lark and was anxious to get on about his mischief.

"I don't know that I can trust you, Bucky," Fanny murmured, looking at him with suspicion. He was altogether too eager to suit. Was there something up his sleeve besides a dirty wrist? "There is a puckish gleam in your eye that bodes ill, my lad," she chided him.

"Fanny, Fanny, I'm an *angel*—a veritable cherubum or seraphim or whatever. Why, there ain't a puckish bone in me body," he protested with a pretense of greatly injured feelings and much innocence as well. "What have I got better to do than help you and Charlotte down the primrose path to wedded bliss?"

"Go!" Fanny ordered with a laugh and a shake of her head. "Get out of my sight, dear boy. The more you say, why, the less I trust you," she wailed in delight as tears of laughter flooded her eyes at his comical manner. "Go to Charlotte and do as you must." She shooed him away as he came to embrace her. "Go on, I shall have to dress. I want to look particularly elegant this afternoon, as you may well imagine."

"And you will, love," Bucky assured her, bending, despite her resistance, to kiss her forehead before leaving on his next mission. "Remember," he admonished from the doorway, "you're out to bag a duke, an' they're not always so easy as they look—a skittish lot, in fact. So get the arrow through the heart before you show the ring you've got in mind for his nose."

"Out," Fanny ordered with a little scream of frustration.

"And look you don't come back til you're a duchess," he scolded with a skip and a wink as he closed the door quickly against the barrage of laughing abuse that she hurled in his wake.

* * *

Young Buckthorpe could hardly contain himself. With more joy than wisdom, he knocked out a cheery tattoo upon the panels of Charlotte Hungerford's door and received for his efforts a clatter of small objects, evidently hurled by the handful, against the door, followed immediately by a heavy thump as well.

Ignoring this harmless but nevertheless implicit attack upon his person with infuriating good nature, he called out sweetly, "It is Bucky, love, bearing splendid news for his petulant little auntie." He bent and called with maddening charm right through the keyhole, "Be a dear and let me in."

"No, go away."

He straightened up to his full six feet and stood his ground, chest to the panels like a drill sergeant about to raid a barracks. "All right, dearie," he called, "but you'll be sorre-e-e. I carry upon these lips a panacea designed to soothe all aching hearts—especially yours—" Bucky warned.

"The devil you do," Charlotte wailed from the other side of the door. Damn Bucky. He was being *such* a beast.

"The devil I do indeed, but no matter. Ta-ta," he called with a light thump of good-bye upon the door.

"Ohhhhh," came another moan from behind the bedroom door.

"Farewell, Auntie, I'm going," Bucky sang faintly, with his face turned away as if he were receding down the hallway.

"No, wait, don't—" Here Charlotte opened the door at last, only to find herself face to chest with her nephew, who had not gone at all, but had stood his ground with maddening tenacity. "You beast, you weren't going at all," she exclaimed, beating her hands on his chest, noticing as she did that he wanted a change of linen.

"No, I stood me ground like a man. Come on, let me in." He pushed his way past her into the sitting room of her suite, which, unlike Fanny's, was still as dark as a cave despite the approach of noon. No open draperies and sunlit breakfast tables for our poor, brooding Charlotte.

"I am in no mood for company," Charlotte warned him testily as she followed him back into the room.

"So I see," Bucky commented mildly with the air of a man who knows that whichever way the dice tumble or the horse runs, he's bound to win. "Sugar lumps! I wondered what it was you were peltin' at me; sounded a bloody hailstorm, don't you know? Ah, the sugar basin as well. Jolly good," he complimented her expansively as he kicked the silver basin out of his path, crushing lumps of sugar into the carpet under the heels of his boots as he strode about the room, surveying its comforts in the dim light. A hairbrush and some few other objects of the female toilette littered the floor in the general vicinity of the doorway as well as the sugar things. He eyed them merrily. "Aunt Charlotte has had a strenuous mornin', I see."

"If you have nothing better to do than take notice of my athletical powers, kindly have done and go away," Charlotte warned him acidly. "My throwing arm is still in good form, you know."

"I say, you missed your calling, I fear. You should have gone up to Cambridge and been a cricketer, Auntie," Bucky remarked placidly as he threw himself across a chaise and crossed his ankles on the upholstery for greater comfort. "Got any toast left?" he asked, nodding idly toward a barely touched breakfast tray. It was a marvel that anyone had got far enough into the room to serve her a meal. It must have been set out before she awoke.

"I may not have missed my calling after all. I may be best suited to nephoocide, you bloody—" Charlotte snarled through clenched teeth as she hefted a teacup in her hand menacingly.

"Now, now, let's not be tiresome, pet. And watch your bloody language kindly. Remember, you're a parson's daughter after all."

"Parson's daughter be damned," Charlotte retorted succinctly, the cup still in her hand, ready for the hurl.

"And well she may be, for all I know. Certainly *one* parson's gel I could name has more credit in the hotter place than else-

137

where. Mebbe it runs in the family, but seriously, don'cha want ta hear me splendid news?" he asked in his most casual of drawls.

"Perhaps," Charlotte countered warily, the teacup still a threat in her hand. "Say on."

"Our Fan's in love . . ."

"I *know* that, you lout," she wailed as she sent the cup hurtling at his head with no great accuracy. Bucky, without moving anything more than his good, long right arm, saved the bit of porcelain from certain destruction against the wall at his back and, stringing it by its handle on his pinky finger, whirled it in idle circles as he spoke.

"Don'cha want to hear *who* she's in love with, pet?" he asked calmly, playing with the cup whilst Charlotte eyed the saucer purposefully.

"I *know* whom she loves, damn you," she muttered through tightly clenched teeth, her fingers closing round the saucer.

"Tut-tut, save the Sèvres if you please," Bucky chided. "She's fallen heels over head for John Darlington, poor Neddy's guv'-nor."

Charlotte put the saucer down with a clatter. "The Duke of Ax—"

"The very same! A corpulent old farter, if what Neddy says about him can be trusted. She don't see Cheng for thrupence. He ain't her type."

"But you said—"

"Well, I was wrong," he countered defensively, his eyebrows raised and a blasé tone to his voice. "She don't like him, but she's mortally afraid o' breakin' the poor chap's heart. Seems he's actin' very peculiar and daft—all sure signs o' lovesickness. Behaved very bad yesterday, she says, and so she's got ta let him down easy lest he think wild thoughts. Can't have a suicide on old Fan's conscience, can we?" he went on blithely, enjoying himself immensely.

"Suicide, hah!" Charlotte jeered. "Why, that man is no more likely a suicide than—than I am myself," she said, forgetting her recent melodramatic contemplations of the hemlock cup.

"Yes-s-s-s," Bucky agreed thoughtfully. "I expect he'd be

more likely to throw a fit—rather like a certain auntie o' mine who's given ta such tempers herself 'pon occasion."

"Well, I cannot help it, Bucky. You know that I am usually a dear—a veritable angel to get on with. All I ask is that I have my own way! When I get it and am content, why, don't I make everyone else's life a pleasure?"

"Oh, aye, that you do," Bucky agreed, biting his cheek til it hurt, "but when you are crossed, God help us all."

"Well, well, then we must all see I am not crossed, mustn't we?" Charlotte said with simple and perfect logic. She was trying desperately to get her head in order. If Fanny did not want Sir Hannibal, all well and good. Now how could she, Charlotte, win him and upon what pretext see him for that purpose, for surely Fanny would take pains now to avoid him?

Bucky watched her anxious face and read it well. Well, best let her off the hook. "Charlotte dear," he said smoothly, "we've just got to help Fanny out o' this pickle, what? She's goin' ta be chasin' after Neddy's papa from now on, and unless I miss me guess, she'll catch him ere long. But meanwhile, Sir Hannibal, who's been very attentive to our Fanny, shall be rather let down, right? He might even lose face a bit, what?" he added with fanciful exaggeration.

"Right—" Charlotte agreed tentatively.

"Well, what say we help old Fanny out and take up the slack with poor Cheng, so ta speak? You know, sort of keep him occupied and distracted with our own charmin' personalities so he don't feel the sting o' her neglect so much. Sort o' let him down easy as it were," he suggested, watching the light in Charlotte's eyes with secret satisfaction.

"Why, Buckthorpe darling, you are positively *inspired* this morning. Why, what a man you've grown lately and how lovely of you to think of such an unselfish and good-hearted thing to help your dearest stepgrannie," Charlotte cooed in delight. "Of course, I myself have even less interest in that peculiar man than Fanny, you know," she remarked with a great pretense of disinterest, forgetting that she had admitted her interest to Bucky through a veil of tears not much over a dozen hours earlier.

"Still," Charlotte went on earnestly, "since I encouraged a friendship between them in the first place, I expect I must, with resignation, accept some of the guilt for the poor man's plight now—mustn't I?" She gave Bucky a look of challenge.

"Of course," Bucky agreed solemnly, rising to her look with a placid façade that hid a myriad of humourous feelings.

"Of course I must. It is only right," she agreed with a shake of her head. "I am honour-bound, in fact," she declared with vehement resolution. She hopped up from the little side chair by her breakfast tray, twitted Bucky lightly upon the top of his head, and drew open the draperies to the glaring noontime sun. She threw up the sash, took a deep breath of the fresh outer air, and began dancing about her rooms like a dervish.

"By the gods, look at this mess! I want a maid to clean up and the girl to get out my things. I must do my hair. Horrors"—she pouted into her mirror—"I look a fright. I shall want rice powder under me eyes this day. Oh, Bucky, I tell you a woman should never cry—never. The toll it takes in puffy lids and blotchy cheeks is not worth the candle, no matter what they say about a good cry being tonic. Gad, I look a hundred this day. Bucky, get out at once—" At which command young Buckthorpe jumped from the chaise and, stifling a fit of the giggles, loped toward the door.

"Where does Sir Hannibal usually spend his afternoons? In the gaming houses, I suppose?" she called after her nephew as she jerked emphatically on the pull beside the mantel.

"Here and there. Hither and yon. No set route as I've ever noticed." Bucky shrugged.

"Well"—Charlotte sighed, pushing pins frantically into her curls—"well, if you should happen to see him, sound him out, ask him to tea on the morrow—I don't care—just do *something*. We cannot have the poor fellow breaking his heart in futile love of Fanny, now can we?" she asked seriously, her eyes agleam with heroinelike schemes and plottings.

"Heaven forfend," Bucky exclaimed with palms upraised and eyes rolling back in his head. "A fate worse than marriage, from which we must vouchsafe to deliver him," he added as he darted out the door, muffling an uncontrolled guffaw in the palms of his hands as he went.

No, there was absolutely nothing in the demeanour of Sir Hannibal Cheng to belie a verdict of lovesickness on the part of young Buckthorpe Vane. He might not be ranting or pacing like a caged lion, but there he was, leaning against the Esplanade with as black and scowling a countenance as ever Bucky had seen upon a living face.

"Hullo," Bucky called out as he approached the Chinee baronet. "How nice ta see a cheery face."

"What's so cheery about my face?" Cheng scowled even more darkly as Bucky stopped beside him unbidden and more or less unwelcome.

"Nothin', now you mention it. What happened? Somebody die?"

"Nobody."

"Well," Bucky rejoined heartily and with an amiable slap on the back, "that's worth bein' cheery about, right there, ain't it? Where's the good Duke Ernest?" he asked when his small attempt at humour met with no response whatever.

"Off last evening to stay a few days at Hove. He's had another of his famous rows with the regent, it seems."

"Ah, what about this time?" Bucky asked, not so much because he was interested—he wasn't actually—but because at least now he had Cheng talking.

"Who knows? Politics, one supposes, although they ain't been on the best o' terms since last winter when George got wind of Ernest's remarks about his ankle. I expect anything'd set 'em off after that."

"We never hear a thing worth the name o' gossip at Wooton-Maggot, more's the pity. What'd he say?" Bucky urged.

"Ah, it was nothing really. A trifle, though it was funny at the time. Seems the regent banged his ankle a bit whilst tryin' to demonstrate a Highland fling for the princess Charlotte of Wales. It may have been an admirable fatherly gesture to try, but being fat and old, he wound up in bed for a fortnight. All Ernest

141

said was that he thought George's illness went *'higher* than the foot and that a blister on the head might be more efficacious than a poultice on the ankle.' As I say, a mere trifle, but it got back to George, and he had fits over it."

"Oh, I say, that was a good one. The more I hear of him, the more I like your friend the duke," Bucky said, laughing agreeably. "So they've had another quarrel and he's gone to sulk on Princess Sophia's fair white shoulder, eh?"

"So I expect." Cheng nodded, growing glum again.

"Ah, yes, I see," Bucky mumbled thoughtfully. "Nice ta have a soft shoulder ta cry upon, what, even if it is only a sister's?"

Cheng said nothing.

"Where's Neddy then?" he asked, trying to draw this infuriatingly taciturn man into some conversation, however slight it might be. It wasn't going to be easy, he could see that.

"He's quarrelled with his pater yesterday afternoon. Now he is searchin' high and low and can't find the old bastard. Wants to make it up if he can—has to save his allowance naturally." Cheng scoffed. "The duke, it seems, has threatened to cut him off without a guinea if he marries your aunt."

"Ah, yes, I heard all about it, but it don't signify anyway. Aunt Charlotte won't have him, of course, so his allowance is safe. There never was a worry about that," he added with a shrug.

"No, I agree. Neddy hadn't a hope, poor loon, though one can't blame him for trying. Your aunt's a real headturner, you know," he put in cautiously. Perhaps he could get Buckthorpe Vâne to talk of Charlotte Hungerford if he was lucky, but he must be careful. Must not say too much and give himself away for as big a fool as Ned Darlington.

"Yes, I know," Bucky concurred. How the devil was he goin' ta get onto the subject of Fanny?

"Yes," Cheng muttered to himself, "and a Tartar according to Duke Ernest. But, pray," he said, suddenly brightening, "how did you hear about Neddy's row with his papa? Was it so loud as to be heard all the way over the road?"

"Naw, I had it from me gran—from Fanny," he corrected

himself hastily, breathing a sigh, relieved that he'd at last got on the subject he wanted. "The Duke of Axminster must have been out for blood, for he came over our way after dressin' Neddy down, bent, so it seems, on layin' down the law to Aunt Charlotte. She bein' from home, he charged in on Fanny."

"Did he? Bellows like a bull, they say. She must have been taken aback, I expect." Sir Hannibal let his eyes wander out across the beach and rocky inlets beyond.

"She wasn't taken aback at all. Handled the old dukey very well, by all accounts," Bucky said.

"What?" Cheng asked abstractedly.

"Fanny! Me stepgrandmama. By all accounts she handled the duke very well," Bucky said, trying to lead Cheng to speak further of Fanny—pour out his heart perhaps.

"Oh, oh, yes. That's good," was all the reply Sir Hannibal could muster.

"Buxom wench that, what?" Bucky suggested with a wink as he tried a new tack. "I have gathered you are quite smitten there, eh?"

"Smitten where?" Cheng asked blankly.

"In Fanny's direction."

"Good God, no!" Sir Hannibal bellowed in alarm, looking around in embarrassment as heads turned to stare at him and wonder at his outburst. "Look you, let's get away from here before the whole of Brighton takes me for a madman." He took Bucky firmly by the elbow, guided him swiftly up one of the narrower lanes off the Esplanade, and led him behind the fashionable section of town to where the trading classes took their ease in their own little public houses.

"How's this?" he asked, nodding toward a modest but otherwise respectable-looking alehouse on the far corner.

"Fine with me, so long as the ale is good and the ham ain't polka-dot green with little iridescent rainbows on it." Bucky grinned toothily. In spite of his dark mood, Cheng had to laugh at that.

The place was nearly empty, it being early yet and the shops from amongst whose clerks and help the house drew its trade were still open. It was all black oak and white plaster with heavy, comfortable chairs and benches and much abused oak tables hacked and stained with years of use, but it smelt tolerably well of ale and stale tobacco and pickled walnuts, so it suited admirably for their masculine tête-à-tête.

Cheng took a table set against a back window which overlooked a sparse kitchen garden whilst Bucky inspected the state of the baked ham sitting out on a sideboard near the bar—all pink and white with lots of cloves stuck in a sticky molasses-glazed top. His mouth began to water like a dog's, and so he decided to risk it. Ordering a plate of ham, bread, and walnuts from the publican's wife, he rejoined Cheng, bent on a good long heart-to-heart.

Sir Hannibal took a pull on his pint, burped fastidiously into a fine linen handkerchief, and looked at Bucky directly in his bright blue eyes.

"Now what's all this nonsense about me and Fanny?"

"You ain't lovesick over her?" Bucky asked with narrowed eyes. "It ain't gonna leave you at loose ends, ready ta fling yourself inta the bay, what with her lookin' in another direction? You ain't smitten?"

"What *are* you talking about, Vane?" By damn, the boy seemed sensible enough til now, but here he was babbling away like a natural.

"Yesterday," Bucky stammered. "Yesterday, why, I saw you meself and Fanny confirmed it later. You came ragin' in, pacin' in circles, roarin' and starin' and generally behavin' like—"

"Like?" Cheng prompted.

"Like a lovesick loon, that's what."

"And?" he asked with a shrug, though his cheeks coloured alarmingly.

"*And?* And Fanny ain't no flighty, heartless little vixen, after all, who takes a fellow's deep-felt feelings lightly. She's afraid you've fallen in love with her, and she don't want ta hurt you. She's all for dallying with someone else instead. No offense intended, of course."

"No, no offense in the world. She just don't like Irishmen,"

144

the Chinese-Irish baronet remarked with sardonic irony. Despite his wealth and refinements, his bloodlines did not admit him to a vast circle of eligible ladies—young or old. "Well, Fanny Hungerford, Lord Vane, may dally with whomever she wishes and more power to her—the Czar of All the Russias for ought I care—but she may not dally with *me*. I am not available. No offense intended, naturally."

"I'm relieved ta hear it for the sake of her conscience and for—" Bucky stopped short of naming Charlotte. "Suffice ta say, I'm relieved ta hear it. She's a good little woman, but then they're the worst kind, I believe."

"Neddy said something to me about Fanny the other night as well," Cheng mumbled, biting absently into a large and dripping walnut speared on the tines of his fork. "Gad, how did everyone get the idea I might be interested in Fanny Hungerford? I mean, as you say, she's a good-hearted and admirable little woman to be sure," he said politely, "but after all, she is my own age, which in a man may signify the approach of his best years, but in a woman? Why, it's all downhill for them after thirty, ain't it?"

"So I've always thought," Bucky agreed, leaning back on two legs of his chair with his feet propped on a corner of the table and sucking thoughtfully on a clove.

"Anyway, she's amiable enough, as I say, but *old,* and *fat,* and, forgive me, Bucky, but not overly bright." After pausing, he added, "I like me women smart and slender—and not girls either, mind. Grown women of sense, spirit, and passion." He said no more, for he had been describing Charlotte Hungerford to the life and was afraid to give himself away by saying another word.

"Nothing ta forgive, old man, nothing to forgive. I quite agree, in fact," Bucky assured him. "Still, I do seem ta remember warning you once that me Aunt Charlotte had you in mind for Fanny, and I know I was tight, but I wasn't so tight that I don't remember you sayin' you were aware and that you thought it was rather a good idea. In fact, now I think on it, I was so surprised at the time I actually got cold sober in seconds—which spoilt the rest o' me evenin', I don't mind tellin' you, and gave me a thumping great headache into the bargain."

"Ah, yes, I remember now," Cheng remarked, ignoring Bucky's bid for sympathy and tearing instead into a second helping of ham. "It seemed a good idea at the time, it did."

"What, marrying Fanny?" Bucky asked, belching a pungent ale breath and motioning for the publican's wife to bring more liquid refreshment.

"No, not marrying her. Going along with your aunt's little scheme. Unfortunately it don't seem ta be workin' out as I had hoped," he added thoughtfully, spitting cloves into his palm with a grimace of disgust. "Ugh, bitter little devils, these."

Bucky leaned back with his boots up and his chair braced against the wall, a fresh mug of ale in one hand and a slab of ham in the other, and studied Sir Hannibal's face for a long time. The poor man was *not* placid. He had some worry or other confusin' what even Bucky took to be a damned fine brain. Damn him if somethin' deuced heavy were not weighin' on the Chinee baronet's mind—and that'd be either empty pockets, a naggin' case o' the "French gout," or a woman. Now Cheng, he knew, was rich as Croesus, did no great amount o' whorin', and certainly didn't look poxy—ergo it must be a woman! What else but a woman causes in a man such wild behaviour as Fanny described in him yesterday afternoon? What else could be causin' his current dark mood? He must be in love and not with Fanny! And if not with Fanny—

Then who? Or *whom,* as Charlotte would insist?

All of a sudden the brilliant blue eyes of Lord Buckthorpe Vane lit like shooting stars in August.

"Oh, you wag," he exclaimed, dropping his chair back onto all four legs and stomping his booted feet on the flagstone floor for emphasis. "Oh, you wicked baronet! Ha-ha, I've got it, I've got it. You rake, you dog. Of course, it ain't Fanny! It's *Charlotte!*"He laughed til he cried. Oh, what a jest! What a comedy of errors—and not a twin in sight. Why, Shakespeare himself had nothing on his aunt Charlotte and her Chinee baronet when it came to farce!

"Shhhhhh," Sir Hannibal hissed in alarm. "For God's sake, keep your voice down, Vane." He looked about as Bucky subsided into a fit of gibbering titters. He looked about, but not a soul was in sight, the good wife being busy in the kitchen quarters and the publican himself dozing in the sun at the far end of the garden with his pipe, a dog, and three pigeons all in close proximity.

"Don't lie ta me," Bucky admonished with a waggling finger in Cheng's face. "I won't believe ya for a minute if you dare ta deny it," he pursued, leaning across the table toward his companion with great determination.

"I shan't deny it," Cheng answered quietly. "You are quite right. I have been able to think of nothing else but Charlotte Hungerford since that day—what?—three weeks ago on the Esplanade. Remember, you and the Duke of Cumberland were conversing as you walked? I was behind, and Charlotte—Miss Hungerford—came toward us and spoke to you? I have been virtually cross-eyed with love ever since—the most terrible state for a man to be in that you can imagine, my boy. I tell you, I'd rather be on the deck of a ship fightin' a monsoon in the Indian Ocean than ta be in the state I've endured these three weeks past. She's so deuced *cool*—so detached. I know she can't see me at all—that she'd probably not even think of me as a—but—"

Bucky said not a word to all this, listening instead with hooded eyes as Sir Hannibal confessed like a penitent the fullest extent of his distraction with Bucky's aunt. His voice was hoarse with emotion; his brow furrowed with the pain of his lovelorn agony; his eye glazed with the vision of his unattainable beloved. Bucky watched fascinated, seeing it all with mischievous delight and a certain philosophical detachment that might be aptly summed up with that puckish comment "Lord, what fools these mortals be!"

Lightning! And it had struck them both at once, Bucky'd bet money on it, but being two such devious, proud, and clever fools as they were, they had not seen it. No, it was too simple for their brainy heads, and so they'd muddled it good and proper. Charlotte had begun by treating the whole situation like a plot to be worked out. Only the gods knew what was in poor Cheng's mind that he had not come out with some sort of declaration or other.

Why, for all their intellect, they couldn't manage as well as simple, honest Fanny, who saw what she wanted and went right after it—the straightest course and the best chance to win. Poor Cheng and Aunt Charlotte, like a pair o' nags with overly clever riders, dodged between horses, lost their wind, and would therefore either lose in the stretch or break down altogether. So much for brains and book learnin', he summed it up to himself and, sighing heavily, decided that ere this race was run, he'd have to do a bit of jockeying for them, or Sir Hannibal and Aunt Charlotte would never finish in double harness.

"So you really love her!" he stated rather anticlimactically when Cheng had concluded his confession—even down to admitting he had read all of Charlotte's novels. "You are stark mad about her," Bucky exclaimed seriously.

"Stark," Cheng agreed disconsolately. He shook his head sadly. "At first sight," he said and sighed like a sick dog til his lungs were empty. "And that's why I played along with her matchmaking betwixt me and Fanny, in hopes that she'd take some notice of me herself."

Bucky smiled sardonically at that but held his tongue. Instead, he warned, "She's the very devil, you know. As high-spirited as any filly bred."

"I know. I saw that from the first as well as her beauty and her brains." He nodded. "It don't matter, old son. Tartar or no, I'm for it."

"Sends the teacups and sugar basins flying whenever she's in a temper," he added gently, his sentimental heart really out to Sir Hannibal in his plight, especially when he saw him motioning for another plate o' vittles and thirds of ale.

"What's the odds," Cheng said with the wry smile of a man who has accepted the vicissitudes of his fate and no longer fights. "I'm an excellent catcher—and I dodge very well, too. Quick on my feet."

Bucky pulled at his ale, feeling suddenly all teary-eyed and beery. It was rather like watching a brave, unflinching comrade-in-arms as he took up his pack and left the fort on some suicidal mission. There ought ta be flags flyin' and a brass band playin' a sad and martial air. The two men grew silent, remaining so for a while, save for an occasional belch or the spitting out of a clove, until Cheng, not used to confiding his innermost feelings, felt a pang of regret at his indiscretion.

He leaned across the table, clapped his broad, square tawny-coloured hand upon Bucky's thinner, paler one, and, looking the younger man straight in the eye, said solemnly, "Buckthorpe, I've bared me very soul to you this day, man ta man. You'll not let me down, will ya, nor betray me confidence to a living soul?"

"Never, old son," Bucky replied, his eyes moist with sentiment. "No traitor I, to me own sex."

"Swear," Cheng urged with a slight hiccoughing into his shoulder.

"I swear," Bucky echoed, slapping his free hand over Cheng's hand, which still gripped him like a vise. "Only one thing," he added softly.

"What's that?"

"Don't ever call me Buckthorpe again, old feller."

"Never," Cheng whispered feelingly. "Never again in this world or the next, old friend."

The publican's wife passed by just then and, seeing the two men whispering as they held hands across the table, hastened back to the kitchen with a sniff of disdain.

"Humph," she said to the cook, "no wonder two such fine gents as them come in here. They're back there holdin' hands like lovers, if you please. Well, they shan't be let in again, I'll tell you. Give the place a bad name, they will, the nances!"

Bucky sat across from Charlotte at supper that night still so nicely stuffed with ham, ale, and walnuts that he could not even be tempted by an admirable bit o' fish.

"Must you do that?" Charlotte asked peevishly.

"Do what?"

"Belch like an overfed mongrel," she snapped back instantly.

"Well, I *am* rather an overfed mongrel, as it happens," he remarked cheerfully, dropping his napkin beside his plate and leaning back in his chair. He gave another hearty burp to back up his statement.

"Ugh, you wretched pig," Charlotte scowled. Clearly being crossed in love did not improve her temper.

"Carp, carp, carp. Don't you want to know why I am so well fed today, and me allowance ain't even arrived from home yet?"

"Not really," Charlotte remarked dryly.

"Aw, go on, ask," Bucky taunted.

"You child," she said, pursing her pretty lips in annoyance, relenting nevertheless. "Why?"

" 'Cause I had a meal with Sir Hannibal Cheng today in the town," he drawled with a pretense of nonchalance.

"Did you? Really? What did he say? Has he heard of Fanny and the Duke of Ax—" And then she snapped her mouth shut, thinking better of her sudden show of enthusiasm.

"He's lovesick all right," he said firmly, which was no lie after all. He merely omitted the true object of that lovesickness. "Feelin' rather lonely. Cumberland's had a row with the regent and went off ta your friend the princess Sophia at Hove, ta lick his wounds, one expects. Neddy's no fun now his papa is here and layin' down the law like Moses to the fatted calf—"

"That's Moses to the Israelites about the *golden* calf, you lump," Charlotte corrected him.

"Whatever." He waved his lacy cuffs. "Anyway, him bein' so low, I took pity and asked him to dinner tomorrow night, and a game o' fantan or cards after. Is that agreeable?"

"A-a-agreeable," Charlotte shrilled in amazement. "Why, it is splendid! I—I mean," she said, calming herself deliberately, "it is only right. After all, it is so sad to see him disconsolate over Fanny, and anything we can do to make amends . . ."

"Exactly my thought." Bucky nodded with an enigmatic smile.

"You know, Bucky, you are really quite a fine young man," Charlotte exclaimed, changing tone from sour to sweet with amazing alacrity. "So thoughtful of others. So magnanimous in your care of your fellowman—"

"Now, now, Auntie dear, don't say another word. You'll swell me head for me." Bucky smirked with self-satisfaction.

"Oh, but I *mean* it, dear boy," she insisted happily. "You have grown up these past weeks, matured! How selfless you've become, thinking first of Fanny as you have recently and now of poor Sir Hannibal as well—and believe me, together you and I shall set things to rights for the poor man—lonely and a widower as he is." She smiled complacently.

Bucky nodded his agreement. "Oh, that we will, Auntie, that we will," he murmured as he was served an ample dish of sherry trifle. "Ah, me favourite. Lucky I made some room, what?" Giving another hearty belch for good measure, he proceeded to wolf down his sweet with piggish delight.

Charlotte smiled with newfound tolerance, suddenly seeing her nephew bathed in the warm light of a golden nimbus. It glowed around his blond head and broad shoulders, endowing him with an almost holy aura. Wonderful lad, she thought, and her appetite thus inspired with renewed hope, she dug into the trifle herself, eventually outstripping Bucky in second helpings.

::9::

Bucky had coached Sir Hannibal well for his role. He arrived at Number 10 Seaview Row promptly at eight the following evening looking low and dramatic, his normally impeccable attire in some slight disarray as an indication of the extent of his distraction. Heaving heartrending sighs, he toyed with his aperitif and stared soulfully into the fireplace.

Lovelorn! There was no other word for it, and Charlotte, thinking that all this heaving and thrashing were over Fanny, sought to charm their guest with witty conversation and gay laughter, hoping against hope that he would forget Fanny and begin to see herself in the light of love. The effort was not easy! It strung her nerves to a fine tautness and made her impatient and jumpy. The mantel clock showed one minute past the half hour already, and still no dinner had been served! A minute late! What was going on belowstairs? When another full minute elapsed, she excused herself to investigate the unconscionable delay.

"I can't do it! I can't go on like this, old feller. It's too hard by half," Cheng whispered urgently as Charlotte left the room.

"You must, Cheng," Bucky insisted.

"But she's so lovely, so distractin'! I want ta tell her right out I don't care a fig for Fanny and never did. Why must I go on with this ridiculous charade?"

"Because every man," Bucky explained, "every chap, every *boy*, with an eye for her has chased her like a simperin' fool—which is what you're beginning ta behave like, I notice—and she's disdained 'em all, everyone. The slower you are to respond, the harder she'll work and the more of a challenge you'll be ta her. She'll fall, I tell 'e, head over heels, and you'll win the day, believe me, where everyone else has failed."

"It all sounds like one of her silly plots ta me," Sir Hannibal mumbled sourly.

"Now you've got it! Exactly. You've got ta play the hero for her, old man," Bucky whispered insistently. "Why, do you think that Maida would have looked twice at Sir Berry de Groat if he had begged—"

"Ravenstock," Cheng put in.

"What?"

"Maida's lover was Ravenstock, not Sir Berry. Sir Berry was Rowena Renfrew's lover in *The Romance of*—"

"Dry up, old son. It don't matter a pin's fee. They don't none of 'em beg a wench in her books, right?"

"No, you're right, Bucky," Sir Hannibal conceded. "There's always a lot o' thrashin' and sighin' and tribulation, lost birthrights, other women—"

"And then?" Bucky prompted.

"And then everything manages ta come right in the end."

"Exactly! At the *right* moment—and not before—the hero does something heroic and sweeps the wench off her feet and right down on her back—so ta speak—with benefit o' *marriage,* mind," Bucky added severely. "I won't have her 'scutcheon smirched, hear."

"Perish the thought. No 'scutcheon smircher, I, Vane, but how the devil do I manage to do somethin' heroic? And *when?*"

"Tut-tut, not to worry. I'll sense the right time coming, stick a burr up her horse's arse—and you can come riding along in just the nick o' time and save her life for her. She'll squeal; you shall comfort her in your good right arm, steal a kiss, and win her heart all in one swoop," Bucky chortled happily.

"Sounds damned silly to me," Cheng remarked doubtfully. He got no further with his remarks, however, for "Shhhh, here she comes back again," Bucky warned in a stage whisper. "Look lovelorn, for God's sake," he mouthed mutely as the door opened. Cheng heaved a passably lovelorn sigh, as he had been ordered and Charlotte, entering the room in time to catch its full effect, murmured "poor man" under her breath.

"Dear me, I hope you two are not entirely ravenous, for dinner has been delayed slightly by a mishap in the kitchen. Another quarter of an hour, and all will be well," she announced brightly.

Sir Hannibal looked up at her and smiled a small, wan smile. "No matter, dear lady. My appetite has been off of late and no doubt I shall just peck . . . like a bird."

"Bucky," Charlotte whispered urgently as Cheng sighed and turned toward the windows, staring out into the quiet street like Diogenes on his quest. "What am I to do now? I am tongue-tied. I do not know what to say. All I long to do is to declare my affection and offer to console him. Why cannot I just be honest with him and tell him how I feel?"

"What, and have him think you are too easy? Let him pine and come to love you for your wit, charm, and disinterested concern with his plight. What would Maida do for a jilted suitor? Or Lady Isobelle?"

"Offer noble understanding and selfless consolation—"

"Exactly, just as you are doin' tonight. Now don't spoil it. Be a heroine like that Rowena Ravenstock," Bucky urged in a hearty whisper.

"Renfrew," Charlotte retorted, flashing a look of menacing coldness at her nephew.

"What?"

"Rowena Renfrew," she reiterated icily. "Ravenstock was Maida's lover, you lump."

"Oh, bother, who gives a fig?" he retorted with a frown of annoyance. "Get over there and offer him a game o' fantan or, better yet, piquet—for just the two o' you," he urged, pushing Charlotte toward the Chinee baronet.

"No, no. I should just die," she whispered urgently as she dug her heels into the carpet. "A game all three of us can play."

"Fantan then," Bucky declared, and then, "Aha," he called out, pushing Charlotte before him unceremoniously. Sir Hannibal turned abruptly from the window, his eyes Lighting on Char-

154

lotte with eagerness. It was on the tip of his tongue to blurt out his heart to her right then and there. Only the spectre of Buckthorpe Vane, standing behind her, shaking his head slowly in a silent warning, kept him mute.

"Just havin' a conclave with me auntie here about how best ta cheer you, Sir H. Got any ideas? A game o' fantan, perhaps, or some tea leaf readin' until dinner? Look inta all our futures, what, an' see what's in store?" he suggested to the mingled delight and alarm of his companions.

Cheng, torn between laughter at the childishness of it all and genuine alarm that Bucky had some new devilment up his sleeve, threw up his hands in despair. "How, Miss Hungerford, do you stand this fellow? He is too much the devil for me and *all too wise as well.*" He laughed amiably, though there was an implied warning in the tone of his last words, which Bucky chose to ignore.

"I agree, Sir Hannibal," Charlotte added significantly. " 'So *wise* so *young,* they say, do never live long.' "

"Ah, you like that obscure and much maligned play, too?" Sir Hannibal declared with evident satisfaction. "There are all too few who even know *Richard III,* let alone who can quote it so readily. Have you ever seen it performed, Miss Hungerford?"

"I regret to say that I have not, though they say Mr. Kean, who tours East Anglia with it, performs the part tolerably well," she answered with a smile, relieved to have hit upon a topic of conversation.

"Indeed he does! I have seen him 'pon occasion, although I must confess I am more partial to his Iago, for I like *Othello,* of all Shakespeare's plays, quite the best," he replied eagerly, feeling suddenly easier. At last they had hit upon a subject, and he could give up the blasted sighing.

"*Othello,* you say?" she remarked thoughtfully.

"I beg your pardon? Oh, yes, *Othello* is my favourite of the Bard's plays," Sir Hannibal explained again. "Not that I don't enjoy Marlowe—and Sheridan amongst the moderns. *The Rivals* is always a delight, is it not?"

"Indeed," Charlotte remarked absently. He preferred *Othello*

—and how natural that it should be so, for like the Moor of Venice, he was something of an outsider in his world, a man of a different background from his companions, set apart, so to speak, by his odd bloodlines. Being thus set apart, he was perhaps more vulnerable and lonely than one might first think. After all, one saw him in the company of dukes and princes. Suddenly Charlotte found herself looking beneath his handsome, exotic exterior, seeing more of him than she had before and liking him no less for it.

"How about a game o' fantan?" Bucky asked rather overheartily, seeing and misreading the thoughtful glaze that had come over his aunt's eyes. Sir Hannibal had grown silent again, as well, after their first hopeful stab at conversation.

"No need, old man," Cheng replied, coming over to sit near Charlotte, "we've got lots to talk about, I think."

"Oh, have we?" Bucky mumbled, sitting down himself and feeling suddenly quite out of things.

"Why does it interest you so, that I should find *Othello* so much to my liking, Miss Hungerford?" Sir Hannibal asked quietly, looking her directly in the eye, even at the risk of losing himself in their utter beauty.

She stared back into his face for a long moment and then, quite unheroinelike, answered with complete honesty, "I had never thought of it before, Sir Hannibal, because I for one have accepted you for what you are—a handsome and accomplished man, wellborn, a hero who has done noble service to your king and country, and a man who has, unlike so many men of similar wealth and station, seen much of the world and led a useful, interesting, perhaps even *Romantick* life—"

"You—you have seen me thus?" Sir Hannibal stammered in subdued astonishment.

"But of course. How else?" Charlotte shrugged. "At first I thought of you as being merely handsome. Yet then I saw you are befriended by Cumberland, the most notorious perhaps, but also the most intelligent and maligned, of all the English royal dukes. Moreover, you are a baronet, not merely by birth, but

156

rather by your *own* heroic accomplishment. And now tonight I learn that you actually use your *head*—you read, you do . . ."

Charlotte trailed off slowly while Sir Hannibal was entranced that this peerless creature thought so highly of him, of him whom he had assumed she did not think at all! *Mirabile dictu!*

"But all this is not what I really meant to say," she went on with a small moue of annoyance at herself. "It never occurred to me before this very evening to think of your *feelings,* and how others may think of you—"

" 'The odd fellow,' 'the Chinee baronet,' 'that peculiar Cheng feller.' 'Too strange a chap to ask ta join our club, don'cha think?' " Sir Hannibal said with a wry smile and the assumption of a typically stuffy Englishman's drawl. Charlotte winced but did not interrupt him. "Once, in my rash youth, I proposed marriage to an English heiress, the daughter of an earl, and she, ever so discreetly, turned down my offer with the remark she could never marry an *Irishman.*" He smiled bravely at the irony of it.

"The little bitch!" Charlotte exclaimed indignantly, and then, somewhat flustered at her unladylike outburst (which had delighted Sir Hannibal), she added, "But I am glad you did not win her hand, Sir H. Such a gel could never deserve you."

"No, I did not win her. I went home to Moondragon instead," he remarked, more to himself than to Charlotte, "and married a little Chinese cousin. I convinced myself that I loved her—which I did not really, I am ashamed to admit—and that I wanted her for my wife." He paused a moment. "I did not make her happy, I fear."

"And then she died," remarked Charlotte, who wished to avoid that kettle of fish and get to the point of things as they were *now.*

"And then she died."

"And *you,* my dear Sir Hannibal, are alive and free to love again, to find that lady—a young, pretty one, I trust—who *can* marry and *will* marry an *Irishman* by the name o' Cheng." She spoke with dancing eyes and a sweet smile upon her pursed lips.

Someone who will love you and cherish you with all her heart til the day she dies, she thought. She stared across at his dear face with brimming eyes and knew suddenly that all would be well. It *must* be well, because of all the men on earth, *this* was the man for her.

"You are very sweet, Miss Hungerford, and—and very kind," Sir Hannibal said slowly, seeing much more in her face than just the beautiful, willful, tart-tongued heartbreaker of his dreams. She was radiant, and she felt for him, understood something of him. No, she was not merely pretty and clever. She was feeling and kind as well. Soft. Suddenly, with his heart fluttering in his breast like a bird against the bars of its cage, he felt that everything would come right. Everything would be as he wished it to be!

"No fantan, huh?" Bucky asked at last as the strange, fitful silence between his aunt and Sir Hannibal grew longer and, to his unpractised sensibilities, rather unsettling.

"No fantan, Bucky," Cheng said firmly, not taking his eyes off Charlotte, who held her own fine amber orbs fixed on the light in Sir Hannibal's black eyes.

"No fantan tonight, dear boy," she added softly.

All at once the three of them laughed together as with one voice, Charlotte in joy and delight, Sir Hannibal in relief and pleasure, and Bucky, the loudest of them all, out of sheer exasperation, not for the life of him knowing what had just happened —or even why. He had to be the very densest Cupid who ever drew breath.

> " 'Corn rigs an' barley rigs
> And corn rigs are bonnie;
> I'll ne'er forget that happy night
> Amang the rigs wi' Johnnie.' "

The sound of shrill singing echoed through the row outside the drawing room windows, floated up the steps of Number 10, and then, the front door having been opened with a latchkey, Charlotte's very own hallways filled with the high, shrill repetition of the old Burns refrain.

"Shhhhh," came a cautioning masculine voice, "you'll rouse the household, Fan."

"'. . . amang the rigs wi' Johnnie.' Nonsense, everyone's awake," came Fanny Hungerford's shrill, cheerful voice. "La, la, see how lovely. The house is all lit like a party, and the drawin' room full," Fanny trilled from just beyond the doors. "Come, come, dear Duke, and see if it ain't."

"Shhhh," the masculine voice cautioned again. "P'raps we shall intrude."

"Fiddle-faddle, come and meet me stepdaughter and me gran —and her nephew," Fanny urged.

"Ho, Fanny," Bucky called out, "I thought the words went 'amang the rigs with *Annie*'?"

"You may go amongst the rigs with Annie, dear boy," she retorted merrily. "*I* prefer me Johnnie," she chirped amidst a lot of sotto voce conversation from the hall. At last, calling a "Come along" over her shoulder, she pushed open the drawing room doors and tripped into the room.

"Fanny!" Charlotte exclaimed, totally taken aback by the sight of her amiable stepmother.

"Oh, I say, Granny, has there been a carriage mishap?" Bucky asked, leapin' to his feet in alarm. And well he might ask, for Fanny Hungerford was in no slight state of dishevelment. Even Sir Hannibal, who rather resented her raucous intrusion, could not help but utter a cry of surprise at the sight of her.

She stood in the doorway, her lovely new high-bosomed rose silk evening dress damp to the knees, one puffed sleeve slipping down off her plump shoulder and half of her coiffure unbound and tickling her neck with long black curls. Her little jewelled diadem sat awry upon her head, the white aigrette at its centre bent to one side and the quills of the plumes set into it all broken. Her cheeks were flushed, her eyes bright as jewels, and her long lace shawl was sandy and damp. In one upraised hand she held a little beaded reticule and her fan; over her other wrist dangled, by their satin ribbons, the tattered remnants of her evening slippers.

"We went to the spa ballroom and danced and danced and danced and—"

"That we did, and me feet shall know it in the mornin'," the seventh Duke of Axminster concurred cheerily, coming into the room in Fanny's wake and looking not much less dishevelled than she. His powdered periwig sat askew, showing a short stubble of cropped gray hair beneath. His cheeks were so ruddy with exertion as to look almost painted, and his stays creaked alarmingly with the mere effort of his breathing. While his evening jacket and waistcoat, his cummerbund and breeches were none the worse for wear, his white silk stockings were water-stained to the tops of his solid calves, and his black patent leather dancing pumps were gray with grit and sand, their finish damaged beyond hope of repair.

"I don't suppose Neddy's here, Cheng, by any chance?" he asked unceremoniously and with not a thought as to how he must look to the company before him.

"No, Your Grace. Neddy's in bed with a toddy and the wee Scotch parlourmaid from Number Nineteen, I think. At least that was his intention when last we spoke. Behavin' himself rather well since you laid the law—" Sir Hannibal replied with a careless drawl and a sly look at Charlotte, who blushed prettily but said nothing.

"Good, good. That's what I like ta hear." The duke nodded complacently. "And here's the little lady herself, eh, Fanny?" he exclaimed, hastening to greet Charlotte with both fat paws extended. He grasped her hand and bent over, squinting to see her face the better.

"Yes, Your Grace, I am the little lady," Charlotte said evenly, showing rather more of her lovely white teeth than was usual with her.

"Well, well. I must say, me Neddy has a good eye, what? No hard feelin's, eh, little lady, if you know what I mean?" he blustered, smiling and blushing and trying to be charming all at one time. By God, she is a comely wench, this scribbler, he was thinking. No wonder Neddy went so daft.

"I am so glad you feel that way, Your Grace. I feared that you would bear me malice when you heard—" Charlotte said sweetly, breaking off quite deliberately, a look in her eye that made Bucky watch her alertly.

"When I heard what, me dear?" the duke asked innocently.

"Why, when you heard it retailed abroad that I cannot stomach your eldest chick and have turned him down so flat," Charlotte answered in an acid tone. "I feared you would think ill of me for not having him," she finished, purring sweetly at the last.

Bucky clapped a hand over his mouth to stifle a whoop of delight. Sir Hannibal, who was not overfond of the seventh duke, made a fencing gesture at Charlotte behind the old gentleman's back and mouthed a silent "touché" at her. Fanny held her breath and prayed.

The Duke of Axminster stammered, his eyes goggling and his mouth working like a trout's. "Oh, yes, to be sure. Well, well, a happy resolve all round, eh?" he said at last. "Neddy's obeying his papa like a good lad, and this little lady keeps her—her—"

"Independence, shall we say," Charlotte remarked helpfully. "I keep my freedom, and Neddy gets the wee Scotch parlourmaid from Number Nineteen. A satisfactory arrangement all round, for we each get what we deserve." She summed it up with a devastating smile. After all, she did not want to spoil things for Fanny by being too nasty to the duke. She had given him just enough discomfort, she thought, to satisfy her honour, and now the matter would be forgotten.

"Oh, ah. Exactly. All's well, eh, that ends well, eh?" John Darlington exclaimed doubtfully as he caught an exchange of glances between Bucky and Cheng, both of whom were figuring on Neddy's getting a lot more than he deserved from the little Scotch maid.

"And I don't mean fleas," Bucky remarked to no one in particular, though his remark was lost on all save Sir Hannibal, who held his side to keep from laughing. "It seems you two had quite a night yourselves," he remarked with a bawdy leer at the duke. "You still ain't said if you've had an accident with the carriage."

"No accident," Fanny sang out, happy to change the subject at last. She twirled about the sofa and, patting Bucky on the top of his blond head, described her evening with the duke. "We danced and danced, and then we walked all about in the public gardens under the lanterns and around the bushes," she remarked, a funny light in her dark eyes as she made a self-conscious adjustment to the sleeve and bosom of her gown. The duke coughed discreetly and turned away.

"Your slippers are ruined, it seems. And your gown appears to be quite, ah, damp?" Charlotte observed with a dry sniff and eyebrows raised to their highest level. It was a feigned disapproval actually, for Fanny looked as happy as the schoolgirl she so often resembled, and blushingly pretty as well, all of which pleased Charlotte greatly, whatever reservations she might have about the blustery Duke of Axminster.

"La, so they are," Fanny agreed indifferently, swinging what was left of her lovely rose silk slippers on her wrist with a faint smile. "We danced them to threads, and then, betwixt the gravel of the walks and the sands o' the beach, why, I guess they are no more." She shrugged, tossing them into a corner. "There is not much left o' me stockings either." She giggled, poking one stockinged foot out from the damp, sandy hem of her gown daintily and withdrawing it quickly like a naughty child showing off her mischief-making with a certain embarrassed pride. In doing so, she nearly lost her balance.

"I say, you shock me, Granny," Bucky exclaimed, reaching out to steady her. "Is that any example to set an innocent boy and his maiden auntie?"

"Of your alleged innocence, Bucky, I have nought to say"—Fanny sniffed with closed eyes and pursed lips—"but as for your aunt, she should be ashamed to be a maiden at six-and-twenty."

Charlotte could not be sure, but there seemed to be a decided snort from Sir Hannibal's direction just then. Certainly Bucky whooped like a red Indian. "Fanny!" Charlotte squeaked in fury. "Fanny, behave yourself, else I shall think you have been drinking spirits," she accused priggishly and as a way of directing the subject from her own undoubted maidenliness to her stepmother's quite possible inebria.

"And what if I have?" Fanny asked defensively.

"Aha!" Charlotte exclaimed triumphantly. "Your Grace, my stepmother has, for the sixteen years that I have known her, been an abstemious, sober, and proper young woman and a model mother to me. One evening—nay, two, I believe—in your suspect company, and she behaves like a—a—" Words failed, for Charlotte really was not half so angry as she pretended to be.

"A what, Miss Hungerford?" Sir Hannibal broke in before either Fanny or the duke could protest. "Like a woman in love? I think, madam," he said, addressing Fanny, "that you are in love and I wish to extend you my *personal* best wishes." He winked and smiled, and Fanny, getting something at least of his meaning, looked relieved of her last small vestiges of guilt over that peculiar fellow. She blushed prettily and waved the tattered remnants of her fan.

"Now you've hit it, Cheng," John Darlington boomed, amazed at the fellow's perspicacity. "It's quite true, little lady, that your stepmama and I did—did tipple a bit o' the fruit punch as we danced—and what harm, I ask you? She's home safe, ain't she? And uncompromised."

"*I* do not doubt, sir, or condemn, but what shall my neighbours think?" she asked with a priggish air that both Bucky and Sir Hannibal suspected of being pure leg-pull. "Mrs. Creevey, up with the boils all night, and peering from her windows across the way, for want of any other amusement, poor tortured soul?" she added with questionable sincerity.

"Enough said, young lady," the duke interrupted. "You are a damned sight too proper for words. P'r'aps it comes from havin' a—" He had meant to say "a tart for a sister," but he broke off just in time, remembering whose son Bucky was. "A cleric for a father," he amended with uncharacteristic diplomacy. " 'On the morrow,' as you say, your stepmother and I—shall I tell 'em, Fan," he asked, looking across the room to Fanny Hungerford with a warm twinkle in his gray eyes, "or will you?"

"Perhaps *you* had better, John dear," she said simply, with a deferential nod.

"Right. Tomorrow we're off ta church to arrange for the banns ta be put up. They'll be read first on Sunday next, I expect and your stepmother and I shall be married in three weeks' time."

"Married! In three weeks' time!" Charlotte was stunned. This was fast work indeed.

"That is, if it is all right with you, dear," Fanny said tentatively.

"Oh, my dearest Fanny, of course, it is all right with me. I am so happy for you if—if." With that Charlotte came across the room and, kneeling upon the stool at her stepmother's feet, put her arms about the plump little lady and looked earnestly into her eyes. "If you love—"

"Yes, I do, my dear. I love him very much. Sometimes one just knows a thing is right. Time has nothing to do with it." With that simple statement Charlotte could not argue, having been a mad thing herself since her first sight of Sir Hannibal Cheng.

Bucky, taking his cue from Charlotte, rose and, harumphing a good deal, approached the Duke of Axminster, who stood his ground, arms akimbo, his stomach well forward and the heels of his ruined pumps dug into the hearthrug beneath him. "Well, well, sir. Ah, you understand, I am the man o' the family, responsible for these ladies, as it were."

"Yes," the duke agreed with an attempt at solemnity, evidently more prepared to be solicitous of Bucky's tender, green manhood than he usually was of his own sons'.

"It's awfully quick, ya know. I mean, I've got ta think o' Fanny's future," Bucky said, floundering a bit and turning nervously to Cheng for encouragement.

Sir Hannibal, stifling a smile, nodded with serious eyes and stern demeanour to reassure the boy that he was on the right tack.

"I can support her nicely, me lad, if that's what worries," the duke put in with a twinkle.

"Naw, it ain't that." Bucky waved the thought aside. "Fanny

don't take much keepin'. It's—it's—well, she's a very good little woman," he said earnestly, "and she's lovin'—and she ain't *old* —if ya take my meaning. She's got feelings and sensibilities and—well, she's *warm*—"

"He means, Your Grace, that the heyday o' Fanny Hungerford's blood ain't tame yet," Sir Hannibal put in helpfully.

"Exactly so—whatever he said—" Bucky agreed in some confusion.

The Duke of Axminster blushed crimson, as did Fanny herself. Everyone else grinned with delight at the sight of John Darlington's embarrassment. "Oh, yes, I see. Well, young man," he said in a deep, rolling voice as he recovered himself, "rest assured that my blood ain't tame either. There's life in this old feller yet—and love, if that's what concerns 'e. I love this little woman, and I'll do me part as a husband—I've been alone far too long, but . . ." Here he broke off softly, looking across the room toward Fanny.

" 'But,' John dear?" Fanny prompted in a sweet voice.

"But I guess I was just waitin' ta meet you, Fan," he burbled gently, holding out his hand for her. She rose with alacrity, nearly knocking Charlotte off the stool beside her chair in the process, and took his outstretched hand to her heart. He whispered in her ear, and she, nodding happily, started to lead him out of the room.

"Where are you two goin'?" Bucky wailed after them.

"Belowstairs for some warm milk and biscuits. I insist that he have something sensible on his stomach before I send him back to his rooms. Good night, Sir H., Bucky, Charlotte dear," Fanny cooed, and leading the docile Duke of Axminster by the hand with a "Come along, John," she disappeared from view.

"Well, what do you make of that?" Charlotte breathed incredulously. "They're to be married—and in three weeks' time, no less—or rather, no more!"

"Did ya see the state they were in? They actually went wadin' in the bay tonight, like a pair o' bloody children," Bucky exclaimed in scandalized wonder. "They're actually wet ta the knees."

"I think it's rather nice meself," Sir Hannibal remarked placidly, forgetting that he was supposed to have been in love with the lady in question. "It's no wonder ta me, love makin' Mrs. Hungerford a gel of eighteen again, but I confess I never thought ta see Neddy's governor, a windy old fart if ever there was one, turn back to a boy o' twenty before me eyes. Your stepmother is a distractin' little woman indeed, ta make John Darlington wake from his torpor an' dance and walk the beaches o' Brighton in the moonlight.

"Yes, she's quite a little woman," he repeated in admiration, reflecting on her buxom little person with kindly thoughts until he caught the dark look in Charlotte's eye. "If ya like the type," he added with prudent haste, "and don't mind her bein' so—so old."

Charlotte nodded sweetly, a complacent smile upon her lips, and Sir Hannibal breathed easier. He'd got out of that one well enough.

It was the mid of night. His Grace the seventh Duke of Axminster had left for his lodgings sometime earlier, feeling pleasantly sleepy, what with his ample tummy full of warm milk and digestive biscuits, his heart full of love, and snatches of lively old airs running through his happy head.

Charlotte was up in Fanny's bedroom hearing all about her stepmother's giddy night of love, dancing, and moonlight marriage proposals whilst Cheng and Bucky, the latter sneezing and scattering snuff in his wake, paced up and down Seaview Row, thrashing out the evening's happenings between them.

"You nearly gave it away, Cheng, old boy," Bucky chided. "You paid her far too much mind, talked too much sense after a while and forgot all about sighing and lookin' lovelorn. By God, what an opportunity you missed when Fanny actually arrived on the scene. You should have looked like a beached whale at the very least," he protested.

"And what, pray, does a beached whale look like?"

"Aw, how should I know? You get my meanin'. Ya should have suffered."

"Lovelorn, be hanged. It had got far beyond that point before Fanny and the old f— and the old duke came in. I'm in love with Charlotte, and there's an end to it. Moreover, while I don't fool meself that she loves me yet, still, she said some very warm and understanding things—things that encourage me no end, so . . ."

"So?" Bucky asked, still sceptical.

"So, I'm not beatin' the bushes round and round anymore, old sock. I'm takin' a leaf from Axminster's book! Goin' ta be direct, you hear? No more obfuscation! I'm goin' over there tomorrow and ask Charlotte if I can pay her my court. It's as simple as that," he said flatly.

"It'll never work." Bucky sighed, kicking a stone along the kerb as they walked. "It's too easy, I tell ya. She expects vicissitudes," Bucky warned him.

"Vicissitudes! Good word, that. I've always fancied it rather. How come you ta know such a word, Bucky?" Sir Hannibal asked teasingly.

"Here now, don't get nasty. I've read a book or two in me day. I ain't a fool, you know," he protested defensively.

Sir Hannibal laughed amiably and clapped an arm around Bucky's shoulder in camaraderie. "Come, come, I'm only chaffin' you. Tell me, how'd ya like ta have a Chinee baronet for an uncle, my boy?"

"Wouldn't mind."

"Wouldn't? Truly?"

"Hell, no. After a cuckold for a pater, a Chinaman's easy, what? Besides," he added brightly, "they say the huntin's grand in Ireland. You'd have me for a visitor now and then, wouldn't 'e?"

"That I would," Cheng agreed warmly. "Boon companion."

"I'd like that." Bucky smiled. "I think you're a devilish good sort, ya know. More my idea of an uncle than that rattlebrained arse Neddy Darlin'ton."

"Here, Neddy's not so bad, old son. Just young and green and under his father's thumb—not like you, eh?—but he's a good sort after all," Sir Hannibal defended his friend.

167

"Well," Bucky conceded with a shrug, "I suppose he really ain't so bad. It's just that he ain't proper metal for Aunt Charlotte. You're what she needs, I expect—someone strong who can stand up to her."

"Standing ain't what I had in me mind." Cheng laughed, giving Bucky a playful punch on the shoulder. Bucky guffawed at that.

"Oh, you wag. Oh, you buck," young Vane shouted before Cheng silenced him. "Oh, to hell with the neighbours. They're abed too early anyway, the old f—"

"No, shhhh, listen," Sir Hannibal ordered as he strained to hear the insistent, urgent sound of hoofbeats clattering on distant cobblestones. They grew louder and louder until finally they came from the very cobbles of Seaview Row itself. Then, out of the shadowy night, a rider appeared, bathed in the eerie flickers of gaslight on the far end of the long, curving street.

"Here, what's this?" Cheng cried, hastening toward the rider. "That fellow's come up to my digs, I think." Sure enough, a messenger on a well-lathered horse had just come to a halt before Number 17, dismounted, and was now in the act of tethering the animal to a ring at the kerb.

"Ho," Sir Hannibal called out as he approached with Bucky in his wake, "who d'ya want at Number Seventeen?"

The rider, they could see, wore the livery of the Duke of Cumberland. "Sir Hannibal?" the fellow asked, squinting against the gaslight of the intervening lamppost.

"Yes. Is that you, Quibbens?"

"It is, sir. I've been sent with a message from the Duke of Cumberland. I'm to wait a reply."

"Well, come in then," Sir Hannibal ordered. Turning to Bucky, who, torn between curiosity and discretion, was slowly taking his leave, he said, "Come along, Vane. I don't know what this can be about, but if it alters my plans in any way, I may need you."

They entered the house, which was dark and silent, the servants having retired, after leaving a few candles in sticks burning on a hall table for the use of any inmates who might return late from their irregular rounds, and hurried along the passage to Sir Hannibal's study at the back. It was neat and well ordered as Charlotte's own, a fact not lost on Bucky, who took it as a further proof of the pair's likeness of mind and temperament. Cheng lit several candles in a stand and, taking the duke's message from the man named Quibbens, read it over hastily once or twice.

> Cheng,
> No time for ceremony. Sophy's in a bad way for reasons I cannot put to paper, but which you may well guess from what I've told you recently.
> Come early tomorrow in time for luncheon, and if you are able, bring the Hungerford girl. Sophy's taken to her, and she may prove a distraction. In fact, bring Neddy or the nephew, Vane, or anyone else you may think suitable, as if it were a lark and nothing more.
> I feel quite responsible, as it happens, and must get her out of this wretched mood. I need your help, dear friend.
>   Ernest C.

He scanned the note once more and then, firing it in the flame of the candles on his desk, threw the paper into the grate, where it burnt to a cinder. Bending to his desk and working in silence, he scribbled a hasty reply, folded it, sealed it with wax, impressed the signet of his ring, and handed it to the man Quibbens.

"Go round to the mews, wake the stableboy, give him your horse, and take another at once. Give this note to the duke with my compliments," Sir Hannibal rapped out tersely.

"Yes, sir," the messenger replied and left, like a good servant, in proper haste.

"Trouble, Sir H.?" Bucky asked, rather awed by the scene which had just transpired—midnight messenger from a duke royal, clattering hoofbeats on silent streets, lathered horse, eerie candlelight on book-lined walls, message burnt in the fireplace grate, letter sealed with a gold signet! Gad, it all smacked of one of his Aunt Charlotte's novels!

"Nothing deep," Sir Hannibal replied dismissingly. "D'ya think your aunt is still awake, Bucky?"

"Lord, yes. Fanny'll chew her ear til dawn, I expect. If a ball can set her chin waggin' til two o' the clock, why, a proposal ought easily ta keep 'em busy til four, the dears."

Cheng was far too deep in thought to smile at Bucky's slight humour. "Go at once, old chap, will you? Ask Charlotte to be ready in the morning for a ride to Hove for luncheon with the Duke of Cumberland and Princess Sophia. She has been invited, and you as well."

"Me?" Bucky exclaimed in wonder. He had never met a princess before, let alone dined with one.

"Bucky, tell your aunt that her friend Sophy is low in spirits and Cumberland wishes us to distract her. Is that clear?"

"As water, Sir H.," young Vane assured him. "Well, I'm off then."

"And, Bucky," Cheng called after him as he hastened down the hall.

"Yes?"

"Tell your aunt that I shall be grateful *personally* for her help in this—and for her company as well. You know what to say."

"Will do," Bucky called over his shoulder as he went out into the night. In the distance he could hear the man Quibbens, freshly horsed, taking off from the stables in the mews behind the houses with Sir Hannibal Cheng's note safe in his pouch. What mystery!

170

::10::

"There is some *particular* sadness in the princess Sophia's life, is there not, Sir Hannibal? Some heartfelt sorrow that has marred her happiness beyond all hope?" Charlotte Hungerford asked thoughtfully, a charmingly serious frown crossing her pretty brow like a cloud crossing the sun. For once she was caught up not in the romance of a fact, but in its reality, Sir Hannibal Cheng observed with satisfaction as he watched her from the back of his horse while it cantered along beside Charlotte's carriage at an easy pace.

"You are quite right, Miss Hungerford. Pray forgive me, however, if I cannot speak further of the matter. Suffice it to say, she is in low spirits from whatever cause—that is hers to explain or not at her own discretion—and the Duke of Cumberland, having seen the cheering effect of your recent visit to Hove upon his sister, has asked that you join us in distracting her. It is most kind of you to be willing," he added deferentially with a graceful nod of his handsome black head in her direction.

"I think the duke and Princess Sophia are lucky to have such a kind and noble friend as they have in you, Sir Hannibal," she returned, looking up into his eyes. "I should count myself fortunate indeed to have—for my own—such a friend as you are to them," she said, speaking in a voice suddenly husky and breathless with emotion. It was a daring remark, perhaps—suggestive even—but she felt spirited enough to risk it, even at the cost of the inward trembling that took hold of her whole person in a most alarming fashion.

Bucky, sleeping with his back to the horses and his legs stretched across the opposite seat, snorted noisily, whether from a stifled snicker or an abortive snore, one may only guess. Charlotte bit her lip in annoyance but managed to ignore him.

"Miss Hungerford, a man could only feel honoured to be counted a friend of yours. Your beauty alone might inspire that loyalty. Your intelligence and sensibilities—dare I say it?—are calculated to inspire in a man far more than mere—friendship." Sir Hannibal's lower lip, full and sensual, trembled slightly as he spoke; his hot eyes flashed over her glowing rose-gold face and amber eyes with a searing look that completely took her aback and left her limp with surprise.

Bucky was snorting in earnest now, his eyes squeezed shut, his teeth biting down on the insides of his cheeks to keep him from exploding. Resisting an impulse to brain the boy on the spot, Charlotte managed to keep her attentions where they belonged.

"Sir Hannibal," she breathed huskily, "I—I—cannot think what to say. You, you quite take my breath away with the unexpected ardour of your remark." She was so frozen with surprise that her words seemed hollow to him, giving him absolutely no clue to the feelings behind them. Had he gone too far?

"Pray say nothing now, Miss Hungerford. I can only hope that by expressing my feelings thus I have not offended you or caused you any pain."

"*Au contraire,* dear Sir Hannibal," Charlotte murmured indistinctly and with an ambiguous frown.

Blushing, terrified that he had perhaps spoilt his chances by going too far too fast, just as Bucky had warned him he might do, Sir Hannibal inadvertently gave his horse the spur. Damn it, he thought, as they took off, horse and man like an arrow shot from a bow. There was nought to do now but to go on, look as if he had intended a gallop, and so, partly to save face and partly to get away from a dicey situation, Sir Hannibal sped down the road at full tilt, which was perhaps as well, considering that he immediately broke out into huge cold drops of perspiration at the sheer terror of having declared himself so forcefully and unexpectedly to the object of his passion. By Jove, what must she think of him? Did she take him for an impetuous fool?

Charlotte, left behind so unceremoniously in the carriage, tried to gather the tumult of her thoughts. She looked grumpily at Bucky, lolling in great dishevelment across most of the seat opposite and commandeering much of her own side as well. He looked to be still asleep, but she knew better.

Giving him a vicious kick in the thigh with the pointed toe of her patent leather shoe, she growled at him, "Do stop playing at possum, you beast. D'you think I don't know an honest snore from a sneaking little snort, you eavesdropper?"

"Who, me?" came the innocent, wondering reply.

"Yes, you. You heard every word, I'm sure, so do not dare deny it. What d'you make of him? What does it mean when a gentleman speaks thus to a lady?"

"How the devil should I know, love, bein' neither one meself?" Bucky replied with a toothy grin, enjoying Charlotte's obvious consternation.

"Do be serious, nephoo. I mean it. I must know," she pleaded in utter vexation. "It seems to me that he spoke very warmly. And there was such a look in his eye . . ." She broke off in a welter of anxiety and then added, "I—I never felt like this before. It is so confusing. Why, last night he was sighing over Fanny."

"I'd say he rather likes you, Auntie dear," Bucky said softly, relenting a bit from his posture of puckish teasing. "He's forgot Fan."

"Does he? Perhaps so, but—but how much?" she wailed. "If he can sigh over one lady in the night and woo another in the day . . ."

"Ask him," Bucky suggested with a shrug.

"You must be mad. I—I daren't do such a thing," Charlotte cried in shock and exasperation, blushing at the very thought of such an action. Would this boy never take her seriously?

"Then don't! Do nothing. Maybe he'll say something further on his own hook."

"And if he doesn't?" she wailed miserably.

"Don't ask me, pet," her nephew answered nonchalantly, adding, "*You* write the romances in the family, not me." For his pains, he received another kick and a pair of white gloves in his sleepy, amiable face just for good measure.

"Not *I*," Charlotte corrected petulantly. "How ever *could* you *write* when you cannot even *speak?*" At this Bucky prudently fell silent.

"I say, you all right, Cheng?" Ernest Augustus asked as Sir Hannibal reined in his horse before the door of Princess Sophia's house and dismounted.

"Yes, yes, of course, why?" he asked distractedly as he handed the reins to a waiting groom.

"Ya look a trifle pale."

"I am fit," he answered abruptly, mortally afraid he would, in his nervous state, confess all to Ernest. Damn, what a raggin' he'd get if the duke suspected he was in love—and with Neddy's scribbler to boot! "Pray say no more of my state, and it please you. Miss Hungerford's carriage should be here shortly. I grew weary of the slow pace," he remarked with a show of boredom, "and rode on ahead. We've brought her nephew, Bucky Vane, along. He's a good sort and full o' fun, as you yourself have seen. Thought he'd distract Sophy."

"Ungh," the duke grunted in acknowledgement.

"Now before this damned carriage comes—driver takin' his time, what?—tell me what's happened that Sophia's so low. She seemed fine when last I saw her—glad of the boy bein' nearby, despite your concerns—and Charlotte says, ah, *Miss Hungerford*," he corrected as Ernest looked at him askance, "says that Sophy was quite merry on Monday afternoon."

"She was, eh?" Cumberland snorted. "I'll tell 'e about that visit and your Miss Hungerford anon, but for now, suffice it to say the boy has got to be sent away. She's seen him every morning this week, and she'll see him tomorrow—but then he's to be sent packing. That's why she's so low, why she wants distraction. Garth's here right now, by the bye."

"The devil he is," Cheng cried. "No wonder you look grim.

174

But why send the boy away now? I can't say I don't agree it's wise, but why so suddenly? His birthday's only a fortnight or so away, and I think she had plans. Why must he go so soon? Is it Garth? Or you?"

"Garth'd keep him longer for *her* sake. It's me, old man, me and that scribbler, if you must know. She started it all on Monday, what with her sharp eyes and thoughtless tongue."

"Charlotte? But I don't understand. You said in your note that Charlotte was good for her," Sir Hannibal protested.

"Oh, aye, she *was*—up to a point. Still is, as far as her way with Sophy goes, but it was something she did—or said, rather—that set off this whole trying situation. Because of it, the boy's to be sent packing." Cumberland went on, to Sir Hannibal's deeper consternation. "More later. I hear the carriage approachin'. Now *smile*, f'God's sake, man. Ya look like death."

Charlotte Hungerford's carriage pulled up into the driveway before the door. Ernest Augustus, Duke of Cumberland, greeted her with a hearty cheer and one of his broad, well-meant, but nevertheless menacing-looking leers. "Ah, my dear Miss Hungerford. How happy I am that you could come. And young Vane, as well, good lad! Marvellous. Sophia will be delighted." He shot Sir Hannibal a cautionary look as he handed Charlotte down from the carriage and, taking each of the new arrivals by an elbow, steered them up the steps and through the house to the garden at the back.

"Sophy, see what a surprise I've brought you," Cumberland called across the lawn with such enforced good cheer that Sir Hannibal was even more upon his guard. Following in the wake of his friend and Charlotte and Bucky, whom Ernest still steered by the elbows, Cheng stepped out the back door of the house and onto the brightly sunlit terraced lawns that overlooked the sea beyond. He found himself momentarily blinded. Once his eyes adjusted to the glare, he saw that a group of as yet unoccupied lawn chairs had been drawn up around Sophia's chaise, which had been carried out from the drawing room for her comfort. She lay in an attitude of lassitude, shading her face from the sun with a small white parasol, all the while listening to the conversation of a man who sat in a chair beside her and leant, until the duke's greeting, quite close to her in an almost insinuating manner. It was a man whom Sir Hannibal recognized instantly, though a dozen years had elapsed since they had met; it was Garth. The purple claret mark across his face was unmistakable.

"Ah, my *dearest* Charlotte—I may call you that, mayn't I?—oh, yes, of course I may! That was all settled on Monday week, was it not? How delighted I am to see you again," Sophia exclaimed with genuine pleasure and a sort of fevered overanimation which Charlotte took to be nerves as she offered a hand to her guest. Charlotte took it at once, noticing Sophia's pale, hollow-eyed look with some concern. Clearly the princess had not been sleeping well of late, the difference in four days' time being very apparent to her.

Curtseying expertly despite the uneven turf beneath her feet, she smiled her most winning smile. "It is my pleasure, Your Highness. Sir Hannibal felt we would all make a jolly party."

"And Sir Hannibal, as always, is right," the princess Sophia exclaimed, turning to the Chinese baronet with an earnest smile. "I cannot thank you enough, dear friend, for bringing this pretty young lady to cheer me. She is a tonic, do you not agree?"

"I would be a wooden block, Your Highness, if I did not. She is a tonic to us all," Sir Hannibal murmured with a small bow as he kissed the princess's hand. Sophia noted at once the reddish tinge that stole over his tawny cheeks as he answered. So that was the way of things? Her eyes strayed to Charlotte Hungerford, whose rosy cheeks corresponded exactly to Sir Hannibal's blush of feeling. Yes, that was the way of things, all right, and why not? They were both young, healthy, and—free.

"Allow me, Your Highness, to present my nephew Lord Buckthorpe Vane, who is the eldest son of my sister, Lady Helena Vane, and her husband, the third Viscount Vane of Buckthorpe Court, Wooton-Maggot, Wiltshire," Charlotte said quite formally, urging her nephew forward with a little push in the direction of the chaise.

176

Bucky, once prompted, stepped forward with a fine display of manly grace, bowed low, and, taking the princess Sophia's outstretched hand with a grandiloquent flourish, planted a fervent kiss upon it.

Charlotte drew in her breath and closed her eyes in despair, but need have had no fear. His manner was impeccable. It was then that General Thomas Garth was introduced, Sir Hannibal nodding curtly with a brief "We've met, I believe," and Charlotte, not knowing for the life of her who the gentleman actually was, responding with a warm smile and a polite offering of her hand as he rose, with some difficulty, from his chair to greet her.

General Garth's sudden proximity gave her opportunity for closer inspection of his person. He was a smallish man in his mid-sixties, rather corpulent, wearing a gray wig and large cloth slippers on swollen, gouty feet. As for his dress, he was quite dapper, in a fine blue jacket of military cut decorated with several small medals of no particular merit, the sort of honours commonly bestowed upon loyal members of the king's household. His features were plain, good English ones, his eyes gray and small, his sideburns full and silvery. What set the little man apart from his fellows was a large and quite disfiguring claret mark which ran across most of his forehead from somewhere above the hairline of his wig and down over one eye onto his cheek, something like a half mask in its effect. Its purple colour was made all the more apparent by the silvery white of his bushy eyebrows and the pallor of his unhealthy-looking skin.

"Charmed to meet you, my dear. Her Highness has been telling me of your visit of Monday last," he said in a reserved and formal tone. "You write books, eh?" he asked, and Charlotte sensed it was an effort for him to be civil.

"I do write books, General Garth, and find myself fortunate enough to have the princess Sophia for a reader of them," she replied with a gracious smile. There was something about this man she did not like, nor did he seem pleased with her, she sensed.

As for Sir Hannibal and the Duke of Cumberland, she knew that for whatever reasons of their own, they would gladly have skewered him on the point of a sword. No swords being to hand, however, they pierced him instead with the daggers of their eyes, until—and perhaps even as a result of their malice—the old gentleman took himself and his mediocre medals and his unattractive claret-stained face away.

Charlotte, relieved that he was not to lunch with them, found herself immediately lifted in spirits. She said farewell with almost more alacrity than was consistent with civility. Cheng and Cumberland were more reserved, but she could tell that they were most glad to see his back.

Only Sophia seemed genuinely disappointed at the old general's retreat. She took his hand and held it long before she finally let him go. "You will be here on the morrow? All of you, you promise?" There was an earnest, unaffected pleading in her voice that was mirrored as well in her pensive face, a need for reassurance that was pitiful for Charlotte to behold. What was this ugly, gouty old man to her that she should plead with him? The Duke of Cumberland was so affected that he had to look away, but not before Charlotte saw tears welling in his undamaged eye. She looked questioningly at Sir Hannibal, but he merely shut his eyes and tilted his head ever so slightly as a warning to make nothing of the scene transpiring before them.

General Garth hovered over the princess solicitously. "We will, Your Highness," he assured her. "You have my word on that."

"Your word as the king's Garth, old friend, dear, dear old friend?" Sophia whispered with an agonized smile.

"As the king's Garth and as . . ." His voice faded to a low, guttural, and inaudible murmur as the company, suddenly feeling as if they were intruders, looked away in embarrassment, surveying lawns, sea, and even the trees in the park surrounding the house, anywhere but on Sophia's face or old Garth's bent shoulders as he stood beside her chaise and spoke to her in that low, rumbling, inarticulate but insinuating whisper.

* * *

Sophia had been listening contentedly to the general conversation for some minutes before she chanced to catch her brother's eye. His baleful look mirrored his deep thoughts, every bit as dark as those she sought to bury. She turned, as if by instinct, to Bucky as Ernest, too, sought other eyes and other tongues to distract him. The first to attract him, no wonder to any who had ever seen her, were the arresting amber orbs of Charlotte Hungerford, "the pretty little scribbler," as he was wont to think of her. Well, she'd cheer him perhaps.

"Any new novels in the works, Miss H.?" he asked intently, rumbling through a mouthful of food at Charlotte.

"Eh?" Charlotte responded dully, coming slowly out of the reverie in which she had been wallowing—a reverie which revolved around the contradictory nature of Sir Hannibal Cheng. What kind of a man was he? Sighing over Fanny one evening and then saying overwarm things to her on the following morning. She had decided to reward his seeming inconstancy with cool disdain.

"Any new novel?" the duke reiterated, showing all his teeth, not to mention a good deal of luncheon as well.

Light dawned, and the benighted problems of Sir Hannibal Cheng were eclipsed by the sun of literature.

"Oh, yes, Your Highness. Two as a matter of fact. *Lady Viola's Revenge* is near complete . . ." Charlotte gushed, colouring agreeably at the duke's sudden attention and, of course, always delighted to take up her favourite subject, to wit, her own latest literary efforts.

"Is it, eh?" the duke replied, "What's it all about?"

"It is the romance of a gentle-born, delicately bred young Huguenot lady who is deeply wronged by French Society," said Charlotte, waxing enthusiastic. "She regains her rightful place in the world only after a series of mishaps upon the Dalmatian coast, where she has been shipwrecked and rescued by a—a—forgive me, Your Highness—a *wicked duke,*" she purred demurely with a devastating smile toward Cumberland.

"Aha, yes, I daresay. All us dukes is a wicked lot." He leered amiably, tweeking his mustaches for emphasis.

"So we ladies like to imagine, at any rate." Charlotte smiled, warming to her subject and twinkling charmingly at the duke. "The duke—Renaldo, Duke of Dalmatia—"

At this point, Sir Hannibal, who had been listening to their exchange with morose fascination, choked upon an olive, turned red in the face, and hacked with tearful eyes into his napkin. All eyes turned to him.

"Are you quite well, Sir Hannibal?" Charlotte asked coolly, annoyed at the interruption, especially coming from Sir Hannibal, who was in Coventry as far as she was concerned.

"Quite," he gasped, reaching for the wine.

"—as it turns out is not *quite* so wicked as he is painted . . ." she went on, not missing a beat.

"Naturally," Sir Hannibal put in dryly as he motioned the butler to refill his glass. He was in a peevish mood now, brought on by Charlotte's contradictory nature—warm whilst riding with him and cold as ice ever since.

"I beg your pardon, Sir Hannibal?" He looked across the table at her and received for his gaze a distant smile—the kind that Bucky said froze honey.

"Nothing, nothing. Pray go on, Miss Hungerford. It is interestin' ta hear an author in the throes o' creation, as it were."

Charlotte relented a trifle in her coldness, though she was resolved not to be distracted by his handsome face. "Ah, yes," she agreed eagerly. "It is indeed the 'throes,' as you say. It is no easy thing, I may say, to have a gaggle of strange persons all thrashing out their several dilemmas in one's head like characters in a Punch and Judy show. I am not complaining, mind, but it does tend to set one's brain to reeling like a whirligig from time to time," she said, smiling merrily at the thought and taking a sip of wine.

"Yes, I daresay, eh," Cumberland agreed pleasantly. "What is t'other book you mentioned?" he asked by way of encouraging her to further converse. He liked the animated sparkle in her eye as she chattered so charmingly. That sparkle, together with the effect of his wine, was making him feel better than he had in days.

"Oh, that," Charlotte replied with a small deprecating gesture. "It is hardly more than a title and the tiniest kernel of an idea really."

"I was under the impression all your novels had the tiniest kernel of an idea, eh?" Sir Hannibal Cheng drawled, grinning sardonically toward Cumberland behind his hand.

"I beg your pardon? Oh, yes, I daresay they are, to begin with," Charlotte replied in all seriousness, for she fortunately missed his point, "but then they blossom into a full-blown plot, you see. It is at that point one is ready to begin the rather tedious process of setting it all down."

"Tedium ad nauseam," Cheng muttered into his glass.

"Sometimes it does seem so," Charlotte agreed naïvely.

"What d'ye call the new one, Miss H.?" Cumberland asked to bring her attention back to himself. He liked the directness o' those beautiful amber eyes. Such eyes were wasted on Sir Hannibal, who was as sour as milk.

"The Sins of Serena Swann, Your Highness," Charlotte replied readily, ignoring what sounded like a snicker from the direction of Sir Hannibal. "It is the story of a—"

"Pray what is that, Charlotte? A new novel, you say?" the princess Sophia called down the table where she had been, til that second, engaged in a bit of badinage with Bucky. Young Vane grinned down the table in his aunt's direction. All was going well, and the princess was certainly being distracted from her mysterious troubles.

Charlotte smiled, feeling quite marvellous and animated. The wine, the company, and the opportunity to speak of her favourite hobbyhorse . . . "Yes, Your Highness. As I was just explaining to your brother, it is just barely in the works, but it shall be entitled *The Sins of Serena Swann.*" Again came that peculiar snickering sound from Sir Hannibal's quarter. Bucky, who sat beside him, gave a sharp look. With slightly more effort than the first time round, Charlotte managed to ignore him. "I was about to tell the duke that it shall be the story of a Roundhead's daughter and her love for a dashing Cavalier—or else perhaps the love of a Cavalier's daughter for an honourable Roundhead —if there ever were such a thing," she added hastily. "I have not exactly decided which it will be just yet," she said, frowning thoughtfully—and very prettily as all the men at table noticed to their pleasure or discomfiture, depending on their several moods. "In the last chapter," she went on, "the heroine is being forced into marriage with a lecherous, libertine Puritan peer who is up to no good at all—"

"Naturally." Sir Hannibal nodded, giving Cumberland a sly wink, the wink being lost on the good duke, who was at the moment utterly fascinated by Charlotte, his natural interest in her female good looks being enhanced by her sudden and promising conjuration of a lecherous, libertine Puritan. Ernest liked that concept, for while he was certainly no Puritan himself, if he were, he would be a lecherous and libertine one!

"You were saying, Sir Hannibal?" Charlotte asked dryly.

"Nothing, nothing, dear lady. Say on. You hold the table in thrall with your literary devisings. Say on," he prompted with a little scuttling gesture of his hand.

Charlotte shot him a withering look, suspicious of his sobriety —or rather the lack thereof—and went on with her remarks, glancing round the table to each listener in turn. "As I say, she is being forced into marriage with the villainous Puritan when—"

"Lecherous libertine," Sir Hannibal corrected with a slight hiccough.

"I beg your pardon?" she asked, turning off the twinkle in her eye and giving Sir Hannibal a disdainful glance. Really, what could she have seen in this wretch? What did it matter that he had eyes like molten onyx and the face of a god? What did that signify, after all, if he was an inconstant wretch—and a sodden one at that?

"You said villainous this time round," he replied, pretending to be quite serious. "Before, you described the varlet as a lecherous libertine. Ought ta keep one's concepts straight, oughtn't one?"

"Indeed! Quite right you are," Charlotte agreed tartly. "Say then she is being forced into marriage with a lecherous, libertine, villainous Puritan," she corrected precisely, looking to Sir Hannibal for further comment with raised eyebrows and a haughty air. He nodded his permission to go on, and she did, hoping he had been silenced at last.

"She's forced into marriage when at the last moment, just as the ceremony is about to proceed—"

"The dashin' Cavalier—or Roundhead, is it?—rides his horse full tilt right up the aisle of the church," the Chinee baronet exclaimed with a great sweeping gesture of his broad arms and a precarious tipping of his chair for emphasis. "And then—"

"Sir Hannibal, you are interrupting me," Charlotte snarled in ill-contained fury. No one else spoke up. Sir Hannibal's behaviour was not only reprehensible but also so uncharacteristic of him as to strike both Sophia and the duke dumb with fascination. Bucky held his breath, knowing that Charlotte would soon be furious beyond all hope.

"Ooops, sorry." He shrugged with feigned meekness, flashing a grin toward Bucky, whose only reply was a slow, solemn shake of his blond head. If there was one thing Sir Hannibal Cheng had better not do if he intended to capture the heart of Charlotte Hungerford—or *keep* it, actually, since he had it already—it was poke fun at her novels. That, even young Buckthorpe knew, was courting disaster at least, if not outright tragedy. Had Bucky ever dared such bantering, why, he'd have been packed like a sausage into the nearest mail coach and sent back to Wooton-Maggot forever. Sir H. was being a fool!

"Pay no attention to Sir Hannibal, my dear. Clearly he is ill-disposed to be serious or literary-minded this afternoon," Princess Sophia suggested soothingly when she saw Charlotte's temper about to flare. "Do go on. We are all attention," she urged, though in truth she had to bite her cheek to keep from laughing.

"Yes, do go on," Cumberland prompted as well, exchanging merry glances with his sister.

"The ceremony is about to proceed when at the last possible

minute, the hero—a dashing Cavalier I expect he shall be—comes riding up the aisle of the church—"

At that Sir Hannibal sniggered audibly into his glass with a muttered "I told you so" to the impassive butler as his wine was replenished.

"—and sweeps the heroine up onto the pommel of his saddle," Charlotte cried with an exuberant and dramatic sweeping of her hand that incidentally sent her water tumbler all atilt. The duke, who sat at the foot of the table on her right hand, caught it just in time to save his breeches.

Cheng let out a whoop of uncontrolled guffaws, and Bucky winced. Gad, he thought, the poor fool is hangin' himself.

"Pray, what is so humourous about *that*, Sir Hannibal?" Charlotte asked, staring at him coldly.

"Nothin', nothin' at all, at all. Only I could say somethin' deuced vulgar about the dangers o' swoopin' heroines up onto a fellow's *pommel*—be he hero or not. Needless ta say, I won't," he added soberly with a reassuring and deferential nod to Sophy and Charlotte. To Bucky and Cumberland he offered a sly wink and a leer

The duke was quick to respond, giving Cheng a poke in the ribs as he roared out, "Well, I ain't sa squeamish, me lad. I'm always happy ta have a damsel upon me pommel, what, what?" he asked with a leer and another nudge in the baronet's ribs. He gave a squint of his good eye down the table toward Bucky, who was not feeling very conspiratorial just then, being engaged as he was in trying to assess his aunt Charlotte's potential for imminent explosion.

Cumberland and Cheng were past noticing Bucky's bleak expression; they were lost by now, dissolved into tears of laughter and titters of glee entirely out of proportion to the magnitude of the jest about ladies and pommels. Sophy was used to her brother's coarse humour and was amused enough to risk a small, sedate smile before resuming the dignified frown she was maintaining for Charlotte's benefit. It really was amusing—not their silly jest, of course—but rather the effect it was having on them, two supposedly grown men, behaving like naughty, utterly adorable schoolboys.

"You are mighty good as a critic, it seems, Sir Hannibal, which is an easy enough task after all. It is an old adage, I believe, that those who *can do!* Those who can't *instruct.* I can go it one better, sir, and suggest that those who *think* write; those who cannot write criticize."

"Bravo, Charlotte," Sophia cried, rooting for the distaff side. The duke chortled, hoping for a good contest in the eternal battle of the sexes.

"Those who think *best* are capable of either writing *or* criticizing. It so happens that I'm a damned fine hand at *both*"—Cheng sniffed—"As I shall prove one day with my great work."

"And what, pray, is the grand opus you intend to write, sir, *one day?*" Charlotte asked levelly, choosing to ignore his jibe at her Puritan.

"*A History of the Cheng Family in Ireland.*" Sir Hannibal sniffed haughtily, recovering his dignity with some effort of will.

"Oh, I say, what a grippin' title, that," Charlotte retorted spitefully, "a title in the tradition of *The Compleat Angler* or *A Diary of the Plague Years,* eh? No doubt, you shall have us all up o' nights burnin' out our tallow ends in a fever o' passion at the outcome of every page."

"Deride me if you will, Miss Hungerford." He sniffed with raised eyebrows and a blasé tone. "I plan to follow the noble tradition of me maternal grandpapa, Valerian Wallace, or my own father, author of *The Military History of the Ming Dynasty,* and create a work destined for the ages—no mere fashionable *entertainment* for the passin' fancy of the hoi polloi. Why, in a hundred years' time, who shall still be readin' *The Madness of Maida* or any o' Mrs. Radcliffe's Gothick nonsense?"

"In a hundred years' time I shall be long dead and past caring. In the meanwhile, what is wrong with entertaining the hoi polloi, as you so contemptuously deign to call my loyal—not to say *royal*—readers, Sir Hannibal?" Charlotte asked hotly, giving a deferential nod toward Sophia, who smiled conspiratorily toward her friend and offered a sally of her own.

"Since I and several other royal ladies are counted amongst Miss Hungerford's most ardent readers, Sir Hannibal, ought we not have the privilege of being called the *roi* polloi?" the princess asked with a self-satisfied little moue of pleasure at her modest play on words. The duke guffawed at his sister's jest. God bless 'em, the little scribbler and Cheng were doin' a fine job o' distractin' her from her sorrows. What a lark, he decided, congratulating himself on the setting up of this little luncheon party. It was perfect.

"Very clever, Your Highness, very witty indeed, if just a little beside the point," Sir Hannibal remarked with a patronizing nod that Sophia forgave instantly, knowing full well he was in his cups and past caring about the small amenities due to her station.

"Then get to *my* point," Charlotte challenged, "and answer my question. What is wrong with entertaining one's readers?"

"Nothing, nothing at all, I suppose," he answered with closed eyes and an infuriating wave of his hand. "Write such stuff, and luck to you, *if* you prefer to waste your talents on panderin' to the cliché-ridden romantic lunacies of a lot of addlepated, overheated females. If that's your highest literary aim, why then, be my guest and get on with it."

"Pandering?" Charlotte fairly shrieked. "Cliché-ridden?" She was almost beside herself now. The princess, who til now had been far more amused than annoyed with the baronet, became indignant as well.

"Sir Hannibal," she snapped with rather more ire than usual for such a placid, long-suffering lady, "you go too far beyond the bounds of decency and decorum to condemn us all—Charlotte's loyal readers—as addlepated or overheated. Romantic lunacies, indeed!" she fumed in a pretty pet that had her brother laughing to the point of tears.

Sir Hannibal was not to be moved, by either Sophia's words or the fine bloom of colour that accompanied them. "Do I indeed? With few exceptions, and I am sure that you are one, Your Highness, for I know your disposition to read great works of a serious and edifying nature," he replied with haughty deference, "any female who reads such silly, florid, overblown romance is certainly addlepated—perhaps even imbecilic." Now there was a gauntlet thrown!

"How dare you, sir?" Charlotte seethed, rising from her place at the table and throwing down her napkin in just such a dramatic gesture as Maida would have mustered under such circumstances. "My readers imbecilic? My novels silly? Florid? You lout! I write to cheer, to excite, to entertain, to take my readers out of their ordinary, mundane daily round—away from their noisy households, insolent servants, and scurvy, whining children! I offer them *romance* because all they have is an unsatisfactory marriage to some fat, lazy, dull-witted husband who—"

"Ha, and what, pray, do *you* know of husbands, my girl? You've never been married," he challenged rather unwisely. By Jove, but the angrier she got, the lovelier she became; her eyes flashed and her cheeks grew red as the bloom on a summer rose, bless her. He took another sip—or gulp rather—of wine and winked at Bucky, who winced, watching this fencing match as it deteriorated into what promised to end as an alehouse brawl. There went all his dreams of a footrace down the centre aisle and a rich manly, amiable uncle-in-law for his very own.

Charlotte spoke with an icy niceness when she finally recovered sufficiently to answer. "No, I have *not* married, Sir Hannibal, being wise beyond my years and certainly no glutton for punishment." This was the man she had fallen in love with? This lout, this literary impostor, this—this *critic?* Never! she told herself firmly. Besides, his shoulders were far too broad!

"Tell me, Miss Hungerford. Did it never occur to you that these ladies'd be a great deal happier if they read less and doted on their spouses more? You fill them with silly fancies—"

"*Silly* again!" Charlotte cried, throwing her arms and eyes heavenward as if in supplication of the Deity.

"—silly fancies, foolish notions o' heroes and titles an' long-lost dukedoms and treasures! Describe these idiotically romantic, dandified lovers—handsome and dashin' and brave—"

"Does she?" Cumberland asked with wide-eyed attention. Mebbe he was missin' somethin' after all by not readin' such tripe. And hadn't Bucky mentioned a deflowered virgin or two?

187

"Why, what man—husband, son, lover—could possibly live up to the expectations you fill their impressionable heads with?" Sir Hannibal proclaimed with a slap on the table. "It's positively insidious."

"You ended that sentence with a preposition, I believe. I hope that such a slip is not indicative of your literary style," Charlotte remarked with deceptive blandness.

"The devil I did? Since when is 'insidious' a preposition?"

"*With*, you dolt, *with*. Yes, it is insidious of me, now you mention it, insidious of me to give my lady readers hope that there may be *somewhere* in the world—not in their little world, mind, for they already know what they have—some fat, lazy man who belches like a Falstaff, scatters snuff like a chimney sweep, and sleeps half the evening away over his pipe and his port, that somewhere there breathes a handsome, brave, noble, long-suffering, and romantic gentleman worthy of all their deepest loyalties and greatest passions. Yes, it is insidious of me, I expect."

"It amazes me, Auntie, that bit about snuff, Falstaff, and port," Bucky said sombrely, breaking in for the first time. "It's me guv'nor to the life—and I didn't think you knew him that well."

"I do not, Bucky. I merely describe the common run of men. Sir Hannibal here would fill the bill quite as well were he a bit fatter," Charlotte said acidly, not taking her gaze from the handsome Chinee baronet who was as far from her description of men as Bucky's pater was near to it. "Fah, husbands," she cried, "a scruffy lot—far too lazy to be dashing or romantic and too unimaginative to be truly wicked. Too dull even to sin, save in the most conventional ways," she added dryly, turning to the princess Sophia and throwing up her hand. "God save us, Your Highness, from husbands. I swear I would not have one of the knaves to save my soul! No, not to save the human race from extinction, look you!" Sophia smiled knowingly. Charlotte was saying too much.

"Methinks she doth protest too much," Sir Hannibal muttered

under his breath, but quite loud enough for Charlotte to hear and take exception.

"What was that, sir? Do you doubt my word?"

"I do indeed. Most women would marry the corpse on the end of a rope just to say they've been wed."

"Hear, hear," Cumberland seconded, tapping his knife against the side of a tumbler.

"And as for meself," Cheng went on glibly, not to be outdone by Charlotte in protestations against the married state—why the devil had he ever considered wooing such a terror?—"I'll be flayed alive before I ever make the mistake o' marryin' again—especially some flibberty, simperin' female scribbler the likes o' you, ya hot-tempered she-devil of a wench." Whoops, perhaps he *had* gone a bit far there. . . .

"Now that's torn it, sir. That has torn it! Scribbler I may be—and hot-tempered as well—but not my worst enemy could call me a *simperer!* I *never* simper, and *neither* do my heroines. You are a cad, sir, and a varlet to boot, and so help me, if this were my table and my china, I should demonstrate my temper by pitching it all—down to the last soup plate—right at your insolent head."

Sir Hannibal roared in mockery, his passions more roused than ever by her fire and her beauty as she stood across the table from him. Thank the gods he was drunk, or he'd never have dared bait her so. "Pitch away," he instructed airily.

"Oh, do, gel, do," Cumberland urged happily. "Don't mind the crockery. It's only rented, eh, Sophy?" Sophia, fascinated by Charlotte and Sir Hannibal, who clearly cared a great deal for each other without the least awareness of it, made a faint sound to shush her brother forthwith. She wanted to see how far the contretemps would go—how long it would last.

"Yes, go ahead, pitch the crockery like the fiery heroines of all your novels. Play at being Maida if it pleases you," Sir Hannibal shot back with such mockery in his eye that Charlotte actually did lift a cup and heft its weight in her hand, though she did not really dare hurl it in such august company.

"You are no hero, Sir Hannibal. No hero and no gentleman.

189

Sir Berry de Groat would not be such a beast. No, nor even Renaldo, Duke of Dalmatia, who is no angel, let me assure you. Not even he—" Charlotte said in a low, cool voice that trembled slightly with pent-up emotion.

"Berry de Groat is an arse," Sir Hannibal roared back at her with magnificent gusto and a wave of his glass that sent a tail of wine splashing across the carpet. "And so is that Ravenstock feller and God knows what an arse Renaldo, Duke of Regurgia, must be—" At first the only sound was a loud moan from young Buckthorpe. And then:

"That does it," Charlotte whispered all but inaudibly, her eyes locked on the molten eyes of Sir Hannibal Cheng, who, if anything, was even more handsome at that moment than he had ever been to her, curse him. "Nobody insults my Ravenstock and lives!" Before Sir Hannibal could duck, he found that he had been struck a glancing blow with the teacup and after it a saucer, both of which, being of a thick, serviceable nature, bounced unbroken onto the carpet behind him. "You are the most irritating—"

"I say, good shot," Cumberland muttered.

"Charlotte, contain yourself," came Sophia's voice, shrill with surprise. She really had thrown it! Bucky laid his head in his hands and moaned eloquently.

"—argumentative—"

"*I* argumentative?"

"—uncivilized brute that ever drew breath. You wouldn't know a hero if he bit you! No, nor a good novel if it was etched into your brain with a hot poker. Out, out of my sight, you viper," she cried dramatically with a wave of her hand. Catching Bucky's eye, she added, "Nephoo, I vow I would not be that man's wife for all—"

"Never fear, Miss Hungerford," Sir Hannibal cried, rising from his chair so swiftly as to knock it over behind him onto the saucer—which remained, *mirabile dictu,* intact. "You are the last gel on earth that I'd ever be likely to ask. You were right, Ernest. She is a Tartar, and I'd sooner be a monk in a cell than have to live—Forgive me, Your Highness. I ask to be excused," he said hotly, bowing low to Sophia and edging toward the door. "If I stay another minute, I shall forget myself and give this wench here the fanny whacking of her young life—"

"You wouldn't *dare*," Charlotte cried in horror.

"Oh, wouldn't I?" Sir Hannibal retorted with a menacing step forward.

"You may leave the room at once, Sir H.," said Sophia. "There has been quite enough squabbling between you for one afternoon, I think. Ernest, Bucky, I expect you had better go with him. Take a ride through the countryside, but see he does not thrash his horse because he cannot thrash his wench," she instructed firmly and with a sly, humourous wink at the Chinee baronet, which caused him to blush and stalk from the room without further ceremony.

Only after the doors had closed behind the men did the princess break out into the merriest laughter that Charlotte had yet heard from her royal lips. Charlotte—does it need saying?—laughed not at all. . . .

"Ohhhh," Charlotte snarled between clenched teeth, her face screwed up most unbecomingly, her eyes squeezed shut, her fists knotted, and her dainty slippered feet beating a tattoo upon the worn carpeting. "I hate him, I hate him, I hate him."

Sophy laughed all the louder at that passionate declaration.

"And you laugh?" Charlotte asked, breaking off her tirade as abruptly as she had begun it.

"I cannot say that you were not provoked, my dear, but you could have been cooler. After all, he was in his cups and simply behaving like a naughty schoolboy to get your attention. You have been ignoring him all day, and I think he was rather hurt—"

"Hurt?" Charlotte cried. "I didn't hurt him half as much as he deserved, the—"

"Oh, silly girl, I don't mean hurt with that cup and saucer—where, by the way, did you ever come by such an arm? You'd do on a ladies' cricket team, you know—I mean that you hurt his feelings with your lack of attention to him. He really likes

191

you, you know," she chided gently as they left the wreckage of overturned chairs and scattered crockery to a gaggle of highly bemused servants.

"Likes me?" Charlotte asked in surprise.

"Yes, and quite as well as you like him," Sophy added as she steered her companion into her back drawing room and closed the doors. "Do sit down now and calm yourself."

"I cannot be calm," Charlotte snapped irritatedly. "Are you actually suggesting that I *like* that wretched fellow?"

"Yes, I am, my dear," Sophia whispered confidentially, as she came across the drawing room to hug the girl. "That is just what I am suggesting—that you like him and like him *very much* indeed."

"Nonsense," Charlotte fluttered, colouring prettily. "Utter piffle."

"Is it?" Sophia asked mildly. "No, I think not. Come now, my dear, 'fess up. You adore him. There's no shame in that, you know. Really, there isn't." It was the wrong tone to take with such a stubborn creature as Charlotte Hungerford.

"At the risk of offending my very dear friend and most gracious royal hostess, I must beg leave to differ. There is nothing to confess. I do not adore him! As far as I am concerned, Sir Hannibal Cheng is a barbarian, as, no doubt, were his pirate ancestors. He is a lout, a beast, and a scoundrel—"

"My, all that," Sophia broke in with a smile.

"—and if it is twenty years ere I set eyes on the man again, why, even that may be too soon." Charlotte spoke quite firmly, avoiding Sophia's eyes, but ending with a deep curtsey to mitigate her stubborn rudeness. "May I beg leave to change the subject to a more agreeable one, Your Highness?"

Sophia looked at her for a long moment, noting the blushing-hot, honeyed cheeks, the frozen look in the huge, lavishly beautiful amber eyes, the stubborn set of the firm jaw, and gave up with a small shrug. "Very well, my dear. You hate him, and there's an end to it. And to keep his offending looks from your sight, I shall send him packing this afternoon before tea. The whole lot of them, in fact: your nephew, my brother Ernest, and the dreadful Baronet Cheng. But you shall stay the night and keep me company if you will for a day or two. I—I have need of a good companion," she remarked softly, remembering for the first time in an hour or more that she would soon be alone, bereft of her secret little son, who was at once the light in her eyes and the ache in her poor heart.

"What do you say? Will you stay and keep me company? Your nephew can ask your stepmother to send some things if you like, though I expect betwixt my ladies and myself we can see to any necessaries you may need. Please say you'll stay," the princess Sophia urged, trying with only partial success to keep the note of pleading out of her voice.

"I shall be happy to stay, Your Highness, for your company and companionship and not out of any wish to avoid the wretched Hannibal Cheng. He is absolutely nothing to me, as I hope I have made perfectly clear."

"Oh, perfectly, my dear," Sophia agreed hastily. "Nothing could be clearer to me than your true feelings for the wretch," she added, stifling the smile that wanted to break out across her face. Surely, she thought, Charlotte cannot be so stubborn as to throw it all away?

But then again, perhaps she was.

Actually it was Bucky Vane rather than Sir Hannibal who was wretched. He felt positively miserable, in fact, as he trailed the Chinee baronet and Cumberland first out of the dining room and then out of the house. They marched solemnly in single file, and none of them spoke til they had neared the stables, at which point Bucky caught up with Cheng, whose long stride had outpaced that of his companions.

"Well, what did you hope to accomplish by that—that wench baiting of yours, you bloody Chinee twit?" young Vane asked sourly as he fell in step with the baronet.

"Ahhh, good question, that, Bucky-me-bucko. I—ah, I'm not exactly sure, old son, but I have established one thing," he remarked dryly, turning to flash a grin at the Duke of Cumberland, who was still recovering from the excesses attendant upon what he regarded as an incident of sidesplitting hilarity. "I've established that Miss Charlotte Hungerford is even prettier when she's furious than when she's not." He leered nicely at Cumberland, who returned it in kind.

"Oh, right, but you should have given her that fanny whackin' you threatened—if only ta see if the bottom's as pleasin' as the rest of her," the duke chortled like a raucous schoolboy. "I'll wager it is," he added with an appraising gleam in his eye.

"Here now, sir, that's me auntie's bottom you're talkin' of in such a cavalier manner," Bucky protested with a wail. How could they take it all so light? He turned to Sir Hannibal, bent on making him see the seriousness of what had passed. "Fat lot of good it shall do you, Sir H., to know she's pretty when angry," Bucky muttered glumly, "if you never get to see her again as long as you live. You have really torn it, you know. No man has ever treated me Aunt Charlotte like that, I'm sure."

They entered the stableyard just then, and the mere sight of them sent the hands scurrying for saddles, horses, and bridles.

"No, probably not," Cheng agreed unruffled, "though I daresay someone should have ere this. It's best to train a woman young, you know, and at six-and-twenty! Why, it's almost past doing." Bucky looked hard at Sir Hannibal and, with a certain perception almost precocious in one of his youth, realized how much of bravura went into that impassive remark. Cheng was spooked. He knew he had torn it, poor fool, Bucky lamented with a sinking heart.

Cumberland, who did not know—did not even suspect his friend's infatuation with the lady—roared with laughter at Sir Hannibal's remark. "Good job you've done, Cheng. Served the wench right. No offense, young Bucky, but we're older, wiser heads, eh? We know a damned sight more, don'cha know, 'bout tamin' wimmen. Always gotta let 'em know who has the whiphand—though"—and here the good duke broke into a new fit of laughter and clutched his side til he bent double—" though she did look mighty fetchin' as she pitched the crockery every which way. Gad, what a spirited gel she is, Buckthorpe."

"Bucky," Bucky corrected automatically as he pondered the

duke's bits of off-the-cuff wisdom about tamin' wenches. When he finally spoke, it was a more carefully posed reply than might seem on its face: "Me old gov'nor. It's what me governor ought to have done to me mater at the very first sign of a variable amongst the Vanes, eh?" He paused. "Should have shown the whiphand, so he should, eh?"

"Precisely," the two older, wiser heads pronounced as they mounted their steeds.

"Now enough o' scribblers! What say we retire ta the Green Bull Inn for a pot or two o' their best ale, eh?" Cumberland interrupted with a hearty motion that in other circumstances might lead men into battle. His suggestion was met with a chorus of seconds.

Some hours later the little trio, roisterously tight and in high expectation of a hearty supper ahead, returned to Hove, where instead of open arms and a hot dinner, they were greeted by the sight of Cumberland's boxes, neatly packed into the boot of his coach and his servants patiently waiting about on the steps of the house, which was locked up tight as a trap.

The duke's man, Quibbens, stepped forward as Cumberland reined in his horse and presented his dumbfounded master with a letter from the princess. He tore it open and read it over, an incredulous expression crossing his face as he squinted his good eye at the words. His mouth worked like a fish, his eye goggled, and he looked across the necks of the horses toward his two companions in a welter of hurt and astonishment.

"I've been turned out. We've *all* been turned out! Sent packin' and not to return til invited."

"That's it. That's torn it forever," Bucky rejoined mournfully. "A spinster til the end of her days," he moaned quietly to himself.

"Looks like I've spoilt things for you, Ernest, old friend. Turned you out of your proper bed what with me damnable temper," Sir Hannibal suggested with a mournfulness that was only slightly tempered by the tipsy grin spread crookedly across his face.

"Oh, who cares, eh?" the duke retorted fiercely. "Wimmen!

They're all a mad lot—silly females full o' pettish ways and fits o' the sulks. Away." He gestured wildly to the coachman and valet. "Get in, get crackin' back to Brighton to our own digs, to a man's lair, where wimmen ain't wanted—or needed," he railed drunkenly, waving a fist toward Sophia's darkened house.

"Down with females. Down with the lot o' them," he called out, reeling his horse about and taking off down the road at a gallop with Sir Hannibal and Bucky, ranting in similar fashion, close at his heels. With much scrambling of servants for seats, the baggage-laden coach, swaying and rumbling under its burdens, took off after them.

"Last one to the Green Bull pays the bill," came a faint shout from far down the road. . . .

::11::

Sophia sighed longingly as she watched rays of orange light streaking the purple waters of the bay. "It is so peaceful here," she said. "One could be so happy in this place if only—"

"If only what, Your Highness?" Charlotte asked softly.

"If only things could be as one wished, if one could have about one the—" The princess mused before she broke off once more. "If only one could have one's heart's desire," she said at last, her face lost in the deepening shadows of evening, only her white muslin dress standing out against their surroundings.

"What would be your heart's desire, if you could have it, Your Highness?" Charlotte asked with no intention to pry, but merely to draw out her companion, who seemed so disposed to speak.

"Ah, that. If I could have my heart's desire, then I should be free to tell you—to tell the world, in fact—just what it was. But alas, I cannot have it and I cannot speak of it either."

"It is so secret as that then?" Charlotte asked, though her tone made it more a statement of fact than a question.

"It is. A deep secret." Sophia's tone was strangled.

"I shall say no more then," Charlotte replied with a nod.

"Pray do not be hurt, Charlotte, that I cannot confide," Sophia pleaded, mistaking Charlotte's discreet reserve. "It is something too, too deep. I mean you no insult," she whispered.

Charlotte, with the protective gesture of a loving sister, wrapped Sophia's shawl higher up about the princess's shoulders and hugged her close. "We should go in," she suggested.

"You may be a mother and a wife and—and—never have to

197

be a princess." Sophia sighed suddenly, gliding away from Charlotte's protective hands and looking out into the night waters, drawing in her breath and pulling herself erect with straightened shoulders and head held high. "My, I am sentimental this evening, am I not?" she said with a dry, harsh laugh. "You must think me wretched company." She wiped a straying tear and recovered herself. "Is that the dinner gong?" she asked with enforced cheer in her voice.

"I think it is, Your Highness," Charlotte answered brightly, matching Sophia's change of tone with a false heartiness of her own. She turned toward the house in time to see a figure silhouetted in the dim light of the french doors leading down onto the terrace. It was dark now, and the windows of the house glowed with the faint golden light of many candles.

"My lady is awaiting us," Sophia observed.

Charlotte was about to speak when a sound, a sudden move in the trees far along the terrace to the left of the doors distracted her. "What is that?"

"What is what?" Sophia asked idly as they retraced their steps toward the house.

"I heard a noise. Something moved in the shadows. *There,*" she whispered urgently, extending a finger in the direction of the trees.

"It is only one of the household. See, she awaits us in the doorway," Sophia suggested.

"No, I saw this after I saw her. Something moved in the trees at the end of the terrace."

"An owl perhaps; some other creature. Do not alarm yourself with shadows, Charlotte," Sophia chided. "Maida would not do so, I am sure," the princess added dryly by way of some good-natured teasing, for she knew as well as Bucky (and now Sir Hannibal, to his regret) how seriously Charlotte took her literary efforts.

"No, I suppose she would not," Charlotte agreed humourlessly, "but she might be suspicious of foul play and lurking strangers."

"Dinner, my dear girl," Sophia said firmly. "This has been a long and eventful day, and for once I have an appetite."

"Your Royal Highness, your wish is my command," Charlotte replied with a deferential curtsey. The two women locked arms and, laughing lightly, walked toward the house.

It was nearly midnight. Charlotte sat in a narrow bed in a narrow room that served as the second best guest room in the princess's house, Cumberland having usurped the best for himself and loaded it with far too much impedimenta to be easily moved. She held a book before her face, but to little avail since the eyes of Sir Hannibal Cheng—the long, wide black eyes of Hannibal Cheng—intruded between herself and the printed page with maddening insistence.

She had behaved dreadfully. He had been the worse for drink, teasing and rude, it was true, but she had behaved dreadfully nonetheless. She should have laughed at him, as Sophia had, teased him back measure for measure; she should never have got angry and never, never hit him with that cup. It was too wicked for words! She had deserved the spanking that he had threatened to inflict upon her person; she had deserved that and more! But now he'd never speak to her again.

She was too upset to sleep. She was not distracted by *Childe Harold*, and yet, without a book to read, she would chew her nails, toss til dawn, and look a fright all the next day long, so, slipping out of bed and donning a borrowed robe to put over her borrowed nightdress, she took up a candle and tiptoed to the door, bent on finding a novel in the drawing room.

The hall was dark, the house silent, as Charlotte crept down the long, shabbily carpeted hall, feeling with little pleasure the dusty roughness of its threadbare surface against her bare toes. The circular staircase yawned before her, a ring of deeper blackness in the dark, silent hall. Slowly, groping for the smooth security of the bannister, she slipped cautiously down the steps, only the dim golden light of her candle's flame keeping away the looming darkness that surrounded her.

Suddenly, she knew just how Lady Viola must have felt on her first, terrifying night under the sinister roofs of Castle Drago as she felt her way, with but one lucifer to her name, down the inside of the stone tower and thence into the damp and secret dungeon where Duke Renaldo kept his—

The drawing room door was no more than an inch ajar—but it was enough! Someone was inside, moving slowly about with candle in hand, for the point of light shifted restlessly too and fro. Charlotte stopped stock-still, her heart pounding.

Who could it be? Suppose it was an intruder? Should she rouse the household? Was there time or would the fellow escape? Then she remembered the shadow she had seen moving on the terrace. It *had* been an intruder, and he was back again now—up to no good!

Regaining her composure after one brief moment of panic, Charlotte carefully removed the candle from its heavy brass stick and took it, mindless of the dripping wax, in her left hand. Hefting the stick and brandishing it over her head like a weapon, she tiptoed the few steps down the hall to the door and, drawing in her breath, slowly pushed it open.

"Your Highness!" she whispered as she dropped the candlestick to her side. Before her Princess Sophia of England stood transfixed as a terrified animal in the light of their two candles. Her nightcap was awry, her nightdress dishevelled, and her shoulders covered only by a shawl draped loosely with its ends trailing the floor. But whatever the disarray of the princess herself, it was nothing to the condition of the small drawing room in which she stood. It appeared to have been thoroughly ransacked.

"Charlotte, for God's sake, help me," she whispered urgently. "Come in and close the door behind you."

Charlotte did as she was told.

"What has happened, Your Highness?"

"What has happened, you ask?" Sophy repeated dully. "I have been ruined, that is all, dear friend. I have been ruined."

"Ruined?"

"They are gone, you see, and in their place—"

"Yes?"

"Oh, dear God, I cannot tell you," Sophia wailed in despair as Charlotte strove to shush her.

"Your Highness, you are overwrought," Charlotte said more to herself than to the princess. Her mind raced, and she realized that before anything else, she must calm the lady down at once lest she become ill. Already Sophia was clutching at her thin chest and beginning to cough softly into her clenched fist. Charlotte took the candle gently from Sophia's hand and set it down on the disordered desk near the back windows. After guiding her like a troubled child to the chaise, she sat the princess down and wrapped the shawl and a throw rug from the fender around her friend. Taking up a decanter and two tumblers from the dining room, she returned quickly, closing the door as she passed with a sharp snap of the latch.

"There, we are alone and cannot be overheard. Now here is your port. Drink it as if it were medicine."

Sophia took the glass and did as she was told, shivering at the bite of the strong, sticky wine upon her tongue.

"I am ruined, Charlotte, ruined. There is no help for it now. All will be known. Scandal, ruin—and not just mine alone. Ernest, the poor king's Garth—the child . . ."

"Would it not be best to send for help, for your brother?"

"Charlotte, I dare not. I could not bear his rage," the princess cried, nearly upsetting the tumbler in her hand.

"Shhh," Charlotte soothed. "Pray calm yourself. If you could only trust me, tell me what has happened. Perhaps I could help you."

"You would help me?"

"If it were humanly possible, yes," Charlotte insisted vehemently. "Can you doubt it?"

"Yes, I suppose you would. Oh, I am too upset to judge aright. You must hear my story, dear friend, and help me if you can, and pray do not judge me too harshly," she cried, imploring Charlotte. "Where to begin? When I was a girl of eighteen or twenty perhaps, young and alive and eager for love, dreaming of a handsome prince or duke or king for my very own. We, my sisters and I, all chafed under the rigidity of our upbringing, all dreamt of being away from court, in lives of our own, with lovers—husbands—homes and children of our own. But Papa, always to be pampered and placated lest the least trouble send him back into his recurring madness, would not hear of any of us marrying.

"We were bound in by rules and hemmed round by waiting ladies who were no better than spies, kept from the company of young men of our own ages—even from the company of our brothers, mind. We were linked to Mama by the chains of her chatelaine like a scissors or thimble or the household keys. It was hell to us, and some of us managed to rebel in our own ways.

"*I* rebelled. I fell in love; I had long been in love, head and heart in love, with the kind of infatuation that only a passionate girl, sheltered beyond all reason, can conceive for a forbidden and unlikely lover. I had, for want of any other opportunities, I suppose, fastened upon one man at court and had adored him from afar for years—all the years of my adolescence. He was my adored and secret hero. You, of all people, can understand that, I think. You who write so eloquently of ladies and heroes, Charlotte," Sophia said, breaking off her monologue and looking to her companion with pleading eyes.

"I do understand, Your Highness. Pray go on."

"In 1798 I took courage and spoke—dared to speak of my love, my adoration, and my—my passion. He was not—is not—to blame, Charlotte. Do not think that. He was a dear, good man, noble and honest—but lonely and so human. It was not his fault if he fell prey to the earnest seductions of the wild and willful young woman that I was in those days. *I* wooed, *I* cajoled, and at last, in spite of all his fears and reservations, I won my lover to my bed."

"Your Highness," Charlotte whispered.

"Do I shock you? Yes, I suppose I must, but then remember, *you* are free to be proper—to accept or reject a suitor as you will. I was a girl in prison. My only chance for life and happiness was to find comfort in the arms of one of my gaolers—and that is what I did. But idylls—especially stolen ones—do not last long, and the price we pay for them is great indeed."

Sophia fell silent for a moment, looking deep into Charlotte's large, earnest eyes, which, in her shock and surprise, had not left the princess's face. Even in the faint light of the two flickering candles Charlotte could see the expression of irony and almost cynical worldliness creep over her companion's pale face.

"The price of my sin was the child I discovered soon enough that I would bear. My lover wished to marry me, and I could have been glad of the marriage and a modest home away from court, but . . . but they did not dare tell my father, who was older, sicker, and closer to madness than ever before. Without his consent, under the Royal Marriages Act, no wedding of mine would be legal, no child of mine legitimate. Yet, those considerations aside, my lover was not considered a suitable match for a princess of England. Fah, how I hate being a *princess of England!*" she cried out bitterly, checking her voice even as she spoke, lowering her tone again as she went on. "You know, of course, all Europe knows, that of all my parents' numerous sons, only one—the prince regent himself—has contracted a legal marriage, and poor George's is a farcical one at best. Of all my father's many grandchildren, only one is not a bastard: my niece Princess Charlotte of Wales, who will one day be queen over us, God willing.

"By the early summer of 1800 I was nearing my time. I was sent to Weymouth for the confinement. My health had never been robust, so it aroused no suspicion that I should retire to Gloucester House for my health—ostensibly to take the waters. While there, I was married secretly in the little Puddlestown Church—a marriage for my honour's sake and that of my lover, a declaration, if you will, of our desire to be man and wife in spite of the world's preventing us. Though it may not have been a marriage in the eyes of the law, it was a true marriage in the sight of God. Since that day I have broken none of the vows I made then, nor will to the end of my days." She sighed. "I am a wife without a husband, a mother without a child. The boy was born that August, and hardly had he been born but he—he was taken from me. For my own good, they said, and I partly agreed, then. I was young, frightened, and in trouble, with no disinterested

203

and wise friend to advise me of what was good for *me*. So I gave him up—gave up the only thing in this world that was *mine*." The bitterness and ferocity of the princess Sophia's self-loathing were terrible to behold.

"You did what you had to do. As you have said, you were not free to choose," Charlotte reminded her gently.

"He is a handsome boy, is he not?" Sophia asked suddenly. "He is beautiful, my son, Thomas, isn't he?"

Charlotte's mouth dropped open. Of course! Oh, what a fool she had been. "Yes, Your Highness," she answered when at last she recovered her wits and composure. "Your son, Master Thomas, is indeed handsome, fine and strong and well spoken," she added, her mind going back to that morning on the beach near the Green Bull Inn. He had been well spoken right enough —to the point of circumspection, in fact. "You must be very proud of him," she added to be kind.

"Yes, in those small ways that I can be, who see him so seldom. He is called Thomas Garth after his father, and he is kept by his father for much of the time. His good, loyal father . . ." she murmured warmly.

"Is he? I—I see," Charlotte asked, vaguely disconcerted. "Is the old gentleman whom I met this morning his grandfather then? General Garth, I believe."

"No, Charlotte," Sophy said, shaking her head sadly. "General Garth is his father. It is General Garth who was my lover and who is my husband in God's eyes, if not in England's," she added, trying to smile through blurred, teary eyes.

"I know what you are thinking, dear friend. I cannot explain it, but I really did love him wildly. Some could not believe my attachment even then—which gave rise to certain ugly rumours. . . . But that does not bear repeating. My sister Mary rather cruelly dubbed General Garth my 'Purple Light of Love,' and everyone who knew of my feelings for him ridiculed us behind our backs. I never cared. He was dear and good and kindly to me. Perhaps it was *because* he was so ugly, because others turned away from him . . ."

"It made him more especially yours in a way," Charlotte

broke in quietly, trying to understand for her own sake as well as Sophy's just why this onetime beauty had so loved the beast. *"You* saw beneath the purple mask to the man it hid, and he, in his turn, loved you for loving him, in spite of his ugliness. Desdemona to General Garth's Othello perhaps?" she suggested gently, thinking of another Othello.

"And my mother the Iago who drove us apart," Sophia added darkly. "We were never alone again, as man and wife or even as parents of a son. . . . Not until this summer have I dared see him alone or have the boy to myself at all. Now, thanks to Parliament, I have a pittance of my own, my father is beyond all help or hurt from me, and my brother is regent, powerful enough to fight for me against my mother's tyranny. This summer all these circumstances have come together and freed me, or so I was fool enough to think, so that I have been able to see General Garth and my son for more than mere minutes at a time. I have been with them for whole hours on end. It has been wonderful!" she paused. "But now I must send him away."

"Send him away?"

"Yes, I shall see him for the last time tomor— This morning actually," she amended, glancing at the small mantel clock, which read twenty past one in the morning. "General Garth shall stay on in the neighbourhood, but my son and his governor shall return to Garth House at Ilsington until it is time for school. He is to be educated for the army like his father and grandfather. I shall not see him often after that. In no time he shall be a man," Sophia remarked with a mournful bowing of her head, "and quite lost to me, I expect."

"He shan't forget you. He shall always love his mother, I am sure," Charlotte said with a comforting pat on the hand.

"He does not know that I am his mother. He thinks that she is dead and that General Garth sees me only as he does the other members of the royal family, out of duty, loyalty, and sentiment, for old times shared at court. He thinks that I dote on him and spoil him because I am an eccentric, lonely, invalid lady who loves children and has none of her own. He does not know that it is only one child—one *son*—whom I love.

"When you saw that portrait of Ernest in the hall and described the child you saw on the beach, I knew at once it was my son of whom you spoke. He has been in the neighbourhood all summer, staying with his father at the seat of some discreet and good friends. Each morning the boy visits with me here.

"He is such a bright child and as handsome as were my brothers in their boyhood, but oh, how much better it would have been were he like his father in face and form. His eyes are like mine and Ernest's. He is fair like us. You saw the startling, unmistakable resemblance he bears to our family, and as you did, others have as well." Sophia lapsed into a momentary reverie, and then, staring into the dregs at the bottom of her tumbler, she went on in a different tone. "I am being blackmailed, Charlotte. Someone has got hold of letters of mine referring to Thomas. They mean to publish them if I do not pay a sum of money."

Charlotte Hungerford's stomach turned over and twisted into a knot. Scandal, ruin. These had not been idle words of Sophia's after all.

"I have turned this room upside down just now, before you came in, looking for my letters, praying that they were just mislaid, but—"

"They are gone?"

"Gone, and left in their place," she said, groping in the pocket of her nightdress for a piece of cheap paper, folded but not sealed. "Read this," she ordered, handing the paper to Charlotte, who snatched it unceremoniously and rose to stand by the candles on the desk in order to read it. "And remember it is a base, base lie, my dear friend. The part, I mean, about my brother Ernest." There was a strangled, wavering note in her voice as she spoke.

"All blackmailers are liars, Your Highness, by their very nature. I shall give no credence to anything I read here," Charlotte replied as her eyes scanned the clumsily written letter.

Princess Sophia, you have a bastard son by your own brother Cumberland and the world will know if letters I hold from him to you be publish. Save yourself. Bring money and jewels—all you have—to the hollow barrel buried by Southwick road. Wait from three tomorrow until a messenger come. Be alone or you will be ruined and your evil brother, hateful Cumberland, also. The English throne will rock.

Avenger

Charlotte took her time reading and rereading it carefully while Sophia, still upon the chaise, fidgeted in impatient, fearful silence. "What do you think?" she asked at last.

"What do I think?" Charlotte fairly shouted, and then, catching herself, went on in a whisper, "I think that this is the vilest, the meanest libel, the most traitorous piece of evil knavery I have ever beheld. It infuriates me."

As if she knew what Charlotte dared not ask, Sophia spoke up, though clearly it was painful for her to do so. "At the time my son was born, there was a gross and calumnious rumour circulating to the effect that poor Garth was not my lover, not Thomas's father, but merely a stalking-horse for the real lover—the real father. They dared imply that Ernest, my brother, was that lover. It was ludicrous and vile, of course, but our own affection for each other and my mother's idea that he was bad company for me served to add fuel to the rumour. She had the idea he was helping me to my transgressions, and so she forbade him all access to me. By doing so, she made our closeness seem to be more than it was. Who forbids a sister to see her own brother—unless . . . You see?"

"I see."

"Then, too, by all reasonable standards, Garth was so old and so ugly. Ernest was young, dashing, and handsome. So the rumour circulated and died—or so I had hoped. Now, with my father mad and George only newly on the throne as regent . . . We cannot afford this scandal—and Ernest! To be accused of such a thing only two years after he has been accused (and cleared, thank God!) of murdering his valet. It would ruin him forever in England, and he might never reach the throne of Hanover."

Charlotte had been listening, but through it all her mind had been bent on what to do, not what had already been done. "Tell me," she said abruptly, "do you know this place? Where this buried barrel lies?"

"Oh, yes," Sophia replied almost eagerly, as if relieved by the simplicity of the query. "It is a well-known wonder of the beach at Southwick—a huge oaken hogshead barrel washed ashore from some shipwreck long ago and, by its half-buried position amongst the rocks on the beach, forming a cave of sorts. It is partly underwater when the tide is high, but quite dry underfoot when it is out. Thomas played a game of hide-and-seek in it with General Garth and me one morning a few weeks ago when I had just arrived at Hove."

"Did he?" Charlotte asked absently, her eyes tracing over and over the wording of the blackmail letter in her hand. "So the place is well known, and the blackmailer, if he had chanced to see you there, would be sure that you knew it, too. It says to come alone. Do you ever go out alone?" she asked in surprise, so used to thinking of the princess Sophia in terms of invalidism.

"Occasionally, in my pony trap. I was at that place in my trap, in fact. I had arranged with General Garth to meet him and the boy there as if by accident. It was from that meeting, arranged for the boy's benefit, that we came to exchange visits here.

"Charlotte, what shall I do? I have no money, hardly any at all—and very little of it here. As for jewels, why, they are mere trinkets and of no great value at all, save to me in my pitiable sentimentality. I do not have nearly enough to buy back those letters. I am sure of it."

"No set sum is mentioned, Your Highness, nor, for that matter, is the prospect of buying them back. You may be asked to buy silence only, a delay in publication perhaps, and not the letters themselves. I cannot tell exactly what is implied, for the wording is hasty and lacking in clear thinking . . . *haste,*" Charlotte muttered thoughtfully to herself.

"Not get back the letters? Oh, Charlotte, that is worse yet.

I—I did not see the import," Sophia cried, becoming agitated all over again. "I never dreamt, but the way that the threat is worded—it is possible. . . . Oh, I should have burnt them."

"Shhh, pray be calm, Your Highness. I must think if I am to help," Charlotte urged. Sitting down to the princess's desk, she laid the letter out and started to make some notes upon a piece of letter paper.

"What are you doing?"

"Jotting down some questions that occur to me. Are you very tired, Your Highness, or do you think you can answer some questions for me in a while?"

"Questions? What questions?" she asked in renewed alarm.

"Your Highness," Charlotte said with a slightly petulant edge to her voice, "if I am to help you to get to the bottom of this—"

"Get to the bottom? How? I must find some money and pay," Sophia asked in bewilderment. "Perhaps General Garth . . ."

"Nonsense. You shall not pay a bent farthing nor so much as a glass bead for your own letters. I shall take your place tomorrow at three o'clock and retrieve them for you; retrieve your letters and your honour—and catch the traitorous scoundrel into the bargain."

"Oh, Charlotte, no," Sophia whispered urgently, one hand raised to her mouth in horror.

"Oh, Charlotte, *yes*," Charlotte Hungerford replied angrily, not lifting her eyes from the desk where she sat, pen in hand, the nib flying over the paper, stopping in its hasty scrawling only for an occasional dip in the inkpot.

"It is too dangerous."

"Dangerous, fah! This 'Avenger,' so called, may be a scoundrel, but he seems a rank amateur as a blackmailer—and not too inspired a one at that. Moreover, he did not realize that he would be dealing with *me*. Do you remember when Rowena discovers the—"

"Charlotte, this is not a novel. This is real life," Sophy pleaded, more alarmed than ever.

"So it is, Your Highness," she agreed. "This is the very first chance I have ever had to do what my heroines do—bring to heel a genuine villain—and I aim to do it, Your Highness, I aim to do it," she added with a thump of her foot on the carpet beneath the desk.

"Or die trying? Isn't that the way such declarations usually end?"

"No," Charlotte snapped. "Only in novels where the writer knows she's going to be killing off the character in the next chapter or two and wants to give him intimations of his own mortality. I have no intention of dying, no intimations of mortality, and no doubt of success. Your Highness, you have no occupation whilst I write. Why not set this room in order so that your ladies and servants are not upset in the morning?" she suggested, unmindful of the impropriety of suggesting such a labour to a royal.

"Oh, oh, yes," Sophia cried in a rather dithery little voice. "You are quite right. It would never do to leave it like this, would it?" With that, she set about to put in order the papers, books, and cushions that she had scattered in her wild and fruitless search for her stolen letters. The small, homey acts involved in setting the room to rights served to relax her, and she worked in a silence which gave Charlotte time to formulate her ideas on paper, in much the same way that she plotted the vicissitudes and triumphs of her beloved heroines.

"Now, at last." She smiled, sighing in satisfaction, casting about the room with a wicked gleam in her eye. "I shall remove to the chaise, Your Highness, and let you take my place at the desk. Whilst you straighten its contents again, I shall ask you some questions."

"As you wish, my dear. I am entirely in your hands."

"Only til we get the letters back, my dear Princess Sophia, and then you are in your own hands again." Charlotte smiled reassuringly, aware for the first time just how high-handed she had been these few minutes past, but starting her interrogation nonetheless.

"Question one . . ."

::12::

While the morning had given brief promise of bringing in its wake a sunny summer afternoon, the noon hour saw a heavy mist roll in off the Channel waters, turning the sky to lead and giving a dank, sodden look to every rock and tree trunk. The temperature, moreover, remained high, making the day increasingly sultry and unbearable. Every creature, from the birds in the trees to the horses in their stalls, shifted from foot to foot with a restlessness that betokened a storm in the offing.

The swift and nasty change in the atmosphere had made Charlotte sullen and irritable. Her mood did not begin to change until she had finally sprung to some sort of action, even if it was only the donning of the same sprigged green muslin dress that Princess Sophia had worn to breakfast with her son that morning.

"Does it fit?" Sophia asked from her perch on Charlotte's bed as the girl emerged from the dressing room, still doing up the laces at her back.

"A wee bit tight, but not too much so. I can still breathe, if that is what you mean." She smiled, a glow of determination in her eyes. At last she was getting on with it.

"We are both wearing patent leather slippers—good enough," she stated. "Now, did you bring a bonnet?"

"Here it is. It suits the dress, I think," Sophia said tentatively, handing a rather dowdy-looking cream-coloured Milan bonnet to Charlotte. It was high-crowned and wide of brim, all tied up with green satin ruching, furbelows, and plumes—of all things! It was so out of fashion—the sort of hat to make Charlotte

211

weep—but still, she was meant to be no fashion plate, but rather an *actress* bent on creating an illusion, the illusion from a distance, at least, that she was the princess Sophia herself. And Princess Sophia—more's the pity—would wear just such a bonnet as this.

She clamped it down upon her head and looked at her image in the mirror. Ghastly, but what the devil! It was only a charade after all. "Have you any more ribbon perchance?" she asked.

"Yes. I brought all I had from my room," Sophia answered, handing her several lengths of wide green ribbon.

"Perfect," Charlotte exclaimed, snatching the longest piece, centring it across the high crown of the hat, and bringing the ends down under her chin so that the sides of the brim hugged close to her cheeks, thus obscuring much of her face. She tied the ends in a large bow under the right side of her jaw, obtaining at once a more fashionable effect and also hiding her features as well. She tucked her chestnut curls up into the hat and looked at the effect with a critical eye. Decidedly unpretty and still not convincing enough to pass for the princess.

"Your Highness, have you any false curls?"

"Some," Sophia answered reluctantly, as if loath to admit so much vanity entered into her modest makeup. "A fringe, too," she added, as if throwing discretion to the winds.

"May I have them? And some pins?"

"At once," Sophia rejoined and went to fetch them.

In five minutes' time, by powdering her face and neck to make them pale and by tucking the blond false curls and fringe under the brim of the bonnet, Charlotte had artfully become a double of the princess. It was only upon closer inspection that one saw the amber eyes in place of blue, the full, buxom figure in place of the thinner, frailer one, the robust stride exchanged for the slower, less certain one.

"It will pass nicely from a distance, do you not think?" Charlotte asked with a certain smugness as they stood side by side before the glass.

"I expect it will, Charlotte. You really are a marvel," Sophia agreed with a smile. It was almost like some girlish game rather than a deadly earnest ruse to thwart a terrible threat to her honour and her family.

"Perhaps we can give a masked ball together one day and go as twins." Charlotte laughed lightly. "But now the casket that I asked for," she added with a sudden down-to-business air.

"Will this do?" the princess asked, carrying from the bedside table a coffer-shaped box of polished inlaid woods set with small gilt-bronze feet and trimmings of ormolu along its edges and over the keyhole.

"It should do nicely. It looks as if it were designed to hold valuables, and it is big enough to look as if its contents were ample. What have you put into it?" she added, hefting its considerable weight.

"Some bent old silver from the kitchen—the kitchen girls thought I was mad to ask for such stuff—but it is heavy and clinks promisingly when the box is shaken. On top I have put some strings of rather good artificial pearls and a packet bound up in strings with the corner of a banknote partly visible, as if it were tied in haste. Is that enough, do you think?"

"It should do quite nicely, and now, for added bait . . ." Charlotte said, pinning to the front of her dress a large gold brooch that had belonged to her mother and sliding on her finger a ring as well. "I shall wear these things to make the lout think there must be real finery in the box if I wear these pieces so casually. It will be a further distraction."

"Oh, Charlotte, do not risk . . ."

"I risk nothing. I am smarter than this Avenger," she broke in with some hauteur. "He is, as I have said, an amateur."

"But dangerous perhaps," Sophia rejoined, her misgivings increasing as the hour for departure drew nigh.

"Perhaps." Charlotte shrugged, adjusting her shawl and taking the little casket under her arm. "But I think not. Is the pony trap ready for me?"

"Yes, waiting at the near end of the stables, just as you asked."

"Then, Your Highness, I am off upon my adventure in the service of my princess. Wish me luck." She smiled, curtseying and winking one eye mischievously as she slipped out of the bedroom and headed down the backstairs out toward the waiting trap.

Princess Sophia, torn between Charlotte's joy at the lark of the adventure before her and her own fears of mischance, sighed deeply and sank down upon her knees to pray.

Sir Hannibal Cheng had spent a fitful night in a too short, too wide bed at the Green Bull Inn, thinking of Charlotte Hungerford and berating himself for his foolish, ungentlemanly, and bibulous behaviour—though, to be sure, he did rather regret not having had a go at thwackin' her pretty bottom for her.

It had been dawn when he had finally fallen asleep, and he had slept deeply indeed, resisting all efforts of his two companions to rouse him from his slumbers the following morning. In fact, sometime just before noon they had given up, and after paying their own bill, they had left a note for Sir Hannibal and hastened off to partake of the pleasures of Brighton; Cumberland was satisfied that he had left his melancholy sister in the safe and distracting company of the little scribbler, and Bucky was happy in the thought of the devilment he could raise in Brighton without his aunt Charlotte's watchful "Wooton-Maggot" eye overseeing his every peccadillo. In fact, he heartily hoped she'd stay the week at Hove, knowing what a mood she'd be in after her fateful row with the Chinee baronet.

When Sir Hannibal did finally rouse himself, he felt surprisingly wonderful, rested and suddenly full of purpose. He breakfasted heartily on eggs, bacon, and hot coffee by the mugful, glad to learn from Cumberland's message that he had been abandoned to his own devices. That was just as well—saved explanations for a start—he decided with satisfaction as he looked out upon the broad, sodden beach and leaden gray sky against which flocks of sea gulls wheeled and shrieked like harpies.

After dwelling long over his estimable meal and browsing through the Brighton papers at his leisure, he returned to his rooms, where he made a very careful job of his ablutions, shaving his handsome face to a nicety and seeing to the winding and tying of his stock as if it were a work of art. His hair alone took much of his time, and only when it had been brushed and pomaded to perfection did he step back from the glass and admire the full effect of his elegant good looks.

"Yes, perfect," he muttered with confidence. "Just about as perfect-lookin' as a funny-faced half Chinee of a feller could possibly look." He grinned back at his image, and it was not so much a smug verdict on his part as a true and honest one. Had he looked terrible, he would have admitted that, too.

Humming something to himself about "Froggy would awooing go," he ordered his horse brought round and settled his bill with the innkeeper.

As everyone in the Green Bull Inn noted with no little curiosity, there was a decided gleam in the long black eyes of the redoubtable and undoubtedly peculiar Chinee baronet.

Charlotte's destination was easily found. About half an hour's ride along the coast road between Hove and the village of Southwick, at a place where the bleak shore sloped down to a series of rockbound coves, an immense hogshead lay upon its side in the sand.

Originally it had been wedged in the rocks at the edge of the littoral, but gradually wet sand had packed around it and in it, anchoring it as firmly in its place as if it were one of the great black boulders amongst which it rested. It was dank and waterlogged; the swollen staves of its base and lower sides were tinged green with moss, those of the top bleached silver-white by the sun and stained with the chalky droppings of gulls.

"No small wine cask, this, but a molasses cask of fully a hundred gallons," Charlotte murmured to herself as she approached the open end, which faced straight out to sea on only the slightest angle toward the direction of Southwick. It was sound enough, the hoops still ringing the staves firmly, the wet-packed sand within giving it a solid, slightly sloping floor upon which to stand.

Charlotte slipped into its cavelike interior and set down her burden, the little wooden casket and a long, rather heavy carriage whip, both of which she placed in the shadows behind her.

As she stood up again, she saw her footprints clearly embedded in the sand at her feet. A line of them was visible, extending from the soft sand of the upper beach right down to the barrel. Whoever comes will be aware of my presence at once, and I shall have no element of surprise on my side, but then what matters that after all? she concluded. At least he shall be sure I have come alone, and that is something, for it may cause him to drop his guard a trifle.

Nervous, impatient to be on with things, oppressed by the humid, stifling atmosphere, Charlotte shifted from foot to foot and finally withdrew her little silver pocket watch. Nearly ten minutes to three. She was early. She replaced the watch and set about the last of her tasks.

With the shaft of the whip she dug a pit and buried the box so that its lid was just barely visible—bait, to be seen but not touched until she was ready to make her getaway. That accomplished, she looped the whip up in her waist, hiding it with her shawl. It might not be the most potent of weapons, but after all, she hardly expected to have to enter into a barefists fight like Tom Cribb and the others of that ilk that men loved to bet upon. The "Avenger," as he chose to style himself, was no wild highwayman, but merely an impecunious, opportunistic, and scurvy-minded young knave of a governor who was clever enough to have put two and two together and got the right answer.

The minute she had read the letter she had known. There was no mystery there. How stupid could he have been? Mark how he had given himself away. *Sofia! Sofia* indeed! Who but a foreigner would misspell an English princess's name like that? And his English was utterly vile; such a want of proper tenses. The man actually dared call himself a tutor! Charlotte grumped, waxing indignant at the very thought. Why, old General Garth must be in his dotage to have hired such a man—or else he really does not care a fig for the boy's upbringing.

She came out of her reverie and, stamping her foot in impatience, took out her watch again. Twenty-five past three and still no Mr. Sellis. How slowly time was creeping by. Her feet were cold, the soles of her slippers wet through from standing on the damp sand, and the wind, blowing off the sea, was rising for a storm, sending first tendrils and then clouds of sopping mist in off the water. The tide had turned as well. In less than an hour the waves would be lapping at her very toes. Damn the fellow to perdition! Would he never come?

Just then, as if in answer to her unspoken, irritable questioning, there was a rumble of carriage wheels and the flinty sound of hooves upon the road above the beach. The "Avenger," it seemed, had come at last. . . .

A smart-eyed stableboy, knowing the Chinee baronet to be free with his gratuities, came running up to Sir Hannibal Cheng as he reined in his horse before the princess Sophia's doors.

"See to the horse, lad, but don't unsaddle him yet. I may not be welcome to stay," Cheng instructed, calling over his shoulder as he leapt up the front steps and brushed past a manservant just as he opened the door. "Where is Her Highness?" he asked merrily.

"Charlotte, Charlotte, oh, thank God you are back—oh, oh," Sophia fairly squealed in dismay. "Sir Hannibal, it is you," she said lamely, having emerged from the drawing room in a frenzy. Now, seeing it was not Charlotte who had arrived, but Sir Hannibal, she slunk back into the shadows of the hall, seeming to shrink before the very eyes of the baronet.

"It is indeed, Your Highness," he answered, alarm in his black eyes, two spots of high colour rushing to his tawny cheeks as he saw the princess so distraught. He pushed her backwards into the drawing room quite without ceremony and closed the door behind them.

"What is it?" he snapped. "What is going on here? Where is Charlotte?"

"Oh, Sir Hannibal," Sophia cried in vexation and mounting anxiety. "I heard your horse in the drive and thought that it must be she. I—oh!" She started as suddenly as if she had been shot when the clock on the mantel chimed the quarter hour. "After three, already. She—she should be back at any minute, I expect.

Oh, Sir Hannibal, dear Sir Hannibal, I have been beside myself this past hour and more."

"I can see that well enough," Sir Hannibal commented dryly. "Now suppose you tell me just what is going on, Your Highness." His tone was icy, his manner reserved, more out of concern for getting to the bottom of things than annoyance with her inarticulate female ravings. They were to be expected, he supposed, under any even mildly unusual circumstances. "Where is Charlotte, for a start?"

"She—she is saving me, saving my reputation from ruin," Sophia lamented with a wringing of her thin white hands. "I should never have allowed it."

"Allowed what?" Hannibal Cheng shouted, truly alarmed now by the state of the princess Sophia and deeply afraid for Charlotte, though he had no idea as yet why he should be.

"I—I." She hesitated. "Here, read this," she said at last, after fumbling with the papers on her writing desk and finally thrusting both the blackmail note and the page of scribbled notes that Charlotte had made the previous night into Sir Hannibal's hands.

He strode to the back window and by the gray afternoon light read the note signed "Avenger." When he had done so twice, he looked up sharply at Sophia, who dared not return his angry glare. He said nothing, however, but instead read over the hastily scrawled questions which Charlotte had put to Sophia the night before and her even more hastily scribbled answers.

Three words leapt out in a peculiar and arresting conjunction: "tutor," "Sellis," and "guv'nor." Two evoked suspicion; the third, "Sellis," was a heart stopper.

"She has gone to get back your letters?" he asked with an almost inhuman calm under the circumstances.

Sophia nodded forlornly.

"What money and jewels had you? You are not well fixed, I think, and have not much in the way of valuables with you here at Hove to begin with?" Still, the voice was deadly calm. That alone was enough to frighten Sophia. She told him about the box.

"Oh, Sir Hannibal, I should not have let her go!"

"No, you should not," he replied coldly, a chill of fear stealing over his heart.

"But I did not know what to do, and she—she seemed so sure—so very sure."

"Yes." He smiled to himself. "She would do that." A pain stabbed through his heart as he thought of her, and he ached to know she was safe. "You should have sent for me," he growled furiously, turning on Sophia in his sense of concern and anger, "if not for Ernest. I can understand you leaving him out. He's a hothead and would have killed the man, but I—I am always at your service as I am at his. You should have known it and sent for me. Why, by God, you even knew that I was still in the neighbourhood, damn it. I told your man when we were sent packing that we'd be puttin' up at the Green Bull Inn. Damn it, Sophia—but never mind. Who is this guv'nor or tutor she mentions? What's that all about?"

"I—I don't know. I suppose she must refer to Thomas's governor whom General Garth hired this spring. He took the boy back to Islington this very morning."

"Did he? And what's his name?"

"I—I do not know. I never thought to ask, and I've never met the man. I have seen him only from a distance."

"And?"

"And?"

"His looks, woman," Cheng snapped impatiently. "What does he look like?"

"Why, he—he's small of stature, perhaps thirty, I should say. Dark and slender. A foreigner, I think, by his complexion."

"Sellis!" Cheng cried, a look of fury crossing his face. "Damn it, the man had a brother somewhere. We knew it at the time but could never find him. 'Avenger.' Yes, 'Avenger' indeed. But how came Charlotte to know his identity?" he pondered.

"His identity? Sir Hannibal, do you really know who this person is?"

"Charlotte evidently thinks she does, and if she is right—which I have little cause to doubt—then this is a far deeper business than you have dreamt. Ruin you, you say! Why, my dear Princess, forgive me for saying it, but ruining you is merely the icing on the cake—totally incidental to the ruin he really intends: the ruin of your brother the Duke of Cumberland and, if he can accomplish it as well, the downfall of the whole royal house.

"Charlotte, bless her darling, brave heart, is playing at heroine right now and does not dream just how deep she has got herself in! If the man is an amateur of blackmail as she supposes—and in a sense he is, I grant her—he is a vicious and vengeful amateur, and a Corsican one to boot! We British have no reason to love Corsicans, have we, given what has been going on over the water these few years past, eh?"

"Corsican?" Sophia repeated dumbly.

"Yes, a Corsican with a blood vendetta against your brother. The man is Anthony Sellis! He is the brother of Joseph Sellis, Ernest's valet who went mad and attacked him in the night. When he could not kill Ernest, he slit his own throat—a very Corsican thing to do, I believe. After all the vile things that were attributed to Ernest and that man, can you imagine what would be made of letters between the two of you that even hinted at an illicit affair? The consequences are not even to be thought upon."

"Charlotte never said a word to me of who he might be."

"She may know who he is—that is, realize he's Thomas's tutor—but she may not connect him with the valet's death two years ago. She may not even know very much about that, in fact. How far is it to this place?" he asked, suddenly changing the subject and lowering his voice, which had become something of a roar as his agitation mounted.

"Half an hour's ride by trap. Less on horseback, I expect. She was to be there by three, but she left much earlier to allow for finding it. She should be back . . ."

"God help me, I hope you are right and I meet her returning on the road, but I am afraid I may even now be late," Cheng said, bounding across the room with a glance at the clock. "Nearing the half hour already. I am off, Your Highness. *You* stay here and pray, for pity's sake. Pray like a madwoman that I am not too late."

He was out the door in a flash, slamming it behind him with such force that the bric-a-brac rattled on the mantel. The clock struck three thirty just then, and out in the court Sir Hannibal could be heard shouting for his horse.

"Dear merciful heaven, what have I done?" Sophia wailed, dissolving into tears and falling upon her chaise. She began to cough in such a fit as she had not had in months. Dear God, Charlotte—Charlotte. If she was in danger . . .

The lather from Regimental's straining neck flew back in little white flecks against Sir Hannibal's black jacket and tense, taut face as he urged the horse along the shore road to Southwick at a headlong pace. From somewhere just ahead, around one of the many bends in the road, he heard a faint scream and an even fainter oath in a foreign tongue. He had found them at last.

Rounding the bend, he came upon an unusual scene. Halfway down the broad beach of a wide, curving cove, the incoming tide just beginning to lap at its entrance, lay the huge hogshead which had been appointed as the place of assignation. The action had shifted however, for farther up the strand toward the road two small figures grappled frantically, both of them slipping clumsily and with almost comic effect in the soft sand beneath their feet. The one was a lady in green muslin, her face partially obscured by a milan bonnet which had been knocked somewhat askew by the scuffle, but nonetheless instantly recognizable to Sir Hannibal by her slim, full-bosomed figure as Charlotte Hungerford.

The man, he could see, was dressed in a shabby brown jacket and trousers, his linen yellowing and unstarched to begin with, but now much torn and pulled about in front by his furious, if ineffective, adversary. He was small, dark, and like enough to the late, demented, and unlamented valet Joseph Sellis to confirm Sir Hannibal's worst suspicions. It was the brother all right.

Unaware that the tutor's own coach waited just beyond a rocky outcropping farther along the road, Sir Hannibal reined in Regimental beside Charlotte's loosely tethered pony trap, dismounted, and ran full tilt out onto the beach, where he promptly fell afoul of the uncertain ground under him and lost his footing.

With an oath, he staggered to his feet and began to run, slowed by sand, rocks, and debris, along the quarter of a mile of beach that separated him from his goal.

By now Sellis had Charlotte by the left wrist and was groping with his left hand toward the bodice of her frock, intent, or so it seemed to Cheng, upon the gold brooch she wore. Charlotte was breathlessly hurtling choice expletives and oaths as wildly as was Sellis himself, save that his were in some unintelligible Corsican dialect and hers in the clearest, most time-honoured Anglo-Saxon English. They carried downwind to Sir Hannibal with bell-like clarity, and despite everything, he could not help but grin at the admirable string of invective coming from the demure lips of his ladylove. Gad, but she was a wench to be reckoned with!

Anthony Sellis had arrived at the cove at a quarter past three, leaving his unwitting master's coach in other hands where it would not be seen. He had walked the rest of the way, cutting across the sand warily until he caught sight of the small single track of lady's footprints far down the beach in the band of damp sand that surrounded the half-buried cask. She must be there already—the sister, Sofia—whose bastard son he tutored. He didn't know or really even care who the boy's father was. What did matter was that the boy was Sofia of England's and that he looked like the Duke of Cumberland as a child. It was a fact, and with these letters tucked so securely in his breast pocket, he had the means to get back at the duke and at all of them—all the royal libertines of this accursed, cold country.

He shivered in the thickening mist and thought of the warm Mediterranean. Damn this country, he thought bitterly. If it were not for that naïve old fool, General Garth, who had a good heart and too little love of Cumberland for his own good, why, he'd still be starving in some rat-infested room in London, unable to find work, hounded by Cumberland's friends, his life ruined and his brother dead. Curse them all. He'd show them. He'd bleed them dry—first this princess here—and when he had all she could give, which was precious little from what the boy

222

had seen in the house, why then, he'd be ready to start on the mighty Duke Ernest himself.

Still, that was far off, for Cumberland was too formidable a lion to beard just yet; he'd have to have money and a better position—which this first effort would help secure—and then he would be able to buy influence and gain the ears of the rich and the powerful. God knew, there were enough such men in England—and no small number of them who had reason to hate Cumberland as much as he did himself. Yes, Anthony Sellis smiled as he approached the hogshead and the waiting princess, he'd avenge his brother's death and bring down the mighty Duke of Cumberland into the bargain.

"Princess Sofia," Sellis called out in a low voice as he arrived at the sodden cask, "have you brought what I asked?" His dark eyes narrowed in greedy expectation as he spoke.

"Are you the man who signs himself 'Avenger,' sir?" came a low, husky voice from the shadowy recesses of the great echoing barrel.

"I am, Your Highness," he said with a wry grin and a mocking bow. "Are you alone?" he asked rather superfluously since no other footprints but his and the lady's were visible anywhere along the beach.

"Obviously, sir, since I hardly wish to broadcast my shame," the woman in the shadows muttered bitterly.

"Where is my money?" he asked, stepping squarely across the opening of the hogshead, arms akimbo in a commanding stance before the shadowy figure of the princess, who, he noted idly, wore the same green frock he had seen her in that morning together with the addition of a milan bonnet from his own part of the world. He smirked at her nastily, thinking what a fool she was and how easily ordered about. His thought was shattered by her next utterance.

"Why, you shabby, shabby little man! Your linen is filthy," she returned in just such a cold and contemptuous voice as one might associate with a certain species of royal lady (though never with the real Princess Sophia, who was far too kind). "How dare you come into the presence of a lady and a princess of the blood in such rags?" With that, the lady in the green muslin frock and milan bonnet stepped forward quite unexpectedly, pushing him away from her with the flat of her hand against his thin chest.

He was taller than she, but slight—so fine-boned as to be almost birdlike—and the sudden thrust caused him to lose balance. He was several feet back before he caught himself and stopped, digging his heels into the wet sand, unmindful in his surprise, of the tide lapping at the uppers of his worn, buckle-fronted brogues.

Charlotte, taking advantage of his momentary stumble, stepped out of the cask and took a few steps up the beach toward the road. She kept her head to one side, wishing to keep up her pretense as long as possible. Her heart was pounding, but she was exhilarated rather than frightened by the adventure. She must only keep her wits til she had accomplished her purpose and fled.

Sellis took a step toward her, angered by what he took to be this imperious princess—this tart with a bastard boy, who dared talk to him so, him with such incriminating and ruinous letters in his coat pocket.

"Stay right where you are," the lady in green commanded. "I may have to deal with you for my sins, you scoundrel, but I'm damned if I have to look upon you as well—or smell you! Have you brought the letters?"

"Have you brought the money?" he countered, unconsciously stopping in his tracks as he had been ordered. All well and good. Charlotte smiled inwardly. A servant with a servant's mind, raised in service and bound to obey even when he does not wish to—so long as the voice of authority is firm enough, the air of command all unwavering.

"Never mind what I have brought. *Have you my letters?*"

"I have."

"Prove it! Place them *here*—in my hand." With that, a slim, elegant, ladylike hand was extended toward him sideways with all the suddenness of a striking cobra.

"I—" he stammered, taken aback by her authority and by the unexpectedness of her gesture. He took a step forward.

"Keep your distance, Avenger," the cold voice of the lady

warned, one hand fingering the end of the horsewhip hidden in the waist of her dress, the other still thrust sideways toward him. "In my hand as I have ordered."

Scowling, but still aware he had the upper hand, Sellis complied, removing a sheaf of letters from the inner pocket of his shabby brown coat and slapping them without ceremony onto the outstretched palm.

Charlotte snatched them with a trifle too much eagerness. Calm down, she chided herself in annoyance with her own impetuosity. You have him under some control now. Do not upset the balance for pity's sake. She riffled through the envelopes. They were addressed to Sophia right enough, and in the duke's own hand and bearing his seal upon the wax. However . . .

"There are only three letters here," she said flatly, hiding her dismay as best she could.

"The others are quite safe, I can assure you, Your Highness," Sellis said with mocking deference. "May I have them back now, please?"

"Have them back? I should say not," Charlotte retorted, folding the letters and placing them down the bosom of her dress. "Did you think that I came to visit them only? They are mine, and I will keep them. Now hand me the others if you will!"

"My money?"

"When I have reclaimed what is *my* property, *you* shall have what you—" She said no more, having an itch to say, "What you *deserve,*" and thinking the better of it.

"I do not have them on my person, Your Highness," Sellis replied suavely.

"Are they in your coach then? Fetch them here at once, I say," Charlotte snapped and then fell silent, instantly regretting her slip.

Sellis was quick enough to catch it at once. His conveyance was far along the road toward Southwick, behind an outcropping and well out of sight. How could she have known he had arrived in a coach? He was wary now, though still slightly confused.

"How could you—" Then, in alarm, he stepped toward her. "Where is my money?" His voice was ominous now.

Charlotte turned heel and began to make her way along the beach toward her trap, which she saw to her dismay had been dragged farther down the road by the pony, which evidently found the grazing more to his liking in that direction. She looked back over her shoulder at Sellis, still not daring to run lest it arouse him to give chase.

"Where is my money?" he reiterated angrily, starting toward her on the run.

"In the barrel. Find it for yourself, you wretch," she called over her shoulder. Seeing him halt and return to the cask, she began to run with all her might, though by now she was in the soft sand of the upper beach, which slowed her progress considerably. Behind her she heard a cry of triumph as Sellis found his prize. She chanced a look and saw him running across the beach toward the rocks that must conceal the carriage, holding the box before him as he ran.

"I have it," he called out, seemingly to the empty air.

"Wait," answered a high, clear voice, "that lady is not my mother. It is someone else. You have been tricked."

Charlotte stopped in spite of herself and looked back over her shoulder in amazement. "That bloody little beast!" she exclaimed, letting fly a string of oaths that would have had her father spinning in the churchyard had he heard her. "His own mother." With that she began to run all the harder, for Anthony Sellis had stopped by now and was smashing the jewel casket open upon a rock. When he saw that he had been duped with bent forks, glass pearls, and blank paper, he let out a roar and took off after Charlotte like a demon possessed. The boy slunk down behind the rocks, where he had evidently been hidden all along, and watched.

Charlotte ran faster now, sinking into the sand, tripping on her skirts, struggling to free the horsewhip from her waistband and from the tenacious webbing of her long crocheted shawl as she went. The wretched tutor was bearing down on her. She could hear his steps in the sand in spite of the wheezing gasps of her breath and the sound of her own blood pounding in her ears.

It was inevitable. He caught her easily, running as he was in trousers and brogues whilst she struggled along in skirts and patent pumps.

"Damn you," he wheezed through painful breath as he laid a hand upon her shoulder and tried to stop her. "Who are you?" he puffed. "I—I think . . . ? Have we not met . . . ?"

"It does not matter who I am, Mr. Sellis," Charlotte interrupted, turning on him in order to try to regain the element of surprise and to catch her breath for the final run to her trap. "We know who you are."

"We?"

"All of us," she retorted bravely, trying for a last bluff. "The princess, the duke—all . . ."

"You bluff. If you all knew, why, this beach would be swarming with people bent on stopping me. You are a waiting lady to the princess, I suppose, and she has *not* told her brother. He has been after me for two years. If he knew where he could get his hands on me, why—"

"I do not envy you when he does have you in hand, Mr. Sellis," and then, catching at an inspiration, "Throw the rest of the letters out of your coach onto the road and get away before he comes—" she suggested all at once and in a confidential tone, taking the chance that the man would think Cumberland really was somewhere behind them on the road and would choose to obey her.

It was the wrong thing to say, for it only reminded him of the letters that she had already reclaimed. "No one is coming, miss. You are alone here, aren't you? All alone," he said, looking along the road to the distant place where the pony now grazed, dragging his light trap behind him. "That is the princess Sofia's cart, and she sent you alone to save her. Give me back those letters."

"No," Charlotte retorted in a shrill of panic, frightened by the look of craft and menace in Sellis's beady black eyes. She backed away from him, suddenly feeling very small and alone upon that deserted stretch of beach. At least, though, the boy chose to remain where he was. If he joined Sellis, then she had no hope of escaping the two of them.

"Yes, the letters," Sellis insisted. "*Now* or by the saints, I shall have them from you myself," he snarled, lunging at her like a dog. Charlotte screamed.

"You wouldn't dare," she cried out indignantly, one hand to her bosom in fear for the letters and therefore, incidentally, for her honour as well.

"Ha, wouldn't I, my lady?" He leered. He grabbed her by the wrist, and the struggle began in earnest.

While Sellis tried to keep Charlotte at arm's length and still manage to grope for what he wanted from her, she gave several smart kicks to his unbooted and therefore unprotected shins, having to be contented with that portion of his anatomy, though, to be sure, she was in fact aiming somewhat higher. Finally, with one pigletlike squeal of absolute frustration and fury, as the ungentlemanly governor's hand found what it sought, pulling the letters from the bodice of her dress, Charlotte hauled around and swung at his jaw, her small, knotted fist landing what is traditionally referred to as a roundhouse right.

The blow did not knock the rogue down, but it did land squarely enough to make him reel back with unfocused eyes. He let go of her wrist. He clamped his hands to his face to shake his head clear, and as he did, a number of vellum sheets and envelopes went scattering across the upper beach, lodging amongst the rocks and fluttering along the sandy littoral. Wheeling about and hiking up her hem to facilitate a scramble, Charlotte began to collect the letters as best she could, cursing Sellis for a bounder all the while.

Sellis recovered his wits and leapt upon her bodily as she bent to retrieve the last of Princess Sophia's letters. The two of them went tumbling over and over in the sand, skirts and false curls flying every which way as Charlotte, cursing like a trooper, strove to keep the papers from Sellis's grasp.

It was at that point that Sir Hannibal Cheng finally reached the rolling, tumbling pair, who grappled in the sand like a pair of scrapping schoolboys.

He almost laughed at the scene, gasping for breath and trying vainly to get a handhold in order to break up the melee. If it hadn't been so serious, it would almost have been funny, he reflected now that he knew Charlotte would be safe; the devil's own Charlotte Hungerford rolling about in a bareknuckles fistfight with the "amateur" but nevertheless dangerous likes of Anthony Sellis, archvillain! Like something out o' one of her silly novels—only more so. Maida had never had to resort to fisticuffs!

At last, his breath caught and his time chosen, Sir Hannibal dug in his boots, reached down, and pulled Sellis to his feet by the scruff of his jacket. He turned the fellow neatly around, straightened him nicely, and, taking an easy swing with his right hand, hit him squarely on the jaw on that same place where Charlotte Hungerford's blow had landed, only this time with somewhat greater effect: Mr. Sellis's eyes veered eloquently from their natural orbit, and he passed out like some plugugly knocked down for the count in the squared circle. Sir Hannibal then let go of the Corsican's coat and watched coolly as the man crumpled to the sand for a nap.

"Wh-what did you do?" Charlotte gasped from her own undignified position as Anthony Sellis landed beside her, unconscious.

"I knocked him out," Sir Hannibal replied, flexing his knuckles in manly satisfaction.

"Why? Why the devil did you have to interfere? I—I was doing just fine," she said with a haughty air not matched by her undignified looks.

Resisting the urge to laugh out loud and thus precipitate another fight like the one that they had had the day before, Sir Hannibal said, "Oh, just fine," with only the slightest hint of irony in his voice. And then: "*Why?* Why, because he is a blackmailer and a blackguard and," he added, lowering and softening his voice almost to the point of tenderness, "and because I did not like the liberties he took with the lady I love." There, damn it, he'd said it at last. He held his breath, expecting some kind of reply to that rather daring remark, but none, it seemed, was forthcoming.

Charlotte said not a word, but instead, ignoring his outstretched hand, she scrambled to her feet by herself and took off pell-mell down the beach in the direction of Southwick without so much as a by-your-leave. So much for declarations of love!

Sir Hannibal gave the unconscious Sellis a quick kick to make sure he was still out and ran off in pursuit. What, by Jove, had got into the wench now? he wondered in exasperation.

"You stay right where you are, young sir," Charlotte called out menacingly to Thomas Garth. He had seen his tutor mishandled by Sir Hannibal from his position amongst the rocks and was now attempting to make his way stealthily toward the road, where his father's coach was waiting. He would have had no compunction about taking the reins and leaving Mr. Sellis to his fate.

But he was caught now. He stopped and turned as Charlotte had ordered, squaring his shoulders, his eyes direct. He was going to try to brazen it out, the little monster, Charlotte realized as she caught up to him, breathless but ready, nonetheless, for any trouble he might offer.

"Master Thomas Garth, I believe," she said with formality, ignoring the fact that she was all over damp sand, her bonnet hanging halfway down her back by its ribbons and blond false curls festooning her own chestnut ones in the most ridiculous fashion imaginable. Master Garth, however, was in no position to find her appearance amusing. His mind raced swiftly as he strove to remember just where he had seen this lady before.

"Miss Hungerford, is it not? Yes, I do believe it is, despite the rather eccentric chapeau," he could not help from adding, straight-faced. "We do seem to meet on beaches, do we not?" he added coolly, not once blinking his large blue eyes. His precociousness did not sit well with Charlotte, not well at all.

"Indeed we do," she said with equal cool as he gave her what he intended to be a winning smile. It had no effect upon this lady as it did upon his mother.

"I—I—" he stammered lamely, losing his composure somewhat under her censorious stare. "It is good you came when you

230

did. I was most awfully afraid of the rogue, you know," he added, recovering.

"Were you indeed?"

"Oh, oh, yes, Miss Hungerford," he wailed with sudden emotion. He would have leapt to hug at Charlotte for safety to demonstrate his point had she not quite neatly sidestepped his cunning manoeuvre. "He—he threatened me if I did not—"

"If you did not what, Master Garth?" Sir Hannibal Cheng cut in as he came huffing up the beach behind Charlotte.

"Sir—Sir Hannibal! How good of you to have come, sir, to the, ah, rescue, sir," the boy stammered. "Ah, if I did not steal my mo—the princess Sophia's letters for him," Thomas Garth mumbled. Two against one was not fair, he thought sulkily.

"And how, pray, did the fellow know of her letters since he had never been in her house?" Charlotte asked pleasantly, her voice disarmingly sweet.

"He—ah—I—I—"

"Precisely! 'I—I—' You were snooping, you little wretch," she snapped, changing tone abruptly, "weren't you? *You* had access to the house; you learnt your true identity—who your mother really is—and you told Mr. Sellis, and between the two of you, you plotted this little piece of knavery—"

"No," Thomas Garth cried out. "No, I—I am only twelve years old," he exclaimed defensively.

"What? A mere innocent? A child, you mean?" Sir Hannibal scoffed. "Don't plead that to me, boy. It won't wash, for I know better. You lie through your teeth—and a boy may be a knave at any age. It don't take a wit to know that."

Young Garth looked at Sir Hannibal's face and began to cry in earnest, knowing now that he was caught past all saving.

"You stole these, didn't you?" Charlotte insisted, waving a fistful of crumpled letters under his reddening nose. "Sometime earlier this week, I expect," she went on as he drew back guiltily. "You and Sellis read them over and thought of how best they could be used. You thought that you had all summer yet, didn't you? Or at least until your birthday early next month, eh? You realized that your poor, doting mama would want you near her for that day in particular, didn't you? You had counted upon it, in fact, but then yesterday you learnt that you were to be sent back to Ilslington at once. You had to act quickly or not at all, so last evening, when you and Sellis should have been at your supper, you sneaked back to your mother's house and planted Sellis's blackmail letter—a hasty, ill-written thing—on the desk where you knew it could not be missed for long." She grinned at him, a menacingly crafty grin. "That was the way of it, eh, boy?"

Charlotte pursued him unmercifully, thinking that he deserved no better treatment. "Your dear mother said that it was an owl I heard amongst the bushes by the terrace last evening, but it was no owl at all, was it? It was a bloody little weasel, wasn't it, Master Garth?" she asked angrily, thinking of her friend, Sophia, Princess of England, and of all the love, guilt, heartache, and remorse that she expended upon this boy. Why, he wasn't worth it! Wasn't even worth a tinker's damn!

"By heaven, I'm going to thrash you," Sir Hannibal roared suddenly, taking a step toward the boy. He, too, had been thinking of Sophy and what she had allowed this boy to mean to her. It was monstrous that a child should so repay a parent with such utter treachery.

"You do," the child shrieked in alarm, "and I'll tell my father you beat me—"

"Ha! I may damn well take a horsewhip to him as well," Sir Hannibal scoffed, half in jest.

"No, Sir Hannibal, he is quite right. You are far too big. You shall do him an injury," Charlotte broke in, restraining the Chinee baronet as he started to remove his coat.

"That is precisely what I had in mind."

"Shhh," she chided him with an eye signal to be still and let her go on. "Now, boy," she continued, turning to the child again, "where are the rest of the letters? Give them up. Come on," she coaxed.

Reluctantly young Thomas withdrew from his own coat pocket the remainder of the missing letters and held them forward.

"Take them, Sir Hannibal, and see that there are three . . ."

"There are," he answered, riffling through them, "and they are all in Ernest's hand."

"And take these into your keeping as well," Charlotte said, handing him the mass of pages and envelopes which she had retrieved from the beach, "whilst I settle things with our young friend here," she added as she reached out for Thomas Garth's arm.

"What are you going to do?" he cried.

"Apply the rod where it belongs, my lad. It has been spared too long already," Charlotte muttered through set teeth as she wrenched the horsewhip free of her clothing at last.

"You wouldn't dare," he shrilled nervously. "I'll tell my mother on—"

"Oh, do! Do that, my boy," she retorted in glee as she sat down upon a rock and turned the squirming boy over her knee. She thwacked him soundly with the handle end until his bottom ached and his tears ran free from pain, if not from remorse. Sir Hannibal, who had folded the letters and placed them over his heart for safekeeping, watched the boy's comeuppance with grim satisfaction, wondering whether he really could have done him any more injury for his size than Charlotte was doing for hers. He rather doubted it, realizing that both of them were furious at the child for the hurt they knew would be dealt the mother when she learnt of the boy's treachery—which, of course, she must quite soon.

"And that is not half what you deserve, you little—" Charlotte exclaimed as she pushed him off her lap at last and into the sand at her feet.

"I'll tell," he whimpered, struggling to his knees and holding his posterior gingerly in both his hands,

"Be my guest"—Charlotte shrugged—"but if you do, it may put some ideas in other heads, me lad. I fancy there must be a horde of souls might wish to queue up behind me for a chance at thrashin' your tender little bottom, Master Garth."

Master Garth gulped and, spotting the sanguine look in the

black eyes of Sir Hannibal Cheng, fell silent, awed by the truth of Charlotte's suggestion.

Charlotte Hungerford stood on the road beside General Thomas Garth's shiny black coach, shaking sand from her damp, dishevelled person and trying to put her hat back on straight. At last she gave it up as a bad job and pulled the thing off altogether, hurling it from her in frustration. It was caught on the rising wind and went tumbling along the misty beach at a fine clip.

It is the world's ugliest bonnet anyway, she said to herself, so what's the odds? Sir Hannibal, who had just seen to the tethering of Regimental to the back of the coach and to the depositing of the equally tethered Anthony Sellis in it, closed the door with a snap on the tutor's prostrate form and on that of young Garth, who of a necessity *stood,* and grinned happily at his ladylove.

She caught him grinning and grew self-conscious. "I vow Her Highness would be better off bald and bareheaded than wearing that monstrosity," she mumbled as she pulled off Sophia's blond false curls and tried to pat her own real ones into some semblance of order Sir Hannibal was watching her every move with *such* a look in his eye; he was too irritating and making her more nervous by the minute.

"I must look terrible," she grumbled testily, not daring to look Sir Hannibal in the eye. What had he meant by that remark down on the beach earlier—"liberties with the lady he loved"?

"You look bloody marvellous." Sir Hannibal grinned, his eyes alight in a peculiar manner.

"Watch your language, sir," Charlotte retorted with a pretty blush. Why was he looking at her like that, and after the bedevilling he had given her just the day before?

"Ha! Wench, you dare say that to *me* after the language you used whilst you were tilting with Mr. Sellis here? For shame, it was enough to make Chaucer blush!"

"Anything in Chaucer is quite all right." Charlotte sniffed daintily. "Chaucer's *classic*—like Shakespeare and Rabelais," she added righteously.

"Agreed. I shan't argue at all, you marvellous, bloody wench." The Chinee baronet grinned, leaning back against the side of the coach for comfort.

"Wench again," she squealed in mock annoyance.

"Yes, wench again—would you prefer 'dolly-mop' perhaps?" Before she could reply to *that*, he went on. "Speaking of classics, *this* is classic, too." He suddenly drew her to him and kissed her hard upon the lips. She squealed once and squirmed twice—as any properly brought up parson's daughter ought—and then gave up the struggle as any sensible young woman would.

"Classic?" she asked breathlessly when at last they broke apart.

"Of course. Kissing's done in all your great works o' lit'rature, don't you know? Chaucer, Shakespeare, why, even in Hungerford, I believe. . . ." He smiled, showing his beautiful white teeth in a thoroughly engaging grin as he winked and pulled her to him once more.

"Sir Hannibal, no gentleman has ever kissed me like—like that."

"I should hope not, Miss Hungerford. No gentleman should ever kiss a lady like that—unless, of course, he intends to make an honest woman of her quite soon after."

Charlotte let forth another of those little squeals. "Oh! Oh?"

"Just so, oh." Here he kissed her again. "See, Miss Hungerford, you are quite compromised and for your sins, you must marry me, I fear—or else . . ."

"Or else?" Charlotte prompted with a smile and a gleam in her eye that was beginning to match his own.

"Or else live as an outcast, shunned by all decent society for having accepted a kiss—two kisses, in fact—and rejected the hand that goes with them." He pulled her close for another kiss.

She tried to push him away this time. "Go to, rogue," she said. "What about your Fanny? Can you so easily forget loving her? Are you so fickle as all that?"

"She's not *my* Fanny, you goose. You're my Fanny—I, uh, that is, you are the one I love and the one I wanted all along. I only endured her flighty company to get round you." He

235

confessed this last against all his wishes. What a fool he sounded to himself, but evidently not to Charlotte. . . .

"*Did* you? Oh, Sir Hannibal, how wonderful!" she exclaimed, leaping back into his arms at once. "Well, Sir Hannibal, you have kissed me now three times running, and you are quite right. I am far too proper a maiden to languish in such an invidious position as that which you have described, so therefore, I am afraid I shall have to accept and marry you, sir." She twinkled her great amber eyes at him in a way calculated to make him go weak in the knees.

"Wonderful," he cried at the promise in those melting eyes.

"My hero . . ." she sighed.

"My heroine," he returned before he silenced her with yet another kiss.

::13::

It was nearing ten o'clock, and the moon, rising full and silver over the waters of the Channel, shone down with such brightness as to pale the glow of yellow candlelight that streamed with uncharacteristic prodigality from every window of Princess Sophia's house.

Within, little pockets of calm or trouble abounded, the atmosphere depending upon whether one was in one particular room or another, whether one was accounted hero or villain. . . .

In the butler's pantry utmost calm prevailed, for the room was presided over by a rather delighted and bemused Lord Buckthorpe Vane, his rump firmly planted in a comfortable chair, the upholstered back of which rested against the only means of egress. His legs were braced, his booted feet firmly set upon a large, heavy Dutch cupboard. In his hand was a pistol, properly loaded, ready for use, and aimed steadily but with little malice at the only other occupant of the room—a small, frantic-eyed Corsican, who sat bound and motionless in a far from comfortable kitchen chair, gagged to silence by a fine linen towel.

Bucky, who could not help but conjure up images of highwaymen and heroes à la his auntie Charlotte's novels, was having a high old time of it. Mr. Sellis, perhaps, was less enthusiastic with his part in this particular *tableau vivant*.

Stretched upon a narrow metal bed in an upper garret lay the boy Thomas Garth, his bottom sore unto throbbing from the thrashing inflicted by Charlotte Hungerford in the afternoon and another, far sounder one inflicted by his own father just an hour earlier. Who would have thought the pater had such strength left in his dodderin' old body? the boy marvelled again and again in his solitude. It was a miracle that the Duke of Cumberland had been stayed from having at him as well. A thrashing from that quarter he would not have expected to survive!

The boy lay dry-eyed and motionless—upon his stomach of a necessity—and contemplated where he had gone wrong in his calculations. He moved slightly, renewing the pain in his bottom, and found tears welling uncontrolled from his burning eyes. Young Thomas Garth cried himself to sleep. . . .

Downstairs, at the back of the house, in the small drawing room which had been the scene of such tempest the night before, all was agitation yet. The room was overcrowded to begin with, and the Duke of Cumberland, a large man in any room, pacing in looming and bull-like fury amongst the clutter of furniture and people, did not help matters at all. Sophia herself sat quietly upon her chaise, her legs drawn up girllike to make room for Charlotte; only her hands, convulsively shredding what had once been a very pretty handkerchief, gave evidence of her great agitation of mind.

General Thomas Garth sat wheezing like a porpoise in an armchair close beside Princess Sophia, his swollen, gouty feet, still swathed in a pair of oversized felt slippers, resting upon a stool before him. His wig was awry, and his eyes were wet with unshed tears of something on the order of shame. He had always kept at a distance the unwelcome spectre of his inescapable second-rateness, but now it stared him in the face: Second-rate in the army, in battle, in the service of his king, as a lover, and now as a father!

"I intend to kill the fellow. No one shall stop me, you hear," Cumberland rumbled all at once into the silence of that room full of people each lost in private thoughts.

Sir Hannibal Cheng, who sat on the edge of the desk between the two back windows with his legs braced and his eyes steady— the calm centre of the storm that raged within the household— spoke up quietly. "You shall kill no one, Ernest. You are already accused, without justice, of having killed the brother. If you kill

238

him, you've torn it. You shall have no credence left at all and be ruined in England for all time. So don't talk so, even in anger."

"Well, what d'ya suggest then? That I kiss 'im on both cheeks for attemptin' the ruin of my sister and the puttin' forth of the grossest of libels upon our honour and our nature?" the duke returned with a fine, grotesque show of his great square teeth.

"No demonstrations of affection either," Sir Hannibal commented dryly. "Remember what they say passed betwixt you and the brother, eh?"

Cumberland shot his friend a look of pure malice but said nothing.

"I am a ruined man," General Garth wheezed to himself rather than to anyone in particular, at which comment the duke snarled and Princess Sophia purred in sympathy. Charlotte, whose sympathies lay elsewhere, merely clucked her tongue and kept still.

The Duke of Cumberland grunted, started to speak, and then thought better of it. He was hot, and Cheng was cool. Better let the cool head prevail.

"I only took pity on the man. He came to me with such a tale. He has been hounded by the duke," old Garth continued, defending himself, knowing, that though none had blamed him, he was much to blame. "He had been unable to find work. He was destitute through what I took to be no fault of his own. What could I do but help him? I have spent half my life righting wrongs done both by and to the royal family. Was I to stop then? And I was in need of a governor for the boy . . ."

At this piece of foolishness, the Duke of Cumberland could no longer be still. "You sentimental, addlepated old fool," he roared. "I haven't hounded the man. I've been searching for him to get him to testify to the fact that Joseph Sellis suffered from an aberration of mind, that he had attacked others before me, and that his suicide was not the first such attempt that he had made upon his own life. I needed his evidence to clear myself of the taint his death has put upon my honour. The lout told me two years ago that this was true—that his brother was, in fact, mad by spells from childhood—but he disappeared when I refused to *pay* him for his testimony in the case."

"Perhaps you should have paid," Garth suggested.

"Oh, yes, and if that had come out, what would have been said then? I can just imagine what would have been made of that!" Cumberland scoffed, rolling his good eye madly at such a damnably foolish suggestion. "And that's the viper you've been nursin' ta strike at this lady here—"

At this, Sophia finally spoke up, silencing her brother and attempting to soothe Garth as well. "It is all over now, and no real harm done. My friends here, Miss Hungerford and Sir Hannibal, have seen to that, haven't they? All will be well after all, I am sure," she soothed.

"Indeed it will," Sir Hannibal agreed, pulling a letter from his breast pocket and waving it toward the duke as a distraction.

"Eh? What's that?" he asked.

"A letter—you needn't read it now—addressed to Captain Clarence Merrick of my merchant ship *The Honoria Wallace,* which is at the Cove of Cork being fitted for a voyage to China." He paused.

"It is a long, slow trip to China, with stops at Hong Kong, Amoy, and Shanghai before the return; plenty o' time for a man to cool his heels and contemplate his sins, eh? Captain Merrick is ordered, in this letter, to take on just such a passenger as needs to cool his heels—to say nothing of his hot head. Said passenger would be kept in the brig til the ship rounded the Cape, after which time he would be set free and treated as an ordinary seaman. Now if this man should choose to jump ship at any port east of Madagascar, why, well and good. If, however, he chose to stay abroad for the return voyage, he would be set at liberty at the port of Gibraltar with his honest pay and a one-way passage to Corsica. Fair enough?" Cheng asked with a shrug as he finished his recitation.

"Too fair, if you ask me," Cumberland answered sourly, "but discreet. I'm for it—with thanks, old friend," he added more gently. "With thanks."

"Nothin'," Cheng mumbled in return.

240

"Nothing? It is too marvellous," Sophia insisted gratefully over one shoulder as she ministered to the comforts of the old general, who was too overcome with his own shame to pay much attention to anyone else.

"So that is why you sent for those pups Bucky and Ned Darlington," Charlotte exclaimed. "You have a job for them, I expect. Imagine! Bucky of all people. The pup seems to be growing up after all."

"Indeed," Cheng agreed mildly. "Pups usually do, and after a certain period of leggy awkwardness, they stop falling all over their paws and become good dogs, too. Noble animal, the dog—good, loyal, dignified, brave, with a stout heart and keen senses. Even some of the mongrels—" he said thoughtfully, breaking off suddenly.

"Mongrels?" Charlotte repeated, not taking his point. She glanced at the princess and General Garth as if for enlightenment, but they were oblivious of the rest of the company, lost in a private colloquy of their own.

"Aye, mongrels," he reiterated. "Think you won't regret takin' on a cur like me—half Irish wolfhound and half Chinese sleeve dog?" he asked with a twinkle.

"Sir Hannibal," Charlotte retorted with equal merriment, "it is probably only the very animal that you describe could possibly put up with a scrappy little English fox terrier such as myself. You're on."

At this, Sir Hannibal laughed out loud and crossed the room to hug her. The Duke of Cumberland screwed up his face and watched them openmouthed. So that was the way o' things, was it? Cheng thought he was goin' ta tame that pretty little Tartar, did he?

Well . . . maybe he could at that. . . .

Lord Ned Darlington arrived at Hove on a steaming horse at a quarter past eleven, only to be ushered with a total lack of ceremony directly into the butler's pantry, of all places, where Bucky still mounted guard, pistol at the ready, over the nicely trussed and dozing form of Anthony Sellis.

"Ain't that the brother? The valet's brother who's been missin'?" Ned drawled in wonder as the shabby little governor, all the shabbier for his sandy, dishevelled clothing and the want of a shave, roused himself from his drowse and stared up into the faces of the men who surrounded him so menacingly. "Here, why's he trussed, and Vane here with a p—"

He got no further before the Duke of Cumberland broke in. "Never you mind, me lad. Safe to say he's a villain, a knave, and a liar to boot."

"Indeed, sir," Neddy agreed wisely.

"Ned, my lad," Sir Hannibal spoke up with an admonitory glance at Cumberland, "and Bucky, too, there's no doubt that this little wretch ought to be in the hands of the king's magistrate at Brighton. However"—here Sir Hannibal gave a baleful look at Sellis, who withered visibly under the gaze of Cheng's fierce black eyes—"however, we have deemed it more prudent to prevent this devious fellow from using our fair and open English courts as a forum for his scandalous lies and mendacious inventions. Therefore, we shall avoid all possibility of such an occurrence by seeing that Mr. Sellis, who is an alien after all, leaves the country.

"I am going to have Mr. Sellis's boxes transferred to the duke's coach. Quibbens, who can be trusted, unlike others who have served His Royal Highness," Sir Hannibal remarked pointedly with a glance at Sellis, "will act as coachman. Bucky and Ned, you shall escort this fellow here to Plymouth, where a small yacht of mine, *The Sea Dragon,* is at anchor. The captain, a young man named William Merrick, will sail you and your prisoner over the water to Cork, where you will deliver this letter of instructions to his father, Captain Clarence Merrick, of my merchantman *The Honoria Wallace.* When you have seen your prisoner safely transferred to the brig of the ship and Captain Merrick has taken full charge according to the orders in this letter, you may return via *The Sea Dragon* to Plymouth, where Quibbens and the coach will await you at the Red Mill Inn."

"Is that all clear?" the duke asked with some gargling in his throat. He was feeling decidedly superfluous at the moment.

"Is it?" Cheng echoed.

"All clear and easy. You can count on me, gentlemen," Bucky assured them both quite seriously, despite the gleam in his eye. Gad, a secret royal mission—exactly like one of his aunt Charlotte's novels. What a lark!

"You can count on us both, old friend," Ned Darlington concurred with a far more manly demeanour than he was wont to have.

Sir Hannibal hesitated. "I have a reason for wantin' you both back in Brighton in three weeks' time. It rather rushes you . . ."

"Oh, yes, you've heard then . . . and it does rather rush me, too, for I have to be back in Brighton for the same reason Bucky does," Neddy cried, with inspiration brightening his stolid face. "In fact, I suppose you've all heard. The pater's marryin' Bucky's stepgrandmama, Fanny Hungerford. They put up the banns on Sunday and marry three weeks from Monday next. I say, that's not far off, is it? We shall have to hop it, shan't we, old son?" Neddy concluded, turning to Bucky, who was suddenly brought up short by the prospect of three weeks in the company of Ned Darlington.

"Ah, Ned, lad, there's, ah—slightly more to it than that . . ."

"Yes." Neddy chuckled. "Poor Bucky's got ta walk his grannie down the aisle, eh? Can't miss that, eh?" he added with a slap on the back of Bucky's head. Bucky fumed but said not a word.

"Walk his grannie and his—his aunt as well, Neddy," Cheng murmured in some embarrassment. He heard the duke snort and wondered idly what Sellis was making of all this nuptial chatter. Sellis, however, he noticed with some relief, was asleep, whether from boredom or exhaustion he knew not, but he was grateful nonetheless. It is one thing to appear a fool amongst one's friends, quite another before an enemy.

"Charlotte Hungerford and I are puttin' up the banns as well. She really wasn't for you, Ned," Cheng hastened to assure him in a rather apologetic tone. "I—I didn't *steal* her. She wouldn't have had—"

Ned Darlington drew in his breath. Well, that was that. His allowance was safe for a certainty now. And without his ever havin' to avoid Miss Hungerford for a second.

"Say no more, old man," he blustered with a conscious deepening of his thin voice. "Miss Hungerford and I, thing o' the past. Plenty more wenches where she come from. Lots to go round," Neddy suggested with the air of a hale-fellow-well-met.

"Here," young Buckthorpe broke in indignantly, "when did you two— Why, yesterday you were fighting like cocks."

"We made up," Sir Hannibal said succinctly. "Now, enough chatter. You two have a job to do, delivering this wretched fellow to Cork."

It was, appropriately enough, upon the stroke of midnight that the duke's monstrous coach, shades drawn down against the gaze of the curious, finally set off on the road toward Plymouth. Only Sir Hannibal and the duke himself stood upon the step and watched it off upon its mission. Cumberland screwed up his good eye and peered into the darkness after the coach, which was already out of sight. "They think they're out for a romp, those pups."

"Cheer up, old friend," Sir Hannibal rejoined, clapping a hand on the duke's back. "Remember they ain't much different from the way we were at that age. Why, I thought back in '96 that I was playin' at toy boats when I took those ships in Bantry Bay. Never thought I might have gotten meself blown out o' the water by some frog sailor no older than I was then. Thought never occurred, I tell 'e, til the shootin' stopped and I started slippin' about the decks in other men's blood. Christ, I thought, it might've been me, and then I wasn't so cocky after that. Grew up right then and there. So did you, in the army, just as I did at sea."

"So?"

"So? Why, so once they're alone on that dark road with only their thoughts and a brace o' pistols trained on Anthony Sellis's skull, they'll see the weight o' it all. They'll do their part and do it well, Ernest, and in fact, I've got a pocketful o' guineas says that they'll be well on their way ta bein' full-grown men by the time they return. Am I on?" he asked with a smile and a wink.

"No, you thief." Ernest of Cumberland laughed, finally breaking into a pained but nevertheless recognizable smile. "You've had the best o' me too many times for me ta take that bet. Besides, I expect you're right."

"Yes," Cheng agreed dryly. "Usually am. Now, if you'll excuse me, I have an assignation with a certain pretty scribbler." With that he was off around the side of the house to await Charlotte on the terrace.

It was cool and refreshing in the brisk night air, and Charlotte found the solitude to her liking after the trials of the past twenty-four hours and more. She had left the boy at the door of his mother's drawing room, but not before she had given him something of a tongue-lashing. She worried that Sophia would be hurt, for the boy was sullen and recalcitrant, yet clever enough to see which way the wind blew and to trim his sails accordingly. He would smile and obey and appear to respond to his parents' guilty attempts to sway him into the paths of righteousness, but he was no innocent to be brought back into the fold. He was too cunning and too wicked already in the ways of the world. He had been too much with servants and the lower ranks, too secretive in his ways for his mother to hope to change his character at this stage. He would simply mature and go on to greater deeds of the same kind as this blackmail scheme which had come to nought. Perhaps other schemes, in future, would succeed. Perhaps other victims would pay, as Sophia, fortunately, had not. Damn the boy! His own mother!

"There you are." A voice, soft, deep, and thrilling sounded across the lawn from the corner of the house. "I wonder you have the strength to stand. It is past midnight of what has been a very busy day." The voice chuckled warmly out of the blackness of the night.

"Oh, Sir Hannibal, you are quite right. It has been a long day, and I am tired unto death—yet I doubt if I should sleep. I am too agitated, too low."

"Low?" he asked, coming to her side and taking her hand in his. "After such a good job done?"

"I have just come from the boy," Charlotte said, as if that were answer enough.

"Ah, I see. You feel sorry for him, I suppose. Most women would. Still . . ."

"The devil I do! It is his mother I pity. She actually entertains hopes of his salvation. But no more, pray, for I cannot speak of it. Shall we walk? Near the water, please?" she asked, pulling the Chinee baronet after her as she strode diagonally down to the edge of the lawn.

"Pray, Sir Hannibal, what will happen to Mr. Sellis? After he is set on board your merchantman by Neddy and my nephew, I mean?"

"Oh, two years or so before the mast"—he shrugged—"if he does not jump ship first, and then, if he's wise—which I think he shall have learnt to be by then—he'll take his pay and free passage from Gibraltar to Corsica. If he behaves, I shall see to it he's enough in his purse for a small farm . . ."

"And if he chooses not to be wise? If he makes more trouble?"

"Then Cumberland or I shall kill him," Sir Hannibal said simply, shrugging his wide shoulders nonchalantly.

"Could you?" Charlotte gasped in some surprise. The men in her novels might talk so, but in life she had never yet met such a man. She stopped at a cluster of white lawn chairs, luminous as a conclave of ghosts against the dark lawn.

"Of course, if I had to. Not gratuitously, of course, or else I should have done it already, but yes, if I had to."

There followed a long silence, during which Sir Hannibal's heart nearly stopped.

"Why? Does that shock you, Charlotte? Do you disapprove?" Curse him, had he put his boot into it again?

"Disapprove? Goodness, no! I was just musing on how utterly, utterly perfect a hero you are: brave, manful, wise, just, and yet, if you have to be, ruthless as well. Just the blend of qualities I tried so hard to get in Ravenstock, but . . ."

"But?"

"Poor Ravenstock," Charlotte whispered, her voice trembling ever so slightly, "is only a paper hero printed on paper pages. You, Sir Hannibal, are very real . . . very flesh . . . and very bl—"

He kissed her long enough and hard enough to prove—as if it were necessary!—the veracity of her somewhat disjointed and rather overheated remarks. She squirmed away from him at last, almost coolly, certainly breathlessly.

"Enough, sir," she breathed with a pretense of her usual hauteur.

Sir Hannibal laughed out loud at that and then checked himself, lest they draw attention to themselves. "Maida," he whispered, "would have said, 'Desist, varlet.'"

"No." Charlotte corrected him in all seriousness. "That sounds more like Lady Viola de Villiers to the Duke of Dalmatia actually."

"Does it really now?" he said with a smile.

"Yes, it—"

"Charlotte!"

"Yes?"

"Silence that pretty mouth and kiss me. We shall discuss lit'rature at another time, eh?"

They kissed again, taking some advantage of one of the ghostly lawn chairs in the process.

"I feel so sorry for her," Charlotte exclaimed suddenly, sitting up and shaking her curls fretfully.

"Sorry for whom, blast it?" Sir Hannibal nearly roared before checking himself. "Lady Violet whatever? Or Maida? Really, Charlotte, can you not let your novels go even for a kiss? Is that what our married life will be?" he growled in exasperation.

"Oh, bother, of course not. I mean the princess Sophia," she cried, adjusting her skirts nicely. "She is so lonely, so bound round by dos and don'ts, by conventions and rules. She is a lady in a cage—and not even a gold one at that. She's so poor, it's got brass bars on it, poor lady. It seems we females are excluded from rather a lot of things—even the future queens amongst us."

"Now, now, you are no Mary Wollstonecraft, are you? I hope not, or God help me!"

"No, no, I am not, but I do not think that she was as wrong or notorious, as they say. I am no pursuer of female rights, but I like to think that the day will come when we ladies may exert our individualities by other means than birthing bastard babies and living out of wedlock with our lovers. Perhaps one day we shall drink port with honour, discuss politics with seriousness—"

"Politics!"

"Yes, why not?" Charlotte asked mildly, raising her eyebrows and blinking. "The great mistresses of every age have practised political influence, always, unfortunately, from the only position in which a man is likely to listen to a woman at all—the horizontal. Would it not be nice for us to be heard from a platform rather? One generally does think better on one's feet after all, and so the results ought to be quite satisfactory."

Sir Hannibal suppressed a smile and urged her on with a nod. This was a new hobbyhorse for a lady who wrote silly novels of romance and suspense. Was there no end to her opinions?

"Why should we not even vote?"

"And you say you are no feminist?"

"Yes, vote and practice medicine, teach at universities, be—be *free!*"

"Free? As if you all are not already!" he scoffed. "Free to spend your fathers' money or your husbands', free to live a life of amiable idleness in comfortable country houses."

"Bosh, sir! Bosh, I say. What freedom is that, I ask? Do you think that Sophia is free? Or my sister? She is so bored and imprisoned by her life that she resorts to the main form of rebellion open to those of my sex—promiscuity—which benefits the man and exacts nine months' penance in the form of backaches and swollen bellies for the lady. Why, I am freer than either of them, I, a parson's daughter, raised in circumstances of utmost convention and propriety. Yet I am freer than either my sister, who is a viscountess with a wealthy husband, or Sophia, who is a princess and the daughter of a king. Oh, Sir Hannibal, I would not be a royal for all the tea in China," she finished vehemently with a stamp of her foot upon the turf of the terrace.

In his love-lit eyes, Charlotte was too adorable for words. What spirit! He smiled broadly. "Ho, have a care, Charlotte, for I trade rather profitably in China tea and a corner on the market such as you describe is not lightly to be—"

"Oh, bother tea. I am being serious, Hannibal," Charlotte exclaimed.

"You goose." Sir Hannibal laughed, unable to contain himself any longer. "You have promised, do not forget, to be my wife. In return, I promise no brass bars—or gold ones either, though I could afford 'em easy enough—and no silken bonds either. Only the wide green sea and a broad-sailed ship to rove her in, remote isles, and faraway nations to see—and a grand big house on Bantry Bay for when we grow weary of wandering and come home to rest."

"You make it sound so—so marvellous," she whispered incredulously. "Marvellous and *romantic* and . . ."

"So it will be, our life together, though sea voyages are slightly less than romantic when the seas are heaving and one has one's pretty chestnut head in a bucket . . ."

"Oh, poo," Charlotte remarked, waving aside his silly words. "And I'd really still be free," she mused aloud.

"Free in every way save one." Sir Hannibal grinned with a wink which she did not catch the meaning of.

"Save *one?* And what one is *that?*" quoth Charlotte, ready to fly at him again.

He leant back in the chair, while the wicker creaked alarmingly, and stretched his boots before him, raising one finger in admonition. "You'd not be free to dally with the local lords like your sister, Lady Helena. All your babies had better look like me." He leered, pulling back the corners of his beautiful dark eyes with his forefingers.

At that Charlotte could not help but laugh. "Oh, no fear. You are all the dalliance I could possibly desire, *but*—the same holds true, sir, for you. No coming home at cock's crow with hay in your breeches, mind."

"I promise—or at least if I ever do come home in such a state as that, you'll be puttin' hay out o' your . . ."

"Enough," Charlotte squealed, pushing Sir Hannibal away as he caught up to her and sought to kiss her once again.

"Go away? Why, don't you love me?" he asked in dismay.

"Of course I do, you silly. Would I have behaved like such a mad thing these three weeks past if I did not? Now go this instant. I want to wear white on my wedding day without having to blush at a lie," she teased.

"You little witch," he breathed as he stole the sweetest kiss of the night. . . .

Monday morning, the last Monday morning in July 1812, dawned sunny and bright, which was as well since happy are they, the brides the sun shines upon . . .

The last mists of morning had been burnt off the gilded minarets and brilliant white onion domes of the regent's Pavillion at Brighton, leaving them burnished and bleached in the sun, as unreal to the eye of an ordinary Englishman as would be the exotic visions of an Oriental pipe dream. It was like some glad, mad, delightful wedding cake of a folly, a confection of spun sugar and gilded gingerbread whipped up in the imagination of an eccentric royal bakery chef, or more than that—a jewelled playhouse perhaps, all pearls and gold in a setting of emerald grass and sapphire sky set against a sea of lapis lazuli, the royal jewellers playing at architect for the indulgence of a spoilt, extravagant prince with a penchant for the droll and the bizarre.

But whatever else it was, the Royal Pavillion was on that sunny day the perfect setting for the gift of a double wedding bestowed by a grateful regent upon a couple who had done noble service to his loving sister Sophia.

Within, dwarfed by the sumptuous Oriental splendours of the great crimson music room, waited an array of guests, the noblest of them all being H.R.H. the prince regent and his only daughter, Princess Charlotte of Wales, surrounded by the ladies and gentlemen of his court. Bucky's papa, the third Viscount Vane of Buckthorpe Court, looking unusually stern and purposeful, stood arm in arm with his wife, Lady Helena, a rather chastened-looking viscountess indeed, being approximately four months gone in an indisputably legitimate pregnancy. Behind them was gathered the neat, handsome crew of Vane children, ranging from a pretty, very demure redheaded girl of seventeen down through a succession of varying sizes, sexes, shapes, and colourings to a large, black-haired, black-eyed infant boy of about eight months. This latter, held in the viselike grip of a nursery maid, had a great wedge of damp toast stuck in his little pink mouth to stifle any untoward outbursts in such august company.

Across from the Vanes, amongst a few cronies of Sir Hannibal and the Duke of Cumberland, stood the eight or ten sisters and brothers of Ned Darlington, a rather unkempt but exceedingly lively group, being herded into a semblance of neatness and order by three unfashionably dressed but very nearly beautiful girls of fourteen, sixteen, and eighteen respectively. Unlike the Vane offspring, the resemblance of the Axminster brood, one to the other, was indisputable to the point of repetition.

The seventh duke, calm but hungry, watched his great brood for a long moment with a gurgling stomach and winced. Perhaps Fanny would take things in hand. Those gels were too lively by half. He looked sideways to his co-Benedict, Hannibal Cheng, and, seeing the poor fellow was near frozen with trepidation, gave him an encouraging wink. Then the music swelled. The Duke of Cumberland, in his capacity as groomsman, gave Neddy, who was his father's best man, a nudge to get his eyes off the pretty redheaded Vane girl, and the doors of the music room swung open upon the bridal party.

Bucky stood within the opening, his arms crooked smartly to admit the dainty, trembling hands of the two brides, Fanny on his right and Charlotte on his left. Behind them, smiling wistfully, was surely the most august and wonderful matron of honour the daughters of a parson and a country squire could ever have imagined—H.R.H. the princess Sophia of England.

He had done it! He had got both Charlotte and Fanny married

off before the end of the season. "All set," he whispered, and not waiting for a reply, he swept them slowly down the centre of the room.

Fanny, a vision in pale blue and white, caught the eye of her duke and pursed her lips prettily, then glanced expertly over all the Axminsters, big and little, mentally cleaning and straightening them one by one, taking note of their best features for future reference. The eldest gel . . . lovely. Perfect for Bucky, she thought with a sly glance at the guileless innocent trodding beside her. Yes, that would do nicely. . . .

Charlotte, trembling like an aspen leaf, saw nothing. All was a blur before her eyes, just as all was butterflies in her middle. For an instant she wanted to bolt. . . . But then she saw Sir Hannibal, his tawny face aglow in the candlelight, his expression so grave and manly. Did he want to bolt as well? she wondered.

Perhaps, but he wouldn't, and neither would she. They were after all, hero and heroine, and like Maida and Ravenstock or Isobelle and Laird Angus, they were committed to the proper ending now. There was just nothing for it but to marry as all heroes and heroines married and to live happily ever after just as all heroes and heroines live happily ever after.

And that, of course, is exactly what they did. . . .

Love—the way you want it!

Candlelight Romances

THE DARK HORSEMAN

Marianne Harvey
author of *The Proud Hunter*

Beautiful Donna Penroze had sworn to her
dying father that she would save her sole leg-
acy, the crumbling tin mines and the ancient,
desolate estate *Trencobban*. But the mines
were failing, and Donna had no one to turn to.
No one except the mysterious Nicholas Trevarvas—rich, arrogant, commanding. Donna
would do anything but surrender her pride, anything but admit her irresistible longing for *The
Dark Horseman*.

A Dell Book $3.25

The passionate sequel to
the scorching novel of
fierce pride and forbidden love

THE PROUD HUNTER

by Marianne Harvey

Author of *The Dark Horseman* and *The Wild One*

Trefyn Connor—he demanded all that was his—and
more—with the arrogance of a man who fought to
win . . . with the passion of a man who meant to pos-
sess his enemy's daughter and make her pay the
price!

Juliet Trevarvas—the beautiful daughter of The Dark
Horseman. She would make Trefyn come to her. She
would taunt him, shock him, claim him body and soul
before she would surrender to THE PROUD HUNTER.

A Dell Book $3.25   (17098-2)